Praise for the prequel to *The Hundred Names of Darkness*

THE WILDINGS

Longlisted for the DSC Prize for
Shortlisted for the Commonwealth Book Prize

"A marvelously spun novel that could well become a classic in its own time."   —*The Sunday Guardian*

"A beautiful re-visioning of Delhi, of friendship and of war. Roy has made the mind-link: her wildings hunt in my dreams."
—Alissa York, author of *The Naturalist*

"A novel for all seasons and ages. . . . Nilanjana Roy has created a savage, dangerous world parallel to our limited, self-centred human one. It is a world of heightened senses and myriad species, a world that seems tangibly real. . . . Roy has her readers on the edge of their seats."   —*India Today*

"Roy's cats bring to mind the creatures of Rudyard Kipling's 'Rikki Tikki Tavi' and Richard Adams' *Watership Down*, and like these immensely popular stories, *The Wildings* has a warm heartbeat. I predict that Roy will win fans from all ages with this delightful debut."
—Kathryn Kuitenbrouwer, author of *All the Broken Things*

"Gripping, humorous and truly immersive."   —*Sunday Indian*

"As much a modern fable as it is a floor-level point of view of cosmopolis, largely through the eyes of cats. . . . A most impressive debut. . . . *The Wildings* is an excellent and assured first novel."   —*OutlookIndia.com*

"A few pages into Nilanjana Roy's *The Wildings*, you'll wish you had whiskers and could mew. Roy is a cat-, cheel-, mouse- and mongoose-whisperer and this is the animals' story, unhampered by human interference. . . . *The Wildings* is a page-turner and charming read."   —*Daily News & Analysis* (India)

THE
HUNDRED
NAMES <u>OF</u>
DARKNESS

The sequel and conclusion

to

The Wildings

NILANJANA ROY

Random House Canada

PUBLISHED BY RANDOM HOUSE CANADA

Copyright © 2013 Nilanjana Roy

Illustrations (pp. ii, vi) © 2013 Prabha Mallya

www.penguinrandomhouse.ca

LIBRARY AND ARCHIVES CANADA CATALOGUING IN PUBLICATION

Roy, Nilanjana S., author
The hundred names of darkness / Nilanjana S. Roy.
(Book two of The hundred names of darkness)

Issued in print and electronic formats.

ISBN 978-0-345-81557-6

eBook ISBN 978-0-345-81558-3

I. Mallya, Prabha, illustrator II. Title.

PR9499.4.R89H85 2016   823'.92   C2015-908557-8

Book design by Kelly Hill

Cover images: (cats) © Anita Ponne, Benguhan, and Ellika,
(peacock) © Koshevnyk, (frame) © Azati1976, all Shutterstock.com;
(arches) © Pooja Arya / EyeEm / Getty Images

Interior images: (peacock feathers) © Kudryashka, (abstract flower) © Ttenki, both
Shutterstock.com; (cats) © Vectorig / Getty Images

Printed and bound in the United States of America

2 4 6 8 9 7 5 3 1

Penguin
Random House
RANDOM HOUSE CANADA

CONTENTS

Prologue   *1*

1   Cat Burglar   *14*

2   A Circle of Senders   *22*

3   Hunted   *53*

4   Crash Boom Bang   *66*

5   The Sender's Run   *80*

6   Into the Grey Skies   *93*

7   Creatures of the Night   *116*

8   Hellhounds on the Trail   *144*

9   With the Bigfeet   *163*

10   The Cat and the Egrets   *179*

11   The Hundred Names of Darkness   *192*

12   Fledglings and Summonings   *210*

13   Among the Mors   *236*

14   The Bonds of the Earth   *267*

15   A Thuggery of Bandicoots   *290*

16   The Sender of Paolim   *302*

17   Ashes and Departures   *318*

18   Twists in the Tunnel   *340*

19   Full Moon Rising   *355*

20   The Belly of the Beast   *374*

Epilogue   *386*

Author's Note   *397*

Acknowledgements   *399*

"Somewhere, in some corner of this universe,
a town is inhabited solely by the spirits of cats.
Surely, it does exist."

—HAGIWARA SAKUTARŌ,
"The Town of Cats"

Prologue

The egret dipped her wings and sheered away from the red roofs. She flew over the village every evening on her way back to the paddy fields, soaring over the tiny bakery, the football fields, the peaceful houses. The rain fell steadily, in heavy silver sheets, but the egret was used to it.

She saw the flash of movement before she saw the cat pad deftly across the slippery red tiles. The egret changed course, calling once to alert the other birds. The rain streamed through her feathers, and the massed grey clouds in the sky told her that the monsoons would take over the night.

That wasn't going to stop the most ferocious hunter in the village of Paolim. Flying back from their evening sorties across the amber hills, the emerald green fields, the egrets stayed well away from the crumbling house with the faded blue shutters, and the ones next to it, knowing that Magnificat owned the rooftops that night.

Though her fur was the blazing white of the feathery clouds that studded the skies over the River Chorize just after each drumming downpour, Magnificat moved with such speed and ease across the roofs that it was hard to spot her. If the birds had only known it, they were safe from the cat. Goa's most famous Sender was on the hunt, but not for birds, or even fat palm squirrels. The previous night, Magnificat had attacked and killed her second cobra of the year, taking on the powerful snake fearlessly, mindful of its venom and yet intent on making her strike. The cobra's mate had slithered away when it saw the blood speckling Magnificat's white-furred jaws. The cat had seen his black scales gleam as the snake sought shelter on these roofs. If she didn't kill the snake, he might bide its time. But he would come looking for her someday, and she couldn't take the chance of being caught off guard. It was yet another round in an ancient war. The snakes of Paolim and the cats who patrolled the fishing boats and launches of Chorize had hunted each other for generations in a deadly dance of predator and prey, where the roles could change in a second.

Magnificat paused at the edge of the roof, curling back into the shelter of the tiles and holding still when two motorcyclists roared up on their pilot bikes. They stopped at the foot of the jackfruit tree, leaning their bikes against the brick boundary wall. On the other side of the wall, damp hens huddled under a sheet of plywood, their red and black feathers soggy in the rain.

The cat knew the boys wouldn't hurt her, but she didn't want to be petted this evening. She loved being cuddled, especially by some of the more animal-friendly inhabitants of Paolim, but she would lose her assassin's edge if she allowed herself to be stroked just before a hunt. She curled up, using her large, fluffy tail as a comfortable seat. Her tail never got waterlogged even in the worst monsoons; a gift from her father, who had been a Bengal swimming cat of some distinction.

The boys chatted, and soon the village priest joined them, and then the baker, the hoods of their colourful raincoats blocking out the fat raindrops. Magnificat watched the bats flutter out and whirl around the jackfruit tree. The roar of the monsoon rains played a tabla beat on the roof. The bats would not go out to dance above the old well and the paddy fields tonight; the storm was breaking over all their heads, and the last of the evening light shimmered out of the grey skies. Night hovered on the horizon, stretching black shadows towards the village.

Then the boys got on their bikes, and in the sudden light of the headlamps, Magnificat saw the cobra's sleek head skim the stubbled green spikes of the jackfruit, his tail flicking as he shot into the upper branches. An overripe jackfruit fell with a dull thud onto the glistening road below, the fermented sweet stink rising from its innards making her pink nostrils twitch. Then there he was, faster than she'd anticipated, his hood rising out from the broken slates in the gutters.

She was up, her paws and claws digging into the red tiles, her whiskers and the long fur on her face quivering in fear. The tiles were so slick with rain that she didn't dare risk moving downwards towards the snake. If she tried to go back up the roof, she'd be at a disadvantage, allowing the cobra first strike.

The wind picked up speed, howling in Magnificat's ears. The cobra's hood gleamed in the light of the street lamps; she could see only the angry spectacles, and the tiny black eyes like the pebbles at the bottom of the river, not the rest of his tail. His tongue flicked in and out nervously, and the cat realized he'd come up too fast. Snakes had poor eyesight, so it was unlikely that he had seen her on the roof. Instead, he must have planned to lie in wait along the tiles. Now he had her scent, and knew she was there. The snake hissed, rearing up, and Magnificat had to stop herself from skittering away across the slippery tiles.

Before he could rise to his full length, Magnificat screamed, letting the battle cry ring out over Paolim, and scrambled sideways, seeking the edge of the roof. The cobra had been about to strike in her direction, but he hesitated, weaving back and forth, uncertain of his next move. The Sender calculated her chances. She could make a run for it—a long leap to the balcao below, then a dash across its broken balustrades towards the palm tree. And if she did, the stalking would have to begin again, the long mornings and days of near-sleepless vigil, the nights of hunting as each of them tried to find the other one first. This was a bad place for a fight, but Magnificat had learned as a kitten that you couldn't choose the battleground, the time of battle or even the opponent. The speed of your paws, the swiftness of your attack—only that was in the hunter's control.

But she had let too much time go by in reflection. The cobra lowered his hood, his tongue jabbing at the air, and Magnificat's whiskers flared up, the long fur on her face prickling despite the rain's steady beat. She caught the snake's jet eye, and realized that he was thinking the same thing. If he flattened himself against the roof, the cat would lose the biggest advantage she had over him: sight. Night had dropped over Paolim silently, and there was only a half-moon in the sky, the light of the street lamps lapping only at the edge of the rusted tin guttering.

The snake would use his tongue to scent the cat, and Magnificat would have to rely on her whiskers and her instincts. The white cat growled softly, her teeth baring as she considered her position—out on the very edge, she would have to hope that she sensed the cobra before he reached her.

Her whiskers bristled unpleasantly, as though an unseen bat had flown by and touched them with its leathery wings. Through the coldness of the rain, the air shimmered with sudden heat; it seemed to the hunter that the winds themselves were parting.

". . . This blanket is too heavy. Curses! Will no Bigfeet rid me of this meddlesome quilt?" The mews came right out of the storm, as though a cat was riding the clouds. Magnificat, her tail fluffed, her whiskers humming with an unpleasant electricity, erected her fur and screamed defiance into the winds.

The storm dropped. The cat was trembling; the clouds had never mewed at her before in a stranger's voice. But Magnificat was a hunter, she snapped back to the cobra—where was he? Had he already slithered up the tiles?

"That's much better, thank you, such happiness to be able to breathe again. Ugh, there's wool stuck in my throat, mustn't swallow . . . Oops, too late! Morning hairball alert, Bigfeet!" said the voice again, making Magnificat's paws curl up, her claws scraping at the roof.

The hunter stared as an orange cat shimmered in and out of view. It appeared to be suspended above the red tiles, rocking in a bed placed just above the roof of the old house. It was a small cat, half her size, and by the look of its ruffled fur, half asleep. Magnificat found the way its paws appeared to hover just above the tiles extremely disconcerting. She yowled, her green eyes catching the light, ready to attack the beast.

A cold fury had begun to replace Magnificat's terror. "My roof!" she snarled. It didn't matter how the intruder had got here, the noisy stranger was going to have to leave. She spat, viciously, and swung into attack stance. The orange cat yawned, and turned over.

But before Magnificat could do anything about her unwanted visitor, she heard the rustle on the roof. Even in the dim light, the black, curved head stood out, a sinister silhouette rearing up behind the tiles.

The cobra's strike was precise; if she hadn't moved just then, it would have got her on the flank. She was sliding towards the end of the roof, she would sail over it and land hard on her belly on the balcao below—she had to turn. Her claws found purchase, and Magnificat spun around, balancing on her forepaws almost entirely. She could smell the serpent's slick scales. He was coming up fast, and instead of trying to see him, the Sender of Paolim closed her eyes, relying on scent and instinct to see her through.

The hunter hooked her left front paw onto the tiles, using them as a slider to let herself swing more to the left. She heard the snake strike again, to her right, the sound reminding her of the way the mangrove roots sprang back when she brushed through them on her long hunts. The cobra was up rapidly this time, but Magnificat had found her balance. She used her left paw as an anchor, and felt the rain beat down hard on her whiskers as she let her claws scythe out. Before the snake could sway in her direction, she had made her first strike, her paw ripping down the length of his throat. It was a bold move, and a dangerous one; it allowed the snake to make a swift strike at her paw, but she was out of danger by the time his head bobbed down.

The hunter struck again, and again, two lightning strikes with her claws, crushing his windpipe and ribs, and the snake collapsed, his tail twitching as he died. The snake opened his mouth and hissed once, the venom dripping uselessly off his fangs. "Ssssswift you were," he said, "ssstealthy and sssstrong." A last twitch, a death-twitch, ran through his massive length, and then he lay still.

Up in the clouds, a small snore emanated from the stranger cat. One of her paws was out, curled around her long white whiskers. The fur on it was neat and dry, her whiskers calm. She was a young queen, probably no more than two winters old, her eyes as green as the hunter's.

"I'll deal with you now," said the hunter grimly, but the orange cat snored with greater intensity. Slowly, the little stranger winked out of view, fading until only the clouds were left where she had been. Magnificat, her paws glistening with blood, was left alone in the night.

THE WHITE CAT SETTLED back on the tiles, puzzled. She let the rain patter down on her; her fur was so long and so thick that it was only in the most ferocious of the Paolim storms that she felt uncomfortable. She began grooming herself, cleaning the blood off her whiskers with one practiced paw. She was fastidious, and preferred her fur to be free of mud, or blood, or any of the other detritus of the hunt.

The air grew heavier, and a familiar crackle lit up the clouds, until Magnificat felt the tug on her whiskers. The swollen rain clouds shone, and parted like gauze, to reveal the solemn, worried faces of a calico cat called Begum, and Umrrow Jaan, a half-Siamese, half-alley cat with slightly crossed eyes. Concern dripped off their fur as they peered at the Sender of Paolim, their outlines shimmering and re-forming in the sky.

"We're so sorry, Em!" said the half-Siamese. "We didn't dare send until the battle was over. I was so scared that if we popped up suddenly as well, you'd slip and fall on those wet tiles, plunging to a horrifying, tragic death like a splattered jackfruit, or that the cobra would weave his wicked way under your guard, plunging his venom into your poor heart . . ."

"Umrrow Jaan," said the calico sternly, her whiskers managing to radiate disapproval even though she was just a formless shape in the clouds, "what did we say about not letting your paws run away with your sense of drama? Shut your whiskers for a moment, will you? Em, we're terribly sorry. By the time she'd started sending, you were already dancing with the cobra, and we couldn't warn you without risking your life."

Magnificat combed her whiskers, bewildered. "I don't understand, Begum," she said. "Who in hell was the orange cat? And what does she have to do with the Delhi Senders? And why was she on my roof?" Her massive, fluffy tail was beating a quiet tattoo on the roof. A loose tile rapped on its fellows and went sideways, letting the rain pour into the old house through the skylight.

The calico sighed. "That orange cat," she said, "is the new Sender of Nizamuddin. As far as we can make out, she has more power in her whiskers than all of the Senders of Delhi combined."

"Oh yes!" said Umrrow Jaan, her ears standing up in sharp points against the clouds. "We could hear her all the way across the Yamuna river and over the dreaming spires and mansions of Old Delhi even when she was a tiny kitten! And then she made friends with the tigers, and she brought one of them onto the link, and you have no idea how panicked we were; I ran helter-skelter all the way through the Chandni Chowk street market and didn't stop until I'd reached the Ridge, and even there, the barbets and woodshrikes were almost falling out of their trees!"

"A kitten? And a tiger?" said Magnificat, curling her fat tail around her in puzzlement. "But I saw no tigers on my roof!"

"Umrrow Jaan!" said Begum sharply, switching her tail. "Put a paw in it, do. I can see we'll have to explain about Mara."

"Yes, do," said Magnificat, with a slight edge to her mew. "I thought I knew all of the Senders in this land, but until this evening, they've had the decency to show their whiskers only when summoned for our meetings! None of them has leapt out of the clouds, disrupted a major battle and disappeared again without so much as a basic introductory miaow! The manners of an alley cat!"

"If this was not a sending, Magnificat, you would be able to smell my regret and our apologies on our whiskers," said

Begum, shimmering among the clouds. "Indeed, we are sorry. The problem with the Sender of Nizamuddin is that she doesn't know she's sending."

Another ripe jackfruit fell from the tree, and the bats swooped out, chittering to themselves. The rain was slowing now, driving in the other direction as the Sender of Paolim stared unblinkingly at the Sender of Purani Dilli and the Senders from Delhi's other localities.

Magnificat hissed slowly. "But how is that possible?" she said.

"She of the long whiskers—the longest we've seen in three generations, mind you—has been sending in her sleep," said Begum. "The worst part is that while we can hear her clearly, the Sender of Nizamuddin is very young, and despite all our efforts, we haven't been able to reach her."

"Except in her dreams," said Umrrow Jaan. "But she thinks we're nightmares and she bats us away. She looks very cute, na? With her paws cycling, just like the oldest kitten from my sixth litter . . . or was it my fifth? You know, the litter I had with that dashing Daryaganj tom . . . or was he the small striped thug from the Civil Lines enclave? It's so hard to keep them straight, after a few litters I forget which kitten was born when, except for the first litter I ever had, remember, at the back of the hakim's shop in . . ."

"Umrrow!" said Magnificat and Begum simultaneously.

"Oh, all right!" said Umrrow, managing to convey that she was sulking even though her image was, like Begum's, a little blurred at the edges, as was normal for sendings.

"As Umrrow said (before she started mewing on and on about her endless litters), the Sender hasn't yet joined our circle," said Begum. "And while Beraal—you know her, don't you, Magnificat?—has trained her not to send to the world at large when she's awake, Mara's whiskers are completely out of control when she's asleep."

The white cat's tail swished, tapping to the beat of the rain on the tiles.

"You're telling me that Delhi has a Sender of such immense power that her whiskers can bring her all the way *here*? In her sleep?" said Magnificat. "And she has no idea that she can do this?"

They had no trouble understanding her meaning. The long-whiskered ones were special. A cat who was not a Sender was confined to the limits of its clan's territory: their whiskers would not go further than the boundaries they marked with their scents. But even for the long-whiskered, there were limits to how far they could travel.

Begum could send to all of the cats in Delhi, but her whiskers would not reach beyond the city's outskirts without the help of the other Senders. Magnificat was Goa's most celebrated Sender, and at her most intense, she could send her image dancing in the skies along a fair distance—ten, perhaps twenty villages. But unless the Senders were linking with one another, letting their whiskers carry them longer distances, no cat could travel so far on her own.

Only a few cats were Senders; in any clan, only a handful would have the ability to transmit their thoughts—and their very selves—so strongly that they could cross space with ease. Their abilities travelled from mother to daughter. Though Senders often produced litter after litter of perfectly normal kittens, every once in a while, a Sender would give birth to a kitten with longer whiskers than usual and know that her daughter was just like her. There was never more than one Sender in any clan, often fewer than four or five in any generation of cats in a large territory. None of the Senders Magnificat had met would have been able to travel from Delhi to Goa on their own. This one, untrained, just two winters old, had made the journey in her sleep.

Begum caught the drift of Magnificat's thoughts. "She has travelled further," said the calico. "She startled the monastery cats the other night; the Rimpuss was shaken out of her usual equanimity and had to take an extra meditation session. We think we should be able to reach her very soon. She has had a long kittenhood, and unlike the rest of us, she had no Sender to train her—Tigris, the last Sender of Nizamuddin, died shortly after this one was born."

A savage gust from the storm sent the cobra's body rolling down to the edge of the roof, where it stayed, limply wedged. The Sender of Paolim looked out into the rain, her eyes straying towards the river.

"You'll have to find a way to contact her soon," said Magnificat. 'We can't have a rogue Sender roaming the seven skies. You must train her, or else her whiskers must be trimmed." Begum's whiskers bristled. The orange stranger's sendings seemed effortless, compared to the steady concentration it took Delhi's entire Circle of Senders before she and Umrrow Jaan could make the difficult journeys to Goa and other places as they followed Mara's erratic wake.

She spoke with finality, washing the last specks of mud and cobra skin off her tail. Begum and Umrrow Jaan made their farewells, and shimmered out of view. Begum thought, just before they pulled back from the clouds and sped away across the emerald fields, skimming the beaches and the palm trees on their way back to Delhi, that the Sender of Paolim was right. They would have to do something about Delhi's rogue Sender before she became a threat to them all.

CHAPTER ONE

Cat Burglar

The fog dropped swiftly across the river, and in the rays of the late evening sun, it brought a fleeting beauty to the black sludge of the canal. The grey winter mist rode through the bylanes of the dargah, the ancient shrine at the centre of the neighbourhood, rising towards the high rooftops of the forbidding new buildings in Nizamuddin proper, creeping around the frozen iron bars of the gates that blocked off many of the colony's roads.

Under the canal, the pigs huddled together for warmth, their bristled coats inadequate protection against the chill. The smallest of the piglets squirmed her way into the centre of the drove, seeking comfort and warmth from her elders. She didn't ask for food; she already knew her mother's teats had run dry, and that the last potato skin and lauki peel had been scavenged from the canal banks. At less than a month old, the piglet did not know what it felt like to have a full stomach. She was tiny, and she rarely squealed, though two of the adults grunted as she pushed her way through. One stepped on another's trotter, and he cried out. The high complaining wail cut through the strains of the evening call to worship from the dargah.

Southpaw paused when he heard the squeal, his ears flicking to attention, but then he placed it: one of the canal pigs, not a cat or a kitten. He padded alongside the second-floor balcony railing, turning his attention back to the Bigfeet, hoping they wouldn't notice him. He didn't think they would. Though he was in his third winter, he was small for his size, and the last few seasons had pared the brown tomcat down to muscle and gristle. He made a thin shadow, invisible in the fog to all but the most sharp-eyed of predators.

When he heard the Bigfeet, he flattened himself, his fur pressed close to the rough bricks of the roof. They came out of the kitchen, talking loudly among themselves, and passed so near the cat that Southpaw could feel his whiskers tingle. He heard them clatter down the stairs.

The cat unfurled his whiskers, listening. But there seemed to be no other Bigfeet, and Southpaw padded into the kitchen. The scents from inside burst over him in warm waves—meat of some kind. Soaring above the smell of the meat, the clean singing freshwater aroma of fish made his teeth chatter in involuntary excitement. He almost missed his leap, because the scent had also made him weak, considering he hadn't eaten in a while.

The fish was a large one, a whole carp, not yet sauced, on a blue china platter. Its scales gleamed encouragingly at Southpaw, and its red gills murmured to him of the taste of blood and the sea, firm, juicy flesh. The cat's nostrils flared as he smelled the fish at close quarters, and felt once again how painfully empty his stomach was. He hesitated. The plan had been to grab as much of the fish as he could in his mouth and run for it before the Bigfeet came back. But he would have to tear the fish into a small enough portion to carry, which might take precious moments.

When he sank his sharp incisors into its silver skin, he knew he was in trouble. The juices from its tender white flesh spurted into his mouth, and Southpaw forgot the possibility of danger, forgot the need to carry food back to the waiting cats. He didn't realize he was making urgent mewing sounds as he tore into the fish, almost inhaling his first proper meal in three days. Four bites, and he had severed the tail and belly. The smell of the fish made his pink nose twitch as he gobbled.

"Out of there NOW, Southpaw! Katar told you not to raid the Bigfeet kitchens!"

Mara's indignant mew rang in his ears, so clear that she might almost have been there, perched on the shelf of spices, perhaps, above his head. But it was just a sending, and though Southpaw pawed at the fish with some urgency, trying to cut through the last flap of silver skin that held the tail attached to the body, he ignored the Sender. It was exasperating enough to know that Mara's whiskers let her travel around Nizamuddin without actually having to leave her Bigfeet's house but it was far worse when she decided to spy on him. Because she left no virtual scent, he never knew when she was on one of her prowls, and the tomcat found this aggravating.

"I'm leaving, I'm leaving," he mumbled through a last hasty mouthful. His belly felt pleasantly full, and he picked up the tail carefully, hooking his incisors through the piece for extra security.

"Right behind you," growled Mara, and Southpaw's fur bristled unpleasantly when he heard the tension in her voice. From the stairs, he could hear the thumping of the Bigfeet as they came up, yammering at each other as they always did, just as though they were kittens who hadn't learned to use whiskers and scent, only mews and yowls. But that, he realized, wasn't what Mara had meant.

There was a Bigfoot in the doorway, staring at him.

"Idiot," said Mara. He could see her now, or at any rate, he could see the Sender's image; an orange cat, bobbing along behind the Bigfeet's head, her green eyes flaring crossly.

The Bigfoot stepped into the kitchen and grabbed a towel off the wooden pegs on the wall. He started shouting just as Southpaw darted to the left, in the direction of the kitchen sink. The Bigfoot followed him, moving faster than the cat had thought he would.

"Not that way, you'll be trapped!" Mara was mewing, and fear had replaced the anger in her voice. Southpaw wanted to tell her he knew what he was doing, but he'd have had to raise his whiskers or open his mouth, and then he might drop the fish. Instead, he watched as the Bigfoot hurtled towards him, as he had hoped, leaving the door unguarded, and then the cat skidded around, using his front paws to propel himself across the sink, across the stone shelves, through the Bigfoot's legs, streaking out of the door. Trapped indeed, he grumbled to himself, as if he would be trapped by one of those dumb Bigfeet, after all these months of being a hunter.

"See?" said Mara, and Southpaw realized she hadn't been talking about the kitchen at all. The other Bigfeet had come up the stairs. Three of them stood in a semicircle outside the door; two stood by the roof, blocking off the approach to the ladder over which he had intended to make his escape. "Mmmmfff!" Southpaw said indistinctly through his mouthful of fish, and skidded for the second time as he did a complete turn.

"Stay away from the kitchen door, he's got something in his hands!" Mara said urgently. "Circle wider, yes, wider . . . Southpaw, run!"

Southpaw heard the stomping of the Bigfoot in the kitchen, but he had his back to him, his eyes fixed on the other side of the roof and the long parapet that he knew ran just beneath. His teeth chattered, not just from the numbing cold and the fog, but in fear; his whiskers and fur stood up despite the damp. He didn't see the Bigfoot make his throw. It was only when his back paws seized in terrible pain and he heard the clang of the vessel bouncing on the roof that he realized he'd been hit. He locked his mouth harder onto the fish, refusing to cry out. His left paw had received the brunt of the blow, and he could feel it dragging behind him. But there was the roof at last; behind him, the Bigfeet sounded close, too close, their cries dangerously loud in his ears. He let his front paws do the work as he limped across the roof, turning for a moment to face the Bigfeet.

The cat made the leap to the parapet just before the Bigfoot threw the kitchen tongs at him, ducking and weaving so that it went past, harmlessly. He could feel a hot, sticky dampness on his back paw, and the smell of his own blood rose higher than the warm smell of blood from the fish he carried.

"You'll have to make the jump into the flame tree," Mara said in his ear. He could tell she was holding her voice steady, but it carried a sharpness that revealed her worry. As he crouched on the edge of the parapet, the flame tree seemed far way. He couldn't rely on his back paws to propel him into the leap. The cat looked down, and the distance made even his brave heart quail. He was three floors up; the fall would be hard.

Above his head, the Bigfeet yells were getting louder. Southpaw risked a quick glance upwards, and saw one of them lean down towards the parapet, wielding a broom that looked ominously prickly—not the soft kind made from dried grasses, but the stick brooms that could cause serious injuries. He measured the distance between him and the nearest branch. He wasn't going to make it, he thought.

"You have to," said Mara. She had changed her position, and her worried green eyes assessed him from the tree. "Drop the fish, Southpaw, it's not that important, and then you can use your whiskers for balance!"

He looked at her and knew she was giving him good advice, but his brown eyes said no.

"You stubborn brat!"

His whiskers twitched a little—yes, they said amicably, he agreed with her. The swoosh of the broom startled him; he hadn't realized how close the Bigfeet were. One of them was climbing down onto the parapet.

Southpaw stayed crouched at the edge, measuring the gap. In the flame tree, the squirrels, woken out of their sleep, gaped at him, chittering as they ran down to the lower branches, well away from the crazy brown cat who thought he could make an impossible jump. The broom thumped down behind him again. The pain in his left paw was intense; it felt like the paw was on fire even as he felt his phalanges crush and the tendon tear. Southpaw blinked, and then he stared deliberately into Mara's green eyes, putting the pain away.

He leapt just as the broom came down, missing his tail by a whisker. The Bigfeet yelled and cursed, but Southpaw kept his focus on the branch. For a moment, he thought he'd reach it easily—and then one of his paws missed, and he found himself hanging on with just the other.

"Drop the fish!" Mara pleaded.

He wouldn't. The cat felt a claw tear, as the bark began to give way. His ribs hurt. The pain was travelling up his left back paw, so brutal after the leap that he could feel his eyes watering. But he kept his mouth clamped over the fish. He had to get down the tree before the Bigfeet managed to get to him.

"Southpaw, if you drop it now, you have a better chance! Please!" His brown eyes met Mara's, and he managed to raise his whiskers jauntily in her direction. He felt the muscles in his shoulder bulge and tense as he made a tremendous effort, forcing his paw up, hooking it over the branch. For a moment, he hung from a branch, eye-to-eye with the hard brown seedpods that dotted the tree. Then he pulled his back paw up, the uninjured one, letting the wounded paw drag behind him, and he slipped into the maze of its branches, moving deftly from the flame tree to the friendly saptaparni evergreen next to it.

"Just wait till you come and see me next, Southpaw, this isn't over," said Mara. "Rats. I have to go, my Chief Bigfoot will soon be here—but you're not off the hook, you hear?" He blinked at her, agreeably. The sounds of the Bigfeet were fading behind him, and as he set off through the freezing night, the squirrels watched him sleepily, their grey tails draggled from the mist. They agreed that he had a swagger in his step, but most of them thought he'd earned it. The only one of the rodents who disagreed was a small brown mouse; Jethro Tail's bright black eyes filled with concern as he noted Southpaw's limp. He had hurt his own paw in a daring raid involving the liberation of some chicken tikkas from their Bigfoot stall owner, and, in the cold, it had taken a long time to heal. He knew the young brown cat, and hoped that Southpaw wasn't as badly hurt as he seemed to be.

CHAPTER TWO

A Circle of Senders

Mara would have followed Southpaw back with a last indignant mew, just to keep him in his place, but there wasn't the time. Though she sent a parting curse in the errant tomcat's direction, she switched her attention back to her own house once she knew that he was safe.

Her whiskers trembled, telling her that she was just in time. The most important Bigfoot in the world was almost at the door. The Sender scrambled down from the windowsill. She shot across the carpet, almost overturning the fancy three-legged table with which she had a series of ongoing skirmishes, and reached the door just as the bell went.

In the past, Mara had tried very hard to use her whiskers to open the door herself, but she had never succeeded. All that had happened was that she'd sent herself to the other side of the door, and sometimes all the way down the stairs, which was not what she wanted at all. The Sender had learned to wait until one of her own Bigfeet arrived.

Her Bigfoot opened the door for the Chief Bigfoot, and Mara forgot that she was a dignified Sender who had seen two winters come and go. She lay on her back, wriggling in greeting, her paws cycling, and then she got to her paws and purred, rubbing her head against the ankles of the most important Bigfoot in the world.

"There, there," said the Chief Bigfoot. "Anyone would think that you hadn't seen me for a week, instead of this morning. All right, here's your cuddle. Okay, you want your chin scratched, too? You want more food? Finished everything in your bowl?"

Mara still didn't understand Bigfeet, but she had picked up a few words here and there, and her ears rose at the mention of cuddles and food. Her own Bigfeet were good at both of these but in an absent-minded sort of way despite all her attempts to train them, and tended to drift off mid-cuddle. The Chief Bigfoot was not like that at all. Mara led the way to the kitchen, purring, her beautiful, fluffy tail waving like a flag.

She held the Chief Bigfoot in high esteem. Compared to her other two Bigfeet, the Chief Bigfoot had far more freedom— she came into the house only twice a day, in the morning and the evening. Her Bigfeet did very boring things around the house, ironing clothes with a large and scary iron whose surface had scorched Mara's paw once, moving books and paper here and there, and generally getting in the Sender's way. The only interesting activity they did was cooking, and much to her indignation, she was barred from the kitchen at those times.

The Chief Bigfoot, on the other hand, was the official wielder of all the items and implements that had fascinated Mara in her kittenhood: the magnificent broom made of soft grasses, the mesmerizing floor swabbing rag that she had loved to chase, all the dusters that she adored pouncing on, especially the feather duster. (The feather duster had come to a messy end, unfortunately.)

Besides, she had never committed the dastardly deed of luring Mara into a small, interesting object that had appeared to be a feline sanctum, but had turned out to be a fiendish form of transportation to the vet's office. The kitten had been too stunned the first time she'd met the vet to do more than express her gratitude to her Bigfeet for bringing her back home, but when they did this again and again, she was seriously upset.

Mara still wasn't talking to the she-Bigfoot, who had taken her to the healer just a few days ago, but that only made her more fond of the Chief Bigfoot, who was far too superior a human to use an unsuspecting cat's very own catnip mouse against her as bait.

As the Chief Bigfoot poured kibble into her bowl, Mara sat there unblinking, and raised her whiskers discreetly. This was an ongoing, and so far, unsuccessful, experiment. Some moons ago, she had been lying on the bed with her Bigfeet, and had wondered what their minds were like. "Could I link to them?" she had asked herself. It seemed possible; she had linked to the minds of monkeys, tigers, dogs, bulbul songbirds, mynahs and moths in the past.

She would never in all her life forget what that first linking was like. Her whiskers had extended, brushing the she-Bigfoot's fingers lightly, and she had tried to hitchhike her way into her human's mind.

It was like falling from the roof and rushing at extreme speed into the swirling rapids of a turbulent river. Within seconds, Mara had been plunged into a maelstrom of Bigfeet thought. Telling Southpaw about it later, she was still indignant: "They don't think the same thought for more than one second! Their minds jump around like the monkeys at the zoo—and it's just as noisy. Noisier! They don't think in smells, either, just images and words, all muddled up so that you can't make out anything!" She had spent hours afterwards shaking her head to try and get the sense of exploding fireworks out of it.

For the last few moons, she had been trying a different tack. If she sent hard enough, could the Bigfeet hear her? Mara was dubious about this. She and Southpaw had discussed the issue, but he felt that the lack of whiskers made it impossible for them to hear cats. "No tails, no whiskers, poor creatures," he had said. Mara hadn't disagreed, but in her opinion, the reason the Bigfeet couldn't hear her had nothing to do with the lack of whiskers. It was because they were so busy dealing with the incessant chatter of their own minds that nothing else could get through.

She had tried very hard to train her Bigfeet, but given up: they were too easily distracted. But the Chief Bigfoot had shown promise. She listened to Mara, for one thing, even if she did forget herself and try to mew occasionally—she had no idea that she sounded like a sick kitten. And though her mind was every bit as loud and garrulous as the minds of the other Bigfeet, Mara had hopes of getting through to her someday. She was experimenting with sending simple images, the way a mother cat might do with her kittens—milk, fish, purring, that sort of thing. So far, she hadn't got anywhere, but Mara told herself that the Bigfeet would take longer to train than the average kitten.

Today seemed promising. She sat on her wooden stool in the kitchen and tried, patiently, to get the Chief Bigfoot to stretch out whatever Bigfeet had in place of whiskers. Mara thought it might be their ears, or perhaps their eyebrows, and she stared as hard as she could at the Chief Bigfoot's forehead. "Hello!" she said to her. "I'm sure you can hear me. Would you like to stop playing with those dishes and the sink and play with me instead? Wouldn't that be more fun?" The Sender waited hopefully, but there was no response. Perhaps she needed to go a little slower. Perhaps just a few basic mews, sent by whisker?

The Chief Bigfoot looked up from doing the dishes once or twice, puzzled by the cat's intense stare. "Ei, Mara," she said. "You've had your food, no?" She went to check, but everything seemed fine in that department. She finished the dishes, and started to clean out the store cupboards. The cat swivelled around on the stool, and after a while, the Chief Bigfoot caught Mara's eye.

They stared at each other, and Mara felt a ripple of hope run along her whiskers. "Hello," she sent patiently. "Can you hear me?" Her whiskers were trembling with the effort she was putting into sending to the Chief Bigfoot, while staying off the Nizamuddin link so as not to bother the other cats. She stared harder, trying to get the Chief Bigfoot's eyebrows to stand up like her whiskers. "Like this," she sent, not sure whether she had actually linked or not. "See? Watch my eyebrows."

She furrowed and unfurrowed them, hoping the Chief Bigfoot would catch on.

Success! The Chief Bigfoot's eyebrows were trembling, and they rose slightly. Mara strained, letting her whiskers unfurl to their maximum length. If she had been sending over the link, the force of her concentration would have carried her well over the Delhi Zoo, far beyond the Yamuna river by now. Was she getting through at last? Mara didn't realize that her small pink tongue was hanging out, or that she was making tiny distress calls from time to time. "Eyebrows," she thought triumphantly. "That's the secret! Focus on their eyebrows, and you have them . . . wait, where's the Chief Bigfoot going?"

Mara had to swivel again, her concentration broken as the Chief Bigfoot frowned down at her and then left the kitchen. "Come back," the Sender sent, trying to see if there was any kind of link, "I'm sorry—was it something I said?"

The Chief Bigfoot reappeared with both of Mara's Bigfeet trotting behind. The Sender blinked. Had the Chief Bigfoot told her Bigfeet about their linking? But she hadn't felt a response, really, just seen the eyebrows rise.

She was turning the matter over in her head when the she-Bigfoot picked her up, making soothing noises. Mara stared hard at her eyebrows, wondering if she could make them twitch, too. But the he-Bigfoot was prodding at her nose, and she squirmed. "Don't do that!" she said. "My nose is perfectly fine. Wet, as it should be . . . ooh! That's my tummy you're poking. Stop doing that, I might cough up a hairball. Wait. The towel! You brought out the towel! Not the olive oil. I hate the olive oil. No, no, I don't need to be dosed. Stop wrapping me up—I'll fight! I'm a warrior, I am! Blast the towel, I can't move my paws, you horrible Bigfeet! Won't open my mouth, so there . . . quit tickling, that's really ticklish, that spot under my chin, mmmrrraaoowwwffff!" The olive oil went down her throat, despite Mara's laments, and the Bigfeet deposited their wriggling, protesting bundle gently on the ground, watching in concern as the cat shot off, her outrage trembling at the tips of her whiskers.

It took a long time to clean the worst of the olive oil off her fur, and Mara knew from bitter experience that it would take a while before the taste faded. The Sender's flanks heaved as she hopped into her basket, resolving to ignore any overtures from the Bigfeet. She kept her back to the door, as a signal to the Bigfeet if they entered the room that they were no longer on speaking terms.

"The perfidy of it!" she thought bitterly. Her Bigfeet were unpredictable, and prone to misunderstanding, but Mara hadn't expected the Chief Bigfoot to let her down so badly. The Sender washed her whiskers to calm herself down, and decided to take a short nap.

SOMETHING WAS TUGGING HARD at her whiskers, so roughly that it was painful. She was out in an open field, unsheltered from the freezing cold. The ground under her was hard, the grass rough. Some things—more than one creature—were circling around her. Whatever was yanking at her whiskers stopped, mercifully.

In her basket, Mara whimpered, turned over and went back to sleep.

The creatures were getting closer. She was lying out in the open, looking up at the wide, endless twilight sky. On the far horizon, the turrets of an old mansion stood guard, as motionless and as massive as the elephants she had seen on her visits to the zoo. The harsh questioning call of peacocks ratcheted back and forth across the great gardens, and a clan of squirrels played games of tag around the massive trunk of a tree so large that its roots lay like thick ropes in the brown and green grass. Mara could hear whispers, as though cats spoke to her in the distance. Cold winds briefly stirred the sensitive filaments inside her ears, but she couldn't make out what the mews said.

Mara stirred, her paws warding off whatever was intruding on her dreams, but though her ears were alert, her eyes stayed closed.

The sensitive tips of her whiskers were being brushed, lightly. It felt as though many shadowy forms had crept up, forming a circle around her, and that each one came up to her in turn, nuzzling her whiskers as they passed. The cold seeped through her fur, reaching deep into her bones. The ground was damp as well as freezing. Through the mist, one of the creatures loomed closer and closer. She felt her whiskers being brushed, again, and then there was a sharp, unpleasant tug.

"What a dream!" said Mara, waking with a start. It must have been the olive oil. She yawned, and her paws shot out, stiffly. The basket was cold underneath her, and hard, and prickly.

"Finally," said a sleek, purring voice. "That took longer than I'd expected."

Mara opened her eyes. She was in her room, in the basket; outside the window, the cheels swooped and called, almost finished with their sorties as night came down over Nizamuddin.

And she was out in the middle of an open field, her fur damp from the chill of the spiky grass underneath. She blinked, and the unfamiliar red ramparts she had been gazing at, with their ornate curlicues and niches, wavered and vanished, revealing only the solid walls of home. She blinked again, and the air thickened.

"Hello!" said several other voices, all of them sleek, but none quite as rich as the first one. A chorus of mews rang out, like a feline call to worship, and the air around Mara filled with the shadowy shapes of a dozen cats, their flickering outlines silhouetted against the rising yellow moon. "Now that the Sender of Nizamuddin is here," said the first voice, the rich husky one, "shall we start?"

This was no dream. Mara scrabbled, pawing the air as she swung for a sickening second between the cold earth outside, the warm blankets at home.

"Don't fight it," said the smooth, purring voice she'd heard first. "Make a choice, and tell your whiskers to stay where you are. I'd suggest you stay with us, because we'll just have to summon you again if you go away. Now that we've figured out how to get you here, we're not letting you go so soon."

Mara took in her surroundings, the quiet lawns, the ancient statues, the peacocks in the distance, the birdsong drowning out the sounds of traffic far away. There seemed to be no Bigfeet about, though they had left traces of their presence. The ancient, mossy bricks of an old wall held birdseed, and some grains and nuts; flocks of crows and mynahs pecked at this banquet at one end, while the squirrels chased each other round and round, their tails fluffed into perky grey fringes against the cold. Doves added their persuasive, soothing crooning to the air, softening the brisk hammering that the woodpeckers produced as they went about their business. A hoopoe trod gingerly along the grass, its bright stripes warming the winter. Two parrots flashed by, leaving brilliant green trails in the sky as they called to each other in eloquent screeches.

"Summon me?" said Mara, wondering if that was what she'd felt—the tugs on her whiskers, the sense that she'd been forcibly lifted through the air and brought here.

"The way you did with that tiger," said another purr, a lively, sparkling voice. "We heard all about it here in Mehrauli!"

"Enough with the chitchat," the first voice said sternly. "Umrrow Jaan, wait for your turn to speak. Mara, stop wavering between Nizamuddin and the Garden of the Cheels, you're making me dizzy with all that shimmering in and out. We have a lot to say to you, and about the way you've been sending in your sleep, but that will have to wait until after the meeting of the Circle of Senders of Delhi. Senders, raise your whiskers, where are your manners? Say hello to the Sender of Nizamuddin, it's her first time inside the Circle."

There were fewer of them than she'd thought—perhaps seven in all. The Speaker for the Circle of Senders was smaller than the voice had led Mara to expect. She was a neat calico, her fur combed down despite the tendrils of mist that clung to it, with sharp, deep brown eyes.

"Begum, look at her tail, curling into a question mark," said a plump tabby, with jaunty and slightly crooked whiskers that gave her a cheerful air. "We're so used to the Circle, but it must be strange for you, Sender of Nizamuddin."

Before Mara could speak, Begum cut in, her whiskers brisk. "There's nothing to it, Mara," she said. "Each Sender comes from a different part of Delhi, and we take it in turns to share about our neighbourhood. Listen to the others, and you'll soon catch up with us, never fear. Shall we start, Senders? We'll go by area, starting with Chandni Chowk—Jalebi, you go first."

Mara took a last, wistful look back at her warm blankets, and told herself to stay with the circle of cats. There was something in the voice of the Sender that made her think there was little point in leaving; the cat's whiskers told her that she'd meant it about summoning Mara again.

"Business as usual," Jalebi was saying. "We had some trouble with the outsiders—this year's railway cats—and the birds, but they listened when Gulab and Jamun explained that the Bigfeet's homes and workplaces were off limits."

"Any incidents?" asked the Speaker.

"Yes, unfortunately," said Jalebi. "Two of the railway cats sneaked into the Jain Bird Hospital and killed a few pigeons before we could stop them."

"That's a risk," said the Speaker, and Mara felt a ripple of assent run along the whiskers of all the cats.

"We were lucky," said Jalebi. "The Bigfeet thought it was the rats who'd done it. But the railway cats have promised they'll do their hunting elsewhere and leave the birds at the bird hospital alone. I don't expect more trouble from them, they're quite sweet, especially Catmandu's crew from Nepal."

"Right," said the Speaker. "Anything else? How are the litters doing this winter?"

"There's enough food for them," said Jalebi. "Some shortages in the Jama area, because they had a sudden rise in the number of stray dogs, so there isn't enough food, not even in the garbage heaps. But the Kashmere Gate side has ample feeding, prey and trash both, so many of the Jama cats have shifted there."

"Thank you, Jalebi," the Speaker said. "The Sender of Hauz Khas, next—anything to report, Baoli?"

At first, Mara listened carefully to the Senders' reports. For a brief space, she couldn't tell whether the cats were actually there, or whether they had been summoned, but after she had heard two or three of them speak, she noticed that most of the Senders had a shimmering outline, and that their whiskers seemed to flicker in the breeze. Jalebi appeared to be present, and so did the Speaker, but she would have said that none of the other Senders were.

Umrrow Jaan's report held Mara's interest: some of the cats had moved after the Bigfeet had built yet another market, Umrrow said, but a few had come down from the Qutb Minar and become market cats, attracted by the prospect of easy feeding from the trash cans, instead of the daily grind of hunting and killing. The Sender from the Embassy area, Spook, was droning on and on, and Mara's attention began to wander. I wonder, she said to herself, why summonings have to feel so real. Isn't there a way to hear and see the Senders without sitting on this prickly patch of grass, in this cold? She tried to wrap her tail all the way around her for warmth and overbalanced, because she'd stretched it too far. But if she wrapped her tail halfway around, the unwrapped flank stayed cold.

"The Sender of Nizamuddin?" said the Speaker.

Mara experimented with wrapping her tail around one flank for a little while, and then switching to the other side, to see if that would work. But all it did was to make both flanks feel cold.

"The Sender of Nizamuddin, we're waiting for you," said the Speaker.

Mara shuffled backwards on the grass, looking for a warmer patch, but the ground was even colder, so she shuffled forwards again.

"Mara!" said the Speaker, huffing.

The Sender flicked her ears at Begum, startled.

"Your report, Mara? As Sender of Nizamuddin?" said the calico cat, her tail beginning to switch back and forth. "Weren't you listening to Umrrow Jaan and Jalebi and the rest of us?"

Begum's fur was fluffing up in annoyance, and Mara thought that despite the differences between the two in terms of their colouring, there was more than a slight resemblance between Begum and Beraal.

But her mews were gentle enough, as she prompted Mara. "Just the basics, then. How are the Nizamuddin cats doing?" said Begum. "On your rounds of the neighbourhood, what have you noticed? Is there any trouble with the Bigfeet? We haven't had any news from Nizamuddin since Miao's death, and we've wondered whether the cats were back to normal after the battle."

"I didn't know Miao was a Sender," said Mara, momentarily diverted.

Begum said, "She wasn't, but she was a good friend to all of us, a keeper of the old histories. She had her ways of sending news across, through the mynahs and the cheels. But we haven't had news of Nizamuddin for a long time."

Jalebi said, "We've been so worried, especially when we heard about Datura and the ferals. Why, there was a feral outbreak once in Chandni, and it took down so many of the clan before they left. Are your cats all right?"

The Circle of Senders waited for Mara to respond, and she found her whiskers twitching nervously.

"I think so," she said hesitantly. "Southpaw doesn't say much, but he drops in every few days or so. The last time we met, he was in trouble, though—he'd gone hunting in the Bigfeet kitchens and injured his paw."

Begum waited expectantly, her whiskers raised in receiving mode.

Mara stared at the Senders, not sure what to say.

"And?" prompted Umrrow Jaan, her crossed eyes squinting in a kind way at Mara.

"Well," said Mara, "he got away, though it was such a big risk. I scolded him, but he doesn't listen to me much these days, he thinks he's as good a hunter as Katar, even though he's half Katar's size."

Begum's tail was twitching uncertainly. "Mara," she said, "I don't understand. Who's Southpaw, and why was he raiding Bigfeet kitchens? How's the rest of the clan? Is Katar managing as clan leader without Miao's guidance? How's Beraal doing with her litter—she was pregnant, wasn't she? Have the Bigfeet reacted in any way after the battle?"

"I don't know," said Mara. "I don't know the outside cats much, except for Southpaw and Beraal."

She saw Jalebi's whiskers rise in incredulity, though the plump cat didn't mew. There was a sudden silence, and overhead, they heard the parrots squawk, as the pair broke out in a squabble. Their green shapes flashed into vivid relief against the old red ramparts.

"Never mind Chancha and Meechi," said Begum. "They've been together for years and their feathers droop if they haven't had three arguments a day. So if I understand you correctly, you don't know the cats in Nizamuddin? You don't patrol the neighbourhood? Mara, didn't Beraal or Miao tell you what a Sender does?"

"I don't like it outside," said Mara. "And the cats don't like me. My Bigfeet love me, so why should I leave the house?"

"Have you never been outside except through sendings, Mara?" asked Jalebi, the plump cat's eyes widening in surprise.

"I went out once," said Mara, "and I hated it." She turned to Begum fiercely. "Beraal kept telling me I should go out, but I don't see why! It's terrifying! Everything's so loud, and the dogs seem so ferocious! The Bigfeet outside are mean and noisy. And the other cats really don't like me. They think I'm a freak. Why should I keep an eye out for them?"

Begum was looking at her very steadily.

"Because you're a Sender, Mara, and they are your clan," she said. "And that is what a Sender does. It's not about summoning a tiger during a battle, as impressive as that was. If you're the Sender, then you're responsible for the other cats, and that's the way it is."

"I don't have to be a Sender if I don't want to,' said Mara sulkily. 'You can do what you want, but I'm not going outside."

"What a brat!" said Umrrow Jaan. "I thought you were such a heroine after we heard about the battle—making friends with tigers, bringing one of them along to help your friends. We all wanted to meet the Sender of Nizamuddin when we heard, you know? But listen to you! So you're scared of the outside, as if all of us aren't! Sending doesn't protect us from the Bigfeet's kicks, or from the sharp teeth of the dogs, or the monkeys, but that doesn't matter, Mara! The reason we have such long whiskers, why we can send and summon, is because we're sup- posed to look after the rest. And here you are, whining about how they don't like you, they think you're a freak. You think we haven't felt that way? But we kept going, we didn't whine about it like spoilt furballs, did we? We were there for the cats of our neighbourhood. But you—you're so spoiled that you don't even realize that if your friend Southpaw was stealing fish, he was probably terribly hungry!"

Umrrow Jaan made a disgusted mew, and turned her back on Mara.

The young queen's green eyes had grown large, filling with shock as she heard what Umrrow Jaan had to say. She stared at the Senders, feeling very small all of a sudden.

"You think Southpaw was stealing because he didn't have enough to eat?" she said, her mew subdued. It was a horrible thought. Mara's tail went down as she considered the last few months, and the memories that came back to her were not pleasant.

Often, she had finished eating by the time Southpaw dropped in; it had never occurred to her to ask her Bigfeet for more food for her friend, because he never said anything, and she assumed he'd hunted well. But she thought of a few occasions when Southpaw had eaten whatever leftovers there were. It came to her, as she sat in the middle of the Circle of Senders, that he had pushed his nose into the bowl with some intensity each time. She thought, too, of how thin he'd been getting, and how when she asked him why his ribs were showing, he'd raised his laughing whiskers and said he'd been overdoing the hunting, leaping and climbing.

"Umrrow, you're not wrong, but you're being too harsh on Mara," said Begum. "She hasn't been trained by Senders; there are none left in Nizamuddin. We had to wait till her whiskers had grown to their full length before we could summon her. I'd like to talk to Mara alone, but before I do, instead of scolding her, shall we link whiskers and show her what it really means to be a Sender?"

Spook, Umrrow, Jalebi, Baoli and the rest mewed in assent. Mara felt power riffle across her whiskers, and then the world changed in the old familiar way.

They were in Mehrauli, among the monuments and the flat rooftops of the Bigfeet settlements that barnacled the ancient ruins. Clowders of cats sat lazing on the walls of Zafar's tomb, and through Umrrow Jaan, they followed the scent trails of contentment and chatter deep into the area. A mother cat played with her litter in the peaceful shadows of Jamali Kamali mosque and tomb; a swaggering gang of toms, led by a proud young queen, made discreet forays on small prey behind the sweetly scented stalls in the flower market. When they saw Umrrow Jaan, their tails went up in glad greeting.

The air shimmered, Mara's stomach lurched unpleasantly, and then they were strolling behind the Red Fort in Chandni Chowk, Jalebi's flanks rolling from side to side as she sauntered down the fragrance-sellers' lane. Sleek grey cats with a military air about their whiskers sat on the wooden steps of many of the shops, acknowledging her passage with a stiff wave. An old tom marched down a crowded alley, winding through the legs of the unheeding Bigfeet. Four young kittens marched behind him, their stumpy legs waddling in his wake. He sent Jalebi a cheerful salute when he saw her, and the kittens raised their black whiskers, trying with less success to emulate their leader.

The world changed again. Fat black-and-white cats with sleepy eyes patrolled the grounds of the American Embassy, scouring the hedgerows for bandicoot runs. Further off, grey cats slipped like spooky shadows in and out of the Chinese Embassy, and three Siamese cats exchanged confidential gossip, their whiskers held secretively low. Their ears flickered as Spook passed by, but she didn't disturb their conclaves.

Begum took the last sending, heading for the banks of the Yamuna, taking the long way around so that they could see the elephants. Curled up together near the great beasts, a cluster of older cats warmed their bones and snoozed in the straw.

The elephants stepped carefully around them. Lower down, on the banks where the Bigfeet grew watermelons and other vegetables in the silty, fertile dirt of the Yamuna's banks, a clan of fishing cats balanced on the edge of an abandoned boat, scooping tadpoles out of the weed-festooned waters. "Join us, Begum, there's plenty!" they called. "Thank you," she called back. "I will, but not today."

Travelling in their wake, Mara felt something buried stir inside. There was a distance between all of the Senders and the other cats, for sure, but her whiskers and fur picked up other things: affection, respect. Wherever they went, the Senders were known, sometimes adored, always liked—even if that respect was sometimes tinged with fear, as it was with Begum's clan. It seemed to Mara that each neighbourhood was held together not just by the clans, and the links between the cats, but by something much deeper, as though the Senders spread a trail of caring as strong as the clans' scent trails wherever they went. They knew their ranges and territories intimately; the Senders with their far-reaching whiskers gave each clan of cats reassurance and comfort in the world of Bigfeet and predators.

"All right, Senders," said Begum. "Time for you to go back. Mara and I will stay a while longer."

One by one, the Senders touched their whiskers to Begum's long grey ones and left, their outlines hanging in the dark winter sky for a few seconds before finally disappearing. Jalebi raised her whiskers jauntily to Mara as she trotted off, but Umrrow's farewell mew was brisk, almost curt.

"Don't mind Umrrow," said Begum, whose sharp eyes missed very little. "She has romantic ideas about battles and

Senders, but she also has a soft heart. Give her time. You'll like her when you get to know her."

Mara's green eyes were troubled. "I don't think she wants to get to know me," she said. "She knows her clan so well, her fur tingles with the names of each kitten and cat. But the Nizamuddin cats and I . . ."

The Sender's whiskers drooped. Except for Beraal and Southpaw, she knew so little of her clan. As each Sender had drawn their maps of trails, marked by the clusters which showed colonies of cats, the borders and boundaries of their territories, even the presence of strangers and ferals, Mara had felt her paws clench at the thought that she did not know the Nizamuddin cats at all.

"Settle down," said Begum. "If the cold troubles you greatly, don't draw your flanks in; that will only make you shiver even more. Fluff your fur out, and let the mists touch you, but lightly. Don't fight the cold and the clouds."

Mara tucked her paws underneath her stomach, and imitated Begum. The two queens faced each other, comfortably fluffed. "Why is it so cold if this is only a summoning?" she asked. "I don't feel the air when I'm travelling to the zoo or elsewhere, but I can feel the ground here. It's hard and damp, too."

"We noticed," said Begum. "And I think Umrrow and Jalebi wondered as well; most of us pay the hunt price for a summoning." She saw Mara's whiskers twitch a question, and explained. "The hunt price—that's the price you pay for anything you want, Mara. If you make a kill, the price is paid in time, and patience, and skill, and sometimes wounds and blood. We Senders pay a price for sending and summoning.

Usually, we feel tired afterwards, especially with a tricky sending. It's easier when we all put our whiskers together, and the burden becomes lighter with time—but there is always a need for sleep, after."

Mara thought of how she had taken to her basket for two days after she had brought Ozzy into Nizamuddin, summoning the tiger all the way from the zoo so that he could help the cats in their battle against the ferals the previous winter. Her whiskers had ached with the effort of summoning, and sleep had closed over her like a giant bird's black wings, blotting out sound, light, the world.

"But your response to being summoned is unusual. Many creatures react with alarm, and find the journey unpleasant," said Begum.

"Ozzy shuddered when I rose with him into the air," said Mara, remembering how strange that had been. Ozzy the tiger had lain quietly in his den, slumbering behind a pile of stones; and Ozzy her friend had risen, his whiskers shimmering, into the air, his claws shooting out in startled reflex as she had tugged him into the skies. He had kept his eyes closed all through the journey, and she had felt the desperate clutch of his virtual whiskers, as massive as cables, clinging to her own slender vibrissae tightly all through that sending, as the Sender and her friend the tiger had slipped from the zoo to Nizamuddin. It was only when they descended to a height that he could bear that Ozzy opened his eyes—and then he had been delighted. But he had not appeared to react to the space around him; it was as though he padded above the fray, close enough to terrify

Datura and his bloodthirsty crew of ferals and yet separate from their world.

"You travelled like an experienced Sender, one with at least four or five winters worth of summoning in her whiskers, though," said Begum quietly. "Once you heard us, you came, and if it was hard for you, it didn't show. You saw what we saw—we didn't have to urge you to look, or coax you into leaving your world, our world didn't emerge gradually for you, nor did you emerge gradually in it. We sent, we summoned, and you came. Your whiskers tell me that this world is as real to you as your home and your Bigfeet are; you can smell and feel what we smell and feel."

"I don't understand," said Mara, her green eyes puzzled. "Isn't it the same for you when you're summoned?"

The calico cocked her ears, and then she rose from the ground. "This way," she said, stretching herself briskly. "The cricketers will be here, and we don't want to be in the way. Come to the old house."

The ruins of the old house mounted guard over the grounds of Old Delhi, its crumbling brown brick rooftops home to a clan of parakeets whose rose-and-green shapes flashed through the air, lightening the grey skies. Begum padded up the wide stone stairs towards a set of recessed niches, from where they could look out without being seen themselves.

They settled in, watching the cricketers as they entered— their cheerful cries and the way they bounded in reminded Mara of the Labradors back home. These Bigfeet had the same energy, the same slight floppiness and eager warmth about them.

Mara inhaled, letting her whiskers flare as her nose followed the scent trails of the gardens. There were the homing trails left behind by armies of bats, the spoor of pigeons who had made their homes behind the cracked and dirty windows of the abandoned bungalow, the warning but friendly reminder of cheels, the dark busy scents from the burrows of rats and bandicoots. But there were no blood scents, nor were there strong predator trails.

"The Bigfeet won't harm us," said Begum. "They're quite friendly, but that ball they whack around the field can break bones and paws and leave a bruise. Don't follow the ball too long with your eyes, Mara, it can have a hypnotic effect, and while we have few predators here, there are one or two birds you need to watch out for. Where were we now? Oh yes, being summoned—no, it's very different for you and for the rest of us. We take time to settle in. First the place we're summoned to shimmers slowly into view; the ground will reveal itself little by little, then the summoner comes into focus, and then the skeins of smells around the place will rise up, and then I know it's all right. But we don't feel stone, or sun, or winds, or rain, where we have sent ourselves or been summoned."

Mara's ears went down. The young queen thought, even here, even among the Senders, I am still different. She said nothing, but Begum watched her keenly, and the calico came to certain private conclusions.

"You have a gift, Mara," she said gently. "What most of us aspire to do with years of training and effort, you can do without effort. It took Tigris four winters to slip so easily from one place to another, to send herself so that she floated between all these worlds; you've done it in your first real summoning. It took Umrow and Jalebi three or four winters of hard training before they could begin to sense rather than just smell and see when they travelled as Senders. But your whiskers reached out to ours, your whiskers sent power to us, and you took in our world without blinking. It was so real to you that you can feel everything I feel. You imagine the cold so well that your fur catches the damp from your imagination, little one. You aren't different from us, but you are special."

"Special," said Mara softly. It sounded better to her than the other words, the ones Southpaw had used, and that she had heard some of the Nizamuddin cats use: "special" was better than either "different" or "freak."

Begum's brown eyes were thoughtful.

"Yes, special," she said. "Nizamuddin yields very special Senders, indeed; Tigris had made friends with the tribes in the air, her whiskers reaching out to sparrows, and bats, and cheels, as much as to her own clan. And now there's you: the only Sender in the history of Delhi who could send to all of the city's cats before she had touched six moons, who could summon a tiger before she had completed a full winter—very special indeed. But you are also, like me and like your clan in Nizamuddin, a cat. You have whiskers, fur, tail and four paws, just like all of us."

She saw Mara's whiskers rise, but she said no more. The two cats, the calico and the young orange queen, watched the cricket match, Mara's eyes widening in pleasure as she tracked the ball, never losing sight of its journey as it arced from bat to hand. Begum kept an eye out for cheels, but allowed herself to slip into a half-drowse. Behind them, Bigfeet chattered as they ambled through the open grounds towards the tangle of alleys that led to the first of many Bigfeet colonies.

Far above the wall, four black specks circled, barely visible against the grey clouds. But the fur in Begum's ears stood up, and she turned to Mara: "Overhead," she said quietly.

As the cheel flapped its wings and plunged into a racing dive, riding the breeze down towards the niche where Mara sat, the orange cat did no more than press her belly down, flattening herself against the crumbling black flagstones that lay scattered across the grounds. Begum had moved back onto her haunches, and was staring at the sky, daring the cheel to come in closer.

The underside of its wings was visible now, the tiny feathers on its stomach flashing white, and so were its claws, their curved talons etched sharply against the dull skies. Mara's tail twitched at its tip, and her green eyes narrowed. She didn't move, nor did she blink as she took in the cheel. It had covered half the gap between sky and earth. It would be with them soon.

Begum rose, hissing, and slashed in the cheel's direction, her paws scything in the air. The bird stayed on course. It was making a dead set for Mara, but the orange cat stayed where she was.

The cheel's claws grabbed at the ruff of orange fur on the Sender's neck; then the bird called out, screeching in confusion, as its talons went right through the cat, brushing roughly against the stones of the wall. It screeched again, tilting as it veered sharply to avoid colliding with the crumbling stones, and then it was off and away, rising into the skies, receding rapidly until all they could see was a tiny black dot.

"Ugh," said Mara, "I didn't think he would get *that* close. Gives me the shivers when they go through me." She licked her fur back into shape, shaking her ears and her whiskers a little to get rid of the feel of the cheel's talons.

"You let the cheel go right through you," Begum said, her mew disbelieving. She was remembering her first brush with a dog as a Sender—a puppy had gambolled into her when she was out on an early sending, in her second winter learning the ropes. Her stomach lurched when the pup's nose passed through her body, and she had broken the sending as fast as she could, leaving with the sound of the young dog's astonished barks behind her. Senders could slip easily through the world they were sending to, but a collision with anything in that world made them feel sick, as she knew—and yet, Mara was washing herself as calmly as though nothing had happened.

"Horrible," said Mara indistinctly as she tried to comb a bit of fur back that had been standing up from the damp. She yanked at the knots. "Makes me feel as if someone combed my fur the wrong way. There. All done now."

Begum stared at the Sender, at the cat who could send with such force that she could feel all of her surroundings, who could let creatures in this world brush past—through!—her without feeling more than slight discomfort. The calico's whiskers prickled as she allowed herself to slide into Mara's skin, and to imagine what it would be like to have the Sender's powers. She loved the freedom being a Sender gave her, just as Jalebi and Umrow and the rest loved being able to stretch a little further in their skins than most cats could. But she was beginning to realize how different Mara was from the rest of them.

She dropped her head and washed her own paws, wondering what Mara felt like when she was sending. The young Sender was back to watching the cricket, and as her alert green eyes followed the ball, followed the quick movements of the Bigfeet, another thought came to the calico cat: what did the Sender feel like when she couldn't send?

"Mara," she asked, "where are you now, back at home?" They were close enough to converse chiefly through their whiskers, only using mews for emphasis.

"I'm in my basket, and the Bigfeet think I'm asleep—oh, good catch, well done, Bigfoot, almost as good as if you were a golden retriever!" said the Sender.

"If the Bigfeet disturbed you, would you still be able to send?" asked Begum, though she thought she knew the answer.

"No," said Mara absently. "I can't send when I'm walking around or climbing cupboards or playing. It takes too much effort and I can't keep my paws straight."

The calico's eyes flashed sudden understanding. "So you can't send if you go out on your own into the neighbourhood."

Mara stopped watching the cricket match. "No!" she said. "I would be . . ." Her mew died.

Begum said, "I understand. But why can't you visit your neighbourhood through sendings? It's not as good as being out on your own paws, but at least it would connect you to the other cats, wouldn't it?"

Mara fluffed her tail out and wrapped it around herself, cradling in its warmth. "I don't want to," she said. "They don't like me. I heard them when I sent the first few times." She stopped, remembering. Hulo's low growl came back to her.

"... *That freak?*" And Katar's voice, the way in which he'd told Beraal once that she was a nuisance, a loud, noisy, alien creature. She had always felt it, the suspicion and the fear from the other cats; seen it in their eyes in her first few tentative sendings, once she was old enough to look closely, and she had overheard their discussions of her when she had crossed six moons.

Begum listened, quietly, not interrupting as Mara poured out her memories of those hesitant, long-ago forays. She had stopped going out after a while, preferring to visit her friends— a clan of tigers at the zoo.

"I smelled it in the air at the battle, too," Mara said. She had huddled into herself, her eyes unseeing as she recalled that day. "They were every bit as scared of me as they were of Ozzy. They thought both of us were freaks. I only did it for Southpaw."

"That's not entirely true, is it?" said Begum, her mew gentle and inquiring.

The orange cat blinked.

"When you came back with Ozzy, when he scattered the ferals, didn't you hope somewhere inside that they would like you better?"

"No!" said Mara. "Of course not! I wasn't . . . I didn't . . . well, maybe only a bit . . . it was so hard, bringing Ozzy all the way there! I thought they'd be pleased but they were only more afraid! I thought some of them would come to the house like Southpaw had and say hello, but they didn't. Only Beraal came, and she thanked me, but she said she had nothing more to teach me, and then she got pregnant and then she stopped coming. And none of them came! Except Southpaw! They didn't want to get to know me! And Miao talked to me, and I thought we would be friends, but then she died and I never got to know her because I'd never gone out, and she said I had to go out, but it was too late."

She was almost whimpering, shaking like a young kitten. Politely, Begum looked the other way until Mara had completed two rounds of washing and drying, and had fluffed her fur and whiskers back into shape. If the Sender had been a little younger, Begum might have comforted her; but she was almost full-grown, and it would have been rude to have treated her like a kitten in distress, much as the calico wished she could.

Mara watched the cricketers, her green eyes darkening with memories. The clouds loomed over the two cats. In the branches of a giant neem tree, a family of cheels swooped and ducked and swerved as they played a complex game of hide-and-seek among themselves, their swerves far more like the manoeuvres of a mock battle than the gentle games of tag the squirrels had played among the roots. Chancha and Meechi ceded territory to the cheels, taking their quarrels off to the roof of the old mansion, soaring down from time to time to squabble with the squirrels for a change over the fruit and grains laid out for them. "Give me one piece! Two piece!" pleaded Meechi, as Chancha nibbled at a nut. "Check your claws!" squawked Chancha. "You have your own already!" Meechi's beak clacked as she considered Chancha's argument. "But that's three piece! Four piece!" she said cunningly. "I want what's in your claw—one piece, two piece!"

Their calls made the place seem friendly, and Begum wondered whether Mara saw the quick lightning glances one or two of the cheels gave her—the tale of the Sender's encounter with their fellow bird had travelled fast, she thought. The cats would not be troubled by the cheels this afternoon, if she was any judge of their behaviour; they were uneasy around this stranger cat.

"Do you remember your dreams?" Begum asked the Sender.

Mara thought about it, her whiskers quiet except for their quivering tips. "I remember seeing cats," she said slowly. "A beautiful white warrior with long fur, who danced with a cobra on a rain-drenched roof; a fat striped one who sat with her paws clasped together. But I thought they were not real, that they were just memories from my sendings. Don't you dream?"

"I don't send in my dreams," said Begum. "None of us of the long whiskers do, though my mother spoke of a cat called Mehrunhissa whose whiskers were rumoured to walk the night. It was only a story, I never knew if it was true."

"Are they really sendings, my dreams?" said Mara uneasily, her ears twitching at the thought.

"We spend a lot of time apologizing to Senders across the length and breadth of the land in your wake, young Mara," said Begum, her tail flicking at the memory.

Mara's eyes were bright. "I'm sorry," she said, though she was thinking with some curiosity of the cats she had met and wondering what the other Senders were like. Were all of them stern, like Begum? "So none of you send in your dreams, except for me."

"I wondered why," said Begum, "and perhaps you're sending in your dreams because you're not going out. I don't know what it is, exactly, but the only Sender we know of who stopped going out was Tigris, and after she became an inside cat, even her sendings became strange. She would send at unusual times, and sometimes she didn't seem to know what she was sending. We're Senders, but we're also cats, like everyone else in the clan. We have to be both. Perhaps we have to use our paws as much as our whiskers."

Mara's eyes were frightened. "I've been out only a couple of times, just a little way down the staircase," said the Sender, washing her flanks in consternation. "But when I reached the bottom of the stairs, each time, I couldn't go further. The outside is terrifying. And now I don't know if I ever will be able to go out again."

"It isn't too late," said Begum, brushing her flank against Mara's to offer reassurance. "It is frightening, yes, the first few times we go out on our own, but we will teach you how to summon us, instead of only being able to respond to our summonings. Then you can walk outside, and we will walk with you; it might be less scary that way."

CHAPTER THREE

Hunted

"Fish!" He had never heard Beraal mew like that, but he had never seen the beautiful black-and-white hunter like this, either. The sleekness of the previous year had disappeared. As she purred her thanks and head-butted Southpaw, the tomcat felt a pang of sadness go through him, sharper even than the pain in his back paw. The long, silky fur that had shone so brightly the winter of their war with Datura and his ferals, just four seasons ago, was matted and dull. Beraal seemed half her size these days, more listless than any nursing mother should be. Her ribs were starkly outlined, and as she curled around him, still purring at the young tom, he felt the thinness of her flanks, saw how the skin hung slack and loose now that the flesh beneath it had melted away.

The jute sacks that he and Katar had dragged out for Beraal and her kittens, making a rudimentary shelter under the rusted Ambassador car behind the Nizamuddin garbage heap, were damp from the night's bitter chill. But Southpaw settled down on the sacks gratefully, happy that there was a layer of comfort between him and the freezing earth. He watched, his brown eyes soft, as Beraal tore into the fish. The bigger kitten, Ruff, made tiny gnashing sounds as he ate, but the other, Tumble, only licked at the scales and then settled back, waiting for Beraal to mash the fish into softer pieces for her. They were both smaller than they should have been, Southpaw thought.

Beraal glanced up from her dinner, her whiskers radiating contentment. "I haven't tasted fish in—since summer, Southpaw! Thank you for bringing this to us," she said. There were scraps of fish on her whiskers, and she cleaned them off with her tiny red tongue before taking another bite. Beraal had always been a fastidious eater, and her delicate habits had survived even the changes of the previous year. "Won't you have some with us, Southpaw?" she asked, remembering her manners. "There's plenty—those two haven't had much of an appetite since the fight with the rats. I think they bled too much, and haven't yet recovered, though they're drinking my milk."

"I've fed well," said Southpaw, "this is all yours." He could have eaten the tail, the belly and sucked the last shred of pink flesh off the last fishbone. If summer and the monsoons had been difficult for the cats of Nizamuddin, winter had been harsh, a lesson in cold, hunger and fear. But the tom took his cue from Katar and Hulo—if they could let their skin sag inwards and suck in their stomachs, saving the few morsels from their kill for the nursing mothers and the young kittens, so could he.

Except for the ferocious gnawing sounds made by the older kitten, Ruff, there was a rare sense of peace and contentment.

The familiar, pleasantly vegetal stench from the garbage heap made up for the harsh stink of burning plastic and rubber from one of the Bigfeet bonfires further down the road. Southpaw ignored the pain in his leg, preferring to focus on the distant sounds of traffic. He found them soothing, the wheeze of the buses, the roar of the trucks, the clipped clatter of the rickshaws. Beraal sat back, washing her whiskers, and then she washed Ruff and Tumble, and combed her fur until it had lost some of its knots and tangles. The kittens squeaked as they made for her stomach, each finding its own particular nipple.

IT WAS ALMOST MORNING by the time Katar and Hulo joined them. Southpaw saw the wince in the grey tom's eyes as he jumped down beside Beraal; the cold stiffened his injured flank and hip. Katar had taken his licks in the battle with the ferals, but more than the scars from last winter, it was the new injuries, the ones the Bigfeet were responsible for, that had weakened him. Perhaps it was only that the fog and the damp of the night had flattened their fur, but Southpaw thought uneasily that neither of the big toms had ever looked so drawn. Hulo's thick black fur had parted in some places to reveal the shiny skin of old and new scars, and he seemed shrunk, as did Katar.

They placed the night's booty before Beraal. It wasn't much at all—a few scraps from the butcher's, carefully collected by Katar, a baby rat, so small that it would make a scant mouthful for the nursing queen. But Beraal touched her nose to each of theirs, her eyes shining in a way they hadn't seen in many moons. Her green eyes gleamed with pleasure as she said,

"I have something for you for a change! See what Southpaw brought us; there was so much that we saved some for you."

Hulo's eyes widened when he saw the fish. Southpaw was astonished when the grizzled fighter let out a mew, as happy as any kitten might be. "Really, Beraal?" he said, "there is enough?"

"More than!" said the young mother, sitting hastily on Ruff, who had popped up to stake his sleepy claim on the last of the fish. He squirmed under her fur, but the warmth sent him back to sleep, and soon he was cuddling with his sibling. Hulo needed no further invitation. "Fish!" he said. "A feast—I had forgotten its taste, it sings in the mouth. Thank you, Southpaw. Come on, Katar, don't you want some?"

But Katar's whiskers were out, interrogating the brown tom. "Didn't I tell you not to raid the Bigfeet houses, Southpaw?" he said. His mew was quiet, but all of them heard the anger behind it, and saw the way his tail was flicking from side to side.

Southpaw said wearily, "You did."

"And yet?" said Katar, ignoring Hulo's hissed invitation to come and eat it anyway, who cared where the brat had sourced it from. His sleek head was lowered, his back arching a little as he padded towards the younger tom.

Anger lit slowly in Southpaw's eyes, but it was unmistakeable. Instead of giving way before Katar, he got to his feet, careful not to let his injured paw touch the ground, and lowered his own head in challenge.

"How many moons has it been since we've been slinking around like shadows, Katar? Scared to even step onto the roofs we used to roam so freely before? And has it helped? Have the Bigfeet stopped trying to hurt us, because we don't go into their houses any more?" The thoughts he'd kept behind his whiskers for so long came tumbling out, pell-mell.

From the park behind the market, the first chirpings of the babblers rose up in the air, telling them that dawn was here, but none of the cats paid much attention to the birds.

"And so you decided on your own, without letting me or Hulo know, to take this risk?" Katar's whiskers were crackling with fury. "We were at the dargah, hiding behind the butchers' lane, when Mara told us. We'd have come back earlier, except that Qawwali and Dastan needed our help. The Bigfeet's demolitions . . ." The tom's mews trailed away for a moment, and then he recalled his anger. "You had no business doing this, Southpaw. You've put us all in more danger, and for what?"

But Southpaw's tail was lashing from side to side, too. "Beraal's been starving for months," said the young tom. "None of us have been able to hunt properly ever since the battle; not even you and Hulo. It's not as though the Bigfeet will change. If they're going to kick us around, and try to poison us, and chase us or hurt us, then the least we can do is get some fish and meat out of them!"

Katar had more to say, but Hulo raised his whiskers, cutting both of them off. "Enough," he said. "The last thing we need is squabbling among ourselves; and you'd better get back on the whisker link, you fools, do you want your mews to bring the Bigfeet here?"

Southpaw saw the terror in Beraal's eyes. Hulo was right. He and Katar never broke their stare, nor did their tails stop lashing, but the sudden silence allowed them to hear the clatter of the Bigfeet from the taxi stand nearby. They were setting up for the day, and the young tom felt a cold prickle of fear touch his spine; what if they decided to investigate? They were safe from most marauders under the abandoned, rusting car, but if they did have to shift, with Beraal's youngsters in tow, the place was a trap. High walls on three sides, no real hiding places, open to the Bigfeet's view. They should have been more careful.

"It's not just me and our kittens who've been starving," said Beraal, using the link that allowed the cats to communicate by whisker over short distances. "It's all of us, Katar. Perhaps Southpaw shouldn't have done it, but you have to admit he had good reason. I hate not being able to hunt, much as I love my furballs."

"None of us have been able to hunt since the battle," said Hulo, his whiskers holding the memories. "Southpaw's right when he says we can't live like this—slinking round like shadows. Though if we paid your price for hunting, you reckless idiot, we wouldn't live for very long, would we?"

"What price?" said Katar. Mara had only been able to tell them that Southpaw had raided a Bigfeet house, before her own Bigfeet interrupted the Sender. They had no details of the raid.

"The brat's broken his paw," said Hulo. His gruffness hid the deep concern he felt. "Bad break, if I'm any judge. You would drag it over the roofs, wouldn't you? Young idiot."

The babblers' voices rose again, in alarm, and the cats stopped to listen. It sounded as though the neighbourhood girls were up early. Sa was screeching her head off in fury, and Re, Ga, Ma and Ni were backing her up in full chorus.

"Pa and Dha are so slow," said Beraal. "They never get out of the way in time . . ." She paused, her ears, keener than any of the other cats, cocked as she listened. "But they weren't hurt. They ducked the stones, not that Sa will stop her screeching." She used her paws to scoop the edge of a sack over her sleeping kittens and went over to Southpaw to sniff at the injury.

"They aren't slow," said Katar. His tail was down, finally, and his whiskers had a small droop in them. "Unlike the other babblers, they haven't got used to hiding from the Bigfeet, that's all. My, Sa's in a fine rage today—she's rhyming her insults!"

"May your skin turn white! May you look a fright!" they heard Sa sing. "When we've covered your ugly mug, you horrid scurvy thug, in scads of fresh bird poo, let's see what you'll do!"

"Droppings on their head," sang Ra in loyal counterpoint. "They'll wish they were dead, and he'll take to his bed, when he has droppings on his big fat head . . ."

The birds' voices soared in unison, and to the relief of the cats, Pa and Dha joined in, apparently unharmed by the Bigfeet's marauding ways.

Hulo hunched over on his paws beside Beraal, watching keenly as she checked Southpaw for damage.

"There's a bad tear in the skin, even if the blood's clotted," he noted. "No smell of the Sweet Sickness yet, you young fool, but it could still happen." If Southpaw's wounds turned septic, the gangrene would spread across his body. It was easy for the cats to spot a sufferer from the Sweet Sickness; the sepsis rotted the flesh, making it smell sickly sweet before the infection spread from the affected limb to the rest of the body. One of the dargah cats had contracted gangrene in his back paws that monsoon, and when the sickness had seeped far into his limbs, he had asked Qawwali to deliver a killing bite, which was done, to spare him further pain.

Katar caught and held Southpaw's eye, though the kitten looked back at the tom defiantly. "Half a moon of pain and discomfort when you won't be able to rely on that leg," said Katar. "And the risk that the Bigfeet will attack any cat they see in the area, not just you. Is that a fair price for your fish?"

Beraal came up to Katar, and nuzzled him gently.

"Stop," she said. It hurt her to see the clan leader like this. First Katar had survived the loss of Miao, and she knew he often thought of the Siamese, often wondered what wisdom she would have offered him in this situation. And then he had slowly realized, as had all of them, that it wasn't only Miao they had lost—it was all of their world.

For many moons after the battle, the dogcatchers' vans had patrolled Nizamuddin, forcing the stray cats and dogs into hiding. It sometimes seemed to Katar that he and the Nizamuddin wildings had paid in their own blood and freedom for Datura's dark war; not just the cats, but all of the strays, the birds and the smaller animals as well. There had been hope in the air in summer, when many of the Bigfeet had forgotten the battle and its aftermath, the pathetic corpses strewn across the grounds of the Shuttered House, Datura and his ferals' killing spree. But then the old houses had started coming down, and the Bigfeet who lived in the towering new buildings had no liking at all for cats and dogs and other small creatures.

"You're being hard on him, because you know he's right. What are we doing—warriors like you and Southpaw, hunters like me and Hulo—living like rats, scavenging from the garbage heaps? How long can we live like this, Katar?"

They thought they had gone too far when the tom lowered his whiskers, breaking the link between himself and his friends. Katar sat with his back to them, looking out towards the rooftops that had once been his domain, as much as the trees and the back alleyways. A lone brown speck did sorties through the lines of electricity wires, satellite dishes and the brightly painted signboards. The tom recognized that precise style—that was Tooth slicing through the narrow routes between the rooftops, the cheel who had once come to the aid of the clan in a time of trouble. Tooth's squadrons weren't around, but the cheel often flew solo when he was trying to unravel a knotty problem, just as Katar took long walks through Nizamuddin's alleys when he was worried about the clan's future.

He wondered whether Beraal's kittens would ever know what it was like to stroll from roof to roof, mapping the parapets, measuring the staircases, wary only of a few of the Bigfeet, some of the dogs. The roofs had been theirs, as the sky belonged to Tooth and the cheels, the trees to the bulbuls and babblers, the roads to the colony's stray dogs. But he hadn't let the others see his rising bitterness and despair, he had cleaned his sadness off his whiskers rather than share it with his clan. No good would have come of letting everyone know how hopeless their situation was becoming. For months, the cats—and the stray dogs, and the cheels, and the bulbuls, the babblers, the mice—had waited for Nizamuddin to return to normal. But now it was clear that things might never improve.

He raised his whiskers once more, coming back to them. "Qawwali and Dastan were telling us that the queens at the dargah haven't kittened this year," he said. "No litters were born except for Abol and Tabol's babies, and they didn't survive."

Hulo said, "They talk about leaving. To Humayun's Tomb, to the roads and parks beyond, where they might find hunting and shelter."

"But there have always been cats at the dargah!" said Beraal. Southpaw was silent, watching the other toms.

"The Bigfeet sent the fakir away some moons ago," Hulo said. "The Bigfeet at the dargah don't feed us or Qawwali's crew any more." The toms had kept this from Beraal, not wanting her to worry. The queen mewed softly, and groomed her kittens as it all fell into place. She understood why the toms had grown so thin that swiftly over the last few moons. Her hunter's mind walked through the lanes of Nizamuddin, seeing with clarity how hard it must have been for them. No hunter could hunt while being hunted himself. And without the small blessing of the meals the fakir used to share with them, they would have had less and less energy to find prey, unless they risked moving into the territory of the Jangpura cats.

"It's no better over there," said Katar. "That clan is sadly diminished. Some have left. Some . . ." He didn't have to tell the other cats what could happen to half-starved strays.

Beraal's deep green eyes turned from one tom to another, moving from Hulo to Katar. What Katar wanted to share with them was trembling on the tips of his whiskers.

The first of the trucks rumbled by, carrying construction material for the new Bigfeet houses. They would come in a convoy for the next few hours, and then the rumble and clang of building would form the backbeat to Nizamuddin's day.

"We can't stay on," said Katar. He had known it in his bones for over a moon now. "We have to find another home. Across the canal, in the dargah—somewhere, but not here."

From their whiskers, eddies of emotions came flooding out—everything that the cats had thought, but not said through the long dry heat of summer, the harsh monsoon rains, the bitter, early winter. Hulo said, "This is our home, why should we leave, no matter what the Bigfeet do?" at the same time that Southpaw said, "We have to leave. This doesn't feel like home any more."

Before the young and the old tom could argue, Beraal stepped in. "It doesn't smell like home to me," she said. And all three cats let their whiskers flare, to take in the truth of what she had said. The scents of the colony were amplified in the winter air. It brought to them the smells from the construction sites: the spoiled-earth scent of the concrete mixers, the sullen metal stink from the welder's torches, and above all, the black, tarry stench that spoke of the Bigfeet's dislike for the rest of the animals.

"Katar," she said, and then her head dropped. "I wish Miao was here."

The tom brushed his head gently against hers. "I miss her too," he said. "Sometimes I see her in my sleep, not the way she was after the battle, but out there, on the edge of the canal, hunting silently, watching all of us, her whiskers whispering the stories she used to tell us when we were kittens."

Hulo blew air out through his nostrils. "Even she couldn't have stopped the Bigfeet," he said. The grizzled tom had stayed close to Katar over the turning seasons, sensing that the leader of the clan missed Miao much more than he would share.

"Miao isn't here," said Katar, and the way he said it made it final.

Beraal's kittens stirred, Tumble raising her paw and turning over, her thin ribs showing. The cats didn't have to say it aloud, but their whiskers rippled with the same thought: what kind of world would Beraal's children think of as home?

"I don't get it," said Hulo, cutting in. "You're saying we have to move. Where? We can't go with Qawwali and Dastan—they would welcome us, give us refuge, but Humayun's Tomb already has its own clan of cats—Ghalib and Ghazal's gang—and they can't have all of us moving in, won't be enough space. Jangpura has the same problems with their Bigfeet that we do. So where do we go, and how will these little ones travel, not to mention the others?"

"But Miao wasn't the only one we had to turn to," said Katar. His whiskers were sparkling with life again.

Southpaw was the first to understand. "That's what she used to tell us," he said. "In the dark times, in the lean years, that's when . . ."

". . . Senders are born," Katar finished what he was saying. "And that's what we should have done before—asked the Sender what the clan should do."

For a moment, as she washed one of her kittens gently, holding the small form close against her stomach so that the little thing could feel the warmth, Beraal felt hope rise.

Then Hulo said, "Ask the Sender? Rubbish! The Sender doesn't even know the clan! She's never stepped outside her Bigfeet's stinking house! What kind of answer would a Sender give when she doesn't know our scent and hasn't even stepped into Nizamuddin once?"

It was all true, Beraal thought. Southpaw's whiskers, like hers, drooped, and his tail switched from side to side in confusion.

But Katar sat up on his haunches. "Hulo, it's true that the Sender doesn't know us, and she doesn't come out of her house at all."

"Exactly," growled Hulo. "How can she advise cats she doesn't know?"

"She loves Southpaw, though, and shares her food and life with him," he said, his mew soft. "If he needs help with that broken paw and the risk of the Sweet Sickness, Mara will do what she can for him. She knows Beraal and she knows Southpaw. And when we needed her, during the battle with the ferals last year, she came, even if she hasn't returned since. Perhaps it's time we went to meet the Sender. She might be able to help Southpaw, and she might even be able to help us."

CHAPTER FOUR

Crash Boom Bang

The day was cold and dreary. Mara wound around her Bigfeet's legs, getting in their way, and batted a paper ball around in a desultory fashion. She had waited all morning for the Chief Bigfoot to arrive, but though the doorbell rang several times, the most important Bigfoot in the world remained missing.

There was little to see in the park, and the Bigfeet didn't seem to want her to help with the papers they were sorting. In fact, after the third time she had helped them, dividing the stacks of paper into smaller piles and chewing the corners of some of the documents that appeared to be upsetting them, they politely refused her assistance, setting her down from the table.

This ruffled Mara's sense of dignity. The Bigfeet didn't seem to realize that she belonged on the sofas and on the desks (and in the cupboards) every bit as much as they did, and she left, her tail raised stiffly to indicate her disapproval. Back in her room, she batted around her toys for a while, but it was no fun being on her own. She sat at the window of her room, and the cold air tickled her whiskers, reminding her that she hadn't visited Ozzy at the zoo in a while. The tiger and Mara had become friends after the Sender's first explorations. She extended her whiskers, letting their tips tremble in the air. This was the part of sending that never grew stale, no matter how often she did it: the moment of lift-off, when she felt herself walk along the comfortable, everyday routes of sense and smell the Nizamuddin cats used, and then walk further, until the skies opened up for her. Her whiskers created a pathway into the world.

When the Bigfeet checked on her, they found that Mara had curled up into a heap, and was fast asleep, her paws wrapped around an old soft toy—her battered orange monkey—for comfort. They had no working whiskers of their own, so they had no way of knowing that the Sender had roamed far away and was almost at the zoo.

MARA HEARD OZZY'S ROARS before she saw the tiger; she was hovering over the langur cage, chatting with her old friend Tantara when the growls tore through the air.

"He's been as grumpy as the bears for the last few days," said Tantara. The monkey's fur had gone a shade whiter in the winter chill, and it threw her beautiful black skin into relief. Mara curled her tail into a question mark.

"The Bigfeet cut the cage in half to make room for a fresh litter of lion cubs," Tantara explained. "Rani doesn't mind so much, but Ozzy likes to pace. And the cubs make him miss

Rudra. You should go over and meet him, it might take the edge off his growl. He's making all of us nervous, especially Eddie." Edward was the youngest of the hoolock gibbons, a solemn ape given to whooping mournfully when he was anxious.

The zoo had shifted Ozzy and Rani's son to the other side of the premises, where he and his mate, Tawny, lived near the sloth bears, in the shade of the towering ramparts of the Old Fort. Mara would have liked to visit Rudra more often, but his mate didn't approve of big cats consorting with real cats, especially Senders who hovered in mid-air. Instead, Mara and Rudra stayed in touch through Tantara and Ozzy; they had met and made friends when they were kitten and cub, and the link between their whiskers remained strong.

Ozzy's roars sounded much grumpier close up. Mara hovered behind the tiger, watching as he paced up and down.

"I don't care whether the bars say it's your territory!" he roared at the lion cubs who goggled at the tiger with great interest. "I marked all of it, you understand? All of it! Raise your stupid heads and take a whiff! That's my land! Mine! Aaarroooof!"

He had paced with such majesty, and speed, that he went smack into the bars.

"He's been doing that a lot," said Rani to Mara. "Then his nose gets hurt and he growls even more."

Ozzy shook his great head from side to side and roared in frustration, the sound making Mara's fur shiver, even after nearly two years. "Whoop! Whoop!" called Edward in the distance. Then the hyaenas started off with their jittery laughter, and they set off the langurs, and soon the zoo was as noisy as the Delhi traffic outside.

"That land is *my* land, you misbegotten, stripeless whelps!" Ozzy growled. "What do you have to say to that?"

The three lion cubs regarded him solemnly. Then the oldest sniffed the air.

"That's where I put my mark," said Ozzy, his roar triumphant. "Yep, right over there, on that rock, and on all of the others—wait! What do you think you're doing? How dare you! Stop that immediately!"

The biggest of the lion cubs was carefully adding her scent, in a copious stream, right over Ozzy's. She finished, and strolled away to her mother without a backward look at the tiger. Her siblings yawned, baring their small sharp teeth, and emulated their sister. One of them turned around and offered Ozzy a polite woof; the other bounded away when he was done.

"Oh no, Ozzy, you're not charging at anyone today," said Rani firmly, padding up to her mate. The white tiger positioned herself so that Ozzy would have to brush past her in order to get to the bars again. "Last time around, the Bigfeet sent in their team with tranquilizers, and I don't want to be knocked out because of your stubbornness. Let them be. It's their cage now."

"Mine!" roared Ozzy mutinously. "Wait till the wind changes and the spring winds come in, then I'll send them enough scent to drench the blasted place, cubs and all!"

"Hey, Ozzy," said Mara, judging that this was as good a time as any to talk to her friend.

The tiger turned, and the Sender felt a sense of shock—now that they faced each other, she could see how greatly he had changed. Ozzy's roars masked the amount of weight he had lost, and his fur seemed rough, unkempt. There was dust from the dry winter ground that he hadn't bothered to brush or wash off, covering the underside of his usually immaculate chin. His gold and black stripes were dull, and for once, they didn't stand out against the grey bars and the clouded skies. He acknowledged Mara with a brief flick of his tail, but it was Rani he addressed.

"We had the jungles to ourselves, Rani," he said, "you in the Sunderbans, while I made the ravines shake with my tread. We learned to measure our paces here, didn't we? We learned to live behind these bars. They took our son, he has cubs you and I have never seen, and now the Bigfeet would erase his scent, would let lion cubs—lions, Rani, not even tigers—place their paws over his pawprints. Must I mince like a wild dog or a jackal around my own home? Aaarooof!"

The tiger's agitation had made him pick up his pace again, and now he began slamming into the bars on the other side.

"Ozzy . . ." began Mara.

"MAY THE GNATS BITE YOUR FURRY LITTLE NOSES OFF!" Ozzy roared at the lion cubs, who had lined up to watch him as he sat back on his haunches, shaking his massive head from side to side to try and ease his aching jaws. He growled again, opening his mouth so wide Mara could see all the way back to his carnassials.

"Ozzy, all you have to do is recalibrate," said Mara, hovering right in front of his whiskers so that he couldn't ignore her.

"AND MAY THE BURRS STICK TO YOUR HIDES!" Ozzy growled. "What was that, Mara? Recalibrate?"

"It's what you do in small spaces when the Bigfeet move their furniture," Mara said patiently. "You let your whiskers lead you around the perimeter until they know the way by feel, and you let your paws learn the new path. It's not so bad, having to learn new things; otherwise you'd always be pacing around in the same old, boring way. Aren't you bored? You've known that old route—twelve paces to the front, fourteen to the left— for so long, your paws can take you around the enclosure in your sleep. It might be fun, trying out new steps."

"But I can't run through the jungle!" said Ozzy, sulking.

"Ozzy," said Rani, strolling back to the shelter by their pool where she liked to spend the afternoons napping to recover from whatever mayhem her mate had caused in the morning, "we've left the jungle far behind. Don't let your memories darken the cage. The lion cubs are smarter than you, they might live behind bars, but they don't let that stop them from playing."

"But they're taking over Rudra's playground!" said Ozzy to Mara, his ears flicking contemptuously in the direction of the cubs.

"You've been missing him, haven't you?" said Mara, her whiskers offering the great cat her sympathy.

"Yes," said Ozzy, his tail sweeping the dust in a pathetic sort of way.

"Wouldn't he have moved into his own range if you'd been in the jungle?" said Mara. "He and Tawny would have wanted their own part of the forests, wouldn't they? It must be nice for you to have cubs around again, even if they are lions."

"NICE?" roared Ozzy. "NICE? Those worm-ridden, undergrown, hairless creatures?"

Mara glanced at the cubs, who were ignoring Ozzy's roars and playing a wonderfully absorbing game of pounce-at-a-Pepsi-can, growling at it as they took turns to shake the hapless can by the scruff of its tin neck.

"You never watch them at play?" she said.

"Of course not!" growled Ozzy.

"All the time," said Rani wearily. "He grumbles about them endlessly, but he spends most of his time on this side of the bars these days."

"I'm only watching them the way you watch prey!" roared Ozzy, infuriated.

"So you're missing out on the fun of having cubs right next door to you, instead of—I don't know—giant sloths who'd sleep all the time, or odoriferous skunks, or an enclosure filled with monitor lizards?" asked Mara.

Ozzy roared, but his heart wasn't in it, and even Eddie, several cages away, didn't bother to whoop in response. The tiger turned away from Mara, stalking over to a fallen tree trunk and scratching his sides against the rough bark morosely.

The Sender wisely stayed silent, letting him work his feelings off, which Ozzy did by knocking over a termite heap with his tail.

"I hate it when you make sense, Mara," said Ozzy, padding back towards the Sender, and flopping his great bulk down on the cold ground. "It ties my fur into knots."

"I'd say your fur's got enough knots of its own without any help from me," said Mara, who was a believer in the benefits of regular grooming. "What's really gnawing at you, Ozzy? It isn't just Rudra or the cubs, or even the smaller cage, is it? You must have known that the Bigfeet would take away some of your space, after Rudra and Tawny left."

Ozzy began, sulkily, to lick his whiskers straight. For a while, he said nothing, washing his paws, the look in his eyes far away, their colour on this winter day a dull, tarnished gold.

"How do you cope, Mara?" he said abruptly. "Living in the Bigfeet house, the doors shut, the windows shut, doesn't it drive you mad? If you couldn't send, if you couldn't travel on your whiskers, would you be able to live that way?"

Mara hesitated, her fur shimmering in confusion.

"I cannot imagine a life without sending," she said, "any more than you might imagine a life without smell or sight."

Ozzy grunted, a forlorn sound, and started work on his dusty chin.

Mara tried to think of what life would be like if she had only the Bigfeet's house. Gradually, it started to steal over her. The web of scents and smells that set her nose twitching from the window, and that she could follow all across Nizamuddin, and indeed, all of Delhi if she chose, that told her how many squadrons of cheels had taken to the air, revealed the existence of cats as far away as Karol Bagh or Mehrauli—that would be gone. She would have to live forever under the roof of the Bigfeet's home, climbing the cupboards and bookcases for entertainment, instead of closing her eyes and following her whiskers wherever they might lead her. She remembered crouching in a drainpipe under the canal as a kitten, hiding from predators; it would be a little like that, the Sender thought, living in a smaller, darker, closed world without much air or light. It made her mew and shift uneasily.

"So you can guess, little one," said Ozzy, softly.

"Only some," said Mara, "but enough, perhaps. Is that how you feel?"

"My fur misses the jungle, more and more," said Ozzy. "It is different for Rani; as the years have gone by, as the seasons chase their tails around the sun, she lets go of her memories of the mangrove forests and the estuaries where she roamed, queen of all she surveyed. She tells me often that we have the open sky above us; we are fed; the Bigfeet do not poke us with sharp sticks or try to kill us with guns. But me, I remember the gorges and the ravines more and more. This dry earth the Bigfeet have given us; how can it compare with the waving grasses, the rivers, the cool black earth under my paws? If I could go home just once, Mara, if someone could bring my home to me only for a day, it would be enough, to let my roar echo through the trees, through the scrub, with no Bigfeet to hear it. Instead, there are the bars, and this stony ground and the Bigfeet gawking at us."

Mara let out a soft mew, watching the way Ozzy's whiskers tautened and quivered at the very mention of the jungles.

"I understand," she said. "This is Rani's home, and perhaps Rudra's and Tantara's, but it is not yours."

The tiger said nothing, but his breathing was calmer as he listened, and the pain of memory was receding from his striped face.

"But is it so bad if you never go back to the jungle?" asked the Sender. "You are not alone in your cage, like the leopard over at the back who moans with such sadness every night; you have Rani. And the cubs could be friends, if you let them be. Will grief hold on to your fur for the rest of your days if you never see the jungle again?"

Ozzy was silent, only the stripes on his flanks rippling as he listened.

"The Bigfeet cannot take the jungle from you, Ozzy," said Mara. "It's between your ears, cradled and precious, every memory of your life in the forests. They can put you behind bars, but if you wanted, you could be free in your head."

The tiger rose, letting his great bulk fill this part of the cage. "The Bigfeet cannot take my jungle away," he repeated, in some wonder. "And until I see it again . . . you know what, Mara? Those cubs need some training. They're spraying all over the place, not getting the hang of marking their territory the way they should, neatly, at distinct intervals. If their mother doesn't mind, I might give them a few lessons, teach them how to behave like tigers, even if they can't be us, poor beasts."

He stretched, his fur looking much brighter, his whiskers back at a jaunty angle. "You!" he roared at the cubs, but it was a happy roar, not an aggressive call. "You over there! Come over and introduce yourselves properly. Come on, come on, line up by size—or weight, one or the other—by the bars, that's right." Ozzy chuffed at the solemn line of lions happily.

Before he strolled over to them, he thanked the Sender. "While we're talking about cages, little one," he said, "time you broke the bars of your own, yes? Sending is all very well. Going for a walk with your whiskers is all very well. Time you went out into the world, Mara, it isn't good for any of us to be locked up."

Mara fluffed out her fur, not wanting to explain to Ozzy all over again how much the outside frightened her.

The tiger bounded off—but then he swung around and padded back to her. "Mara?" he said, and his growl was low, so that only he and the Sender could hear what he had to say. "I can't break the bars of my cage. But you have no bars to break. It makes me angry to see you caught in a cage that you have built around yourself, little one, when you could have what we can't."

"The outside?" said Mara, preparing to go back to her Bigfeet.

"Freedom," said Ozzy, and then he was off, his magnificent and freshly cleaned stripes lighting up the gloom and fog of the day.

MARA SLEPT POORLY WHEN she got back from her sending, and her dreams were filled with tigers and their ominous roars. When she finally slept deeply, she dreamed that the hyaenas were cackling as they circled her, their slavering jaws ready to bite. She woke up; there were no hyaenas, there was only the peace of her basket, the safety of the closed windows, and the chatter of her Bigfeet. The cat stretched, letting the aches in her spine ease, and slept again.

The sky was falling on her head. It had been a dull afternoon sky, touched with pale-green clouds, and as she bounded around the house in the dream, a rending sound had made her look up. When she did, the sky was pouring into the house through a hole in the roof. Grey clouds roared towards her with a clatter and a clang, and then, just as the sky descended on her, the clouds blanketing her terrified face, smothering her whiskers, forcing their clammy tendrils into her pink throat, Mara woke up.

There were no clouds in the room, only the suffocating folds of the blanket. She had slipped beneath it in her sleep, and she relaxed, stretching her back, yawning pinkly. Then she opened her eyes very wide—the winter sun, weak as it was, had risen high into the sky. She had slept the morning through; her Bigfeet must have left the house while she was still deep in slumber.

She had just started to wash her paws when she heard it—a roaring sound, a crash, a clang, a clatter! For a moment, it seemed to Mara that her dream had followed her right into the house, and that the skies and the clouds were raging in the drawing room.

The clangour trebled, and Mara's fur fluffed as something crashed to the ground. "Help!" she mewed, but no one heard her over the racket from the other room. Then she heard the scolding voice of the Chief Bigfoot. Mara abandoned her morning ablutions—given that her fur was standing up from fright, they wouldn't have done much good anyway—and raced into the drawing room, glad to hear anything that sounded familiar through the crashes, bangs and thuds.

The Chief Bigfoot was standing in the room between two swaying stacks of newspapers. "There you are!" cried Mara gladly, and she put her tail down in relief, heading towards her friend.

She was halfway across the carpet when she heard him. The fur on the back of her neck prickled, and the long white whiskers above her eyes stood up. He was a large Bigfoot, and when he saw her, he dropped the load of old magazines and cardboard boxes he was carrying, astonished.

"Who's he?" said Mara to the Chief Bigfoot, just as the magazines and boxes hit the ground with horrendous thuds and thumps.

The sounds, so close, made her head spin, and she scrabbled to get away from the Bigfoot. She ignored the Chief Bigfoot's yelled explanations—"Calm down, relax, don't be so scared, it's only the kabadi wallah, he's here to pick up the old papers and pots and pans"—as she streaked up the bookcases, shot across their length and surfed the room's pelmets, going flat out as she went round and round the room.

"Come down!" called the Chief Bigfoot.

"Stay up there!" called the kabadi wallah, who held strong opinions on cats, especially ones that streaked like greased lightning through the room.

Mara had no intention of coming down ever, but as she took off from the edge of a pelmet, aiming to land on the top of the door, the kabadi wallah backed into a pile of dishes. CRASHBOOMBANG!

The orange cat twisted in mid-air and landed on the sofa, bouncing hard, just as the kabadi wallah pushed a stack of magazines onto the floor near her. She sprang off the sofa, terrified that he would come for her with his sack.

"Mara!" called the Chief Bigfoot, trying to reassure the frantic little cat.

"Marrrrrrrrrrrrrrowwwwrrrrrr!" yelped Mara, running full tilt into a tower of old buckets and plastic mugs. They crashed all around her.

"This way!" yelled the Chief Bigfoot in Hindi.

"That way!" shouted the kabadi wallah in Punjabi.

"Yowwwowwwowwwwowww!" yowled Mara as she headed for the front door like an orange rocket.

"Oh no!" said the Chief Bigfoot in alarm, but it was too late. The door had been left open to allow the kabadi wallah to bring in his weighing scales. A vivid orange streak shot out, down the stairs, at full tilt, and the last the Chief Bigfoot heard of Mara was a faint echo in the stairwell.

CHAPTER FIVE

The Sender's Run

Mara shot out and down the stairs, into a waking nightmare. The world, held at bay when she watched it through the window or from the stairs, was inescapable; it rumbled at her, sending scent trails blasting in her direction. The Sender felt sick as the sounds and the smells jumbled together: the deep blare of bus horns, the vegetable seller's rising chants, the clanging bells from the nearby temple, the menacing black ropes of dog scent that told her of the movements of the neighbourhood pack, the sharp feathery grey scents of hornbills, bulbuls and cheels, the warm tar stink of the tarmac.

The road was at its busiest, and the roar of the traffic made her head throb. Her paws skidded as she narrowly missed a cycle rickshaw and dodged just in time to avoid a rogue auto driver. She pelted down the road, keeping to the verge, her paws sweating with exertion and fear. The cars seemed to scream at her; the scents jumbled into one another, sending her head swirling. She would have kept running, just to get away from the horror and chaos of the noise around her, the relentless tide of images that assailed her mind. But then, she smelled it—a clean, fresh scent, so different from the coal and burning stench of the outdoors. There it was, rising across the wide frightening expanse of road—the cool, green, beckoning whisper that spoke of grass and earth.

Mara made herself stop, even though her paws had mixed feelings about coming to a halt. The Sender backed behind the wheel of a car. Her flanks were heaving, and her pink tongue hung out in terror, but she tried to follow the scent trails through. The stench of dog was thick where she had stopped, so heavy that it made her fur prickle in unease. In front of her, the traffic roared and belched fumes of smoke so disgusting that the smell—and feel—of it made her feel both deafened and dirtied. The road ran on in both directions, as straight and long as the paths she took in the sky when she was sending. She could not see an end to it.

A small part of her mind whispered that she didn't know how to get home, but she shut it down. That thought was too large and too scary to be allowed space. For now, she wanted to get away from the road, from—she ducked behind the car tire—these massive, rumbling vehicles that wanted to kill her. The Sender stared at the road, and a memory stirred, of rushing water under the canal, of a day when she had opened her eyes and stared at the black shining waters under the bridge. To the eyes of a tiny kitten, the canal had seemed vast, and the suck and ebb of its black waves had been the steady purr that had rocked her to sleep at night. The road seemed as vast to her as any canal, as turbulent as any river.

The heavy stink of dog filled Mara's twitching nostrils. She stood stiff-legged and wary, shrinking so that only her whiskers and her green eyes showed from behind the car's reassuring tire.

If the reek of the traffic had started to make the Sender feel nauseous—it was an overwhelming onslaught, tangling her whiskers up in so many sounds and smells that her stomach had begun to do ominous somersaults—the dog's scent throbbed like a dull warning light in her head.

She remembered backing into the damp earth under the canal bridge. She remembered the sound of barking dogs, so close that she hadn't been able to stop shivering. She remembered the heat coming off a muzzle that had been thrust into their home, the cold, ferocious eyes, the hoarse barks, the sight of long, sharp, yellow teeth. She remembered calling out to her mother as the dogs snapped and snarled at them, and then she remembered being lifted up by the Bigfeet, struggling in their gentle hands, crying out again and again to a mother who had said nothing at all, who had stopped responding. She had felt so small, so helpless, so alone.

The dog, who looked like an Alsatian from the front and like a lot of things from behind, was further up the road from her. It raised its toffee-brown head and their eyes met, his startled brown ones, her terrified green ones. "No," she said, to herself as much as to him, "please don't cross the road. Please, stay away from me."

The dog cocked his head. Then he narrowed his eyes, and scanned the flow of bicycles, three-wheeled rickshaws and assorted flotsam coming from one side, the few buses trundling down the road in the other direction. He waited, assessing the traffic, and when a bicycle ran into the seller of roasted corn, scattering golden cobs everywhere, he padded confidently onto the broad black tarmac.

"Perhaps he hasn't seen me," Mara thought. "Perhaps if I close my eyes very tightly and make myself very small behind this wheel he won't see me. Perhaps he'll be run over by a bus."

The dog had reached her side of the road. She felt her heart stop beating as he glanced in her direction, and then he turned casually away, and bounded towards a tree, scattering a family of squirrels in all directions. They chittered crossly at him as they darted up the branches, two taking to the safety of the bougainvillea bushes.

"Oho," said one of the squirrels. "No need for speed, Jao, it's only Doginder Singh."

Jao popped her head out, and gave Doginder Singh an indignant glare. "Some dogs, Ao," she said with immense significance, "might look all grown up-shown up, but they're basically just puppies."

"Watch it," muttered Doginder Singh, "who're you calling a puppy then? I didn't mean any harm, it was just a Bounding Alertness Check. You could have been in a lot of trouble if it had been a real . . . I mean, a nasty strange ferocious dog, yeah, then you'd have thanked me for keeping you on your toes . . . paws. Whatever."

"Bounding Alertness Check," said Ao, his grey-striped head radiating the dignity due to an elderly squirrel who was pretending he hadn't just been chased up a bougainvillea bush. "Like the Car Alarm Check you and your friends carried out the other night, which had all the Bigfeet up and tramping through our homes just before dawn?"

Doginder's jaunty tail lost a little of its bounce. It had been enormous fun, cannoning off the hoods of the Bigfeet's cars, when he had discovered that you could set off their car alarms in a pleasingly musical pattern. But it was no use explaining this to an unmusical neighbourhood; the Bigfeet had been very unappreciative, and the entire babbler clan had been markedly cold to him, cursing him and all of his tribe in rhyming couplets.

Doginder folded his ears back. "I can see that my attempts to improve the neighbourhood are wasted," he said coldly. "Never mind, I'll go where my talents are appreciated. I hear they can do with a good guard dog, a Ferocious Attack Dog, over in Jangpura."

The squirrels watched him march off, his paws clicking smartly in indignation. They let him get some distance before Ao called out: "Oh, Mr. Ferocious Attack Dog? You might want to brush the bougainvilleas off your backside."

"Leave him alone," Jao said, chittering happily. "We are only civilians, no? He is probably covering himself in pink, purple and white floral backside special camouflage for Ferocious Attack Dog Squad dogs."

His heart too full to let him speak, or even woof a stern fare-well, Doginder marched with dignity down the road, ignoring the minor detail that he was showering the pavement with blossoms as he trotted along.

Mara thought she might be sick. The dog had viciously charged at a pack of harmless squirrels, and left them trapped in the branches of a tree. She couldn't imagine why he hadn't shaken them out of the tree and eaten them, but perhaps he was storing his snacks for later. It did seem odd that he had bougainvillea blossoms stuck to his coat, but the expression he bore as he marched in the young cat's direction was murderous.

She felt her whiskers tremble, and her paws started to shake. She knew she should turn and run, but she couldn't make herself move an inch. Mara clung to the tire, which had begun to feel like her only source of stability in a swiftly tilting world.

She made a tiny and pathetic figure as she crouched by the car tire, and Doginder felt his spirits rise. Here was a chance to show Ao and Jao that he was serious about his duties as a member of the Neighbourhood Watch Squad. True, the squad had only two members so far—Doginder brushed away the niggling voice that said the black beetle wasn't really a member, the fellow hadn't objected when he'd been recruited, had he?—but all big movements started small, he reminded himself.

He wondered if he should chase the orange cat, perhaps just as a reminder to the squirrels that he really was a Ferocious Attack Dog, but his hunting instincts refused to kick in—she was such a small, quivering scrap! He would be, he resolved nobly, brushing a stray bougainvillea off his flank, a Rescue Dog. Perhaps she'd lost her clan, and needed to be led back to them. Perhaps she might want a Neighbourhood Watch member to show her the sights of Nizamuddin. Doginder brightened and his tail went up as another thought struck him: perhaps she might even want to join the Neighbourhood Watch! He bounded towards the kitten, barking his greetings, his tongue lolling out in a happy smile.

Mara watched the slavering beast approach with a shudder. Those wicked teeth! That killer's smile! She wondered if it would hurt very much, being eaten. A bus thundered by, juddering as it went, and she realized she was trapped.

"Hello there, cat!" said Doginder genially.

The orange cat stared at him, her green eyes growing larger and larger, and then she wailed into his surprised face.

"Kill me now!" she cried.

"Excuse me?" said Doginder, deciding he hadn't heard right.

"I can't stand the suspense!" the cat howled. "Just strike me down with those large paws of yours already, and rend the flesh from my poor bones. It's cruel to keep your victims hanging like this."

"Victims?" said Doginder, his woof anguished. "Here! No! You've got it all wrong!"

"WOE!" said Mara, and her whiskers spread to their full extent. "Oh woe is me, to die like this, so young, before I have seen anything of the world, at the paws of a vicious, hardened, savage killer."

"What? Me? But . . . no, no, no. Never harmed a cat in my life. Chased a few up trees, yes, of course, all self-respecting dogs have to do that, you know, but I'm a Ferocious Attack Dog, not a vicious, hardened . . . what you said."

"Here!" said Mara, who had a tendency to get carried away when she was excited. "Rend my throat mercilessly if you must! Woe that I ever left my house! Woe that I ever abandoned my Bigfeet! Woe to this road and the ugly beasts on it."

"Now wait," said Doginder, "my tail's a bit on the fluffy side, true, and I'm not one of those pedigreed chaps, but ugly—that's a bit harsh, isn't it? Ugly? Really?"

"LOST!" cried Mara. "PERSECUTED BY BIGFEET, HUNTED BY NASTY TRAFFIC, AND AT THE MERCY OF A VICIOUS, SAVAGE KILLER . . . OH, SOUTHPAW, OH, BERAAL, WHY DID I EVER LEAVE HOME? WOE! THIS IS THE END!"

"Whoa!" said Doginder, dazed. Mara's sending had twanged through the air, shaking the bats in the old monument in the park awake, bringing even the squabbling of the squirrels to a sudden, hushed pause, reaching all the way down to the pigs at the canal. He had to shake his ears vigorously; at such close quarters, he'd received the full force of the Sender's powers.

"Woe!" said Mara, exhausted. She eyed the dog as she trembled, from the winter chill as much as from fear. "Why have you not yet pounced? Are you going to draw this out? Ozzy told me about predators who play with their prey. I wish I'd never left my house and the Chief Bigfoot and my nice basket. I had a soft toy of my very own, a monkey, and the lizard was my friend, and my Bigfeet have very kind hands and now I'll never ever see them again because you'll kill me and put my young life to an end, oh it's too cruel. Where are you going?"

Doginder was backing away. "Mad," he said to the air with conviction. "As crazy as a coot, like that goat fellow down at the animal shelter who hasn't been the same since he survived Bakri-Id, the traditional goat sacrifice. A little young, to be this loopy, but perhaps she had a head start."

His backside connected sharply with the white Ambassador next to the car Mara had been sheltering under. Mara, intrigued by the killer's odd behaviour, watched him with bemusement.

"I haven't met any goats," she said. "Only Southpaw and some tigers."

"Tigers," Doginder said to the world at large. "She thinks she's met tigers. If you ask me, she's full-crack, not half-crack."

"Hello?" said Mara, forgetting her fear in the warmth of her indignation. "I'm not the one talking to the air, am I?"

With the whine of a giant mosquito, a motorbike vroomed up the road. The driver was going so fast that he skidded, and Mara yelped as the bike's tires came frighteningly close, spattering mud from the verge onto her fur.

"Too close," said Doginder, "hang on a tick." He bounded down the road behind the bike, barking and growling for all he was worth, snapping at the speeding rider.

"Ha!" he said when he got back to Mara. "That'll show him. Did you see the way he sped off when he saw me? That's the thing with Bigfeet—you have to show them who's boss."

Mara was about to say that she wasn't sure the biker had heard the barking over the roar of the traffic, or noticed that he was being followed. But Doginder looked so pleased with himself, and his tail thumped so hard against the car bumper that she decided to keep her opinions to herself.

"Well, can't spend the day hanging around here," said Doginder, quite chuffed by his success with the bike. "Let's get you to the park, it's much safer there." A cycle rickshaw went by, skidding through a puddle and sending a spray of slush in the direction of the cat and the dog. "And," he added, looking with distaste at a splash of mud on his coat, "less . . . less . . . ah, sloppy. Come on, cat."

"Do you take all your victims to the park to kill them?" said Mara, torn between her own terror and genuine curiosity. She could understand, she felt, why a self-respecting assassin wouldn't choose this spot—so close to the traffic, so exposed, so filthy.

"Grrrrr!" growled Doginder, startling her. "Oof! That wasn't supposed to be a menacing growl, it just came out that way. I don't take my victims to the park, you stupid cat, because I hate that whole killing business. I mean . . . no, no, of course I don't hate killing, I'm a Ferocious Attack Dog, trained killer, lethal weapon, hahahaha, my growl slays them before they even see me. It's only that I'm, er, retired, you know? Never mind all that. Are you going to hang around this tire all day, or are you going to cross the road with me? Oh good show! That idiot of an auto driver, he's taken the corn seller's stall down for the second time—come on, let's go."

Mara found herself rushing forward pell-mell when Doginder barked and bounded onto the tarmac. It felt sticky under her paws, hard and unpleasant, and she felt the gravel cut into her footpads. "Ouch!" she said, and then she froze. Lumbering towards them was a bus.

It had turned the corner slowly, edging past the auto and driving over a few stray half-roasted corn cobs, and it was the only vehicle on the road. The grill gleamed menacingly at Mara, and the headlights seemed massive to her, each one larger than Doginder's head. The lights weren't switched on, but the sun bounced off the metal, and to the Sender, it looked as though the bus had turned its full glare on her. It rumbled as it drew closer.

"Keep moving!" called Doginder. "You've got to keep your paws moving or . . . don't tell me. You've stopped. In the middle of the road. And there's . . . Cat, there are bikes coming at you, from the other side."

He was almost across, and though he had turned to look for the cat, he kept going.

"Move, cat!" he called.

The Sender stood in the middle of the road, paralyzed, even though one paw was raised to take the next step. The bus driver, who'd been wrestling with the gears, finally got them to pop into place. The rumble turned into a roar as the bus driver stood up, shoving the gear into place as though it was the oar of a rowboat, and touched the accelerator.

Doginder turned and barked at her, but the cat stayed where she was. Her green eyes were open so wide that he could see the water from winter puddles on the road reflected in their depths.

"Rescue Dog," he muttered to himself. "Should've stuck with Attack Dog, if you ask me. Much less work. Why am I doing this? It's contagious, madness is. I've caught it from her."

Then he gathered himself, keeping a wary eye on the bikes, shot back into the middle of the road until he was behind the cat.

"Move," he said. "Now." His usual cheerful yappiness was gone. Doginder shivered slightly as he took in the narrowing distance between the cat and the bus, the speed at which the bikers—a group of four—were shooting around the other side of the park; they would soon be here.

An ugly growl broke from his throat.

"Move!" he said. The growl did the trick.

Mara threw her head back and yowled at the bus. She lowered her ears and charged.

"No!" growled Doginder. "Idiot cat, not *at* the bus—away from it! Bikes! Bus! Cat! I'm getting out of here!"

He shot after her, and he and Mara streaked all the way down the middle of the road, causing the bus driver to swerve violently when he saw the dog chasing the cat.

"Wrong way, wrong way!" barked Doginder. "The park's over there! Watch out for the bikes, mind you!"

Mara flattened her ears as far back as they would get, and skidded left, finally heading in the right direction. Doginder, taken unawares, went past her.

On their bikes, the Bigfeet gibbered at each other, swerving around the pair.

"Don't stop, keep going, you're almost there, we're almost at the park . . . Cat! Quit running with your eyes shut, you'll slam into the railings and you won't like it! Open your eyes, you little idiot!"

The bus driver, who had rumbled up the road and was about to take the turn towards the school, glanced into his rear-view mirror. The animals were almost across the road, nearing the park, but something was very, very wrong. Then he realized what it was and he swerved violently for the second time, narrowly scraping past the Tarzan Tribes Brass Band, who were making their way towards the park for practice. He needed a word with his doctor, he decided. Either he needed to change his tonic or his glasses, but one of them had to go. He had seen a dog chasing a cat, and then it had turned into a cat chasing a dog. And the dog was running for all he was worth, like he was about to join the Delhi Marathon. It must, he thought, be his spectacles, perhaps he really should exchange them for a nice pair of contact lenses.

Doginder barked as Mara neared the railings, but the cat kept her eyes tightly shut.

"Survives traffic," he panted between barks, "comes to a tragic end, smooshed against the iron bars . . . Ah! Magnificent! Well done, cat!"

At the last possible moment, Mara opened her eyes, blinked, and slid so smoothly between the bars of the park that it looked as though she'd been practising the move all her life. She was off the road, the soft, sweet grass cool and welcoming under her paw pads.

CHAPTER SIX

Into the Grey Skies

Tooth waddled across the grass, his talons disliking the spikiness of the blades. The uneven slope of the ground made him wobble awkwardly as he walked, and from time to time, he bobbed his head up, to check for Bigfeet and other predators. He didn't think he would be disturbed—except for the occasional visiting pig, the Bigfeet and the stray dogs stayed away from the rough, unkempt strip of grass and mud that ran alongside the length of the canal.

The smell of sulphur from the canal's filthy, clogged waters kept the Bigfeet away; the dogs preferred to hunt for their prey or to raid the garbage heaps inside Nizamuddin, because the gravel and stones on this ragged strip hurt their paws. Even so, the cheel's feathers were ruffled. He preferred to scan the ground for predators from high above. Being down here on the earth made him feel leaden-winged, as though he had been evicted from the sky. The cheel's sharp eyes narrowed as he scanned the horizon far above, and he gave the few birds soaring in the blue a wistful glance. They formed a net, like grappling hooks harnessing the air, and he wished he was among them.

There was a rustle from the straggling ficus across the road, and the cheel swivelled, his tail feathers quivering furiously. "Dive!" he ordered. "Take cover now!"

He waited. "I meant right now!" he said.

"What-evah," said a small cross voice. A ruffled head, its miniature golden and brown feathers disarrayed, poked up from behind a pile of discarded bricks.

Tooth spread his feathers halfway out, shaking out his plumage in exasperation.

"Dark is the night, and full of . . ." he began.

". . . Bigfeetanddogs, got that," said the fledgling, opening its beak in a yawn.

"Hatch!" said Tooth wearily. The ficus bushes rustled again, and a small black rat darted out, running as fast as it could when it caught a whiff of the two raptors.

"What?" said the fledgling, exuding sulkiness from his drooping feathers. "The last time you sounded the alarm, Dad, it was a lizard, and the time before that it was nothing but a posse of ants. I didn't want to be here anyway. It's much warmer back home in the nest."

Tooth eyed his son, wishing that his mate, Claw, was here to handle Hatch's tantrums.

"You know why we're here, Hatch," he said, waddling on again. He cast a wary eye up to the heavens, but dusk had dropped over Nizamuddin, and most of the cheel squadrons had completed their manoeuvres for the day.

"Idontwanna," said Hatch to a passing beetle. The beetle waved its antenna back at him nervously and skittered off. "It's stupid. I'm fine just the way I am."

Tooth folded his wings and turned, glaring at his son. His beak tore at the white-edged leaves from a spider plant in frustration, ripping them into lacework.

"Hatch," he said, "you're not fine just the way you are. Your sister's been out of the nest for almost half the winter! And you haven't even started flapping your wings!"

"You're always picking on me," said Hatch, his skinny legs skimming the ground far more gracefully than Tooth's clumsier ones. "You like Mach better, she gets the fattest grubs from Mom."

"Hatch, Hatch," said Tooth grimly, "you know that's not true. Mach and you snapped at the grub together, and she won. Fair's fair. You're a cheel, you have to fight for your food. Especially if you're not out there actually hunting it down."

"I hunt!" said Hatch, his beak clacking in injured tones.

"Worms," said Tooth, "beetles, things that crawl on the ground. Nothing from the trees yet, son, none of the fat grubs which nest high in the branches of the bael trees, or even the rats and mice who scutter on the ground. You don't hunt those because they have to be hunted from the air . . ."

Hatch raised his wings and called out in annoyance, his keek-keek still so unformed that it sounded to his father's ears like a kitten's mew.

"What-EVAH!" he said. "Dad, you're such a bore. As if you haven't said this a gazillion billion trillion times."

Tooth plucked at his feathers, wondering whether his father had ever felt as exasperated. Probably not, he thought.

Conquer had been of the old school and had left most of the child-rearing to his mate, Stoop. That grim old commander would have used his talons to clip the tail feathers of any of his offspring who had said "Whatevah!" in that tone.

Tooth had admired his father, especially Conquer's gifts as a leadership commander, but when his own mate, Claw, had become broody, Tooth had promised himself that his chicks would have a kind, gentle and understanding dad, exactly the sort he'd secretly wanted for himself. He had done his best to keep his promise. Though every so often, he wondered whether it would be so terrible if he clipped his beloved son hard over the pileum.

"Daa-aad?" called Hatch.

"Yes, son?" said Tooth, proud of the way he kept his feelings out of his voice.

"Can we go home now?"

"No!" said Tooth, his feathers flying up again. "We're here for a reason, remember, son?"

Silence answered him, and Tooth peered worriedly around.

"Son? Hatch? Where have you got to?"

Hatch's head popped out from under a discarded plastic sheet.

"There's no need to shout," he said. "I was taking a nap."

"You've spent the day napping! You need to stretch your wings!" said Tooth. "You're a cheel! We rise at daybreak, before morning in the bowl of night has flung the first stone of night, because we are the hunters of the east. And no matter what, we don't go to roost until we've slipped the surly bonds of earth, at least once. Your mother and I explained all of this, remember?"

"What-evah," said Hatch, yawning.

Tooth stomped ahead, placing his talons on the bumpy ground with some force to try and relieve his feelings.

"Here," he said, indicating the spot with his beak. "Line up beside me."

"Do I have to?" said Hatch, dragging his talons moodily over the stumpy grass.

Tooth turned, and this time there was a decidedly unpleasant glint in his yellow eyes. "Of course you don't have to," he said, his keeks losing their shrill edge and acquiring a dangerous sweetness instead. "We'll go back right this moment to our lovely warm nest, and you can explain everything to Claw. Shall we?"

Hatch stared at his father, his eyes black and opaque. "Explain to Mom?" he said.

"Yes," said Tooth, preening his tail feathers, inspecting the hooklets and then the calamus of each one with great care. "I'm sure she'll listen very, very carefully to everything you have to say."

Hatch glowered at his father, but remained hunched over, a small stubborn ball of brown and gold feathers standing his ground.

"Or," said Tooth, "since we've come all the way here, we could get in a bit of practice."

Hatch stirred, and slouched along the ground to the starting point, his belly collecting dried leaves and other debris.

"There," said Tooth cheerfully. "You might even enjoy this, if you'd let yourself."

Hatch closed his eyes and ducked his small head so that only the very top of the pileum was visible above his wings.

"What-evah," said the pileum crossly to Tooth.

"Quit making a fuss," said Tooth, "you know you like this bit. Now, we're going to do this together. Though you'd normally spread your wings and take the plunge from the nest, there is another way for us to get airborne off the ground."

Hatch made a noise at the back of his throat that Tooth chose to interpret as a sound of assent.

"Here we go!" said Tooth. "First, spread your wings out and give them a nice long stretch. That's right, that's right, shake the dust and the twigs out of them. Then, press your talons into the earth, feel the connection, very good, very good, young Hatch. You could start flapping your wings at this point—no? No problem, mustn't rush these things, we'll do it your way."

Hatch had unfurled his wings, and was bobbing up and down on his talons, stretching his tarsus in delight.

"Excellent!" said Tooth. "Here we go! Spread your wings out—that's right, watch out for the bougainvillea, don't let them get tangled up in the blossoms—and now, we start the run-up!"

A squirrel shooting down the bark of an ancient neem stopped to watch, astonished. Two cheels bobbed up and down, waddling faster and faster on their legs, flapping their wings as they trundled along the grass and mud.

"Perfect!" cried Tooth, his keek-keek soaring through the freezing evening air, making beak-shaped clouds of mist ahead of him. "You're going to do it, Hatch!"

"Yes, Dad!" cried Hatch, whose wings were held straight out in classic fashion, echoing the perfect form of the last few cheels far above them in the sky.

"You are?" said Tooth, forgetting his run-up and wobbling in surprise.

"Yes, Dad!" cried Hatch, bobbing up and down as he ran.

"Here we go!" cried Tooth. "Flight pattern: domestic hopping flight, short distance only, first target, edge of canal bridge, to the left of the big black pig. Got that?"

"Got that!" called Hatch.

"Prepare for lift-off!" called Tooth. "Wings unfurled, pinions ready, talons off the ground. Got that?"

"Got that!" called Hatch.

"One, two, three . . . lift OFF!" cried Tooth. "Reach for the skies!"

"Reach for the . . . nope, sorry, Dad. Changed my mind," said Hatch.

"You . . . what?" called Tooth, who had soared into the air and was heading for the bridge. "Hatch, you did it again."

The cheel circled the canal, ignoring the filthy sludge and the promising scutter of prey on its banks, pretending not to hear the questioning calls from the last few cheels left in the sky, relieved that none of them were from his squadron. His eyes photographed the scene back on the pavement that ran along the edge of the canal. Illuminated in the glow of the streetlights, bobbing up and down—like a duck, like a blasted duck, not a cheel, he thought furiously—and racing along the grass, with his small curving beak carving a wobbly trajectory through it all, was his son. Hatch—child of two of Nizamuddin's best-known raptors, son of the cheel known for his deeds in the battle of the ferals, descendant of Stoop, who had been one of

Delhi's fastest, most ferocious aviators—had failed to get off the ground again.

Tooth couldn't bear to go back right away. He did a backflip in the sky, letting the thermals waft him all the way down the canal route, until he had to flip himself over and swing through the maze of electric poles that lined the alleys leading to Nizamuddin's ancient dargah. The cheel shot up above the roofs, heading for the safety of the high skies. And then he changed his mind. "Figures of eight," he said to himself grimly.

He sliced through the darkness, letting himself drop like a stone until he was almost level with the tops of the electrical poles. Then he unfurled his wings, just in time, shooting up again, slipping and sliding between the electrical lines, between the poles. It eased his heart a fraction, so he did a few slaloms, a few shimmies, just for fun. His aerobatics were so dazzling that the cheels roosting along the roofs of the dargah poked their heads out to watch the show.

Tooth saw a young Bigfoot, the butcher's apprentice, come ambling out of a lane. The boy spotted him as he swung between three poles, flying almost parallel to the ground, the barest of gaps between his wingtips and the lines whose hum spoke of danger. Tooth hesitated; he had always told his squadron to stay well away from the Bigfeet. But there was only this one, and he was a fledgling Bigfoot, not at all dangerous, whispered a little voice in his head. "Anything goes," said Tooth, half to himself, and then he flashed all the way down until he was skimming the lane. He shot past the boy's head, watching the stunned, fascinated eyes, and he circled the boy, brushing the Bigfoot's head lightly with the tip of a feather.

The boy flinched, and that brought Tooth to his senses. The cheel turned on his side and skimmed out of there hurriedly, hitching a ride on the thermals. As he shot out from above the roofs, he could see other Bigfeet faces turned up in his direction, and then the earth shrank, receding, leaving him back in the skies that he loved so much.

He sped towards the canal, but he felt the air change behind him, and turned to greet the cheel who had swooped down from behind the winter moon.

"Later, Slash," he said to the old fighter. "I have things to do."

Slash flew by his side, giving Tooth his space, but not going away, either.

"This can't wait," said Slash.

"It has to," said Tooth. "Like I said, I'm busy."

"Do you understand the risks you took back there?" said Slash, swerving so that he and Tooth were almost wingtip to wingtip.

"Look, Slash," said Tooth. "I appreciate this, but . . ."

Slash cried out once, a battle cry, a warning of attack, and shot past Tooth until he was a cloud's distance away; then he turned so neatly that Tooth almost plunged downwards. Slash hovered in front of him now, challenging his old friend to look away.

"No, you don't," said Slash, as the two cheels circled in the sky, staring at each other. "You spent so many of your years as a fledgling trying to live up to the Commander—yes, you did, Tooth, I watched you grow up, and I was his Group Captain just as I'm yours now—that you didn't grasp the truth."

"What truth?" said Tooth, as the winds swiped at them, and both cheels rocked sideways, trying to retain their balance.

"You were trying so hard to be like Conquer," said Slash, rising so that he was slightly higher than Tooth, "that you didn't realize you were exactly like Stoop."

"My mother?" said Tooth, startled. "But there's no resemblance."

Slash's laugh cut as sharply as the wind chill factor, his keeks slicing through the air.

"I flew with her for years," he said. "And you fly exactly like her when you're upset or angry. The aerobatics. The control. The precision. And the high wings take your feathers, you stupid cheel! Tooth, the risk-taking!"

Tooth fluttered his wings, keeping an eye on the tiny blob far down below that was Hatch. They were approaching the canal bridge at speed.

"Calculated risks," he said. "I knew what I was doing. I have to go now, Slash, my boy's down there alone."

Slash did a barrel roll to work off his emotions, and when he came back up, his feathers were calm. He flew alongside Tooth for a while, neither of the cheels calling out or speaking.

"I've known you since you were a fledgling, Tooth," he said. "I've watched you grow up, I saw you handle some things that would have torn the wings of a lesser bird apart. But you have to know this: you aren't helping your boy by taking the risks you did back there. Those were electrical wires, some of them live. Those were concrete poles you were swinging around at that speed. That area is crawling with Bigfeet."

Tooth turned his beak away, and when he spoke, his voice was even, though his keen eyes glittered.

"I know what I'm doing, Slash," he said.

Slash folded his wings and dropped down hundreds of feet. Then he soared back up, getting right into Tooth's flight path, forcing the other cheel to slow down.

"So did your mother," Slash said drily. "Stoop knew exactly what she was doing, and calibrated every risk she took, and got away with it."

"Well," said Tooth, preparing to dive back down to Hatch. "You're the one who said I resembled my mother."

"Every single risk," said Slash, "until the day she did a triple roll through those wires, and hit a live one. Don't carry the resemblance too far, Tooth. Your son doesn't need to find out the way his father did what it's like to lose a parent."

And with that, the old cheel was gone, speeding away, a fading black dot that melted into the night sky.

Tooth did a double roll, but his heart wasn't in it. It had been a dreary evening. He flapped his wings, slowly, and began the long dive down. The dot on the ground far below had been joined by another dot. Tooth made himself think of landing patterns. He thought of the way Hatch's head had looked, the sticky feathers forming a plume, when his son had popped out of the shell, following his sister Mach into the world. He concentrated on his low flight over the bridge, where the tarry waters of the canal heaved and foamed sullenly, and on the buzzing pigs who stood shivering on the banks. He concentrated on everything he could call to his mind, except for the empty space in the sky near his left wingtip where Hatch should have been flying.

One of the dots he'd seen lifted off the earth, and soared up into the sky, expanding into a brown ball and then an arrowhead shape. Tooth watched his daughter, noting the clean trajectory, the ease with which she caught and rode on the back of the winter winds. Mach had a knack for reading the sky; she took after Claw, who could map the most unknown terrain in one sharp glance, letting the bristles on her beak tell her the secrets of the thermals and the clouds.

"Dad," she called as she drew closer, "there's a cat down there who wants to talk to you."

Tooth dipped sharply, peering in Mach's direction.

"You left your brother alone with a cat?" he said, his call harsh.

"Chill, Dad, you worry too much," she said. "It's that dude, the one who chats with Mom and you every so often, the grey tom."

"Katar," said Tooth, his feathers relaxing, his talons uncurling in the air. "Yes, we met at the battle of the ferals." He thought of the friend who had brought them together, the wise Siamese cat who'd given her life trying to save Nizamuddin's little ones. After the battle, Katar had approached him, stiff-legged, his hackles wary; but there was gratitude in the tom's whiskers, and he offered Tooth the thanks of the Nizamuddin clan, for the way in which the cheels had come to the aid of the cats. They had talked about Miao, sharing their memories of the Siamese, Tooth perched on a flame tree branch, Katar curled up on the railing of the balcony that ran alongside the flame tree. The two had sensed a connection. They were both warriors and leaders by nature, and they had similar instincts: the clan came first for Katar, the squadron's well-being mattered most to Tooth.

The cat and the cheel were careful not to intrude too far into each other's territory, but a friendship of sorts had sprung up between them. And while Katar and the dargah cats still stalked the young fledglings every year, and Tooth and his squadron made the occasional sortie, dive-bombing the cats so that they had to scatter, it was understood that this was just business, nothing personal. Hatch would be safe in Katar's company.

"Dad!" said Mach as they approached the earth. "Stop brooding! Don't let your feathers get into a tangle. Hatch will get it one of these days."

"You've been out of the nest and flying for more than a moon," said Talon, circling close to the tops of the trees and the straggling shrubbery. He hated coming out of the sky, losing the speed and the effortless grace he took for granted; the ground pulled at him, holding him down, making him exchange soars and swoops for that graceless waddle.

Mach touched her wingtips to her father's larger wings, brushing them lightly.

"He'll fly when he's ready," she said. "Look at him! He's so happy racing along the ground!"

And indeed, Hatch made a funny sight, scooting along and zigzagging, his wings dipping crazily from side to side as he chased a cobweb spider under the branches of a fallen tree.

He looks like a partridge or a pheasant or a peacock, not a cheel, Tooth thought sadly, but for his daughter's sake, he said nothing.

Hatch came to a halt as the two cheels landed, and while he raised his wings in greeting, he didn't look his father in the eye. Tooth took a quick look around; Katar sat some distance away, on an abandoned concrete pipe, giving the cheels their privacy.

"So," he said carefully, "what happened this time, Hatch? Did something scare you?"

The fledgling hunched his shoulders, still not looking at Tooth, and started to walk backwards, leaving tiny talon marks in the soft earth.

"Na," he said. "I wasn't scared."

Tooth waited, his feathers fluffed against the cold. Mach watched the two, her eyes inscrutable, her beak tucked into her left wing.

"You had a perfect run-up," said Tooth. "We'd discussed your flight path. You had it memorized. All you needed to do was spread your wings and let go."

"Whatever," mumbled Hatch, picking a flea out of his feathers.

Tooth lost his patience, letting out an angry series of keeks, flapping his wings.

"Your mother and I have been so patient with you, Hatch," he said. "We haven't pushed you out of the nest—all right, not after that one time when you plummeted straight down and Claw had to catch you on her back. We've walked you up and down this stretch of ground for what seems like most of winter. Mach is flying! She's doing double rolls already! Most of this year's fledglings are airborne! You're the only one stuck to the ground, and I have to ask—is this the way you intend to spend your life as a cheel? Scurrying around like a beetle?"

Hatch had pulled his plumage over his eyes, so that he looked like a small furry ball shuffling along the ground.

"Idontwanna," he said. "Flying's so silly. Just because we've done it for generations doesn't mean we have to keep doing it. You might want to flap your wings and disappear into the sky, but I don't like it. The sky's so empty! The ground's much nicer. You can't fall out of it, for one thing."

"You can't fall . . ." Tooth began, his beak opening and shutting, but Mach intervened.

"Dad, you'd better talk to your friend, he's been waiting for a while," she said. "Why don't I take Hatch off to the nest? Then you can take your time, fly up whenever you're ready."

"Sure," said Tooth bitterly. "Take that freak with you. Hop along the ground instead of using the wings you were born with. I wish . . . never mind. Go on, you two."

Except for the sounds of the Bigfeet's handcarts—the vegetable seller, the fruit seller and the rest who were trundling home, done for the day—there was very little noise in Nizamuddin. Tooth glared at the retreating backs of his chicks, both of them waddling along as they made for the nest. Then he turned away, folding his wings sadly, and walked with his legs awkwardly splayed over to where Katar sat.

He was too far away to hear a short exchange between Mach and Hatch.

"Mach?" said Hatch, his stumpy legs working hard to keep up with hers.

"Yeah, brat?"

"Dad said I'm a freak."

"Dad says anything that comes into his head when he's angry. Don't get your feathers in a twist."

"Mach?"

"Yeah?"

"Suppose I never want to fly, ever?"

"It's okay," said Mach. "I'll look after you."

"Ah," said Hatch.

They waddled along the banks of the canal.

"I mean, you might be a freak," said Mach, "but you're my baby brother freak."

"Take it back."

"Freak!"

"I hate you!"

"Is the widdle fweak a cwybaby birdie, then?"

"What-EVAH!" said Hatch crossly, and he lowered his head back into his feathers as they stumped up to the base of their tree.

KATAR APPEARED TO BE absorbed in the activities of a colony of termites who were expanding their territory in daring fashion, marching towards the very edge of the concrete wall that separated the canal from the road.

As he joined the cat, Tooth remembered something his mother had said to him, in one of the years when the population of dargah cheels and Nizamuddin cheels had hit a record high. "Sometimes, it's more polite to fold your wings and learn how to stare out, seeing only the wires, only the trees, giving the other cheels their own, private piece of the sky," Stoop had said, as they'd watched a cheel family fluff their feathers protectively around each other in the monsoon rains.

Katar raised his tail in greeting as Tooth flew up to the branch above his head.

"Cold night," he said cheerfully. "That flight must have warmed you up nicely."

"It did," said Tooth, realizing that his feathers had lost the damp that clung to them from the winter fog. No matter how hard the winter bit, the thermals always dried his wings out—except in the monsoons.

"I see your daughter up there often," said Katar. "She is a born rider of the winds, that one."

"Thank you," said the cheel, grateful that the tomcat hadn't mentioned his hopping, earthbound son. His keen eyes took in the tomcat's thin flanks, the way in which the grey cat's ribs were showing. "It has been some time since we've met, Katar. The winter has been hard for your kind?"

"The Bigfeet," Katar said briefly. "We've lost many of our old feeding grounds. In fact, that's what got young Southpaw into trouble. You know him, I think?"

Tooth raised his beak, his wings fluffing out in remembrance. "Everyone in Nizamuddin knows him!" he said with affection. "He tumbled in and out of trouble as a kitten—wasn't he the one who fell into the Shuttered House? And then he climbed the Cobra's Tree; I remember how Hulo and you dusted his backside for him! But if I am not mistaken, he has grown into a fine cat, has he not? One of your best hunters—yes, I saw him sneak a few rats right before the slavering jaws of the stray dogs, they hadn't expected a cat to be that fast, that daring. And he is the Sender's friend, too?"

"It's the hunting that's got him into trouble," said Katar. He told Tooth the story of Southpaw, the fish, and the young tom's injuries.

"Hulo feels in his whiskers that Southpaw might have broken his paw," he said in conclusion. "It didn't look so bad last night, but it has swollen up this morning, and we fear the Sweet Sickness."

Tooth shivered, his wings closing around him involuntarily. There was nothing more pathetic than a cheel with a broken wing—or a cat with a broken paw. They would be at the mercy of predators, unable to defend themselves, out of their chosen element; he had seen many animals die of the Sweet Sickness, and it was a miserable path to the lair of the greatest hunter of them all.

"My beak is sharp," he said, "but if you wish me to administer a killing bite, I will have to ask another cheel to do it. It is hard to stab at a cat I've watched growing up, and it would not be good if my aim is untrue. But if it must be done, I will see if Slash will do it."

Katar licked his whiskers, trying to conceal how deeply moved he was. It was an honour for a cheel—or any raptor—to offer to put one of another species out of his misery, and Tooth could not have found another way to express how close he felt to the cats. His liking for them had been cautious, starting with a wary truce between him and Miao; but the battle with the ferals had brought them all closer.

"Truly, Tooth," he said, "Miao said you cared about our clan, but I had not expected such kindness from you. We are honoured, though if we can get Southpaw help, his paw may heal well. The injury is bad, and festers. But he is young, and as Hulo says, that cat could fall from the roof of a six-storeyed building, and all he would do is bounce off into the bushes."

"What kind of help?" said Tooth, puzzled. Gashes could be treated, sometimes with spittle, sometimes with good clean mud, if it was available. But a broken wing or paw, especially one that had swelled, was beyond his ken.

"Beraal and I feel he should go to the Bigfeet," said Katar.

"The Bigfeet!" Tooth let out a sharp keek. Except for a few of the butchers in the old lanes of the dargah, who sometimes left pieces of gristle and leftover scraps out for the cheels, he had no love for the Bigfeet. The paper kites they sent up every so often, like poisonous letters sailing into the sky, had deadly tails made of string and glass that could slice a cheel's wing into tiny pieces; the young Bigfeet threw stones at the cheels if they swooped too close. Tooth would no more go near a Bigfoot, under normal circumstances when his mind wasn't so unsettled, than he would place his head between the jaws of a dog.

The wind changed direction and the fog rolled in across the river, making both of them shiver.

"The Sender's Bigfeet," said Katar, settling himself more comfortably on the rim of the concrete pipe. "They know Southpaw and sometimes put extra food out for him. He says they're kind to the Sender, and they have never harmed him or Beraal. Besides, you remember the times they've taken the Sender out in a cage?"

Tooth shuddered, fluffing up his feathers. He remembered very well. No creature in Nizamuddin was likely to forget the first time the Sender had been carried out of her house, yelling her head off all the way down the stairs and all the way out of the colony in her car. She had reverted, on each of these visits, to her old habits, broadcasting her distress at unbelievable volume.

"I remember," he said. "So does every creature between here and the Yamuna river, Katar, she was that loud!"

"Well," said Katar, "Mara's impressive at high volume. But never mind that. Southpaw says as far as he can make out, the Bigfeet took her to a healer each time. And we thought we might get the Sender to explain to her Bigfeet that Southpaw needs the healer."

Tooth thought about it. The idea of any of them having anything to do with the Bigfeet made the tiny feathers on his neck stand up, but then again, the Sender and her Bigfeet were different.

"Yes, yes," he said. "Though tell him not to yell the neighbour-hood down when they put him into that cage thing."

Katar washed his paws, glad that the cheel hadn't flown off at the mere mention of the Bigfeet. It made his whiskers twitch to think of going so close to the Bigfeet's house, but once they had the Sender's attention, she could take over and do the explaining.

"The thing is," he said, "we've brought young Southpaw this far, but he's in terrible pain, and he can't limp along any more. He's back there, resting in the shadows, and Hulo's standing guard over him. The Bigfeet house is in the next park."

He waited, the whiskers over his eyes beseeching. He didn't want to have to ask the cheel for something Tooth might not want to do, or might not be able to do. But it had been heartbreaking, watching the brown tom crawl these last few yards, and Southpaw was pretty much done for. He wouldn't be able to fight off a limp sock from a Bigfoot washing line, forget about a pack of dogs. Nor could he and Hulo do much more for the younger tom, beyond making sure that Southpaw wasn't attacked. By now the swelling had begun to smell. Predators in the area would pick up the scent of the sick tom very soon, and Katar feared that as the night deepened, Southpaw would be marked down as prey.

"That was what I smelled," said Tooth. "Not the Sweet Sickness, but sickness, yes, and pain. I thought it must have been a dying bandicoot. He does not yet smell of great weakness, but he will soon. Over there, you said?"

The cheel took off from his perch so smoothly that Katar found himself admiring the bird's flight, despite his fears for Southpaw. Tooth was a beautiful short-distance aviator. He threaded through the bushes and the trees deftly, his wings now unfurled, now held close to his body so that he wouldn't tangle with the leaves.

Hulo's matted head shot out of the oleander bushes in a snarl, but he retracted his claws the moment he realized it was Tooth.

"Ha! It's you, Tooth—the young one's sleeping," he said to Katar, not bothering with the formalities of greeting. "He won't be going anywhere tonight."

Hulo padded out of the bushes, using his bulk to hold the branches back so that Katar and Tooth could see.

Southpaw was curled into a listless heap, his coat grubby with mud and tree bark, his whiskers drooping. The paw was badly swollen, and Hulo growled at a line of ants who had marched up to it to investigate. The ants swerved off, waving their mandibles at him.

"Not.for.long," they said. "We.will.be.back.soon.His.fur. is.warm. When. it.turns.cold.we.will.be.back."

Hulo sat down, holding the bushes away from Southpaw's sleeping face by the simple expedient of placing his rump on them.

"I ate an ant's nest once," he called out to the retreating column. "Delicious! Peppery but crunchy."

The ants maintained a dignified silence.

Tooth drew closer to the tomcat, his beak hovering close to Southpaw's whiskers.

"The ants are right," he said to Hulo. "The fever has him in her claws, he has gone far beyond the healing you could provide with grooming or licking his paw. You say the Bigfeet can help him?"

Katar raised his whiskers in appeal. "If we could get him to the Sender's house," he said. "But the fever lets him move only in fits and starts."

The cheel said, "The Bigfeet . . . faugh! They make such a racket, and they build their houses into our sky, and send up their planes like lumbering fat birds, so that even there we are not undisturbed. But once, some years ago, Claw tangled with a kite in the sky, cutting her talons badly on the glass and the string. I did not see it myself, the squadron and I were elsewhere, but she told me that she fell to the rooftops and lay there, dazed, in pain, until some Bigfeet found her. She thought it was the end of her—Bigfeet kill as easily as they breathe, you know. Instead, they raised her up and took her to a place far away, where many birds fluttered around her, telling her she was safe, she would be well. When she vanished, we thought we would never see her again; but two moons later, she had flown back to us. Her wounds were healed, and she said it was the Bigfeet's magic. Perhaps they can heal the kitten, perhaps not. But I'll get him there for you."

The cheel said to Hulo, "You go ahead to the Bigfeet's house and wait for us on the stairs. Katar, wake him up, there's a good fellow. Wait—let me test the grip."

Tooth sunk his talons, with delicate care, into the ruff of fur on the back of Southpaw's neck.

"Perfect," he said. "Wiry and rough, enough pile to sink my claws into, and, yes, as I had guessed, the weight's fine."

Hulo didn't know whether to bare his teeth in warning at the cheel or not.

"It's absolutely fine, Hulo, don't worry," said Katar, and Hulo smelled the sudden relief on the grey tom's fur and whiskers. "You go ahead and take the route across the park. We'll give you a bit of a start. It might take a while to wake Southpaw up, anyway, but we'll join you once he's come around. Wait for me, because I won't start until they do. Meet you at the Sender's house, then?"

"The Sender's house?" said Hulo, his tail swishing uncertainly.

"Yes," said Katar, stretching his paws and padding over to Southpaw. "You take the highway; I'll follow soon enough. They're going by air."

Once again, Tooth sank his talons into Southpaw's fur.

"See you there, Hulo," he said. "Short haul flight, with hand luggage. It's a breeze."

CHAPTER SEVEN

Creatures of the Night

Doginder leapt the railings, his tail waving in the air like a brown, furry banner. A pink bougainvillea flower waved along, stuck to his tail's feathery plumes, but he didn't notice; he had his paws full trying to avoid landing on assorted members of the Nizamuddin laughing yoga society.

"HahahahahahahahahahahahahaHAHAHAHAHA!" they said to him in accusation.

"Haha! Haha! Haha! Haha!" said their leader, a man whose wizened face radiated gloom, pessimism and unrelieved despair when he wasn't leading the laughing yoga club in their rounds. He eyed the dog, who had disentangled his paws from one hapless member's cotton checked lungi and was trying to back out of their gathering. "Ha? Ha?" he said to Doginder.

"I do apologize," said Doginder in a meek bark, backing into the lap of another seated laughing yoga enthusiast.

"Hahaohohohohohoho!" the seated man said.

The leader stopped his hahas. "Excuse me," he said stiffly. "Ohohoh or hohoho are not being part of the laughing yoga technique. It is only hahahahahahaha. Or Haha! Haha! Haha! as you please, but please understand, no ohohohohohoho."

The seated man felt he had to explain. "The ohohohoho was because of the dog, sir," he said, equally stiffly.

"The dog," said the leader with immense dignity, "is not a member of the laughing yoga group. Therefore, you will please not address any ohohohos to dogs, especially if they are non-member dogs. Kindly oblige. Only hahahahahahaha! No ohohohohohoho!"

"Haha!" said the seated man, glaring at the leader.

"Hahahahahahahahaha!" said the leader, restoring the group to its normal levels of activity.

"Where's that cat gone?" said Doginder. "Oh no. Please tell me she isn't . . . but of course she is."

Mara had skittered away from the laughing yoga group, frightened by the seriousness with which they emitted their explosive hahas! But her eyes brightened when she saw a Bigfoot family playing badminton on the other side of the park.

"Hello!" she mewed, and before Doginder could stop her, she had sprinted across the park, forgetting her scare on the road.

"Uh-oh," said Doginder sadly. "This isn't going to end well."

He trotted after her, feeling that a Rescue Dog's job was inordinately demanding on some days.

Mara ran towards the family, mewing for all she was worth. "Greetings, Bigfeet!" she said. "I'm so glad to see you! Do you know my Bigfeet? Can you take me back to them?"

"Come back, cat," said Doginder, his tail drooping. But Mara, who had almost reached the badminton courts, wasn't listening. Her green eyes were bright with hope, her tail was up, and as she went up to the Bigfeet, she purred.

"Get that filthy animal off the court!" one of the Bigfeet yelled to his teammate. "She's ruining my serve!"

He scowled, waving his racket menacingly at Mara.

"Hello there!" the cat said, glad that the Bigfoot had stopped running around the court and was looking in her direction. "I suppose I should introduce myself?"

"Oh no!" said Doginder, from the edge of the court.

Purring, Mara went up to the Bigfoot.

"Ugh!" said the Bigfoot in shock. "Get it away from me! Shoo! No! Stop it!"

Mara wound her way around his legs, rubbing her head against his sneakers in joyous greeting. "All hail, Bigfoot!" she said. "Could you take me home, please?"

The Bigfoot stamped his foot and glared at her. Puzzled, the little cat looked up at him, her tail curving into a question mark. "You know my Bigfeet, don't you? They're really nice to me. I miss my house a lot, it's somewhere . . . hey! No! Don't do that!"

The Bigfoot swished his racket through the air, but when the cat continued her mewing, he lost his temper. "Animals shouldn't be allowed in the parks!" he snapped, and viciously, he kicked out.

He caught her in the ribs, and the pain flared through Mara's body, taking the cat by surprise. Her big eyes stared at the Bigfoot in disbelief. She had never been hit, beyond a few light finger-taps on her bottom, and more than the pain, the shock of it kept her immobile.

"Little one," said Doginder quietly, "get off the court. He's going to do it again."

As if in a dream, Mara watched the man step back and take aim, his foot ready to deliver the second kick. The pain was a burning fire under her ribs, and she could feel it radiating along her spine, all the way down to her back paws. She didn't wait; she turned and ran, putting her ears back, making for the shelter of the hedges.

The Bigfoot had kicked her.

She had done nothing, only tried to talk to him. It didn't make any sense.

The Bigfoot had hurt her.

She hadn't attacked him or bitten him, and he had hurt her.

The Bigfoot had been ready to hurt her again.

Her Bigfeet had never hit her. This Bigfoot had kicked her.

The thoughts whirling around in Mara's head were as painful as the injury. The little cat trembled as she squeezed herself as far back as possible, between the friendly roots of the hedges. In the distance, she heard the blare of trumpets—out of tune—start up as the Tarzan Tribes Band began their practice. A large doggy snout poked its way into the branches of the hedge, and two worried brown eyes surveyed her.

"Are you all right, cat?" Doginder asked.

Mara said nothing for a while. She hadn't really checked to see how bad the injury was, but then she took a few cautious breaths and tested her ribs. They would be all right; nothing had broken. The bruises would probably be as bad as the time she had tumbled off the bookshelf chasing the house lizard—possibly worse—but she would heal in time.

"Yes," she said, her mew numb. "The Bigfoot kicked me."

"Yes," he said, "they do that to us strays, you know. You have to be very careful around Bigfeet. You can't just go rushing up to them, they're cruel. I'm Doginder Singh, by the way. Now that we've gone running together, we might as well introduce ourselves."

"But Bigfeet aren't cruel!" Mara said indignantly. "Mine are lovely! They cuddle me, and they put out extra food for Southpaw, and they wouldn't harm anyone, ever! I'm Mara, since you asked. Pleased to meet you."

Doginder sat down near Mara, backing carefully into the hedge so that he wouldn't have Bigfeet stumbling over his paws as they did their rounds of the park.

"I lived with Bigfeet when I was a pup," he said. His brown Alsatian eyes stared off into the distance, as though the Tarzan Tribes Band and the Bigfeet joggers had melted away.

"So you understand," said Mara. "What's wrong with that Bigfoot? He isn't at all like the rest of them. None of my Bigfeet would ever hit us."

"Mine did," said Doginder sadly.

Mara stared at him, her tail twitching under the lantana leaves.

"The Bigfeet you lived with hit you?" she said. Her mew was subdued. She couldn't understand it at all.

"Mara," said Doginder gently, "most Bigfeet don't like us, you know. You're lucky if they don't notice us, but when they do, it means trouble. One of my Bigfeet was very nice—he was young, too, so we both played together like pups. But the others hit me if I asked for more food, or kicked me if I was in the way. Not hard, but I never knew when a blow or a kick would arrive."

"My Bigfeet . . ." Mara started, and then she stopped, wondering how to explain. She had been so frightened when the Bigfeet had picked her up from the canal drain. They boomed at her in their giant voices and took her away from the dogs, but the hands of the Bigfoot who had carried her off from her home had been gentle, his grip firm but soothing. She remembered how they had sat with her that first night. She had whimpered and cried, missing her mother, and they had talked to her as she had shivered under chairs and beds. She had snarled at them when they got too close to her, but been comforted by their presence, by the gentle concern in their voices. And when dawn came up, it had found Mara sleeping in the warm hollow between the two Bigfeet, the beginnings of a tiny purr escaping her throat as they lightly, lovingly, combed her fur.

"They love me," she said, her whiskers rising in what was almost surprise. Mara had taken it for granted that the Bigfeet loved her, and that she loved them back. It was the same with the Chief Bigfoot, who had watched with approval as Mara stalked and successfully fought the household dusters and brooms; they had stared into each other's eyes, cat and Bigfoot, and acknowledged the beginning of a beautiful friendship. Though she had met a few visiting Bigfeet who were scared of cats, she had never met any who had hated or disliked animals.

"Southpaw—that's my friend—he hates Bigfeet, too, but when he spent some time with mine, he understood that they're not all bad. Perhaps it's only a few Bigfeet who don't like us," she said to Doginder. "Perhaps the rest of them do, and we only met some of the nasty ones."

Doginder said gently, "See those two strays running across the far end of the park? Now look what happens when they meet the Bigfeet who're walking around, Mara."

There were a few Bigfeet, walking in straggling clumps, two or three of them abreast at the same time. As Mara and Doginder sat in the hedges, watching them, the park squirrels chittered a rapid-fire warning to the young pups who were bounding across the grass, barking exuberantly to one another. Two of the pups shied away from the path nervously, but one strayed too close. The Bigfeet stopped; even at this distance, Mara could smell their disgust and could sense their dislike. The pup wagged his tail and bowed, trying to indicate that he was no threat to them. He had moved hastily away from the path, and was backing rapidly. But one of the Bigfeet picked up a stone and chucked it in his direction. It hit the pup on the flank and sent him off yelping.

Mara's whiskers radiated incredulity. "Why did they do that?" she asked as the pups scurried for cover, their tails hanging down, their barks hushed and muted.

There was a rustle in the bushes, a curiously silken sound, as though someone had drawn a claw lightly across the surface of the leaves. The cat's nostrils flared, as the air filled without warning with the scent of cedar and something more disturbing.

"Stay where you are," said Doginder's voice in Mara's ear. His growl was quiet, but urgent. "If you run or show fear, she'll attack, otherwise you're safe."

At first, the cat could see nothing, though she sensed the keen eyes of a watcher in the undergrowth. The hedge was thick, its roots running deep along the park's stone wall. Mara peered through the tangle of roots, her keen eyes adjusting quickly to the shift between the glare of the sun on the stone path, and the deep, dark, cool shade at the back of the hedge.

The creature's head was sleek, brown fur edged with silver. The amber eyes caught and held Mara's own with no fear, and the black nose twitched. Mara felt her own fur prickle at the tips in warning; she glanced at the creature's paws and noted the wicked nails, smelled the dried blood matted under the killing curves of those claws. Her eyes stared unblinkingly into the mongoose's eyes, and she felt her heart race; her blood was up, but she could not have said whether her need was to flee or to attack.

"The Bigfeet are confusing, are they not?" said the mongoose. Her voice was silky and Mara caught the whiff of satisfied bloodlust in it, as though the creature had come into the park fresh from a kill. "They are not like the cobras, who kill when cornered; or like my kind, who kill for food and for the love of a good fight; or like Doginder, who kills not at all. Do you kill, little stranger? I have not smelled your scent before, no, I have not."

The talk of killing nudged Mara's memory.

"You must be Kirri, the hunter," she said. The amber gleamed in Kirri's eyes, and some instinct made Mara raise her whiskers in respectful greeting, though she held her ground, fighting a sudden urge to turn tail and run away from the mongoose. "Southpaw told me about you. He said you were a mighty kill . . . a mighty hunter, and that he had learned much from you."

Southpaw had also said that the mongoose terrified him, but Mara wasn't about to repeat that.

Kirri's claws slid lazily over the hard wood of the roots, making small clicks as they went. "Careful," said Doginder, and Mara could smell his wariness.

"Little stranger," said the mongoose politely, "I am not used to speaking with those whose names have not been offered to me."

Mara saw the tiny flames leap in the mongoose's eyes, but she kept her own gaze steady.

"Forgive me," she said. "You called me a stranger, and so I am. I'm Mara, and I've lived with Bigfeet most of my life, so I don't really know cat customs. It's my first time out, you see. But I didn't mean to be rude, my lady mongoose, truly I didn't."

And something made her add, "Though Southpaw spoke the truth—I can tell you must be a mighty hunter!"

Kirri stopped stropping her claws, and the tiny flames in her eyes dimmed, though the embers remained. A rambunctious group of schoolchildren ran up the path; the three creatures pressed back into the hedge, Doginder ducking well into the branches out of instinct, Mara following the example set by the other two.

When she spoke again, Kirri sounded reflective. "You have given me your name; mine is Kirri, you may use it freely. Manners and customs are not the same thing," she said. "You may have no sense of our customs, but you have pretty manners, little stranger. Do your Bigfeet not let you out, then? Have you come to join us outside?"

"Oh no!" cried Mara. "I've never been outside before, it's so cosy at home with the Bigfeet, and it's safe; I'm happy inside.

But the kabadi wallah came today and there was *such* a noise that my head started to hurt, and then he ran this-a-way and I ran that-a-way, and before I knew it, I was out of my house . . . and now I'm here."

"Lost," said Doginder cheerfully. "I had to rescue her and bring her into the park, otherwise she'd have been stuck under that car for ages."

"How clever of you," said Kirri crisply, her attention never veering from the cat. "So, little stranger, you have no liking for all of this? You prefer your Bigfeet house, the roofs and the walls instead of the free air, the grass and mud under your feet, the danger, the battles, the thrill of hunting your own prey?"

She waited, her sleek head cocked to one side.

Mara raised her whiskers, letting them taste the air of the park, its cacophony of yells from the children who played in one corner, the brisk thumping of the Bigfeet on their walks, the loud squabbling of the Tarzan Tribes Band.

"Have you ever lived with Bigfeet, Madam Kirri?" asked Mara. The mongoose didn't respond, but her sharp brown eyes considered the cat carefully. "Doginder tells me that his Bigfeet were cruel to him, but it is not so with mine. They take me into their bed if I cry out at night in my sleep. They feed me the things I love most, and they play with me for hours. I have a comfortable bed, the calm and safety of the house; and the world comes in through the doors and windows. My whiskers let me know everything I need to, and if I am bored, I can go on long sendings while I sleep in peace on the bookshelves, or in a basket. Why would I need the outside at all? Here we have to hide from the Bigfeet in the hedges, even Doginder who's so much bigger than you and me. And it's cold and wet—there are no blankets, no soft-lined baskets. Your world is filled with predators, Madam."

"I see," said Kirri softly. "But this is your first time out in the world, is it not? Is there nothing you like about it? Your Bigfeet must be good people; but do you not miss your own kind? Does your blood not sing to you to climb the trees and race along the rooftops, to challenge every other young queen who claims this park as territory, to find a tom of your own to mate with under the silver moonlight? I ask again, little stranger, is there nothing about the world that you might love?"

Mara blinked, her green eyes troubled. Doginder watched them both. He would have liked to have told Mara how unusual this was. The mongoose was one of Nizamuddin's most famous warriors. Kirri's world was divided sharply into predators and prey, with a small space reserved for neutrals. Her attention was rarely caught by any creature that couldn't be battled or eaten.

The Sender spread her whiskers out, scenting the air. The young queen's whiskers were unusually thickly clustered; above her eyes, the whiskers grew as long as one would expect of a warrior tom who had seen the earth turn for five or more winters.

For a long moment, the three stayed still under the hedges. A family clattered past them, the baby carriage bouncing on the old flagstones. Overhead, the birds cleared their throats, the bulbuls practising a few early evening alaaps, the parrots calling in mock urgency to one another, warming up for the storm of chirrups and chatter that would signal the end of another day. The keek of a cheel sounded once, high above the treetops, and the traffic roar deepened, as the Bigfeet rush-hour started.

Then the Sender broke the spell. "The air you breathe is different," she said. She blinked, and raised her whiskers again. "I can hear the birds as well as I could hear the passing stray dogs, the squirrels and the cats, without having to send. The Bigfeet's cars stink—their roads stink—it rasps across my nostrils, their love of concrete and tar and metallic things. But the grass is soft under my paws, O Huntress, and the chill on the breeze whispers to me of the lives of so many more creatures—it is frightening, it is overwhelming, but it is full of life, this park. And the sky . . ." The cat shivered.

Kirri's fur stood up ever so slightly around the muzzle. "It seems vast to you?" the mongoose inquired. "Without limit, without end?"

"Yes," said Mara, her mew hushed, but there was doubt in her eyes. "There are no roofs here, and you have to look up such a long way, it makes my head spin. It is scary."

Kirri's eyes had gone black, opaque and unreadable. Doginder could not tell what she was thinking, and he found his hackles rising. He barely knew this young cat, but he felt responsible for her; she was as helpless outdoors as a kitten, or a pup. If the mongoose went for her, he thought, he would have no choice but to fight, however deep his distaste for battle. He lifted his large paws, and shifted his haunches, so that he could spring at need.

Mara hadn't noticed. Her eyes were shut; she breathed in through her pink nostrils. "Huntress," she said, "that is not all, though. I have travelled through the night on my whiskers, but it is only here, outside, that I have truly looked up at the night sky."

"What do you see when you look up?" said Kirri. The mongoose was still, but her body was coiled taut.

And Mara's mew rang out, eager, intense; it was as if she had forgotten that the Bigfeet were close by. "It is not what I see, Kirri," said the Sender. "The darkness may seem empty and vast, but my whiskers say it is criss-crossed with the paths of the birds—can you not feel them? High up, the rough drumbeat of the cheels carves broad highways above the clouds; over our heads, across the trees, you can trace the soaring songlines of the bulbuls, the trails left by the sharp swift sorties of the parakeets, and even the dark purrs of the Bigfeet's clumsy aircraft. It makes me dizzy, but I can scent the bats, the mynahs; the trees rustle and whisper. The skies are vast, but they hold so much more than I had thought."

Doginder let out his breath, as silently as he could. He smelled the change in Kirri; she had gone from kill-ready to peaceable once more, and now the mongoose smelled of cedar and wood bark rather than blood and ice. She stood down, curling her tail comfortably around her.

"Once, Mara," she said softly, "I met a cat who did not like the sky. It is a worrying thing in our kind, to be afraid of the very air around us. Those who start by fearing the sky often end by hating those who live freely under the clouds, who walk in the sun without shuddering. The night hides more than predators until we know it so well that we can speak its many names without fear; and yet, we live most keenly under the wing of darkness. It is good for you, O Sender of Nizamuddin, that you can pad past your fear and let your curiosity ride on your whiskers instead . . ."

Kirri would have said more, but something at the opposite end of the park caught her attention, and the mongoose stood up, her neat round ears on the alert.

"Prey!" she said. "I must go, or the bandicoots will start to believe that they own the night. How they strut, how they brag, until they meet our kind."

"Our kind?" said Mara uncertainly, wondering what Kirri meant.

Kirri was about to leave the hedge, but she stopped. "The Sender has old whiskers, but her fur is young," she said, half to herself. "Our kind, Mara. You're a predator like me. Do not forget."

"I wish you good hunting," Mara said politely, and then, as the mongoose slid off, a final question occurred to her. "Before you go, Kirri . . . what happened to the cat? The one who was scared of the sky?"

The mongoose paused, her claws backlit by the lamps in the park, which were lighting up one by one.

"His story ended as it should," said Kirri, and her eyes met and held the Sender's.

Doginder, who had allowed both creatures their say, saw the mongoose turn to leave, and could not hold himself back any more.

"Wait!" he barked. "O Kirri, you can't leave us hanging like that. What do you mean, his story ended as it should?"

Kirri turned one last time. "Badly," she said. "For him, that is. I enjoyed the dance."

And then there was nothing but the shadows and the light from the lamps. The mongoose was gone. There was a pause, a moment's hush. Then the sun dipped below the horizon, and the birds' low squabbling swelled and rose, until it had become a melodious but deafening chorus, an evensong that ushered in the winter night.

"Just as well Kirri took a liking to you," he said gravely. "But if I might drop you a bark of warning: don't go off chatting with any mongoose you see. They're killers by nature, and Kirri is no exception."

"I understand," said Mara faintly. "Doginder, how many Bigfeet houses *are* there?"

As the darkness slipped down over the two of them, the lights in the windows of the Bigfeet homes glowed bright, and the dog dimly intuited the Sender's despair. He was used to the long lines of Bigfeet dwellings, but she had only known one home. And she knew little of the harshness of the outside world, as he had seen. Doginder felt Mara shiver beside him; even the cold that he took for granted was alien to her.

"Do you remember the house at all?" he said. "It has to be close to the park, since you couldn't have run that far. Perhaps you could recognize it now?"

But as Mara stared at the row of houses and Doginder felt her whiskers droop, caught the arid scent of exhaustion on her fur. "No," she whispered. "I've never seen it from the outside. They all look the same to me—and it's no use asking me to send, the Bigfeet can't understand whisker or mew." The Bigfeet couldn't even understand Junglee, the basic language of gestures and grunts that every animal used when talking to other species. She shrank back when she heard the loud voices of Bigfeet boys and scrabbled to get behind the shelter of the roots again.

Doginder hesitated. If he left now, a traitorous voice in his mind whispered, he would be in time to drop in at the local dhaba, the food stall where they kept stale rotis and leftover gravy and bones for stray dogs. But only, said the insidious voice, if he left right now, or else the other dogs would finish every last delicious meaty shred. He had done his bit, hadn't he? He had rescued the cat—twice!—once from the traffic, once from the mongoose.

"Doginder," said Mara's quiet mew from the hedge. "I've been thinking—you know, my Bigfeet will probably come looking for me in the morning. And the hedge is quite comfortable, so if I settle in here for the night, I'm sure I'll be safe. All the bandicoots are on the other side of the park, aren't they? So if you have dinner plans or anything, you should go. Thank you for everything."

"Rats!" said Doginder.

"I'm sorry?" said Mara. "What did you say?"

"Oh, nothing," said Doginder, but another of the voices that often barked at him inside the privacy of his head was in full swing, reminding him that a true Rescue Dog wouldn't run off and abandon a helpless cat to the predators in the park, a true Ferocious Attack Dog would stand guard over her, wouldn't he?

"Bother being a Ferocious Attack Dog," he said crossly. Then he sighed, tucked his jaunty plume of a tail in so that it wouldn't pick up too much bark and earth, and dug his way back into the hedge.

"Don't you have to go?" said Mara uneasily. She had a very clear idea from her Bigfeet of the importance of mealtimes, and indeed, now that the shock of being outdoors had worn off, her stomach had started to remind her—persistently—that it hadn't been attended to since morning.

"Not at all," said Doginder, lying gallantly and trying not to think of the fact that tonight would have been offal night at the dhaba. "Nothing I'd rather do than spend a night out in the park. You can look up at the moon and get a nice spot of baying and/or barking in if you're so inclined, and then there's the Chasing of the Cars after midnight, and we can always snack on woodlice if we're really hungry." He ignored the twigs that were poking at his flanks, and tried to ignore the chill seeping upwards from the damp earth.

They heard a last round of cheerful yelling, a clatter, and then the last of the Bigfeet left the park. There was only one Bigfoot remaining, a man who lay stretched out on a bench like an untidy heap of clothes. Every now and then, he snored in a rising, loud arc, with a question mark hanging at the end of the snore; it seemed unlikely that they would have to worry about him.

Doginder felt Mara shiver again, and thought that the cold would bite as deep into the little cat's bones as any predator. She needed shelter, better harbour than the park could provide; she needed, he thought, the shelter of her own kind.

"Mara," he said, "Kirri mentioned that you were the Sender, and all that talk of whiskers—can't you let the other cats know you're here?"

"The other cats?" said Mara. He could feel her whiskers twitch in incredulity.

"Why not?" he said. "Your sending earlier in the day was

loud enough—I'm sure they would hear you—good heavens, I'm sure they heard you all the way across the canal in Jangpura, for that matter! And no Nizamuddin cat would refuse the Sender shelter, surely."

"No!" said Mara. "I couldn't. They don't like me, Doginder! They've always thought I was a freak—no, I couldn't ask them."

Doginder put his ears back and looked at her questioningly. "But it would only be for a night," he said. "And you *are* the Sender, Mara—their Sender."

"Oh, you don't understand!" Mara cried. "They don't trust inside cats, Doginder, and then my whiskers and my sendings make me strange in their eyes—do you think I haven't heard them? I stopped sending in Nizamuddin because Southpaw and Beraal were the only ones I could talk to. And Beraal can't move around, she's just had her litter, I haven't seen her in weeks, and Southpaw's been badly hurt, I won't send to him."

Doginder listened, and there was something in the depth of his brown eyes that Mara couldn't read, even though they were well illuminated by the lamp that stood directly over the hedge.

"Beraal is your friend?" he said.

"You know her?" Mara said.

"Yes, we all do," he said. "She's one of the finest warriors and most respected of the queens in the neighbourhood, second only to Miao—but you never knew the Siamese, she died last year in the great battle."

"I met Miao before she died," Mara said quietly. "And Beraal was my teacher, before she had to go away and have her kittens."

"The world is not a sending," Miao had told her. "The world is real, and it is more than the four walls of your house." She had thought often of the Siamese cat's words, and more than once, she had sat on the windowsill, letting the world come to her, wondering whether she should heed Miao's advice and go to it instead. Fear had held her paws back at the sill, at the doorway, at the top of the stairs, for many moons now. Perhaps, thought the Sender, too many moons.

Doginder looked at her steadily. "You puzzle me, Sender," he said. "You have power of your own, you have much politeness, and yet you know so little of your own world. You say Beraal was your teacher, but you have not visited her or her kittens?"

Mara sat back and washed her fur hurriedly, not wanting to meet Doginder's gaze. She kept her attention on her paws, and on the circles of yellow light cast by the lamps in the darkness, and the rustles and squeaks from the small prey in the park.

"No," she said, her voice muffled as she combed out her tail. "I don't go out much."

She was afraid of what Doginder might say, but he surprised her. The dog lowered his head and blew air out of his nostrils, a soft, resigned gesture.

"There was a time when I grew so used to the Bigfeet and their beatings," he said, "that I stopped caring about what happened to me." Imperceptibly, his voice changed, his bark shifting to mimic the timbre of his puppy days. "Days went by, and I would barely look up when the door was left open; instead of watching the animals who went by, the cows and the rat packs, I spent the hours slumped on my blanket, waiting to fill the time between one meal and the next, one kick or cuff and the next."

It seemed to Mara that the tendrils of winter wrapped closer around them as the dog spoke, the night chill seeping into her bones. Doginder's scent had grown heavier, thicker, so different from the sunny, cheerful smell his fur had carried all day. She could see it in her mind—not Doginder as he was now, a great bouncing fellow who carried his plume of a tail as a banner. Instead, the Sender saw a young pup, his ribs thin and bruised from the rough treatment he'd received; she could smell the sadness seeping out of his fur, see the wariness leach the trust out of the young dog's brown eyes as he rested his head on his thin blankets.

"Days went by before I realized that the Bigfeet were growing careless," Doginder said. "They didn't bother to tie me up most days, only slipping the chain around my neck at night— sometimes, if the man doing that was in a bad mood, he would slip it tight, so tight that—oh well, what's the point returning to the stink of yesterday's sadness? But most afternoons, I would be unleashed; and do you know what I did when one day I realized I was free of that hateful leash?"

Mara brightened. "You ran," she said, her whiskers rising as she thought of the pup's gladness, his joy at being able to finally escape.

Doginder sighed, and his breath came out in a puff of white fog, hanging in the cold air.

"No, Mara, I didn't run," he said. "I didn't even think of running. It had been so long that I had stopped wondering what the air would smell like on the other side of the wall, whether the street would feel different under my paws when I could walk freely, without someone shoving a stick under my belly or jerking my head back if I tried to follow my nose. I had forgotten how to want to be free."

He turned his head and cocked his ears as a bandicoot hurried by, but then he returned to the past. "One day, a pair of parrots swooped over the wall. They called to one another: 'Can you come? Can't you come?'—and they made bright green flashes against the red bricks. One flew over my head, so close that I could see the barbs of its feathers on its undercoat, and she called: 'Can you? Can't you?' I stood up and walked a few steps. It felt odd, not to feel the restraining tug of the leash, the dour bite of the chain. 'You can't? You can!' her mate urged me, and slowly, my paws wobbly, I found myself walking away from the house, the Bigfeet and everything I had known. The door was open, and I stepped out into the world, and after many moons my nose started to twitch again."

Mara could see it so clearly as Doginder shared his memories. It was early spring; the new leaves were coming out on the trees, soft clouds of silk cotton whirled and played in the breeze, tangling themselves in the fur of the young pup's legs and tail. He had padded faster and faster, breaking into a run when he realized he didn't want to go back to his Bigfeet any more. The welcoming smell of the pigs foraging at the canal, the scurrying trails of the rat pack along the lanes, the promising aroma of food wafting out of the Bigfeet homes—all of these whispered to the young Doginder in greeting. In the far distance, he had heard the joyous barks of a pack of street dogs, and Doginder knew that he had found his kind.

Mara went over to the dog and rubbed her flank along his. Instinct told her not to lick his face—no matter how friendly they had become, he was still a dog, and her blood warned her not to test his automatic responses. But she purred as she brushed past him, and touched, Doginder bent down to press his cold, friendly nose lightly against her orange fur.

"All right, all right," he said hurriedly, "enough with the sappy stuff."

"I wish your Bigfeet had been more like mine," said Mara, "but I'm glad you left yours. They sound awful."

"Mara," said Doginder, "I'm going to go off now and find some food for both of us. Look, I didn't tell you my story because I wanted you to feel sorry for me. I told you about my life because chains and leashes are strange things—sometimes you don't know when they've slipped off, leaving you free. Anyway, time to get down to some of the old hunting-foraging business, cat, I'll be back soon. Stay right here, mind. Don't budge. Don't go for a walk, don't try to chat up stray predators, don't run off with a strange mongoose or three. Okay?"

"Yes, Doginder," said Mara. She heard him bark as he bounded off into the night, loud, joyous woofs that expressed how happy he was to stretch his legs after the last few hours.

Now that the dog had gone, Mara let her whiskers stretch out, tasting the night air. She felt them tremble at the light silken tug from far above, where the bats had come out for their sorties. Their intelligent chirrups wafted down to her, transforming the blackness of the sky into a more friendly place. The earth under her stomach was damp and crumbly, but despite the cold, Mara felt a kind of contentment seep through her limbs. It was comfortable enough under the hedge, and her whiskers and nose brought her news of the park: a posse of stray dogs patrolling the canal roads well into the distance, the thump of Bigfeet machinery as a concrete mixer rumbled into life for some late-night construction work, the purposeful, stealthy scurry of the bandicoots in the far corners of the park.

The warm, glowing squares that lit the Bigfeet homes caught her attention. In one of the houses, a Bigfoot came out onto the balcony and stood there for a moment, looking down into the park. It was not one of her own, the smell told Mara that much. But there was something about the way the Bigfoot stood that reminded her of her own Bigfeet, and a pang of longing took her unawares. She would have been curled up on the sofa next to them at this hour, batting at the pages of the books they insisted on reading when they could have been doing the sensible thing and cuddling their cat.

Her stomach would have been full, instead of rumbling and empty. Perhaps there would have been a set of war games—battles where Mara's duty was to stalk the feathers, balls of wool and other objects that represented, had they but known it, deadly threats to the Bigfeet. They seemed to think these objects were innocuous, but Mara knew better; she had watched their shadows grow and lengthen on the walls, and knew they were not what they seemed, even if the Bigfeet refused to take her wars seriously.

It felt to her that the lights in the windows made the darkness under the hedge in the park even thicker. She wondered whether her Bigfeet missed her as much as she missed them. And for the first time since she'd left her home that afternoon, she wondered if she would ever find her way back to them. The thought made her mew softly and sadly to herself; it was unimaginable. They were her clan, even if they were lacking in the whisker department.

Her ears swivelled at the sound of a familiar voice. Doginder was still some distance away, but his bark was excited, carrying far in the cool night air. Mara's nose whiffled as she scented something else: who was it? A fully grown tom with a swagger, exuding confidence and something else, the alertness of the practiced warrior.

". . . So you heard the Sender calling for Southpaw and Beraal?" Doginder was saying.

"Heard it? Everyone in the blasted neighbourhood heard it, my eardrums felt like a Diwali firecracker had gone off in it—but she's always been a noisy nuisance of a beast." The tom's voice carried clearly over the park to Mara.

"I guess she totally nails 'loud,'" said Doginder. "But poor thing, she was scared. First time she's been outside, as you know, and she's feeling lost without her Bigfeet."

The tom made a dismissive mew, as the dog and the cat turned into the road at the head of the park. Even at this distance, from her position under the hedge, Mara caught the contempt in his hiss.

"If you ask me, a Sender that never pokes her precious nose out of her stinking Bigfeet house isn't much of a Sender. We don't think much of her around these parts—what kind of scaredy cat stays shivering inside her own house, choosing to consort with our enemies instead of spending time with us? She's a disgrace, this so-called Sender of ours, leading her pampered, soft, cushioned life, never getting her paws dirty with the mud and soil of our world. She's a disgrace to Senders and a disgrace to cats—hanh? What's that you're saying? She can hear us? She's right there? All right, all right, I'll save it for later, let's see what we can do for her. If this is the first time she's come out on her own, she'll be cold and in need of feeding, Sender or no Sender."

Doginder leaped gracefully over a wandering bandicoot, startling the rodent, and ran down the path, Hulo keeping up with him effortlessly despite the dog's longer strides.

"Hey, Mara!" he called. "Brought you a relative. Come on out and say hello to Hulo."

There was only silence.

"Hello to Hulo," said Doginder cheerfully. "I thought that was pretty good, didn't you? Come on, little one, there's no Bigfeet around, don't be shy."

Hulo was prowling around the roots, cautiously sniffing at the air.

"She's not here," he said. "She was, until a moment ago, but there—in the earth—her paw marks."

Doginder cocked his head.

"But I told her not to leave," he said, puzzled. "I said I'd come back with food for her, and help."

The light caught Hulo's grim, scarred visage. There was an unhappy gleam in the old fighter's eyes, and he brushed a few tangles out of his thick, unkempt fur.

"You realize what happened, don't you?" he said.

"Oh no," said Doginder. "You think . . .?"

"Yes," said Hulo grimly, his tail plunging downwards. "She must have heard what I said, smelled my dislike. The pawmarks are widely spaced—she ran out of here, ran as fast as she could. The Sender's gone into the darkness, into a neighbourhood she doesn't know, and it's all my fault."

The tom's fur was ruffled, his sense of balance upset. He had no love for the Sender, and had considered her a nuisance from the time her infant yowls had interrupted his peace, his long hunting nights and Nizamuddin's most promising catfights. He had argued that the Sender was just another outsider, and should be culled as was the practice with unwanted kittens who didn't belong to the clan—it was Beraal who had fought him and won his promise that he would let the little stranger live. Before this night, Mara had always been the Sender to him, the unwanted stranger who set his beloved Nizamuddin by the ears.

Until now, he had never seen her as a kitten, or thought of her as a young cat—she would be, he guessed, only a few moons younger than Southpaw, whom he and Katar had steered through that orphan's often-turbulent childhood. Disliking Mara from a distance was one thing. Scenting the fear and sadness of this small, lost, sharply unhappy young queen, so much like the many Nizamuddin kittens he had gruffly helped to bring up, was another.

The fog touched the tips of his crooked whiskers, and the light reflected in his eyes burnished them to a golden sheen. He lowered his head, sniffing at Mara's tracks.

"Doginder," he said, "how many of your kind are out in Nizamuddin tonight?"

The dog's ears folded forward.

"Too many," he said. "We've had a few rough beasts slouching in from the animal shelter. Some of them are rogues who don't belong to any pack, and who'll snap and snarl at the world because they don't like it. Not like the local strays at all."

Hulo's great head with the torn ears, scarred from far too many brawls, was lowered as he listened.

"You should go and get yourself some dinner before the dhabas shut down," he said.

"I can't," said Doginder. "I'm sorry, she's from your clan, not mine, but smelling the trail of the Sender's sadness—I can't go off knowing she's all on her own in this darkness."

"You go on," said Hulo firmly, his whiskers alert, his tread brisk. "I'll handle this."

Doginder hesitated. He wasn't sure what Hulo meant by "handle this."

"I only met her today," he said, "but I have to tell you, I liked Mara. If you mean her any harm . . ."

His words trailed off into a growl. He wasn't quite sure what he would have threatened Hulo with, since his definition of being a Ferocious Attack Dog focused on the "ferocious growling" much more than the "vicious attacking" side of things, but he felt strongly about the subject.

Hulo was padding off, out of the park, towards the roads that led to the front of Nizamuddin.

"No harm," he said as he left, "I'll find her and keep her safe until we can take her to her Bigfeet. You needn't worry, Doginder. It was my doing that she ran off; but from this day on, the little one will come to no harm at my paws or claws or teeth."

Doginder found the words comforting; they had the ring of an oath to them. He watched Hulo disappear into the darkness, the tomcat's black fur merging with the night, and the park fell into silence again. The only creature that moved was a brown mouse, almost invisible among the roots. Jethro had spent a relaxed day in the company of his friends, a group of genial beetles, until their chatter had been interrupted by the arrival of Doginder and Mara. The beetles had been alarmed, waving their mandibles in agitation, but then they had quietened down when Jethro pointed out that neither the dog nor the cat appeared to be interested in hunting. He had heard Hulo's loud approach, too, and seen Mara's distress just before she had run away.

The mouse looked in the direction that the orange queen had taken, but he didn't go after her. Instead, he considered the matter, nibbling on the end of his tail, and then he scurried off, following the path the black tomcat had taken.

CHAPTER EIGHT

Hellhounds on the Trail

The words had struck her like stones, each one leaving its hurtful mark. ". . . a Sender that never pokes her precious nose out of her stinking Bigfeet house isn't much of a Sender . . . . choosing to consort with our enemies instead of spending time with us . . . never getting her paws dirty with the mud and soil of our world . . ."

Mara whimpered, and backed out of the hedge, trying not to make a noise. She could smell Doginder's embarrassment. She didn't want to meet him. "She's a disgrace to Senders and a disgrace to cats," she heard, but the young queen didn't stay to hear the rest of what Hulo had to say. Her whiskers quivering in distress, her pink nose tremulous, she cast a wild look at the road, checking that there was no traffic, and pelted away from the park. She ran flat out, her ears back, pinned to her head, letting her nose and paws guide her. I have to get away, the Sender thought, I have to get away.

The asphalt cut cruelly into her paw pads, which were soft, unaccustomed to negotiating anything harsher than cool marble and stone or the silken pile of carpets. She ignored the pain, flitting like a ghost under the lines of parked cars, veering once to avoid a cyclist, putting as much distance as she could between herself and that harsh, scornful, contemptuous purr.

An uncomfortable but insistent part of her asked: Hulo's words were unkind, but could they be true? She thought of small incidents she had packed away in her memory: Beraal's gentle mew, asking her to come out and meet the clan; Miao's understanding eyes as she told her that there was a cost to staying safe; Southpaw's hurt brown eyes when she refused to come out and play with him, for the umpteenth time. He had stopped asking after that, Mara remembered, and her fur prickled with discomfort.

She had thought the Nizamuddin cats hated her, and now she knew they did. But, asked the uncomfortable voice in her head, had she given them a chance to get to know her? Beraal and Southpaw had accepted her. Southpaw had given her his friendship. Beraal had given her everything she knew about fighting and war, had patiently borne Mara's tantrums and fear of the outside, had fought for the Sender's right to live. Would Hulo have hated her as much if she'd strolled with him on the rooftops, crossed his path when he was out hunting?

She found a gap between two sets of buildings and turned into a cobbled lane, one of the old snaking alleys that connected the Bigfeet's homes. The cobblestones were more comfortable under her paws, their rounded surface caressing, but they forced the Sender to slow down. Gradually, she became aware of her surroundings. The clicking sound she had registered came from her own paw pads catching on the cobbles. Above, the Bigfeet sat out on their terraces, or chattered at one another; the windows creaked as shutters were pulled to for the night. There was a subtle, oily trail of scents lining the gutters: she thought of furtive night creatures, slinking about in the dark. It made her uneasy, and she slowed further, not wanting to be caught unawares by another animal.

Then Mara's whiskers rose and her heart gave a glad thump as she caught the familiar scent of sun-warmed fur—Doginder was here somewhere! The young queen's tail rose, her head tilted up and she padded eagerly towards the end of the alley. There he was, silhouetted against the tube lights from a Bigfoot shop. He stood at the entrance of the alley, his plume of a tail raised in friendly fashion.

"You found me!" she cried, forgetting her embarrassment in the delight of seeing her friend. "I'm sorry I ran off without saying goodbye, but I couldn't face you and Hulo after what he said. Not that he was entirely wrong, about my never going outside . . ."

Her mew trailed off, and her paws skittered on the cobblestones. The dog moved forward. His eyes were a dirty yellow. His fur smelled singed; his tail was raised, not in welcome, but in menacing warning.

"You're not . . . you're not Doginder," Mara said, her whiskers tremulous. The fur at the back of her neck was prickling in terror, her claws became so soaked in fear-sweat they started to slide on the cobbles, losing their grip. She had to . . .

"Run, prey," said the dog, his growl deep and terrifying. "Aren't you going to make a run for it? Most of my prey does, before I catch them. I haven't seen a cat come down this alley in months, most of them know this is my territory. Mine, you understand?"

He opened his dreadful mouth, and bared his fangs at her. They were unclean and Mara could smell traces of dried blood on his muzzle; he had already killed once this evening.

"Please," she said, "I was . . . I was lost. I didn't know this was your territory. Please don't hurt me."

He laughed, a rough sound between a howl and a growl. "Please don't hurt me!" he mimicked. "What do you think dogs do to cats? Feed them, play with them?"

Then his muzzle was down and he was barrelling towards Mara, so fast, too fast.

She knew she should turn and run, but she was staring at his jaws, flecked with spittle and blood. She thought about those curving teeth coming down on her hindquarters and flinched; she could almost hear the crunch her broken bones would make, feel her paws snap. It would be her neck next. She stood there, not mewing, her eyes bright green with terror, fixed on the predator's slavering jaws.

"Aren't you going to run then? It makes no difference to the outcome, but it's more fun for me when prey runs," said the dog, panting as he clattered across the cobblestones.

"Prey?" said Mara. He was very close now. She imagined that it would hurt a great deal when his paws slammed into her body, when his jaws snapped down on her neck.

But that word he had used: prey.

There was something wrong with it, she thought. It had to do with Kirri. "Our kind," the mongoose had said. "You're a predator like me. Do not forget."

As if in a dream, she watched the dog open his mouth, heard his victory howl raised to the night skies. "Death!" he called. "Death to rats! Death to cats!"

And she opened her own pink-tongued mouth in an ear-splitting scream. "Nooooot soooooooooooo faaaaaaassst!" she called. Her paws were no longer frozen to the ground. As the dog's jaws snapped shut, his teeth met only the air. Mara had leaped, just in time.

"What the blazing bandicoots!" the dog growled. He spun around, seeking the creature.

"Over here," said Mara. She stood in the entrance to the alley, her tail lashing back and forth. "You want a piece of me?"

The dog's eyes lit up, greedily. This was more like it. She was backlit by the tube lights; he preferred to have a clean view of his kill.

"Yes!" he growled, bounding towards her.

Just as he reached, Mara screamed again, right in his face, and he flinched involuntarily, closing his eyes. He only closed them for a second, but it was an expensive mistake.

Mara felt the dog's hot stinking breath ruffle her whiskers, pulled her head back so that his teeth narrowly missed grazing her furry neck, and extended all her claws. She slashed twice, raking his muzzle across the snout the first time, leaving five wide scratches across his neck the second time.

"I'm nobody's prey," she said, her mew soft and venomous in his ear. "I may be lost, but I'm a predator, you hear me?

The mongoose said so."

The dog moaned, scrabbling to get away from her claws. Mara slashed him once over the ear, just to teach him a lesson. He stared at her, his eyes filled with hatred and wariness, but he backed all the same.

"I'll remember you," he said.

"I can't say the same for you," she said. "You're just another dumb, vicious stray, nothing out of the ordinary."

The dog lunged, and she saw the scars on his forelegs, scabbed over, mementos of other fights. Time slowed; as if in a dream, Mara watched her adversary come closer, his claws scrabbling for purchase on the hard cobbles.

She was flattening her belly to the ground, crouching low. Memory brought her Beraal's voice, as strong as though the warrior queen who'd been her teacher was standing there, watching from the sidelines. It had been Mara's second lesson on the Art of the Claw. "You may use the element of surprise only once, Mara, and then, expect to be attacked. Protect your belly. Keep your back rounded, your belly to the ground. Scream when they get close, and then you must run or kill your opponent." Mara had watched her teacher, her eyes widening at the speed at which Beraal turned, and crouched, and sprang. Her long black fur was a blur on the steps outside the Sender's house as she demonstrated defensive positions to her wide-eyed pupil.

"What if you can't kill your attacker, if he's too big? And you can't run because you're scared?"

Beraal had hissed, bringing her head so close to Mara's that the kitten could see her teeth, and smell the adrenaline in her teacher's fur. "Then die," she had said.

And then there he was, looming over her, so close that she could see the thick matted bristles on the underside of his belly. Mara pressed herself so close to the ground that she felt the cobbles and stones press into her stomach. She heard the dog howl, heard the snap of his teeth, felt a brief searing flash of pain as a clump of fur ripped loose on her flank. He had overshot, but only barely. He would turn, and snap again, and this time, she would lose more than fur.

Every nerve in her body told her to freeze, to stay still and close her eyes, to hope that her attacker would leave her alone.

Mara rose, slashed at the dog's back paws, put her ears back and ran without waiting to see if he would follow or not. Her desperate swing had connected; she had felt the telling tug of tissue as she yanked her paw free, and part of one claw had broken off, left in her attacker's flesh. A small part of her mind hoped it would leave a festering scar, but then the little queen let her nostrils flare, let her whiskers ride up and out, concentrating on escape.

She was running past a line of shops, the corrugated steel of their shutters forming crisp barriers. A startled goat popped its head out of a lane, bleating sleepily as she went past. Mara flattened her ears and tried to lengthen her stride, hoping that its bleats would not alert the dogs.

Far behind her, she heard her former assailant bark, once, twice, questioningly; then another dog joined in, and a third. An image from the past flashed in front of Mara's eyes—the memory of a time when a pack of strays had surrounded a bandicoot in the park behind her house, stalking it, playing with it, killing the creature. She shot around the corner, another line of shops to her left, a large Bigfeet taxi stand sprawling to her right. The pack howled; it seemed to her that they were getting dangerously closer.

She changed direction, heading for the taxi stand. Her paws were aching, and though she didn't want to stop to check, she could feel the warm trickle of blood on her paw pads.

There was a blare, so loud that it thrummed through her bones, making her head spin, and the glare of white lights rushing towards her. Mara mewed, a piteous sound. She was only halfway across the road. The car had turned fast down the road that led from the petrol pump; it rushed towards the cat at high speed. She could smell the acrid fumes from its engine. They choked her; the lights blinded her; her paws would not carry her as fast as she needed to go. The car's horn sounded again, hurting her ears and making the hairs in them stand up painfully; the howling of the dogs was far too close.

The car would hit her, Mara thought. It would all end here, and she felt a sudden pang of loss, for her Bigfeet, for Southpaw's beloved brown-striped face, for the Nizamuddin she had never explored. The Sender turned to face the car; she raised her whiskers, whether in defiance or out of some reflex, she could not say; and she tried to send a plea to the car's engine. Now she could see the steel grill, like a maniac's grin. She could smell the anger of the dogs, who stood on the corner of the pavement she had pelted across from, their frustration that their prey had found another, cleaner death. Then she saw only the car's burning white lights, bearing down on her, and Mara closed her eyes.

Something hit her squarely in the ribs, knocking the breath out of her small body. She felt herself borne into the air. It must have been a short flight, but it felt endless to the little queen. "Am I dying?" she wondered. "Is this what dying feels like?" Her whiskers tingled and then she opened her eyes. The world spun around, the ground one way, the black sky another; then it righted itself and she came down with a thump that shook her thin frame.

The car roared past. She saw the treads of its massive black tires, noticed a triangular grey pebble stuck between two of the grooves, smelled the astonishment of the Bigfeet who were jabbering at each other inside the car. The dogs were scattering on the other side of the road, their attention caught by the appearance of a pack of grey rats who had swarmed out of an empty concrete pipe. The rats bolted; the dogs, barking and howling, followed their quarry, leaving the roads empty again.

Mara wondered why her bones hadn't broken. Her ribs felt sore, she didn't have the breath to summon up half a mew, but she was lying on something soft. Something soft, and wriggling, and swearing in fluent, ripe-from-the-gutter, street-cat curses.

Mara scrabbled, and found that her claws were caught in a tangle—more like a thicket—of black, matted fur. Whatever was under her undulated and shook, and another rich stream of oaths—some of which she hadn't heard even on her visits to the monkey house at the zoo—poured forth. The breath came back into her lungs, painfully, but she could move her paws, and Mara got to her feet. She had landed a short distance from the taxi stand, at the edge of the road. She appeared to be standing on a large, fur-covered sack. Gingerly, she walked forwards.

"Gerroff my head!" said the sack crossly.

"Sorry!" said Mara, backing as fast as she could.

"Gerroff my tail!" said the sack, heaving. "You're tickling me," it added.

Mara stepped off just as the sack stood up. They stared at each other, the orange cat with the green eyes, the black-furred warrior tom with the crumpled ears and the battered face.

Her legs stiff, her whiskers lowered in distress, Mara began to back away.

"Oh no, you don't," said Hulo. "I'm not going chasing after you a second time, you blasted brat, you might galumph around the colony making as much noise as the bloody goats, but you run fast! Damn nuisance trying to catch up with you! If it hadn't been for the mouse—Jethro Tail, you've met him? Decent fellow, told me where I might find you. Oh, don't look like that. No, no, there's no need for your whiskers to quiver. No! I said no running off, and I meant it!"

Before Mara could run away again, Hulo tackled her. An orange-and-black blur rolled along the earth, coming to rest near one of the taxi cabs. The orange was underneath.

"Gerroff me!" cried Mara.

"Yes, yes," said Hulo, a little worried because Mara was so much smaller than him that she had disappeared. He didn't want to smother the brat, he grumbled to himself crossly, just to stop her from sauntering away. "First, promise you're not going to run off."

"Mmmmrffff!" said Mara.

"Is that a yes or a no?" said Hulo cautiously.

A pair of orange ears popped out from under his stomach, and Mara spat.

"Your fur was in my mouth!" she said. "Don't you ever comb it? And yes."

"Of course I comb my fur," said Hulo, stung by a complaint that one or the other of the Nizamuddin cats had made all too often. "Once or even twice a week. No need to overdo these things, I'm not a blasted poodle."

"I said, 'Yes!'" said Mara's head, the mew exasperated. Hulo felt her squirming under his belly. It was not a pleasant sensation.

"Yes, you're going to run off, or yes, you're not going to run off?" he asked.

"Yes, you big fat furbag," said Mara, squirming harder. "I mean, yes, I promise I won't run off—now get *off* me, I can't breathe!"

Hulo hastily rose.

"Had to make certain," he said. "Couldn't have you bobbing around and around the place again, what with the dogs—what was the need to go off and have a fight with Motu, while we're on the subject? He's the nastiest of the lot!"

"I didn't start the fight," said Mara indignantly, trying to comb some of Hulo's black fur out of her own. Hulo's fur had a tendency to come off in clumps and migrate everywhere, like the silk cotton balls that would herald the coming of summer.

"Well, he sure as hell knew he'd been in a fight by the time you'd finished with him," said Hulo with some respect. He'd seen Motu's torn ears and scratched muzzle. It was, he thought, excellent work for a novice who'd never been out of her house.

"Really?" said Mara. "You saw him?"

"He was whimpering in a corner, complaining to his filthy pack of curs that he'd been set upon by an entire coven of tomcats," Hulo said in disgust. He had no liking for cowards, of any species. "But I saw the marks on his nose and his face. Nicely spaced, and he'll carry the scars for the rest of his time. You're a natural, Mara."

The Sender's tail flicked back and forth uncertainly. Her eyes glowed with pleasure, but her whiskers radiated wariness. She licked the fur down on her neck where it was standing up, and Hulo could tell that she was wondering whether to stay or go.

"Looks like we started off on the wrong paw," he said gruffly. Awkwardly, he approached the little queen, lightly brushing his furry cheek against hers in a tentative head rub. Mara's ears went up, the fine whiskers over her eyes shaking in surprise.

"Can't do this touchy-feely business," Hulo mumbled. "Sender, I'm Hulo, from your clan. I'm sorry you heard what I said about you in the park. I hide nothing behind my whiskers. I carry my feelings on my fur. But I was just grumbling to Doginder; my mews were not for your ears. When you ran away, I was sorry that you'd heard."

He blew gently at her through his nostrils, a gesture of heartfelt apology. She smelled his sincerity on his fur. The tomcat, rough as he was, hadn't meant to hurt her.

Two Bigfeet motorbikes roared into the neighbourhood, and both cats ducked instinctively.

"Get under the car if more of them come in," Hulo said

urgently to her. "Sometimes they'll veer so that they can hit us, if they see us in their headlights. Many of the dargah cats have been badly hurt that way, you know."

It was warmer under the car. Mara caught the scent of Bigfeet, but when she raised her whiskers questioningly at Hulo, he was reassuring: "They're sleeping—out there, on the sturdy woven-rope cots. Besides, the taxi drivers are friendly enough, for Bigfeet. They don't feed us, but they rarely harm us. More bikes; we'll have to wait here till they've all gone by."

The bikers hooted and whooped to each other as they roared past, reminding Mara of the packs of stray dogs whom she had watched from the staircase of her house. Some strays, she knew, were kind enough—big, overgrown fellows who barked exuberantly and chased leaves around as though they were kittens. But some, like the vicious pack she had seen, were out to hurt anything they could find, especially if it was small and helpless.

When the echo of the last vroom and cough from the bikes had died away, leaving only them and the night, Mara put a tentative paw on Hulo's flank.

"Thank you for coming after me,' she said. Then she added, "You speak with roughness, but I can smell the truth on you. Do all the Nizamuddin cats hate me as much as you said you did?"

Hulo turned his great head, so that he met her gaze squarely.

"Beraal does not hate you," he said. "Southpaw does not hate you. We don't hate you either, Mara, but we don't know you the way they do. All I knew of you before we met in the park was that you were the Sender, and that you refused to come and meet us, as though living with the Bigfeet had made you too good for us. When you came to the battle, you hovered above our heads; you could leave the field unbloodied, untouched by the war that took Miao and that ravaged so many of the little creatures. Until I caught your scent in the park, I didn't think of you as one of us, you understand?"

"Yes," said Mara. Her voice was low, her mew subdued; she smelled both the truth and the hurt in Hulo's whiskers. "Perhaps I do understand. But what made you come after me? You spoke with such harshness; I could feel your contempt in your whiskers, and your fur shook with your dislike. And yet, you followed me here. You saved me from the car. Why would you do that?"

Hulo's paw stirred, catching her smaller one and covering it.

"You stank of Bigfeet, back in the park," he said. "But you also smelled small, like the kittens who come tumbling into our lives each year. And you smelled afraid, and though you stink abominably of Bigfeet and the indoors, you also smell like one of our clan. But why did you never come out?"

Mara spread her whiskers out, trying to make him understand.

"The outside doesn't frighten you, or the rest of the clan," she said. "But I was born under the canal, my earliest memories of the outside were full of violence and death and then I lived in the Bigfeet house. My life always had a roof to it."

"You didn't come out because you were scared?" said Hulo. His tail rose, echoing his surprise. "You? The Sender who walks with tigers?"

"What use are my sendings under this vast sky?" said Mara. "What use are my whiskers against the teeth of a dog, the cruelty of one of your Bigfeet? And none of you liked me, right from the start."

Hulo was startled. "How do you know that?" he asked.

"I heard," she said simply. "On my first sendings, I raised my whiskers and listened. I heard you and Katar one day, and I heard the dargah cats another time."

Hulo let out a gruff exhalation, thinking back. "You heard me and Katar . . . that must have been when you were a kitten, Mara? A few moons old?"

"Yes," she said, and though she said no more, the tomcat's ears folded down in some sadness. For the first time, he thought of what Mara's life must have been: brought up by Bigfeet, fearful of the outside, aware that her own clan held her in suspicion.

The sliver of the moon that had cast a pale veil of light across the night sky was hidden by the clouds that would bring yet more winter rain to Nizamuddin. The darkness around them was absolute, and to Mara, oppressive. With no light to see by, her other senses were sharpened. But the scents that wrapped themselves around this part of the colony were all harsh, ominous—concrete dust mixed with the fretful dreams of Bigfeet, the tar of the roads smelled cold and hard, and the air was cut with grease and lingering smoke, as though cars, cement mixers and rumbling trucks had replaced trees, birds and hedges. The winter wind had a sawtooth edge, cutting through her fur to the bone; and the darkness wore down on the Sender, making even her whiskers droop with its heaviness.

"Hulo," she whispered, "The dark—it doesn't bother you?"

The tomcat shifted in the dark. She felt rather than saw him turn his head to her, and then his rough tongue licked her shoulder and her neck, in heavy, soothing strokes. Mara turned her head up to the tom, in wonder and surprise: she had not expected such gentleness from Hulo. He did not groom her for long, but the scrape of his tongue across her fur did more than calm her down—it was a reminder that she was not alone in the night.

The steady thump of a Bigfoot's tread became louder, counterpointed by the thud of his heavy wooden walking stick. "Just the night watchman," said Hulo. "He's a Bigfoot who walks around the neighbourhood every night. We think he would like to be a cat, or perhaps an owl, because he calls out every so often in longing, but he is trapped in his clumsy Bigfoot body, poor fellow. He'll leave soon." The Bigfoot's tread faded, but then a bark tore through the darkness. Mara and Hulo stiffened, simultaneously, as a pack began howling. The baying was loud, ferocious, and remembering the pack which had loped after her, Mara shivered.

"They're out for blood, yes," said Hulo's reassuring purr in her ear. "But they're hunting near the canal, we're safe." The squeal of a piglet went up, chilling Mara to the marrow, and then they heard—far away, as far off as the howls—the challenging grunt of adult pigs. The grunts and the baying tore the peace of the night. Beside Hulo, Mara shivered so hard that he could feel her slender flanks shake.

"I wish Southpaw was here," she said. "I tried to raise him when I was in the park, but perhaps my whiskers don't work that well at linking or sending when I'm outdoors."

She felt Hulo shift so that his massive bulk steadied and warmed her; and then she felt his rough tongue lick her paw.

"Southpaw didn't get your sendings because he's not well," said Hulo bluntly.

"That wound!" said Mara, forgetting her fear of the dark. "The injuries to his paw—I saw him limping after the Bigfeet threw things at him. Is it bad, Hulo?"

"Very bad," said the tom, grimly. His mind was on the danger at hand, and he shared his thoughts freely. "So bad, Mara, that we took him to your house, thinking that your Bigfeet could help. Only you weren't there. I suppose Katar will manage."

"Southpaw's at my home?" cried Mara. "Oh Hulo, can't you take me there?"

Hulo's ears twitched in response. "Not now," he said. "It would take my paws some journeying to get there again, and you and I are both tired. We'd be targets for the dogs, or the Bigfeet—no, best to hide out and get some rest."

He struggled out from under the car, his belly brushing the ground. "Besides, you have to meet her, it's been too long for the two of you."

"Her?" said Mara. She had raised her head, trying to see if she could sniff out the scents of home, and her wonderful Bigfeet, and Southpaw, but the night air carried nothing on it.

"My head's gone wandering, like a stray cuckoo!" said Hulo. "Come, Mara, let's not stay here much longer. The Bigfeet will be up at dawn, and that's not so far off—we should have gone to her house before, we should have, but my whiskers have been on crooked all night. Oof, but the rats have left such a mess behind, Katar and I must do something about them—here we go! Here's the entrance!"

"The entrance?" said Mara, who had followed Hulo out obediently, as he padded under the cots. It was a wide space, cluttered with the abandoned, rusting hulks of cars and other Bigfeet litter.

Mara caught the oily trails she had smelled before, and wondered whether these were made by the rats Hulo had mentioned. It seemed likely; the tracks had a grey, furtive feel to them.

"She'll be awake, one way or another, and she won't mind that I didn't link to tell her, she's not formal at all. The problem is that the two mites don't sleep at the same time, or her life would be a lot easier, but that's kittens for you," said Hulo, ducking behind a tarpaulin and going inside. He didn't seem to notice that he had collected quite a lot of the litter: sweet wrappers, dust balls and pieces of string adorned his coat, lending him the air of a cat in fancy dress.

Mara would have asked more questions, but she had to scramble to keep up with the tomcat. Her shorter paws got tangled in the tarpaulin, and the Sender had to heave her backside up and over.

She uttered a sharp mew as she somersaulted over the tarpaulin, twisting in mid-air so that she would land on her paws. Something had got into her ears, and her nostrils, and she sneezed, releasing chunks of cobweb and a dismayed spider into the air.

"Hello, Hulo! So what have you brought me at this hour of the night?" said a familiar voice.

Mara's whiskers tingled, then she was running to bridge the short distance between her and the cat whose mew was so familiar, so loved.

"Beraal!" she called. Her mew had become a kitten's mew again. "Oh, Beraal, I missed you! There was the Chief Bigfoot, and Southpaw came, but I didn't know how much I'd missed you until right now."

"There, there," said Beraal, her mew husky. "I missed you too, little one."

Hulo settled down, shaking the string and dust out of his tail.

"Go on, go on, don't mind me," he said. "I'm not much for headrubbing and that kind of nonsense myself, but nothing wrong with it, if that's the kind of thing you like. Beraal, can you get this little chap of yours to stay away from me? I'm not going to groom him. No! Tell him not to snuggle up to me, I don't do snuggling. Oh, all right, little fellow, no need to let your tail droop like that. Oh, all right, just a smidgen of grooming, if you insist. Stop complaining, your face needs a good washing—what's that? Yes, yes, so does mine, but everybody knows you shouldn't comb your fur too often, it falls out."

And though the earth was freezing, and though there were no bowls of milk or food, Beraal's home was soon so filled with the purring from the three adult cats and her kittens that it felt warm to Mara, as warm and welcoming as any home she'd ever known.

CHAPTER NINE

With the Bigfeet

Crouched under the bed, trying not to sneeze as loose strings from the underside of the mattress tickled his nose, Katar wondered how he had got it so wrong.

His plan had been simple. Once they had found a way to get Southpaw to the Bigfeet's house, the Sender would take over. She and Southpaw were friends, and she would never refuse to help him. He and Hulo would mew until they had her attention, Mara would tell her Bigfeet that Southpaw was sick, and the Bigfeet would bring out their cage, whisking Southpaw off to be healed. It had the clean scent of simplicity to it; Katar distrusted plans that smelled risky, or that smelled mixed-up and tangled.

The first part had gone off perfectly, even if it had taken them some time to wake Southpaw up and explain that Tooth would be carrying him off. Sick though he was, Southpaw's fur had quivered at the thought of such an adventure. "I wish

I wasn't feeling so ill," Southpaw had said. "I've never flown before, imagine what Mara will say when she hears how I got to her house! What do I have to do, Tooth?"

"Relax your body, don't look down, and don't wriggle or bite me," Tooth said tersely. The cheel was wondering whether he could pull this off, though he didn't want to share his doubts with Katar. He was used to carrying prey, and prey was either limp because it was dead, or limp because it was terrified. If Southpaw wriggled too much, or mewed in fear, Tooth knew that his instincts would kick in, forcing him to drop his passenger.

But he needn't have worried. As he gripped Southpaw with his talons, taking care to wrap them around the cat's body instead of tearing his flesh, the kitten winced in pain from his injuries. Southpaw did not pass out, but he was not quite conscious, either. When cheel and cat rose into the air, Southpaw's brown eyes glazed over, staring out at the sky. The pain did not allow him to think about the journey at all, and he barely noticed when they rose above the shrubs. He offered Katar down below a tiny twitch of his whiskers, indicating that he was all right, and then the cat stayed limp in Tooth's talons, keeping all of his attention focused on not passing out from the ache in his ribs.

KATAR STIFFENED AS FOOTSTEPS went past the door of the bedroom, growling nervously, but it seemed that the Bigfeet would not come in. He pressed his ears down against his head, disliking the closeness of the space. He was relying on smell and sound to tell him where the Bigfeet were, since he could see little in the dim light.

When he'd padded up the staircase that led to the Sender's house, he had found only Hulo and Southpaw's sleeping form. Tooth had not stayed, though he had politely accepted Hulo's thanks. His wing and breast muscles were aching, he explained, and would need to be rested. Southpaw had murmured his thanks, too. But as Tooth had left, Southpaw's head had lolled back. The flight had tired him out.

Under the bed, Katar fluffed out his fur and whiskers, retracing what had happened. "No Sender?" he had said in a disbelieving mew to Hulo. "But she never goes out! Have the Bigfeet taken her, then?" The babblers had squawked, eagerly telling him and Hulo how they had seen the Sender escape, disappearing in the park.

The two toms had both looked instinctively at Southpaw. Katar's nose had told him that the flight had made perhaps too many demands on the brown tom. He smelled of sickness, and of exhaustion; even when his paws were nuzzled, he did not wake up.

The staircase made him and Hulo nervous. The place stank of Bigfeet, and they felt vulnerable, exposed to the gaze of any creature who happened to look down from the roof, or up from the park. "He cannot be moved or woken," Hulo had said, sniffing at Southpaw's muzzle. "Nothing to do but wait." The place made Katar uneasy, and it hadn't helped that Southpaw's fur felt warm—far too warm—to the tomcat. Hulo had dropped into the patient crouch of a seasoned warrior, settling against the flowerpots for shelter, letting his breathing slow. His stubby whiskers fell to half-mast, alert but not quivering with anxiety.

Katar had been unable to follow Hulo's example. The tom-cat's tail had twitched ceaselessly, back and forth, back and forth, mirroring his deep sense of unease. He could smell the Sender's scent, on the stairs, on the mesh of the kitchen door. He made his tail stop its restless twitching, and for a moment, he had stood there, his ears cocked, his nose flaring as he tried to see if he could catch the Sender's trail. Perhaps she had been frightened enough to run away, but her dislike of the outdoors was so pronounced that she might be in the vicinity, Katar had thought. His nose was keen, and he picked up a great deal—the Bigfeet's mingled scent trails, the spot by the kitchen window where Mara normally sat, but a few moments was enough to let the grey tom know that the Sender was nowhere close.

When Katar had finally settled down, Hulo's eyes were open, watching him. "Your whiskers are quivering with your thoughts: if only the Sender hadn't chosen this day of all days to explore the world," said Hulo.

The grey tom's ears had flickered. That was part of it, but not all of it. He could feel Hulo's need for rest and sleep. Even with Tooth's help, it had been a demanding journey. To go halfway across Nizamuddin with an injured comrade, when all three of them were half-starved—Hulo's exhaustion scented the tom's fur, and Katar knew his own would feel just the same.

Southpaw stirred, fretfully, his back paws scrabbling. Katar rose, but Hulo was already there, his whiskers raised.

"The heat rises from his fur," he said. His mew was contained, but Katar understood, and felt despair scorch his insides. He had thought the hard part would be getting Southpaw to the Sender; it had never occurred to him that the Sender might not be in her home. Without her help, they could do little for Southpaw.

"I didn't bring him here to die!" he said. Katar had not meant to mew aloud, but he found that he had, and that his tail was switching back and forth again.

"We can keep him company," Hulo began, his whiskers dropping down in dejection.

But before the tom could finish, the call had rippled through the air, resounding in his ears, making even Southpaw's tail rise, feebly. "PERSECUTED BY BIGFEET, HUNTED BY NASTY TRAFFIC, AND AT THE MERCY OF A VICIOUS, SAVAGE KILLER . . . OH, SOUTHPAW, OH, BERAAL, WHY DID I EVER LEAVE HOME? WOE! THIS IS THE END!"

They were up before Mara's mews had died away, Katar's ears swivelling, Hulo's fur rising as he sniffed the air eagerly.

"Not here," said Hulo, "she's nowhere near the park."

"But she's out there somewhere," said Katar, "towards the front of her house probably, in the central park. And she sounds terrified."

Hulo started forwards involuntarily, and then he hesitated, his paw raised in mid-air, turning to look at Southpaw.

"Go," Katar had said to Hulo. "Find the Sender, and if you cannot find her, speak to Beraal, to Abol and Tabol, to Qawwali and to the dargah cats. Let them know she's out, alone, and will need help."

That, he thought now, had been the right thing to do. But then, after Hulo leapt up onto the park's boundary wall, and headed briskly off towards Beraal's home, Katar had found himself restless, his whiskers performing an impatient tremolo.

All Katar had done was brush against the wire-mesh door in frustration, no more, and it had swung invitingly open. His whiskers twitched, suggesting that poking his nose around the door just to see if he could smell the Bigfeet might not be a bad idea. His paws had obligingly carried him in, and then the door swung shut behind the grey tom. The click of the latch told him that he was done for. Southpaw was now on the other side, outside on the staircase; he was stuck inside, on his own.

Then he heard the soft boom of the Bigfeet's voices echoing across the house. The tom's fear made him forget Southpaw's plight. He crawled, trembling, under the sturdy wooden table that formed an island in the centre of the room, shaking at the stink of the Bigfeet, who were so close.

The low roofs and the lack of sky oppressed him; the house stank of the Bigfeet's trails. But as his eyes grew gradually accustomed to the gloom, the tom found his fear of the Bigfeet subsiding, replaced with a creeping sense of urgency. He lifted his whiskers and sniffed at the air. If it had been Hulo on the other side of the wire mesh, they might have been able to link through their whiskers, but Southpaw was drowsing, caught in the fever haze. Cautiously, listening for the Bigfeet, Katar crawled out from under the kitchen island and padded over to the door, which had swung shut behind him.

Katar raised a paw and batted at the wire mesh experimentally, but it was firm wire, the kind that would cut through his paw pads if he tried too hard. He nosed at the edge of the door, willing it to swing open; but it stayed firmly shut.

He smelled fresh air, coming in from another part of the kitchen, and turned to see where the window was. He located it—right above the sink, an easy jump away. It was covered with wire mesh, too, but perhaps he could nose it open, Katar thought.

He had leapt up onto the drying board, and balanced awkwardly, his paws splayed between a pretty china bowl and a set of plastic plates. Then the tom felt the fur on the back of his paws start to erect. His tail went up, switching back and forth in unease. Before he caught its scent, he knew.

The Bigfoot stood just inside the kitchen doorway, watching him with interest. Katar scrabbled frantically, trying to get down, but his paws slipped on the stainless steel of the sink. The tomcat yowled, partly out of fright, partly as a warning to the Bigfoot.

The Bigfoot walked towards the grey tom, slowly, with his hands spread out. He was saying something, but then Katar's paws slipped, and he found himself scrabbling to get out of the sink. His claws scraped helplessly, sliding against the shiny, smooth sides, and as the Bigfoot reached a hand out in his direction, Katar growled, ready to defend himself if necessary.

The Bigfoot's hand hovered above his head, though, not descending beyond a certain point. The grey tom shivered. Then the hand came down, avoiding Katar's snarling teeth. The Bigfoot was making soothing noises, and dimly, the tomcat sensed that its smell was not unfriendly.

He had intended to attack, to defend himself as fiercely as possible, but he had never been this close to a Bigfoot. Two instincts warred in the tomcat's head. All his experience with Bigfeet told him to get away, to use his teeth and claws as weapons. Bigfeet had thrown stones at him and Hulo; Bigfeet had tormented some of his litter mates; Bigfeet set the stray dogs to yelping; Bigfeet had built their homes across their old hunting grounds, and chased his clan out of the backyards and garbage heaps where they had once reigned supreme.

But Katar had a keen nose, perhaps the keenest of all the clan's hunters. And as the Bigfoot came closer and closer, the scent told the tomcat that he would come to no harm at the hands of this one. The hands broadcast kindness, and gentle inquiry; all those smells swirled around with two other scents, the scent of another cat, probably the Sender, and the scent of sadness.

The Bigfoot was trying to talk to him, Katar realized, and instinctively, the cat raised his whiskers, forgetting that the Bigfeet had their limitations. Their eyes met, and the tomcat read nothing but concern in the Bigfoot's gaze.

When the Bigfoot touched the cat, Katar shivered and backed against the sink, but he did not scratch. The tom cowered as the Bigfoot gently scratched his ears and then his forehead, too scared to enjoy the touch, but aware that it didn't hurt.

When the Bigfoot picked him up, Katar froze into a rigid circle, his paws and whiskers stiff with his fear, but though he made a few warning calls, he kept his claws retracted. He felt the Bigfoot's arms around him, and he closed his eyes. He felt himself being carried out of the kitchen. The smells changed. They were moving through the house, down the corridor, past the bedroom. He kept himself curled into a small ball, and he kept his ears flat, his paws ready to ward off a blow should the Bigfoot decide to hit him after all.

The Sender's scent was growing stronger and stronger, though the tomcat's experienced nose reckoned it was not fresh—at least a few hours old, possibly even half a day old. He felt the hand come down again on his fur, petting him, and though he shivered again, he registered that the touch was meant to be reassuring.

He opened his eyes as he was carried into the Sender's room, and the tomcat's heart gave a great lurch. There was another Bigfoot sitting on the bed.

He yowled, and twisted until he had worked himself free. Two Bigfeet were too much for Katar to handle; he fled under the bed, and crouched there, growling. The sides of his jaws were dabbled with froth—he had bared his teeth at the second Bigfoot, and the terror had made him slaver.

He saw a pair of legs settle firmly at the edge of the bed, joining the other Bigfoot. They were sitting side by side, talking, their voices low and incomprehensible to him. For a while, Katar could do no more than crouch, grimacing, his lips curling in flehmen. From time to time, he issued growls, to warn the Bigfeet off.

The Bigfeet made no move to come towards him, and gradually, the tomcat stopped fluffing his fur, letting it come back to normal. The sounds above his head faded into a murmur that was almost comforting. Katar let his ears flick forwards as he listened, and let his whiskers roam the room. This was where the Sender lived, he thought. He could smell her basket, and the toys scattered around the room—assorted feathers, balls, what looked like a battered stuffed monkey—carried both her scent and a trace of Southpaw's scent, too. The meaty smell of food from her food bowl made his nose twitch, his belly rumble.

As his fear ebbed and he grew calmer, Katar's sharpness returned. There were soft cushions, blankets, even a scratching post etched with the Sender's claw marks. The room smelled of contentment, and it came to the tomcat that the Bigfeet had taken as much care over the Sender's surroundings as a mother cat would for her litters. He began to wash himself, slowly, as best as he could crouched under the bed, letting his tongue rove over his fur as he considered the Sender's life. His days as an outside cat were full, and after Miao's death in the battle of the ferals, survival and the needs of the clan had occupied his thoughts. He had not raised his whiskers much in Mara's direction, disliking the way she had held herself apart from the clan. He had thought often of the Sender's skills; but he had never wondered about her life with her Bigfeet. When Beraal or Southpaw had spoken of the Bigfeet and their love for the Sender, those mews had gone in through one whisker and out the other. Beyond learning how to avoid Bigfeet he had no interest in their habits.

But the Bigfeet left complex scent trails, and as he washed his tail, holding it with both of his paws to groom it more thoroughly, Katar's nose prickled into life. He smelled their sadness in the air, as strongly etched as though he was receiving it on his whiskers. He smelled their criss-crossing paths, the way they had walked up and down through the house—and gone outside, if he was any judge—radiating thick waves of concern that still lingered in the air.

Cautiously, he put his nose out from under the bed, staying well away from the Bigfeet's legs.

He smelled the sorrow of the Bigfeet, their fears for Mara, their grief and concern. He smelled the emptiness that she had left behind, just the way the death of a kitten who had survived its first nine moons diminished the clan. He smelled their Bigfeet tears, which had as strong a scent as sadness on a cat's fur.

Katar came out from under the bed, warily, prepared to go back to his shelter if the Bigfeet attempted to harm him. They stopped talking, and he could tell that they were watching, so he stood stiff-legged for a while, his tail flicking in warning. The Bigfeet stayed where they were, though, and tentatively, he began exploring the room, keeping his whiskers up so that he could bolt back if required. He sniffed at the cushions, and they spoke of Mara and Southpaw, sleeping with their paws and whiskers entwined. He sniffed at the toys, and they spoke to the tomcat of hunting and chasing games; he could not smell mice or rats, so he assumed that the Sender had to make do with these feathers and bits of string. Then he approached the food bowl, turning once to see if the Bigfeet would smack him. But they sat on the bed, talking to one another in their incomprehensible tongue.

Cautiously, Katar sniffed at the rim of the bowl, and then he tried to shove his head into it, because the aroma was too tantalizing to bear. It smelled of the choicest of meat, like fresh mouse haunches on a rainy day and the fattest part of fish-belly combined, like ripe bulbul eggs just-cracked from the nest, like the crunchiest and plumpest of pigeons. The hunger that had gnawed at his stomach for so long took over. Katar forgot the watching Bigfeet, forgot Southpaw, forgot his mission: his flanks shook as he gobbled the few pellets left in the bowl. They were stale and old, but after a diet scavenged from trash heaps, they tasted like the finest of viands to him. He was shaking like a kitten at its first solid meal, making guttural noises at the back of his throat, scrabbling at the empty bowl with his paws, his tongue pistoning in and out as he tried to get to every last scrap of goodness.

He felt their shadows before he saw them. The hands came down lightly on his flanks, holding him gently but firmly in place. For the second time that day, the Bigfeet had him.

Katar flattened his ears and yowled, trying to break free. The grip tightened; he struggled, trying to get away. "Let me go, I'll bite if I have to," he warned the Bigfoot, but she continued crooning to him, and he realized she didn't understand his mews. The other Bigfoot was crouched next to him, too. Katar flinched as he felt the gentle pats and strokes, pressing his ears down in an attempt to protect his head against the blows he was sure would follow.

But the two Bigfeet made no other attempts to hurt him. They sat next to him, one on either side, chattering away in the language that sounded to him like chirrups, and their hands steadily groomed him. Katar's flanks began to relax. Their touch felt reassuring, even pleasant. Warily, battling his apprehension, he sniffed at the Bigfoot's hand. The fingers combed through his fur, and stretched out to scratch his neck and chin. He felt waves of pleasure ripple through his body, and heard a familiar sound. It took him a few moments to recognize that the low rumble he could hear was his own purring.

The Bigfoot rose and left the room. Katar watched him go, his whiskers uncertain, but when the man came back to pour more food into his bowl, the tomcat needed no invitation. He ate his fill, his whiskers spread out to scent trouble, and he did not stop the other Bigfoot when she scratched behind his ears.

They sat next to him as he washed, and he watched them as he stretched out his hind paws to perform his ablutions. The two looked steadily back, meeting his gaze with wide, interested eyes. Katar finished washing and then he sniffed at the Bigfoot. He smelled of exhaustion, as though he had been up all night. Both the Bigfeet smelled the way the toms sometimes did when they had kept vigil over a lost kitten: anxious, forlorn, grieving. Katar thought of the many years when he had received nothing but harshness from Bigfeet. And Southpaw's words came back to him: "Not all Bigfeet are bad, Katar, or why would there be inside cats at all?"

Tentatively, the tomcat reached out and butted the Bigfoot's hand gently, nerving himself up to run if she screamed or tried to harm him. But he heard a laugh instead, and then he felt their hands reach out towards him. He sniffed both hands, registering the friendliness. Awkwardly, his whiskers shaking out of his nervousness, he put his rough tongue out and licked the Bigfeet. He heard them exclaim, and then he was being lovingly cuddled and stroked, the Bigfeet taking care not to alarm him.

Katar felt warmth and wellbeing spread through his fur. His purrs became louder until they filled the room, and he smelled the sadness of the Bigfeet ebb just a little. The tomcat's tail swished slowly back and forth as he came to a decision. He nudged their hands, and mewed till he was sure he had their attention.

Then he padded towards the door of the room. He sat down in front of it, turning once to look at them questioningly. The Bigfeet murmured at each other again; then the door swung open.

They followed him to the kitchen, and when he sat down next to the wire mesh door, he sensed their sadness. The Bigfeet crouched down beside him. He listened to what they were saying, his ears straining to catch anything that made sense. But then he gave up, and let his sense of smell and his whiskers take over.

When the Bigfoot gently stroked his head, scratching the line of fur all the way from his whiskers down to his forelimbs, he understood. They thought he wanted to leave because he'd eaten enough. And they would let him, he realized, watching the Bigfoot rise to open the door.

Katar brushed his head against their legs, winding back and forth, hoping they would understand how grateful he was. He had never expected kindness from Bigfeet. The most he had hoped for was that the Sender's Bigfeet would not kick him or throw things at him, the way normal Bigfeet did.

Then he stepped carefully into the gap between the door and the staircase. But instead of leaving, he stood there, mewing, pointing his nose and whiskers towards the line of pots where Southpaw lay concealed.

The Bigfeet seemed puzzled. One of them poured more food into a bowl and held it out towards Katar. The tomcat gave him a quick head bump as a thank you, but padded out a little further and mewed harder, turning and fluttering his whiskers out in appeal.

The Bigfeet stared at him. Katar raised the filaments on his forehead to explain, forgetting the Bigfeet's limitations for a moment. The tomcat wondered how Bigfeet managed, without Junglee, without whiskers, with only as much sense of scent as a three-week kitten with a cold. They were a strange species.

He caught Southpaw's scent, and mewed in real distress this time. The scent of sickness and fever filled the cold air, sending an ominous warning through Katar's mind. Forgetting about the door, the tomcat went over to the line of flower pots.

Southpaw lay there, silent, his eyes closed, his teeth bared in a grimace of pain. But the thin flanks rose and fell with his breathing. Katar stood over him, licking the orphan's fur where it had been ruffled by his journey. He washed the brown tom, and then he turned and mewed again. If the Bigfeet did nothing, he would wait by Southpaw's side, until the tom's scents changed enough to tell him that his watch was over.

But the Bigfeet were coming out. They exclaimed, and Katar, his ears keen, alert, picked up on their concern. They pushed the flower pots back, to see Southpaw better. Katar backed when one of them came closer, but he bared his teeth in warning when she dropped to her knees, reaching out to touch the young tom. Then he relaxed his vigil, marking the gentleness with which both the Bigfeet handled his friend.

There was a difference in their touch with Southpaw and with him, thought Katar. They were more sure with Southpaw, handling him just as gently, but with greater familiarity. It came to the tomcat, slowly, that the Bigfeet were fond of the Sender's friend. He wondered if perhaps they had petted or fed him, given Southpaw some of the love they had given Mara.

He watched the care with which they treated Southpaw, but couldn't help shivering a little when they brought out the cage, not wanting to imagine what it would feel like to be shut up in such a small box, to have the roof to your world close in so tightly around you. When they lined it with newspaper and sheets, he understood that they were making a nest for Southpaw. They picked up the sleeping tom, and placed him in the cage.

Before they shut the wire door and took his friend away, the Bigfeet squatted down and talked to Katar. The tomcat stretched out his whiskers, wanting to understand, unable to make head or tail of what they were saying; their talk was as meaningless as the sound of water rushing from an open tap over the cobbled stones of the alleys inside Nizamuddin.

But as they bore Southpaw off, taking charge of the cat who had tumbled in and out of trouble ever since Hulo had found the tiny orphan blundering around on his own, the tomcat felt relief steal over his fur. These Bigfeet had smelled of caring and concern, and he understood, without understanding their language, what they had tried so hard to tell him. They would take care of his friend; he was not to worry.

As he padded down the stairs, his belly full, his tail up again at a happier angle than it had been for days, Katar thought that despite their lack of whiskers and their other obvious limitations, the Bigfeet were not so bad.

CHAPTER TEN

The Cat and the Egrets

Awhile later, curled up in between Beraal and the older kitten, Ruff, Mara raised her sleepy head. The kitten made a tiny glowing dot of warmth on her belly; Beraal's comforting length warmed her back. To their right, Hulo dozed, while the second kitten, Tumble, slept on his shoulder, her tiny paws hooked possessively into his fur.

The ground was cold and harder than anything Mara was accustomed to, but that wasn't what woke her. She had stirred in her sleep, still purring with happiness at being with Beraal, and at having Ruff and Tumble fall all over her in vocal welcome; and then she had thought of the Bigfeet at home. It felt wrong not to be able to pad over to their beds, to greet them with the gift of one of her most precious toys. She would wait patiently until one or the other of her Bigfeet turned over in their sleep, and then push the toy gently into either their ears or their mouth, whichever was more convenient. This gift, offered with such love, always woke up the Bigfeet, who conveyed their delight with loud cries of what Mara chose to interpret as joyous acceptance.

She wondered when she would see them again, but this was dangerous territory; if she closed her eyes, she could imagine them beside her, imagine the softness of the sheets, the pleasure of being stroked by their gentle hands, the murmur of their voices over her furry ears. She thought of Southpaw, ill, in need of help, and hoped that she was right about her Bigfeet, that they would look after him. She wished she could be there to purr him back to health herself.

Thinking of her friend made her want to call out like a lost kitten, and so she pushed the images away, taking in her surroundings instead.

Mara didn't dare to move, for fear of waking Ruff or Beraal from their slumbers, but she lay there with her eyes wide open, her thoughts wandering. Beraal was so thin, much thinner than she had ever seen the fierce warrior, and neither Hulo nor Beraal seemed to be discomfited at the scarcity of food. She hadn't liked to mention it, but her stomach, empty for so long, had begun to send her urgent reminders. Would no one come to feed them? Perhaps Beraal would tell her, or Hulo would, once they were awake.

She told herself that the cold and the hunger were an adventure—part of being an outside rather than an inside cat, to be taken in one's stride, like meeting a mongoose or fighting with dogs. Her gaze rested on Ruff and Tumble, and Mara thought that they seemed frighteningly small, too, their tiny ribs showing up so sharply that they made outlines against the fur.

From the branches of a distant tree, a nightjar called: "Did you see it? Did you see it?" The bird's call was harsh, splitting the night, and two others joined in, from further away: "The dark is deep! The dark is deep!" "Did you see it? Did you see it?" "The dark is deep! The dark is deep!"

Mara felt the fur on her paws prickle, and slowly, as sleep left her and her eyes became more accustomed to the low light she became more aware of the night around them. There was scant shelter for Beraal and her kittens: a patch of tarpaulin hid them from the prying eyes of the Bigfeet, but the sheet of tin that covered part of their home was rusted and pitted with holes. The dark poured in through the holes, and came stealing in past the edge of the makeshift roof.

The cough of a bus engine starting up made Mara shiver; she was unused to these sounds so close. When the engine roared into life and the bus started off, the Sender closed her eyes and ducked her head; it felt so close, as though the giant, menacing tires were spinning around right next to them!

Behind the market, the dogs set up their howling again. Mara whimpered, a very slight sound, but though she was ashamed of herself, she couldn't help it. She looked away, but that was no good, either; the pre-dawn darkness had a coal blackness to it, and it seemed to her that if she stared at that heavy pall too long and saw no stars, the night would reach out its arms and wrap them around her whiskers and nose, stifling her. The thought of sending into the dark was terrifying; she would stumble around blindly, she would never find her way back home.

"Mara?" said Beraal's calm voice. "I'm here. I'm right here, right beside you. You smell of fear and anxiety. Did a predator

181

come in? Did the Bigfeet stir, is that what woke you up?"

Mara let out a silent sigh. She had taken such care not to twitch her whiskers or her paws, but she hadn't lived among her own kind—of course her scent would give away her agitation.

"It's nothing, not a predator," she said, her whiskers betraying the awkwardness she felt. "It was just . . . never mind."

Beraal raised her head, watching Mara, and her eyes followed the track of her former pupil's gaze. How odd their meeting had been; she had been sent to assassinate the cat whose powerful sendings were ripping through Nizamuddin, upsetting the wildings, and they had ended as teacher and beloved student. She remembered how she had felt trapped in the Bigfeet's house; how its roofs and walls had glowered down at her, making her feel that she had been cut off from her world, that she would never see the sky again.

How would her world seem, she wondered, to a Sender who had never lived under the sky?

Beraal remembered how her older kitten had responded the first day he had tumbled out of their shelter. His eyes had only just opened, and still held a tinge of blue; and he had looked up and mewed for all he was worth. "Mama!" he had called out to her. "Look! The world has no covers!" The sky had scared him, as was only right for their kind—he would need to learn, as all kittens did, never to forget the world above their whiskers, and what came out of it: the crows, the cheels, the bats, stray missiles hurled by Bigfeet. But he had also loved it, as they all did, the freedom and the openness it promised.

"Is it the darkness that troubles you, Mara?" she asked. "That must be new and strange for you, to have no roofs between you and the night?"

She felt the Sender's flanks relax, felt the little cat's breathing start to slow down and come back to normal.

"Yes," said Mara. Her green eyes were fixed on the blackness of the night, and her mew was as small as Ruff's might have been. "My whiskers reach up and there's nothing between them and the clouds; it feels as though the night rushes down them and seeps into my fur. Kirri said that the night contains more than predators; she says that we live most keenly in the dark."

"That is true," said Beraal. "The day is mostly for Bigfeet, but the night belongs to us."

Mara leaned against her teacher, feeling Beraal's thin fur rise up and down. Ruff mewed in his sleep and turned, his paws cycling at some dream.

"But how do you make friends with the night?" said Mara miserably. The damp had made her whiskers feel soggy, and her fur felt as though it would never know what it was to be warm again.

Beraal purred at her kitten, who splayed out his paws at the sound of her voice and purred back sleepily. Ruff scrambled over Mara's neck, walked across her protesting head, balanced on one of her ears and successfully made the leap across to land on his mother's belly. He bounced once, and snuggled into her fur.

"By learning its names," she said.

She caught the question on Mara's whiskers. Ruff squeaked.

"He likes stories," Beraal explained.

Mara's tail flicked in interest. "So do I," she said hopefully.

"This one," said Beraal, "has a long history. It was told to me by Miao, and Miao said it was told to her by Tigris"—Mara raised her whiskers at the mention of the name of Nizamuddin's last Sender—"and Tigris said it had been passed down to her by other Senders."

Ruff kneaded his small paws against Beraal's belly, his skinny belly rising and falling against her black-and-white fur. In his sleep, Hulo grunted, the tomcat's whiskers twitching at their murmured mews. Beraal curled around Mara, and using her whiskers as much as her voice, she began her tale.

Once, there lived a cat who liked to follow her whiskers: when they twitched at the breeze, when the scent of something new and strange murmured to them from the back of the east wind, her paws would twitch too, and she would go where her whiskers and paws carried her.

When the spring winds spoke to her of fish with silver mouths and fat juicy bellies to be found in the frog-speckled silt of the mangrove forests, her paws took her to a river boat, a light, lean craft, whose planks she warmed for the length of the summer.

When the summer sun of the river deltas walked its fingers through her fur, whispering to her of the rains that drummed on the red tile roofs of Goa, the plump crabs and frogs that swelled the paddy fields with their croaking, the cat listened to the sun's whispers. Soon, she was stowed safely in the back of a truck, perched high on its bales, sleeping snugly in the thick knotted coils of the ropes that trussed its cargo, sharing the truck drivers' milk and meat until they had reached the other coast, where the skies roared and the dark clouds lay with their full bellies pressed against the green land.

When the monsoon rains slowed, the last of the rain and the wind caressed her ears, and she heard about the friendly house-stoves in the mountains, where there was always room for another cat or three. And her paws twitched and stirred, and though the owner of the shack by the beach would have gladly fed her fish curry and rice for many seasons more, she thanked him, purring as she rubbed her head along his sturdy legs. She found a berth in a train whose wheels clacked along, singing of the high hills and the birds soaring in those great empty skies. The bearers on the train made her a pillow from some old torn sheets, and let her curl up to warm her belly on the flasks of tea when they reached the colder slopes of the hills.

Her whiskers rested for many moons, and she found a village nestled in the high ranges, where there was always place for her and the friends she made around the curve of the potbellied clay stoves. And so it went for many years; the cat's whiskers would twitch after the turning of the seasons, and the winds would rustle the names of far-away places until it had smoothed them into her fur, and her paws would uncurl and take her where she needed to go.

Sometimes, the tortoiseshell—for she was a torty, Mara, they have twice as much curiosity in their paws as the rest of us—thought she had come home. She settled for a long space in a fishing village that nestled like a sleeping kitten alongside the broad curved back of the ocean, and learned to climb coconut trees and hunt the slippery fish who darted in and out of the stalks of the emerald green rice paddy fields. But then the wind changed, and curiosity set her moving again. In a large city, she found a place near the racecourse, loving the comfortable smells and warmth of the stables, making friends with the fastest horses, hunting the mice and rats who were lured there by the perfume from the straw, the carrots, the sweat of the thoroughbreds themselves. But the wind changed yet again, and she moved on.

One spring, when the winds came dancing joyously across the muddy banks of the river where she lived on the stone steps leading down into the water with the other cats of the riverghat, she padded out to greet them, as she always did. But she hobbled a fraction, and perhaps her fur seemed a little thinner than usual, and it is possible that her whiskers had the smallest of droops to them.

The east wind, scented with jasmine, murmured of other villages and towns on the banks of rivers she had not splashed her paws in yet; the west wind, heavy with mango blossom, brought her news of ships that travelled up and down the coastline. But though the tortoiseshell thanked the east wind and the west wind, she padded quietly back to her home, which was an upturned, abandoned boat that kept her snug on the riverbanks. She slept that night, and her paws did not twitch, nor did her whiskers point the direction she should take.

The north wind came swooping down the next day, carrying the last of the chill from the distant mountains in its arms, and it spoke to the cat of roaming with flocks of sheep, in places where only the marmots popped their heads out to gaze at strangers in wonder. The cat thanked the north wind, and padded back to her boat.

The south wind stirred her fur the next day with stories of golden sands, tipped with black rocks, where the fishermen's nets were anchored by sleeping cats, their stomachs rounded with the catch of the day. And the cat put her whiskers up, a little sadly, and she thanked the south wind, but she went back to her boat.

When the white egrets who had become her friends came curving out of the skies that evening, one cried to the tortoiseshell: "Where are you off to this year? Which of the great winds will you follow these next few moons? Will you be back?"

"I don't know," said the cat slowly. "The winds spoke of many beautiful places, but my whiskers have not stirred, nor do my paws twitch."

The egrets looked at each other, and they flapped their beautiful shell-like wings, landing on the edge of the cat's boat. Their thin long legs held them easily in the river mud, so that they walked with grace through its thick ooze, unlike the other birds.

"It is the sickness," one said to the other.

"What sickness?" said the tortoiseshell. "It happens to some of us birds, after too many migrations," said the egrets. "Our hearts do not soar any more as the weather changes, and when the chill sets in, we do not want to ride the high winds, to set sail for the lands across the oceans and the rivers, because the wings in our heart will not beat as fast at the thought of the journey as they once did."

The cat's whiskers rose in recognition. "Yes," she said, "yes, that is it. My tail does not quiver in excitement; the fur on my neck does not rise in hopeful anticipation any more. I am tired; perhaps I am old."

"Oh no," they said, "you are not yet so old, your eyes are not rheumy, your joints are not yet stiff and aching. All you need is another kind of journey."

"Another kind of journey?" said the tortoiseshell in wonderment, her nose quickening. "But my paws can only go left or right, forwards or backwards; what other kind of journey is there?"

The egrets rose into the skies again. "We will ask the winds for you," they said. And they flapped their wings, and like unfurled sails, they skimmed high above the river, calling out to the four winds.

She watched the two egrets as they rose higher and higher, until they flew so high that there was nothing between them and the sun. They made dazzling white shapes against the gentle azure of the sky, and then the sun's rays shone even brighter, and the egrets in all their brightness seemed to shimmer and vanish.

For two nights, there was no word from the egrets, and though the tortoiseshell heard the soft songs of the other river birds, the calls of the ferrymen bringing their passengers to and fro across the river's broad back, she did not hear their high, wild cries.

On the evening of the third day, the egrets came home. They flew slowly, but they flew straight, and gradually, their shapes emerged from the deep blue. Soon they were flying so close overhead that the tortoiseshell could see their white, dappled feathers, their thin black legs glistening in the evening light, the way slender black driftwood branches gleamed in the river water.

"It was a long journey," said the egrets, dropping down to rest on the welcoming curve of the boat. "The winds had travelled further, and we had such a time of it, trying to catch the north wind."

The tortoiseshell brought out some fish for them, and the egrets fed gratefully, cracking the bones but leaving the tails for her out of politeness. By the time they were done eating and preening their feathers, the sun was almost setting, its fading reflection casting intricate nets of flaming oranges and reds across the river. The familiar sticky scents of marsh and mud, wood and rotting leaves and water, wrapped their comforting hands around the three friends.

The cat settled, stretching her bones, wrapping her tail around her paws.

"We spoke to all the winds," said the egrets, "and this is what they said. The south wind whispered that you might want to follow your nose to land's end and settle by the last black rock, letting the sea lap your worries away. The east wind lifted us and spun us around, and she said that the rabbit in the moon would show you where to go, if only you would follow the moonbeams where they fell. The west wind grew slow and still, and said that he didn't know where you were going, but that you should follow the rain and the rainbows back home. And oh, the north wind! She had rushed off, and what a trail she left behind her! The tempests! The gales!"

One of the egrets raised his wings involuntarily, remembering what it had taken to sail those choppy high seas, to ride out the storms.

"But we found her, resting in between a cyclone and a bitter freezing spell, caught in the cleft between two of the low hills. And when she heard what we had to say, she stopped blustering and blowing; there was a lull, a quietness. She let out her breath, and she said, 'Tell your friend that she must go in search of the cat who lives on the other side of the night.'"

The egrets stopped, shuffling uncomfortably on their twig-like legs.

"We are sorry," they said. "She said no more than that. We asked, but where must she start? And we asked, how will she recognize the cat? And we even asked, but how do you cross to the other side of the night? But though she sent us back on a floating bed of clouds, minding that we were safe from the lightning and thunderstorms, she said no more . . . but where are you going?"

The tortoiseshell's tail was raised in glad enquiry, and her whiskers were held high as she sniffed at the twilight sky.

"Thank you, my friends!" she cried. "There is such a tingling in my whiskers, it's as though the skies themselves are tugging on the line! And my paws are itching, and dancing, and eager to be off! Wait, here is something for you—the fish I had caught, thinking we would share it in the days to come. Please take it, with my gratitude. Now I must go."

And, brushing her head tentatively against each egret's slender neck—for they were birds, after all, and she a cat, and it was wise to remember that fact, no matter how many moons they had been friends—the tortoiseshell hurried away. Her eyes had lost their tired gleam. Her paws had the spring of a kitten's bounce and the eagerness of a young cat's first explorations. She did not know, any more than the egrets did, what the north wind had meant, but her whiskers called to her urgently to come along, and she followed. She looked once at the river, with affection; its black length glistening in the moonlight and the stars twinkling above its snaking curves and bends. Here she had found shelter, and friends, she had revelled in the small daily adventures that came with accompanying the fishermen, or watching the herons, or stalking the mice and shrews further inland. She had lived well enough under the friendly curve of the boat, but now she left it as freely as she had settled under it so many seasons ago.

CHAPTER ELEVEN

The Hundred Names of Darkness

eraal broke off to give Tumble, who had woken up and crawled over to her mother's side, a quick washing, until the kitten grunted in satisfaction and went back to sleep, her paws resting on her brother's stomach.

Mara had been listening, rapt, her ears prickling with each turn and bend in the story. There was the sudden rustling of something in the tarpaulin, a fluttering sound that became louder and louder.

"It's only the bats," said Beraal. "There's a large troupe who used to live up in the banyan tree, until the Bigfeet cut down the fig trees and banyans. The counts will probably roost at the back—Drac and Basie like the peace and quiet under the wall—but the girls are much more lively. If they're bothering you, I'll ask them to turn it down . . . Theda? Helen? Pola?"

The fluttering stopped, and Mara's ears flattened against her skull involuntarily as they were replaced by a chittering, an oddly impatient sound, like the rapid clicking of claws against glass.

Beraal made a soft sound back into the night, almost like the maternal chirrups she used to soothe her kittens, and to Mara's relief, the clickings grew softer, too. The chittering of the bats had felt like quick taps that came from inside her skull. The Sender shook her head several times before it cleared. Her teeth, she realized, were bared, the fine hairs over her eyes painfully taut. She thought there were words and phrases floating through her mind, but they seemed to go by too rapidly for her to understand them. She closed her eyes, and then she bared her teeth, chattering in fright—sharp little teeth, pink tongues, bright questing eyes set in the faces of miniature wolves glared back at her.

"Mara!" said Beraal urgently. "Could you stop sending to them please! You're frightening the vamps, they say they can see your teeth chattering at them in vivid close-up."

With a start, the Sender opened her eyes. "I'm sorry!" she said. "I didn't mean that to happen."

"Pola says your whiskers are on their frequency, and that you're making her ears buzz—oh good, she thinks it's very nice of you to apologize."

Mara stared at Beraal, her ears turned to the older cat questioningly.

"Kittens squeak, bats squeak," said Beraal. "Different species, but it's more or less the same language. Though the bats aren't half as demanding. They'll chatter among themselves for a little while, but they'll be fast asleep before dawn."

Mara settled back, but she was uneasy. She didn't want to look up; the night was a strange new place, and it harboured all kinds of creatures. She felt as though she had crossed the frontier from one world into another at sundown.

Beraal took up her tale again, and the Sender listened, her head resting on her paws, grateful for the sound of that familiar voice. It made the darkness feel a little less threatening.

"The cat who lives on the other side of the night," thought the tortoiseshell, and little by little, as her paws hurried her on, and her whiskers tugged at the night breezes, she felt her heart beat faster. Over her years of travelling, the cat had mated with many toms, and spent many nights in that slow circling dance of desire and battle. She had challenged a line of mountain cats, refusing to mate with any but the strongest, the one who bested her in battle; she still had the scars from a year spent in the company of a fierce seafaring cat who had been her equal in their hunts and in other ways.

She had dropped some litters of kittens, and brought not a few up, only leaving once they had found homes, and loving hands to cuddle and feed them. But she had preferred her own company at all times, and always, no matter how loving and loud and long the calls that sang through the nights, there had come a time when her paws had sung a new song of the road, her whiskers had called, and she had bid farewell to whoever she had been with, tomcat or kitten.

She padded up the riverghat steps, taking care to avoid the Bigfeet. Her lithe, small shape glided silently through the night as she headed North, away from the river up towards the long low line of hills; she was adept at keeping out of the moonlight. Her paws were used to the river mud and the damp grass that grew on the roads, and she used the clumps of purple-headed sarkanda for cover when she heard the scurrying thumps of a larger animal or the careless shuffle of a Bigfoot.

The ground beneath her paws was changing; she could feel loam instead of clay on her paw pads. The night was gathering close around the little traveller. A locust played the fiddle on a blade of grass and she started, pausing with a paw raised in mid-air: she could no longer hear the familiar murmur of the river's rushing waters.

The moon had shone as brightly as the egrets' snowy wings when she had started out, lighting her path and making it easy for the cat to see the pebbles, stones, thorns and other small hazards. But the winds sighed in the tortoiseshell's ear, a mournful whisper that set the hackles rising on her fur and on the backs of her legs, and all at once, the frogs croaked in alarm, their voices breaking as they implored: "Go bac-ack-ack! Go bac-ack-ack!"

The cat shivered, but she went on, picking her way carefully as the ground began to slope upwards. The mud gave way to stone, a hard stone that had an obsidian feel under her paws.

A few sullen stars had appeared in the sky, one glittering a baleful red, sprinkled against the blackness of the night. The frogs stopped their pleading, and as silence fell, a cloud, as mottled and purpled as an old bruise, drifted across the surface of the moon. It was joined by another cloud, as grey as the belly of a dead fish, and another, the colour of the dank mud that lay at the bottom of the river she had left behind. The light from the moon dimmed and dimmed, and darkness fell all around her.

The winds picked up speed, whistling around her ears, forcing her to lower her small head as she struggled up the rocky mountain. She could not see where she was placing her paws, and when she slipped, the black blades of the rock cut without mercy into her paw pads, making her mew in pain.

Her voice echoed back at her, taken by the massive rocks and flung back into the freezing air until all she could hear was her own pain, carried by the wind, and all she could feel was the stickiness of the blood that streamed from her paws.

The cat thought she should stop, but when she turned, she could not see what she had left behind her, any more than she could see what lay ahead. She shivered again, her whiskers trembling, her fur no protection against the sharp winds, the cold of the mountainside.

"Perhaps," she told herself, "I should call out to the cat who lives on the other side of the night. Who knows where the other side of the night begins or ends? Perhaps the cat who lives there is asleep; perhaps he (or she) will not know that I have passed by; it is only good manners to let her (or him) know that there is a stranger in the area. I would want to know, if a stray came into my territory."

She sniffed at the breeze carefully, but no whiff of predators came back; only the scent of ice, and blood, and the mothwing scent of darkness.

The cat offered a tiny mew into the night, and then a louder one.

"Greetings," she miaowed. "Can anyone hear me, or smell me? I'm looking for the cat who lives on the other side of the night . . ."

Her mews were caught by the rocks and flung back at her.

Greetings, the rocks said, mockingly.

And the echo said: Eating . . . eating . . . eating . . .

The cat kept walking, though her paws felt as though they had been torn into shreds. She felt the blood run so freely that it had soaked into her paws; making them sticky and cold. But the pain was not the worst thing of all. As she walked and walked, stumbling and staggering when the slope rose too steep, what made her fur stay spiky and her bones feel cold was the silence.

Except for the winds, which dropped and rose, howled and lapsed into absolute stillness, there were no sounds from anything at all. The locust had played its mournful fiddle a long time ago.

Time passed, how much time she was never to know. It could have been as much time as it takes to raise your tail and stretch out fully, it might have been as many moons as it takes to whiten your whiskers. And it seemed to the cat that she was the only creature who walked under the heavy wing of this night.

She stumbled, and this time, when she fell, she felt her claws give way on the smooth glassy surface of the rock. The cat slid to the very lip of the rock, too winded to mew, and when she rose, her flank was raw and hurting where the skin had been flayed by the sharp stone. Her courage almost gave out, then, and once again, she turned around, and once more, she saw only blackness behind, blackness ahead.

She had forgotten about the cat who lived on the other side of the night, forgotten about the river, and the egrets, and her life under the boat. Her tongue was dry and swollen with thirst and fear. Her paws and her flank streamed blood. She wanted only to be away from the night, back under the warmth and light of the sun. Yet still, she made her paws move forward. As the winds howled and tugged greedily at her fur, the chill cutting like giant claws into her back, making her whiskers ache with the cold, the cat kept walking.

The silence fell around her as heavily as the darkness. But gradually, so slowly that it took her tired mind a while to believe her senses, the cat understood that there was something walking behind her.

It was quite a distance away. She turned again, but she could see nothing. And then she caught it, carried on the back of that cold wind, a smell that made her nostrils twitch in terror, the unmistakeable stench of matted fur, flesh and dried blood that spoke of a predator.

The paws padding along behind her seemed to quicken. The cat looked up at the night sky, but the clouds gathered so thickly around the moon that the darkness seemed to deepen, seemed to settle on her whiskers and curl into her fur, reaching its fingers all the way down into her skin and bones.

The tread coming up the mountain was growing heavier and heavier, and the cat felt her blood go cold. She put her ears back, and she kept her tail up rather than allowing it to droop. She did her best to hurry, but the rocks were cruelly sharp.

Behind her, she thought she felt the wind shift, the coolness lifting so suddenly, it was as though something much, much larger than her had taken a deep breath and let it out, the hot exhalation stirring the fur on her back paws.

There was the scrape of claws on the rock, closer now . . . closer still.

The cat scrabbled at the rock, but she could not run, not with her paws so badly injured, not with the blood that had streamed out of her already. She looked up, to see how high the mountain was, and though she could see nothing, it seemed endless.

The cat's terror grew. She feared the hot breath that would whip across her hindquarters, the paw that would lash out, severing her tendons or ripping out her guts, the teeth that might cruelly crush her bones. All that fear and terror began to rumble around in her head, until it shrieked as loudly as the wind.

She almost mewed; and then she thought of the egrets, of their soaring flight across the blue skies, her calm and placid days by the riverside, the joy with which she had chased tiny crabs across the mud, just to see the skittering patterns they made in the clay. And slowly, the terror she felt began to shift, and began to glow, until it had become a kind of anger.

The creature was close, its tread quickening. The cat could not see in the dark, and she could not feel anything except for the slick knives of the rock, and the heavy stickiness of her own blood. She held her fear balanced in her head for a moment, the way she had once held bird's eggs carefully cupped in her mouth, and then she released her fear into the night's blackness.

She stopped walking. She turned, her eyes blazing, her back arched.

"You who follow me up the mountain into the night, you whose fur I can smell, but whom I cannot see, why do you say nothing? Why do you not growl, or grunt, or call out? Do you mean to kill your enemy in silence?"

The heavy tread slowed, and she felt a shift in the air, as though the winds held their breath.

"Yes, you," the cat called, her mew more assured. "What kind of hunt is this, where there is neither light nor level ground, where I cannot even see you or offer you a fight? If you mean to kill me, so be it. All of us must meet an end, and I have handed many over to the care of the greatest hunter of us all; but I faced my prey, and you hunt yours in silence. May I not look on your face?"

The winds stirred uneasily. The cat raised her whiskers, questing, searching, probing; it seemed to her that something in the darkness stood, hunched, on the mountainside just beneath the rock where she was crouched. She shivered, because it seemed to her that the creature was very large.

"May we not fight?" she said. "May I not be given one last battle, one chance to bare my teeth, to use my claws?"

Below, something stirred, and suddenly, the air filled with the strong stink of wet fur, as though a great animal had dropped to its hind legs. The winds sighed, raising the fine hairs in the recesses of her ears; and a cloud drifted to a side, letting a dull silver gleam through the darkness. The cat could see nothing on the mountain, but even that faint light, that curved sickle sliver in the sky, was better than the implacable blackness.

The silence stretched out between them. She could smell her own blood, and knew that the creature could smell it, too.

"I would die fighting," she said, wishing that her mew had come out less plaintive. "But before I die, might I know your name?"

The winds gusted down the mountainside so furiously that she had to crouch low, her belly flat to the rock, or she would have been blown around like a ball of dust. Another cloud sailed away, and now the cat could see the baleful moon, the merest glimmer emanating from its dark-red, almost black orb. The winds moaned and howled, dancing around her ears, making her wounds throb painfully.

She felt the creature move. The cat, lying flat against the rock, raised her head fearfully, and something made her look up as high as she could, even though she could see nothing in that darkness. Her whiskers throbbed, hurting her. She felt a harsh, hot breath scorch the fur on her face, and almost mewed in shock. She could smell meat and stale blood on the creature's breath. The cat could not see it; but its bulk and its breathing made her flanks shiver.

When it spoke, its voice was very quiet, but it rasped across her bones, and made the cat feel raw, as though a rough tongue had passed over her paws and her face.

"You ask for my name?" the creature said.

She shivered, her blood running cold. But she said, "And I offer you mine in exchange, if you wish it."

There was an exhalation, so harsh that it singed the cat's whiskers. She felt the creature come closer, so close that its fur—with the stink of meat and bones on it—brushed against her side. The cat almost cried out, because the rough bristles scratched her wounds so, but though her whiskers shook, she stayed silent.

"Names," the creature said at last. "Yes, I have a name."

The winds howled again, and the blood-red moon cast its chilly light on the mountainside.

The cat caught a flash, a glimpse of yellow teeth inside a massive, yawning mouth. There was something else too, but she quickly closed her eyes and told herself not to think about that.

Then the creature rose, and the cat felt her tail sink, her paws curl up, as she saw how it towered into the night sky. Its face was not visible yet, but she could see the outline of its great paws, sense the gigantic tail swishing in the distance.

"Cat, little cat, little creature of the river, small traveller who followed the moon all the way into the maw of the
night," said the creature, "you may guess my name. If you
guess right, I will kill you swiftly, and if you guess wrong,
I will—well, it will not be swift." And the creature bent its
massive head, and the cat held herself absolutely still as
she felt that great, rough tongue dabble at the blood on
the rocks—her blood, the blood that had dripped from
her wounds.

"Ah," it said, straightening up, "that was tasty. Now
start."

"Wait," said the cat. "I will try to guess your name,
but you offer me only death, one way or another. But I did
not come this far to be killed by a creature whom I cannot
see and do not know. I came to meet the cat who lives on
the other side of the night. Before we start, before you kill
me, O creature, tell me—how close did I get? Was I anywhere near the other side of the night?"

The creature seemed to shake, and then it threw its
head back—she saw the ugly mane form a rough halo
around it—and it howled.

"Close, and yet far," it growled. "There, and nowhere
near."

The creature's howls had ripped through the night,
echoing back off the rocks until they reverberated through
the tortoiseshell's body and through her head.

"If you please," she said, though it was painful after the
creature's howling even to attempt a mew, "could you—if you
meet him or her—could you tell the cat I'd come this far?"

"Enough!" growled the creature. "Begin!"

The cat shifted her paws, nervously, and her tongue stuck out for a moment.

"Very well, then," she said, her whiskers assessing the animal's bulk, thinking of the other big beasts whose habits linked them with the night. "Are you called Metoh? Lupin? Amaguk? Ursa? Parictis? Mamut? Quagga? Almas? Gigas? Pithekos?"

The creature bent its head again, and this time, she felt its fetid breath in her whiskers, fouling her nostrils. There was the stench of something else, a dark excitement that the cat found distasteful. Its tongue rasped the ground near her paws, and she watched in horrified fascination as it drank more of her spilled blood.

"Tastier," it said thickly. "Soon, if you guess in this fashion, I will have fresh blood to drink."

The cat put her paws together, trying to ignore the smell of her blood emanating from the creature's curved fangs. She let her whiskers reach out into the night, and she looked up into the sky, and thought.

"Perhaps," she said, "you were named for the stars, after all."

The winds sighed and sobbed, but the creature squatted, looming over her.

"Was I?" it said, in its quiet voice. "Which ones?"

The cat named the stars, choosing the ones that made up the giant, the bear, the monster, the were-tiger, the prowler, the beast, the dog, the panther, the ghost and the hunter.

The creature panted, its breath warming her freezing fur. It let one paw drop heavily on her flank.

"You entertain me, cat," it said. "I will enjoy tearing you to pieces. But go on, you have more guesses."

The winds sobbed and sighed, and crept through her fur.

The cat washed her paws, and thought, and named ten kinds of shadows next. And the creature licked blood from her paws, and its hot breath made her feel sick.

The cat named ghosts, then, and after that, she named ten kinds of fear, and when that, too, met with the creature's mocking taunts, she named the ten birds that carry death on their wings, and the ten weapons of the gods, and then the ten guardians of the deepest rocks in the hot centre of the earth, and finally, she named the ten dark angels.

The creature bounded to its feet, and it threw its head back, exposing the ring of fur around its throat, which was the size of a tree trunk.

"I have drunk almost all of the blood spilled from your wounds," it cried. "Wait, let me clean the trail." And it bounded rapidly down the mountainside, licking as it went, until it had licked up every last drop of blood that had fallen from the cat's flank and paws.

"It tastes so good," it said, running back up, its paws making the mountainside shake. "You will taste better, because your blood, even old, spilled blood, tastes good, little cat."

The cat felt the strength drain out of her flanks, and for a moment, she thought she would not guess any more names. It would be better to put an end to it. The creature had settled, licking her blood off its paws, and then it yawned, and its teeth gleamed black and yellow in the shifting light of the moon.

The creature stood up. "And now I must sharpen my teeth," it said, shambling towards the cat.

The cat wanted to flee, but the blood from her wounds had congealed, and her paws were stuck to the rock. She hissed and arched her back, but there was nothing else she could do.

The clouds rumbled in the distance, and juddered across the sky, covering the moon.

It was by her side; there would be no escape. She felt a claw, bigger than she had expected, sharper, too, rake her fur lightly, and then not so lightly. She turned her head, and far off, she saw a tiny gleam of light reflected from the black, glassy rocks on the next mountainside. The last of the visible stars winked at her from high above, and as the winds rushed down the mountains once again, shrieking in sorrow, the cat felt a pang of sadness: she had not met the cat who lived on the other side of the night, after all.

The creature raised its paws to the skies, and she felt its breath rasp across her whiskers.

"Wait," she called. "I have one last name for you."

The creature laughed, a rusted, tumbling sound, like bones being clanked together.

"Go on, go on," it said genially. "I am of the night, as you so cleverly guessed, little cat, but you will not find my name among the names of night."

She raised her whiskers up as high as she could, forgetting the ache in her flanks, the pain in her paws, the pain yet to come.

"That is true," she said. "Your name is not one of the hundred names of darkness, including Darkness itself."

"Is that all you have to say?" said the creature. "Hurry up, you must guess fast. The morning will be upon us soon, and I would rather eat before dawn."

The cat made an immense effort, and freed first one of her paws, then the other, then the rest, from the dried blood.

"What are you doing?" said the creature uneasily as she limped in its direction.

The cat brushed her head against its awful, tangled, matted fur, and then she gently licked its paw.

"Stop that!" the creature said.

"It is part of the naming," she said, purring so deeply, so warmly, that the winds stopped their howling.

"No!" said the creature. "I have no name! I always win this game, because I have no name at all!"

"You have a name," she said, and she purred harder, and she rubbed her bloody, wounded flank along its rough, filthy fur, and she washed its paws as the moon sank and the first glimmer of the sun began to lighten the night sky.

"I don't!" said the creature.

"You do, friend," said the cat.

"Friend?" said the creature, as the sun started to come up from behind the mountains.

"Friend," said the cat. "I have named you my friend."

The creature raised its shaggy head in bewilderment, and then the sun rose above the black mountains. And as its rays touched the great misshapen creature, it shook and shook and shook, until it had shaken its fur and its skin and its fangs off.

The creature's pelt lay on the ground like an abandoned shell, and then the skin shook once more, and a sleek black cat stepped out of it, preening his whiskers and shaking his paws out.

He sat down next to the tortoiseshell, and he purred over her wounded paws until the pads healed; he touched his whiskers lightly to her poor, battered flanks and the fur sprang back again, over the newly healed pink skin. Gently, his tail reached for hers, and joyously, her tail entwined itself around his.

"So you were what was on the other side of the night," she said in wonder, and the two cats sat together, on the highest ridge of the mountain. Their tails stayed entwined, as they watched the dawn come up and as the birds sang in the sweet, green valley below.

EVEN THE BATS HAD fallen silent. They stopped their chirruping when Beraal reached the part about the egrets and the four winds, so that they could listen to the story. When she finished, they rustled their leathery wings like velvet curtains, to indicate their thanks for the tale.

The kittens were both asleep, curled up against their mother's stomach with their paws hooked into her fur for comfort.

Beraal had smelled Mara's absorption, felt the Sender's whiskers go taut in apprehension as the creature followed the cat up the black mountain. She could feel Mara's breath ease as the story reached its ending, and smelled the young queen's relief.

"Sleep well, little one," she said in a soft mew to Mara. "See, the dark has lifted." It was not yet light, but the hour of the dawn was almost upon them.

Mara folded her whiskers down, stretching her back before she curled herself into a heap. "It was a good story," she said, her mew growing heavy. "Will the sun be up soon, Beraal?"

"Yes, it will," said Beraal. "And then Hulo can take you back home, to your Bigfeet. He knows the house."

"I would like that," said Mara, in a sleepy mew, and then she yawned, her pink tongue curling outwards. And then there was no sound in Beraal's snug makeshift home except for the occasional purring of the kittens, as they were washed by their mother. The Sender's long day had come to an end. She dropped into sleep as a stone drops into a deep well, knowing in her fur and her bones that all would be set right in the morning.

CHAPTER TWELVE

Fledglings and Summonings

Beraal's kittens played hide-and-seek in the shade of the pile of bricks and sand that had replaced the long park at the back of Nizamuddin, near the canal. The black-and-white huntress lay sleepily in the silver sand, keeping her ears alert for any signs of Bigfeet activity. She ignored the cheels overhead, only checking from time to time to make sure that no strangers had joined Nizamuddin's flying squadrons. Ruff and Tumble had been introduced to Tooth, Claw, Slash and the other Wing Commanders when Beraal shifted her quarters to the comparative safety of this spot near the canal.

The squadrons would leave the kittens in peace, unless one was foolish enough to venture out on his or her own, in which case, their unofficial truce would no longer stand. The raptors made allowances for the kittens and birds they knew, but any young creature found alone would be considered legitimate prey.

The whisker link crackled to life, and for a moment, Beraal felt her fur rise in hope. "Sorry, Beraal," said Hulo, pre-empting her questions. "The dargah cats haven't seen him, and there's no sign of him down at the shelter either. I only linked to let you know that I'll stop here for a bite with Qawwali, didn't want you to spend the morning waiting for me and Katar to report back from daily patrol."

Beraal sent her thanks back to him, but she knew that the tomcat would catch and understand the disappointment that travelled from her whiskers along the link. A moon had come and gone, winter's severe cold had given way to this early, burning summer heat, and there had been no news of Southpaw. The first few visits to the vet had gone so well, she thought, her tail twitching in sad remembrance. The Bigfeet had nursed him patiently, Mara had sat by his side night and day, keeping vigil after her return to the house. Beraal had gone to visit the young tom, and even Katar and Hulo had ventured up the staircase; Katar, indeed, was on cautiously friendly terms with the Bigfeet.

And then the Bigfeet had come back with an empty cage. "The door had a faulty latch," the Sender had told them later. "I didn't know, but then Southpaw's heavier than me. From the scents in the cage, all I can tell is that he was startled by something, and he sprang at the door. It must have opened. Perhaps the Bigfeet's car had stopped somewhere; I can't smell that bit very clearly. I've tried and tried to reach him, but he can't send, and he wouldn't be able to link at all once he'd left Nizamuddin. But I know that wherever he is, he's safe. He'll be back some day."

"How do you know he's safe, Sender?" Katar had said, the harshness of his mew betraying his anguish. "How do you know he hasn't come to any harm?"

The Sender had flicked her whiskers gravely, considering the question in all seriousness. "I don't know," she said. "I can't reach him, or tell where he is. But if he were dead—that is what you're afraid of, Katar—my whiskers would know. If I hadn't been so frightened when I fled my home, I would have felt his illness before. He is alive, even if I can't locate him."

For the first few days, they had hoped and watched the boundaries of Nizamuddin, expecting to see Southpaw's cheerful form, his jaunty tail, sail forth from some unexpected corner. But the days had tumbled along, like the brown leaves that fell from the trees, and gradually, Beraal had grown less and less sure that she would see the young tom again.

Her nose caught a familiar scent, and she sat up, greeting Katar with a friendly nuzzle. The grey tom flopped down beside her, glad of the coolness of the sand. The heat had made matters worse for the clan in one worrying respect: the Bigfeet had built over so many of the parks and green patches in the colony that the animals who lived there had fewer water sources this year than ever before. The canal water was not safe. Even the pigs wouldn't drink it, for fear of the many illnesses whose greedy mouths lay in wait for the unwary under its black surface. The Bigfeet had taps scattered around the colony, but only the bravest of the stray dogs would dare to lap at the water that pooled on the stones underneath.

The Bigfeet's guards would thrash any animal they saw drinking at the taps without mercy, and one of Motu's gang, an evil-tempered creature, had been beaten so hard he had whimpered for days afterwards. They had to steal water from the birdbaths, which meant more risk at the hands of the Bigfeet, or to shift their shelters so that they were closer to the few remaining gardens and could drink from those hoses. Hulo and some of the dargah cats were strong enough, and daring enough, to balance precariously on the slippery surface of the fat concrete pipes that ran alongside the canal, carrying drinking water to the Bigfeet; they would drink from the many leaks in the pipe to their hearts' content. But the canal's sluggish waters were treacherously deep, and those who lost their footing were seldom seen again.

"I was about to link to ask Hulo if he'd heard anything from the dargah," said Katar. "But he had the same luck as me— nothing from Jangpura, Beraal. I'll wait till my fur cools down, do another patrol along the market areas, and then I'll link to let the dargah cats know."

Beraal understood that the tom didn't expect to hear better news.

"If the cheels haven't spotted him yet on their sorties, if Jethro and his band of mice haven't heard anything, then we aren't likely to pick up his scent," said Katar, his whiskers exuding tiredness. "If it wasn't for the Sender . . ."

He didn't finish his mew, nor did he need to.

"Mara says he's alive; she can feel it on her whiskers," said Beraal quietly. "And if any cat can use up his nine lives and still have nine left, it's our Southpaw. Sometimes there is nothing we can do except fold our paws and wait . . . Ruff, stop biting Tumble's tail, you know she'll smack you back and then you'll come meeping to me!"

"What on earth is that?" said Katar, staring in the direction of the banks of the canal.

The cheel squadrons filled the skies, as they usually did at this time of the day, like a fleet of black ships set against the brilliant blue. The cheels flew in precisely judged manoeuvres, not in arrowhead formation, but in a more loose if distinct set of patterns. Their flight paths often ran parallel to one another, and the speed at which they crossed each other's tracks in the air made Beraal blink to see it, but they almost never crashed. They wheeled and turned, creating a skein of patterns in the sky, as though they wove the air into nets that could be thrown across the mottled brick rooftops of the dargah.

Far below the daring acrobatics and complex sorties of the cheel squadrons, a small brown shape hopped along the canal's concrete rim. It seemed to shoot into the air every so often, but it came down awkwardly, landing in a waddle rather than in a graceful dive.

"Oh, that's only Hatch," said Beraal, deciding to end the argument between Ruff and Tumble (the kittens were spitting at each other) by cuffing the brother and nipping the sister. "He's learning to fly. That's Tooth circling overhead, trying to get him to rise into the sky."

Katar stared at the fledgling, who was almost fully grown. He was a handsome bird, his plumage a rich brown flecked with gold, his plumes slightly longer at the back of his pileum, lending him a pleasantly rakish manner. But there he was, hopping along the parapet, like a mynah, taking those gawky flights in the manner of a duck, not a cheel.

"Shouldn't he be part of a squadron?" he asked. "Mach's a Squadron Leader already, isn't she?"

Beraal had started grooming Ruff, over his increasingly vociferous protests, so she answered with the barest twitch of her whiskers.

"Yes, but he doesn't want to fly," she said. "It's driving Tooth mad. Look, he's circling us."

Katar felt the sudden coolness on his fur as the raptor passed overhead, the cheel's shadow falling briefly on the cats. Tooth drew closer, but changed tack, dipping his wings and veering off towards the canal. He hovered for a few moments behind his son. Hatch took off in another awkward burst, skimmed the parapet, and returned to his hopping.

Tooth didn't alight near Hatch, and Katar guessed that the fledgling hadn't seen his father. The cheel banked left, flying over the canal's waters over the Bigfeet of Jangpura, who were out sunning themselves on their charpais in the bustling lanes of the colony across from Nizamuddin. He took a long wide loop down the length of the canal, and it was a while before Katar heard the steady flapping of the raptor's wings overhead.

Tooth perched on the top of the pile of bricks, spreading his feathers out so that they caught the sun.

"No word of your runaway," he said. "I flew as far as the overpass on the roads outside the dargah, but the cheels who live in Khusro Park hadn't seen a tom with brown stripes. They speak politely enough, that lot, but they have forgotten how to be cheels. They forage like rats in the Bigfeet's garbage; few of them hunt any more, as though we were made to use our claws for nothing better than picking up leftovers!"

He ruffled his feathers, shaking the upsetting encounter with the scavenger-cheels off them.

"Should we stop sending out patrols for Southpaw, then?" said Katar.

"No," said Beraal. "The Sender says . . ."

"The Sender says, the Sender says! For all her confident mews, she doesn't know where he is, does she?" Katar's fur was almost as ruffled as Tooth's feathers. He hadn't expected to hear news of Southpaw, but as the days padded by, the tom missed the younger cat more and more sharply, and sometimes his whiskers were heavy with the ache of it. Southpaw's hunting skills had been much needed, in these lean seasons. More than once, Katar had raised his whiskers to summon the brown tom, sent an absent-minded message to Southpaw through a quick spray at the fence that they used as their regular meeting place in the park, only to be reminded that the youngster was missing.

That morning, when Tooth had risen into the skies, Katar had sat on a rooftop, watching the cheel until he was lost in the glare of the sun, and allowed hope to seep through his fur. Perhaps Southpaw was on his way back home; perhaps the cats they didn't know that well, the ones who lived on the Golf Course or the fat cats who made their sleek progress through Sujan Singh Park and Khan Market, would have caught his scent. He hadn't realized how confident he had been that the cheel would come back with some sort of encouragement; his fur bristled with disappointment.

"Southpaw's whiskers are not a Sender's whiskers," said Beraal, calmly washing Tumble back to sleep. "He cannot link to us or to the Sender once he's crossed the scent boundaries in Nizamuddin, but I trust Mara when she says he's all right. I trained her, and her whiskers reach much further than ours ever could. You, of all the hunters of Nizamuddin, should be able to keep your paws still and wait—you were always the most patient of us, Katar, except when it came to Southpaw. It's because you miss him so much that your whiskers can't stop twitching now."

"But it's hard when it's your fledgling in trouble," said Tooth unexpectedly. "I smelled your fur that day when you asked me to help carry Southpaw, and you smelled like an anxious father, Katar."

Katar gave his whiskers a tiny twitch, suddenly amused at a thought. "Most of the Nizamuddin kittens are trained by the queens," he said. "Miao used to take us all on our first hunts, Beraal teaches the younger kittens the art of the brawl. But from the time Hulo found him, Southpaw was brought up by him and me as much as by Miao and Beraal. I suppose we are his fathers, our whiskers are closely linked."

"You feel it in your feathers, from your barbs down to your quills, if something goes wrong with them," said Tooth, and they saw how his pinions drooped.

Beraal watched the cheel intently. "Some kittens take a long time to use their claws, to step into the world," she said gently. "It does not mean that there is anything wrong with them. They learn at a different pace, that's all."

Tooth raised his head, and they saw that his keen eyes were following the squadrons circling overhead.

"There is no room for laggards among our squadrons," he said. "We fly together, sometimes wingtip to wingtip. We fear nothing except falling out of the sky, and we trust each other so greatly that we can fly blind, one cheel's wings brushing another's as we twist and turn, our eyes fixed on prey, not on each other's movements. There is no space for the weak-winged in the squadron. Hatch must leave the nest before the monsoons, a few moons from now. When the first rains fall on his wings, he will no longer be a fledgling, and if he cannot fly then, the squadrons will put him down as prey."

Katar's whiskers trembled in sympathy.

"That is never easy," he said. "Hulo and I have culled kittens, in seasons when the litters have been too many, or when kittens who do not carry the clan scent have strayed into Nizamuddin territory, and though it must be done, it leaves a dark stain on us. It is not like killing prey, though the only way to do it is to pretend that it is."

Tooth flapped his wings and called out, a keek-keek of despair that echoed over the canal, startling some of the cheels and making them swerve questioningly.

"Ah, Katar!" he cried. "I have promised Claw that I will do this when the time comes, because we both know that if he cannot fly, we cannot feed him forever. She said only, "Keep your beak sharp, and do not flinch when you drive your talons home, or else I will take your place," and cleaned her feathers. But her flights have been longer and longer this last moon, as though the only place she finds comfort is in the silence of the highest part of the skies, where even the winds and the clouds are beneath your talons."

The tom's ears were flicking in sympathy. "Hatch is your first-hatched, is he not? You and Claw haven't had chicks before him and Mach?"

"Our first babies," said Tooth hoarsely. "We had a cluster of eggs once before, but I had chosen the nest badly, and the rats carried them off. This time, we chose better. Our nest was high up on an abandoned telephone pole, on the banks of the canal."

The memories brought the fierce glow back to his eyes.

"You've seen how fast Claw can fly, haven't you?" he said to Katar and Beraal.

"Indeed," said Katar, his tail waving at the tip as he remembered one of Claw's more daring flights. He and Beraal had been on their way to the fakir's shrine, where Nizamuddin's clan had been fed by the gentle keeper for years until the Bigfeet had made him leave. A sharp sound had made them look up as they picked their way carefully through a narrow alley. Claw had flashed through, turning so that she went sideways, one wing to the earth, one wing to the sky; she went so fast, Katar remembered, that she had disappeared in the time it had taken him to shift from one cobblestone to another, his paw still raised, his fur standing on end.

"I heard her call from the other side of the clouds," Tooth said, "and I knew it was our time. I called back, urgently, wanting the squadrons, the crows, every other bird up there to clear the way. Then she called out to let me know she would not wait. And the squadrons scattered at her command, Slash and the rest retreating to the roofs of the dargah respectfully."

He brooded, stretching his great wings out.

"There is no season for mating except the winter, you cannot swoop and dive the same way in the heat. Our skies are so crisp, so cold, and that contrast—the light touch from the tips of her wing feathers, the softness of the feathers that lie clustered so thickly on her neck, the warmth that leaped from her to me—snared me. And tormented me, because Claw did not allow herself to be touched until she had extended her talons in invitation. First, we chased each other along the edge of the clouds, we tore through the air, hitching rides on one thermal after another, slaloming dangerously over the tops of the flame trees and rising again until we thought we would reach the sun. She called, and I answered; she called, and she flashed once around me, letting her wingtips graze the edge of my back, my neck, my throat, my quivering wings, and then she met my gaze, folded her wings and dropped. I knew what she expected; I did not plummet with her, instead, I aimed beneath her, like an arrow, ignoring the electric wires, ignoring the gliders who came up from the airfield below.

"Before I could claim more than one cry of victory, she was off again, spinning upwards—upwards, mind, Katar!—in a triple reverse. What could I do but follow, and then I swung around the flame trees at the edge of Safdarjung's Tomb, went low just to teach her a lesson, just to show her that she wasn't the only aerobatics expert, I looped the loop around the electric wires and shaved the roofs of a few Bigfeet cars. Claw only called again, a mocking question—is that the best you can do?—and matched me, two loops to one of mine, and there we went again, spinning upwards, making for the open expanse of Safdarjung airfield, challenging the gliders to a duel, and this time she let me fly almost beak-to-beak with one of the Bigfeet's craft. It was only when I went straight for the cockpit, raising my wings high to show her I would not back off, that she cried out in alarm, until she realized I had always intended to shoot upwards at the last moment, clearing the glider and its backwash effortlessly. It was so cold—freezing—my tail feathers would have stiffened if we hadn't been flying that hard, that fast, and Claw had her revenge, chasing the glider, dancing the fandango with its wretched tail until I was the one pleading with her to stop."

Despite the warmth of the summer day, Katar felt a sympathetic chill in his fur; Tooth made that winter day come alive, and the cheel shivered slightly, spreading his tail feathers out as he recalled their dangerous dance across the skies.

"Then she taunted me, chasing me up and down the thermals, rising higher and higher every time I thought I had her by the wings. Claw made the muscles under my wings work harder than they had in any of the squadron's sorties, diving, forcing me to follow her on the treacherous switchbacks of the winds, twirling and teasing, feinting and fencing until my wings and the winds had fused together; one could have been the other, I could not tell them apart. This time, I turned away, making for the edge of the horizon, trying to reach out and touch the sun with my wings, forcing her to chase me. I went vertical, high up into that part of the sky we love so much, where the air feels thin and rare. You leave the heaviness of the ground behind, because here there is only the sky and then, if we could keep flying long enough, the stars."

Beraal stretched, Tooth's talk reminding her of the nights she had spent challenging her mates, the joy of the combat that came before the lovemaking, the way in which she would whirl at the last moment, watching the hope and watchfulness in the tom's eyes. They could never tell what would come their way, the low resounding purr of invitation, or a slash from her paw that would leave them with a memory scar for life.

"I thought I had lost her," Tooth continued. "She folded her wings and dropped, her body heavy as though she had given up—sometimes the earth reaches up, sullenly, pulling us back to the ground because it is jealous of how we live in light and air—and how I wanted to follow her, but I could not. If Claw was to be my mate, if she and I were to be as well-matched in the nest as we were in the squadron, I could not drop down myself; she would have seen that as an insult, and her beak would have ripped through my wings in chastisement. I pushed my wings, forcing them to carry me higher and higher, calling to her imperiously, demanding that she match me, not asking or pleading for her company any more, but my talons told another story . . . They reached out silently to her, spread as though I would yank her up to me with my claws, if only I could.

"She had dropped so far that through the layers of blue, I could no longer see my Claw, and it seemed to me that I would spend this winter, too, without a mate, for if I could not have Claw, I did not want any of the others. I called as I sped through the air, reckless in my desire and my sorrow, and from behind the clouds, bursting out and upwards at a speed that almost froze my beak, my mate answered! 'Yes!' she cried, 'yes, I will, yes.' And then she looped once downwards again, swung out and around the top of a transmission tower until her feathers crackled at their tips, and there she was. My Claw, rising to meet me as I sounded my barbaric keek across the roofs of the world, my talons spread out to catch her, her muscled brown wings ready for me, and then she flipped upside down in surrender, flying with her head towards the ground, her talons fastened to the very stars themselves."

The summer had slipped away from Tooth; he had even forgotten Hatch, who was resting unhappily on the concrete rim of the canal's parapet.

"The shock when our talons met sent ripples through the air. We hit a bad thermal then, and had to ride the bucking ocean of air; I did not dare lose my grip on Claw's talons, and then as the pleasure rode upwards into my feathers and skin, I did not want to ever lose her. I understood what the lightning must feel like, as it shoots through the skies; we held and released each other, Claw dipped and swerved and zoomed, turned upside down and then spun me around as we made love to the four winds, to the clouds, to the very air itself. We were lightning and thunder, we were hail and storm, but even though the rest of our mating sent pleasure shuddering through my wings, I never forgot the moment when our talons touched for the very first time, as we tumbled through the skies that day, and then that night, and the next day."

Beraal's kittens stirred, Tumble mewing in her sleep. The sound, tiny as it was, made Tooth turn and blink. The faraway look in his eyes stilled, as he returned from the skies to the earth, and looked once again in the direction of the canal, where the squadrons wheeled and skimmed and swooped, while his son clung with his talons to the concrete.

"Hatch and Mach were born of that mating," he said to Katar and Beraal, anguish roughening his hoarse call. "When Hatch broke through the shell, he came out with his beak opening and closing in astonishment at the world, and the first thing he did was to try to raise the tiny bits of fluff that would grow into his wings. Mach came before him, but I had thought Hatch would be the first to fly, he was so curious about everything. Except the air. It scares him, he fears falling out of the skies. There is nothing wrong with his wings; it is his fear that keeps him tethered to the ground."

Beraal paused; she had been combing her own paws.

"He fears falling out of the skies," she said, her purr meditative. "Where have I heard something like that before?"

Tooth hunched his wings together. "Who knows," he said. "The only creatures silly enough to fear the skies are the pigeons, and they are no more than winged rats, we do not count them among the birds at all."

"Not the pigeons," Beraal said. Her green eyes had sharpened, her tail flicked away a few of the flies that were a hazard of the summer. "It is strange, is it not, Tooth? Your son fears falling out of the skies; and until her adventure, the Sender feared coming outside. Not now, she would say to me, her mew frightened, her whiskers defensive, her paws unwilling to consider moving out of the shelter of her Bigfeet's home, not now. And yet, when she found herself outside, even though her long whiskers were of no help against the dogs and the creatures of the dark, she did well enough."

Katar sensed the small return of hope that made Tooth's wingtips spike up slightly. The sun was high overhead, and the cats would soon need to find shelter from its rays, to rest far away from the heat so that they could use the night to find food and water.

Hatch had woken from his nap. He waddled along the concrete rim, looking ridiculous. Two cheels, visiting from the neighbouring squadrons of Defence Colony, very smart in their military correctness, not a feather out of place, flew lower, their beaks agape at the sight. Tooth, Katar and Beraal heard their mocking keeks, like derisive laughter, as they skimmed the canal twice to get a better look at the waddling cheel.

Tooth stretched on his talons, preparing for flight. The happiness had seeped from his feathers, and he held his wings taut.

"If my son hasn't found a way to conquer his fear by the monsoons, if his wings cannot lift him above this sullen clay," said the cheel softly, "I will keep my promise to Claw and kill him myself." He took off, and soon he had flown so high that Katar could no longer pick Tooth out from the rest of the cheels who circled overhead.

"SPLISH-SPLOSH, SPLISH-SPLOSH!" SANG CHANCHA, squawking in pleasure as the parrot sprayed water over her feathers and over every other creature who happened to be near the ornamental birdbath. "Wash well, wash well," scolded Meechi, who used the residual spray from Chancha's ablutions to scrub out her own feathers thoroughly. "So much dust on your feathers, I thought you were moulting, it was quite revolting." Chancha splashed water vengefully over Meechi.

"You're growing old, you're such a scold," she said. "Screechy Meechi, preachy Meechi." Enraged, Meechi flew at Chancha and soon the two parrots were chasing each other around the domes of the old mansion.

The cats clustered around the statue of a man on a horse, scattering themselves on the plinth around the hooves, ignored the parrots and the twittering peacocks who were mincing along on the other side of the park.

"The Sender of Nizamuddin?" called the calico cat who sat with her tail primly curled around her paws. "And if you don't mind, Mara, could you come down to the plinth? It's very disconcerting listening to you while you're hovering over the horse's tail, and if any Bigfeet happen to come this way, they mustn't find you like this."

The orange cat had been shimmering in and out of view, experimenting with popping up behind the statue of the Bigfoot who sat on the horse and hovering over the horse's head before settling on the spot above its stiffly sculpted stone tail. She came down hurriedly, and settled herself between Jalebi and Umrrow Jaan, meekly extending her whiskers in apology.

Begum washed a patch of fur on her flank, taking her time over it, her back turned until Mara had settled down. She gave Mara a curt twitch of her whiskers, finally, indicating that she could start. "This won't take long," Umrrow said to Jalebi, not bothering to keep her whiskers down to hide what she was saying. "Can't expect much from a Sender who stays home and lets her whiskers do the travelling all the time."

Begum's tail swung from side to side, and Umrrow subsided into silence. "Let's hear from the Sender of Nizamuddin," she said. "In silence, if you please. There's enough screeching from the parrots without us adding to it."

Mara stretched out along the plinth, her tail and fur unruffled. "The clan of Nizamuddin faces a hard summer," she said. "The winter has whittled them down till they slip around the lanes like shadows of their former selves, and the clan has thinned out. At the dargah, Qawwali and Dastan reported that most of the winter's litters didn't survive; the few kittens that did make it through are runts, tinier than they should be, and some have begun sickening in the heat. Beraal and her kittens are scraping by—she hunts sometimes at night when Hulo or Katar come in to catch a few hours of rest and check on Ruff and Tumble—but Tumble is frighteningly small. Abol and Tabol have widened their territory, hunting on the banks of the Jangpura canal, but this might not last if the Jangpura clan needs those hunting grounds at the height of summer. The Nizamuddin clan faces three urgent threats: they have lost many of their old water sources, my friend Doginder says the numbers of stray dogs are on the rise, and the Bigfeet are building in the lanes near the dargah, also in the marketplace. The clan's safety is increasingly under threat. The summer will stretch the clan to breaking point, so say Tooth and the cheels. Kirri—she's a mongoose—says that there is little prey in Nizamuddin, and she has shifted to Humayun's Tomb for the summer, along with many of the other predators."

She combed her whiskers, her green eyes filling with sadness at what she was about to say.

"My friend Southpaw has not been found yet, though I spend every evening, and every hour away from the Bigfeet, combing through the lanes of Delhi, sending and searching through my whiskers for him. If he could send back to me, I would find him; but his whiskers are short, he is not a Sender. Katar and Hulo are beginning to lose hope—Hulo has stopped saying Southpaw's name, and will find excuses to hunt or to wander away if Beraal shares her memories of him. I . . . we hope we will find him, some day. Soon. We will find him soon."

The Sender stopped, and her whiskers drooped for a second; then she pulled herself together, washing her flanks and her paws briskly.

"Anything else you'd like to know, Begum?"

"That seems very thorough," said Begum. The calico's mew was a little dazed, and for once she seemed discomposed. She stretched out a paw, stuck it behind her shoulder and began to wash it, to hide her surprise.

Umrrow was less circumspect. The half-Siamese purred so loudly at Mara that she sounded exactly like the ancient lawnmower one of the Bigfeet was pushing across the grass.

"You're going out like a proper Sender!" she said, kneading her paws in a pleased way. "How absolutely wonderful, and I'm so sorry I spat at you last time . . . well, I only hissed and spat after I'd left, and it wasn't really at you, it was at a dunderhead of a Bigfoot who almost stepped on my tail, imagine, just after I'd washed it really, really well, and it takes ages to dry, and it almost went into a puddle, too—oh, all right, Begum, no need to raise your whiskers at me like *that*, I can take a hint." But she continued purring so loudly, her crossed eyes beaming fondly, that Mara felt her own tail rise slightly in response.

"Is it still difficult, going outside?" Jalebi asked. The plump tabby had listened to Mara's report with as much surprise as Begum, both of them remembering how afraid the Nizamuddin Sender had been of the world outside her Bigfeet's house. "When I was your age, Mara, I had to get used to being a Sender twice over—first I had to get the hang of sending, wrestling with my disobedient whiskers wanting to walk towards my left paw when I wanted them to take me right!—and then it felt strange, stepping outside and knowing that the length of my whiskers were of no use in the Bigfeet's streets and markets."

Though it was just a sending, not an actual meeting, Mara felt her fur warm at Jalebi's kindness.

"My paws curl up at the sill of the door every time I leave the house," she said, feeling a rush of relief at being able to share her experiences with fellow Senders. "And my paw pads sweat in nervousness, but it goes differently with my whiskers, as they scent the air outside."

Begum made an understanding purr. "They stand up in eagerness, don't they?"

"Yes," said Mara. "They tingle, and they whisper to me that the night is young, and the darkness holds much else besides nightmares. And there's Doginder, or sometimes Hulo—we go out together, so it's not so bad. My Bigfeet worried about me at first, but now I think they're used to it; they leave the window open so I can return at the first light of dawn."

Umrrow and Jalebi caught the same thought on one another's whiskers—trust the Sender of Nizamuddin to sail forth accompanied by a canine companion!

Begum asked, "You haven't tried summoning yet, have you, Mara?" The Sender's dreams had quietened, and there had been no complaints from Magnificat, or from the river cats of Madhya Pradesh, or from the mountain Senders for many moons.

"I have," said Mara, her ears flicking as she tried to explain, "but not exactly with Senders." She had dropped in often to chat with Rani and Ozzy, but the great tiger had settled down with his mate, letting the lion cubs amuse him. He no longer pushed so hard against the bars of his cage. She never took Ozzy along for a walk again. But she had once startled the bats by summoning an unsuspecting pair of hyaenas from the zoo in one of her midnight experiments; the hyaenas had appeared high up in the air, and Pola and Helen had bared their pearly fangs at her, squeaking indignantly.

The Sender of Nizamuddin gave the quiet gardens a quick once-over, her whiskers checking for Bigfeet, but in the summer heat, the only residents of this Old Delhi park who were active were the parrots and the peacocks, and a few darting squirrels. Even the cheels were resting, waiting for the relative coolness of the evening before they made their flights.

"Perhaps I could practise here," she said, and before Begum could stop her, Mara raised her whiskers.

"Wait till you have your first lessons . . ." Begum began, the calico's tail waving in alarm, but the Sender's green eyes were already squinting in concentration.

The earth whispered, and a few grains of dust kicked up as heat waves shimmered in the air.

"Mara, I hope you know what you're doing!" said Umrrow, her ears pinned far back to her sleek head.

A dry, hot wind rose out of nowhere. The peacocks scattered, calling as dust clouds boiled up, spreading their dull yellow over the green gardens. The heavens opened up, shrieking at them, and the searing winds howled in their ears. There was dust everywhere, in their fur, in their tails, stinging their pink nostrils and getting into their ears, and then the dust formed into a whirling ball. The dustball spun in the hot winds, growing bigger and bigger, and Begum yowled as it formed teeth and whiskers, hissing at them.

The infamous hot wind of Delhi's summer scorched their paws as a furious white cat shimmered in front of the statue. She held a tiny, wriggling, silver fish speared on the claw of her left paw, and her beautiful tail lashed from side to side.

"I might have known it was too good to last!" Magnificat hissed. "It's you, isn't it? Sender of Nizamuddin, what have I ever done to you that you should interrupt the best day of fishing I've had in the last two moons?"

Mara's whiskers flattened in apology, and the dust storm abated, the winds slowing until their fur was no longer on edge.

"I'm so sorry!" she said to Magnificat. "It was an accident! Let me take you back home, Sender!"

"Oh no!" said Begum.

"Careful!" said Jalebi.

But they were too late. The skies opened up, and the Senders felt themselves pulled through the air, as Mara unfurled her whiskers and let the tips reach upwards. The park whirled around them, and dimly, they heard the startled squawk from Chancha and Meechi, the cries of the peacocks, the hoarse alarm from the tree of the cheels. And then the Circle of Senders shimmered and disappeared.

There was a roaring in Mara's ears, the harsh judder of some sort of machinery, and then the lapping of water. The Sender opened her eyes, gingerly. She could see an orange lifebelt, and hear the lazy cry of an egret somewhere in the distance.

"Well done, Sender," said Magnificat grimly. "I've never had a ferry crossing like this."

The Circle of Senders hovered above the deck of a large ferry boat. The engineer bustled around in the cabin where the orange lifebelts hung in cheerful pairs. Egrets called to one another in consternation at the cats who appeared to float in mid-air. The sun shone down on the river, making its waves dance in the light, and fish leapt to the surface, staring at the Senders, their mouths opening and closing in surprise.

"It's the fine-tuning," said Mara desperately. "All I need to do is twitch my whiskers a little more to the side—yes, I think I've got it now. Sorry, Magnificat! See you soon. Ah. Perhaps that wasn't the best way to put it."

The Senders felt themselves rising again, as though they had been scooped up by one of the fluffy clouds that hung like a tempting loaf of fresh-baked pau over the river, and then they shimmered out of view again, all of them except for Magnificat.

The last thing they heard was Magnificat's cross mew: "See you soon? See *you* soon? Don't you dare, Sender of Nizamuddin, if I see you again in my dreams, I'll turn you into a tailless Manx or my name isn't Magnificat!"

Then they were back on the plinth, crouching near the hooves of the statue.

Mara's paws were trembling.

"Is summoning always so exhausting?" she asked Begum.

Begum stared at the Sender of Nizamuddin.

"Only if," she said, trying to keep her mew steady, "you try to shift an entire Circle of Senders at one go across a distance of who knows how many whisker lengths!"

Mara's whiskers were still vibrating from the effort, but they caught her puzzlement.

"Let me explain," said Jalebi, who had been cautiously grooming her fur just to make sure that nothing of her had been left behind on the river. "Most of us, when we're working on summoning, do it differently."

"Yes," said Umrrow, her whiskers quivering. "We summon one Sender at a time!"

"Sorry," said Mara. "I guess I'll have to practise some more."

"Under supervision," said Begum hastily. "If this is what you can do as a novice to summoning, I don't want to know what havoc you'll create once you've had some training." She washed her paws, and then gave the Sender of Nizamuddin a more kindly glance.

"You should end this sending and get some rest, Mara," she said. "Your fur smells of exhaustion."

Mara hadn't stopped trembling; she didn't argue with Begum. But she raised her green eyes to meet Begum's deep brown ones.

"I should go home," she said. "But perhaps I should ask all of you Senders, before we end this sending: what can the

Nizamuddin clan do if things get worse?"

Begum and Jalebi sat back and considered the question. It was what they had been thinking about, before the business of the summoning had distracted them.

"How bad is it in Jangpura, across the canal?" Jalebi asked.

"Worse," said Mara tersely, not wanting to talk about the pathetically thin strays she'd seen, listlessly mouthing scraps along with the rats and pigs on the canal banks.

"Then they can't go there," said Begum. "But from what you've shared, the scent of Nizamuddin has turned sour for the clan, has it not?"

"It's either shift the Bigfeet or shift the clan," said Umrrow. "Not that clans ever move out of their homes, though. I can't imagine leaving Mehrauli ever."

Begum could sense the tiredness on Mara's whiskers. "We'll pat the problem around for a bit, Mara," she said.

The Sender of Nizamuddin shimmered in the air, beginning to fade out. "I have to go," she said. "My Bigfeet are calling me."

"Don't summon them!" said Begum, only half joking. The Senders watched the youngest and most powerful of them leave, and Begum wondered privately what or who Mara would end up summoning next.

"Begum?" asked Jalebi, her tail up. "Have any of the Delhi clans ever died out?"

"Often," said Begum, "especially the smaller and more vulnerable clans. Many across the river have flourished only for two generations or three and then vanished, when the Bigfeet have built more of their hutches; the Ghaziabad clan dwindled years ago, and the malls killed off half the Gurgaon clans. But the old clans always survive, and Nizamuddin is one of the oldest in Delhi."

Umrrow's crossed eyes were sharper than usual.

"Some of the older clans haven't had Senders for generations, have they?" she said. Her purr was low and thoughtful.

"When times are good," Begum said, "clans can have generations of litters go by without a Sender. I can smell what you're thinking, Umrrow, and you're right: it works the other way around, too. All of us were born at times when our clans had special need of a Sender's whiskers."

"And this Sender," said Jalebi, catching on, "has very long whiskers indeed. Long, and powerful."

Begum and the Senders were silent for a few moments, considering the matter.

"The Sender of Nizamuddin is the most powerful Sender Delhi has seen in years, isn't she?" said Umrrow.

"Yes," said Begum, her whiskers reflecting what was on all their minds. "And if the clan of Nizamuddin is in the kind of trouble where they need a Sender with such long whiskers . . ."

The calico didn't complete her mew. She stretched, and jumped down from the plinth. The other Senders left with her, but though they shimmered out of the park, their shapes melting back into the air, the scent of unease hovered in the Garden of the Cheels and clung like dust to the leaves for a long time.

CHAPTER THIRTEEN

Among the Mors

Southpaw clung to the branches of the neem tree, ignoring the sharp tugs at his fur from the dust storm that had sprung up a few moments ago. The sudden wind had brought the car to a standstill, and they had huddled inside, the Bigfeet and Southpaw, waiting for the dust storm to pass. "Jackal winds" Miao used to call them; the first of the hot, dry storms that signalled the end of winter, the start of summer. A jackal wind slid in sneakily like the beast it was named after, blinding everyone in its path with fine, grey clouds of dust.

If it hadn't been for the cyclist, he might have stayed in the car. But one of the Bigfeet had got out to check on Southpaw, worried that the cage would be covered in dust. Inside the cage, the tom's fear had increased when the Bigfoot began to pull a sheet over the container. "Stop!" he'd mewed. "I can't see and it cuts down on what I can smell—please don't,

I'm suffocating." But the Bigfoot had murmured something incomprehensible.

It had happened so fast. Southpaw, mewing and turning in the cage, trying to reach his paws out to tell the Bigfoot he was scared, felt the cyclist come up near the open car door. But he wasn't prepared for the bell, and the sound made him panic. He lunged for the door—and pushed it open. For a moment, he and the Bigfoot were at eye level, and then Southpaw had cried out in terror, as the cyclist peered into the car. He fought his way out from under the sheet, wriggling and yowling, and shot out from under the Bigfeet's arm. The dust scoured his whiskers, confusing him. The other Bigfoot called out, urgently; he bolted away from the roar and clatter of the traffic on the road, heading for the neem tree that grew out of a brick wall.

The branches swayed dangerously in the breeze, but the tom stayed where he was, wrapping his paws around its trunk and digging his claws in. He looked down and his whiskers rose in incredulity. The dust howled across a vast expanse of green, but before he could take in the rolling acres of grass, the endless lines of trees and scrub, a high eldritch screech rang out, making the fur on his ears tremble.

It sounded close by, as though it had come from under the rose-and-black dome of the monument that stood alongside the neem tree. It was not a friendly sound, and the tom shivered, wondering what creatures lived here.

There was silence for the next few minutes, and slowly, Southpaw began to relax. He moved his bottom more snugly into a knot of hard wood on the trunk, and settling himself so that he wouldn't slip, the tom allowed his eyes to close for what felt like the first time since he'd been placed in the cage and taken to the vet. His injured paw throbbed slightly, but when he flexed the limb, it seemed to be doing all right.

The wind shifted, and to his relief, the dust clouds veered the other way. Where were the Bigfeet? The tom turned to look at the road, and his heart gave a great thump.

Cars stood like lines of shiny beetles on the side of the road. Bigfeet walked up and down the pavements, many of them. He could not tell which ones belonged to the Sender's Bigfeet. Perhaps they would be angry with him for running away. They had never hit him or Mara, but they had shouted when he'd left, and he didn't want to risk finding out whether they would be just like the other Bigfeet in Nizamuddin, after all.

He wondered whether he could settle in the tree for the night; trees made for excellent climbing, but bad shelter. There didn't seem to be birds roosting in the high branches, but Southpaw had a feeling they would come back when twilight fell over this place. Nor could he sleep in the branches; he would fall out. But he could rest, he thought, and the tom placed his head down on the bark, giving his whiskers and fur time to get back to normal. He had been flehmening; his teeth were still bared, and he realized he was growling. He stopped, and he did what Miao had taught him to do on their hunts. The tom brought his attention to the tips of his whiskers, concentrating on calming them down. He felt his breathing slow and come back to normal. The storm was passing; soon, there would be only the fading glow of the day's heat. These branches were as good a place as any to rest; he could climb down once he was over his shock. At least, the tom told himself, there were no predators.

Harsh and wild, piercing through the silence, the high, terrible screech rang out again. It was coming from right under Southpaw's tree. Very carefully, he opened his eyes, and quickly shut them again. His paws quivered as he tightened his grip on the tree, grateful that his injury had healed well, and he could feel the fast, ratatatat thumping of his heartbeat. He looked down . . . into a mottled blue face, surmounted by electric blue plumes, a sharp pearly beak and a cold, considering pair of brown eyes, with a dashing streak of white under each eye. The creature's plumes were the size of the giant rose bushes back in Nizamuddin, and they formed a shimmering, vivid blue-green cloak, moving every time it took a step forwards or backwards. It was the largest bird Southpaw had ever seen, monstrous and beautiful.

Its beak clacked, and Southpaw cringed, his sensitive paw pads clutching the bark of the tree. Then the bird opened its beak, and to the tom's surprise, he spoke in Junglee.

"Right," he said, "step down guards at the sixteenth hole, no cause for worry. It seems to be a tomcat, probably didn't know that it was tripping the alarms—what? No, not one of our regulars, this one's probably an outsider, m'yes, of course I'll check. Tell Any and Much to relax the bunker guards, there's a good girl."

The feathers swung splendidly as the bird gestured with a flick of its neck at Southpaw. "Come on down," he said, "I think we'd better have a wee chat, what?"

Southpaw stayed right where he was. Katar had said nothing to him on the rules of engagement when it came to monsters, and after the day he'd had, he wasn't sure he wanted to take any more chances.

The bird let out a sharp hiss and stabbed, successfully, at a luckless earwig. "Come on, then," it said. "I'm not going to eat you—peacocks sup on rat snakes, kraits, finer fare than kittens, mmmm? It's hurting my neck, all this squinting upwards: wrinkles, y'know. Mustn't risk wrinkles, doesn't look good. Now, suppose you scoot down that tree chop-chop and we find you a decent billet for the night, whatsay?"

Southpaw relaxed his paws a trifle and considered the offer. He could take his chances with the bird—there seemed to be only one of the monster within view, and he was sure he could run for it if he really had to. Or he could stay in the tree. Which, given the whippy nature of neem branches and his natural curiosity, wasn't the best option.

Cautiously, he scooted down to the fork of the tree, where he was more or less at eye level with the peacock. It was even more impressive, and even more terrifying, close up—each feather was larger than his head. But the eyes, though they were keen and considering, seemed kind.

"I'm Southpaw," he ventured. "I'm not really from here."

The peacock nodded. "So it would seem, young Southpaw, so it would seem. The name's Thomas—Thomas Mor, but feel free to call me Thomas. Not Tommy. Can't abide nicknames. Ate the last feller who tried to call me Tommy." He caught the hesitation vibrating on Southpaw's whiskers as the cat began to wonder whether he should scoot back up the tree after all. "Bug," he explained. "Or beetle. Damned Madagascar hissing cockroach—blighter travelled here in some Japanese golfer's set of clubs, found him perched on the feller's niblick, a nine-iron, hissing at my brother Henry in an over-familiar sorta way. Nothing to do once he called me Tommy but eat the feller. Damned odd taste."

Southpaw's head began to spin. He had no idea what a "golfer" or a "niblick" was, but it seemed clear that the peacock—Thomas—was trying to reassure him. Gingerly, he attempted to scoot the rest of the way down, hit an unforeseen knot with his bottom, yelped, and landed in an undignified heap at Thomas's clawed feet.

Thomas sighed, but he pretended to look the other way, preening three of his many feathers absently, as Southpaw attempted to apologize, licking his tail into shape, and getting bark out of his fur.

"So," said Thomas once Southpaw was done. "Tour of the place—tararumpumpum! We're on the eighth hole, so we'll double back via the fourth and the third to the first, and you can meet the other fellers. Got lost, did you?"

"I was on my way back from the vet," said Southpaw, "when the dust storm happened and the Bigfeet opened the car door." He didn't feel up to explaining that they weren't his Bigfeet, only the Sender's Bigfeet, but Thomas asked few questions.

The peacock set a cracking pace, covering the ground at surprising speed with his claws. Southpaw wisely and instinctively kept up with Thomas's head and body instead of getting tangled up at the back with his long, now furled feathers.

Thomas, as leader of the peacock Patrol, had enough to keep his beak full at the best of times, and he planned to hand Southpaw over to the few cats who lived on the Golf Course. "Heads up!" he said out loud, looking up into the blue sky. "Southpaw! Go left and duck, fast!"

"Wha . . .?" began the cat, but the peacock had already stretched a wing out and knocked him sideways. Two inches from his nose, a large white egg soared down and settled with a thwack into the turf.

"Easy, easy now," said Thomas. "We've got a minute to clear the ground, what? No reason to run. Can't stand it myself when the younger peacocks start galumphing around—galumphing is for the deer, I always tell them, not for the birds. Come on, young 'un, this way. Before the next chappies tee off, come on, then, look sharp."

Southpaw looked up and saw another egg appearing from the far horizon, hanging high up in the sky—and following the egg was an entire band of Bigfeet. He didn't wait to be told twice; putting his ears back, he streaked after Thomas into the shelter of a long line of trees and undergrowth. Peering out from behind the brush, he saw to his horror that the Bigfeet were brandishing weapons.

"Why are they hitting eggs?" he asked Thomas. The peacock looked aghast. "That's a golf ball!" he said. "Don't you know the . . . no, how would you, you weren't born to the course, like the other cats. Anyway, it's a kind of game the Bigfeet play. They tee off and what they're trying for is a birdie or an eagle, though most of the duffers end up with bogies . . ."

He glanced down at Southpaw and sighed. "Never mind. It's a noble game, and we, of course, have our part to play in it. We must present ourselves at ritual moments, and receive the homage of the cries of their priests: ancient, strange cries known only to men, but how they stir our blood, as they intone the age-old incantations of 'Get Away!' and the holy hymn of 'Damn That Bird!'"

The peacock had a faraway look in his eye now, and his blue-and-green plumes flashed in the sunlight with even more magnificence. "There are no exceptions," he continued. "Every Mor, for generations past, has had to face the test of the third hole, where you cannot see the white ball that might strike you down from out of the bunker, or the eighth, where you face your Bigfoot squarely, daring him to strike you amidships. It is a test of courage, old chap, a true test. But all you need to know is this: steer clear of the golf balls and the Bigfeet, and the freedom of the course is yours. Step carefully around the bandicoot burrows, there's a good fellow. They've been overdoing the burrowing this year for some reason and you don't want to feel their blasted snouts snuffling around your paws."

Southpaw watched for a while as the Bigfeet played the game, his feline brain registering the speed and weight of the ball, and recognizing how deadly it might be to a bird—or a cat. He shuddered at the thought of deliberately facing into one of the Bigfeet's golf shots.

"You said every peacock has to face the Bigfeet's shots," he said, his fur relaxed and questioning as he looked up at Thomas.

"Yes," said the bird, "unless he wants to be called a bad egg."

"But doesn't it hurt if you're hit?" asked the tom.

Thomas's feathers rose involuntarily into a terrifying fan, and the cat shrunk deeper into the bushes.

"Yes," he said, more hoarsely. "It hurts a great deal. It can . . . kill. Over there, to the right, is the ninth hole, shrine to my uncle, who stood bravely through his time of ordeal as a young feller, never knowing that the ball would strike him square on the neck. He was dead before we could reach him, and now we all honour the courage and glorious end . . ." his voice quavered, "of the best uncle a bird ever had." Recovering, Thomas said, "Since his death, every peahen has brought her chicks over to the ninth hole, and told them never to forget the name of Noah Mor."

As they padded on, Southpaw found that he was enjoying himself. He walked stiff-legged every time clumps of Bigfeet emerged, but Thomas seemed to know the best routes around them, and the grass was cool and soothing under his paws. Southpaw inhaled the rich scents of the Golf Course. The wind brought him tales of mice and bandicoot families, living for generations in the hedges and ditches, dodging the pythons and the ancient rat snake tribes. As he padded along, the winds whispered the history of the three-generation feud between four Cinnamon Babbler families and the standing detente between the mynahs and the partridges. And trailing grey tendrils through all of this were the murmured tales from the cats—tales of long, lazy days spent in the sun, mouse and rat hunts, playing artful dodgers with the golfers, and of sleek mornings cadging scraps off the clubhouse tables.

Thomas kept up a comfortable slow run, his beautiful tail parallel to the ground, feathers flicking like a boat's sail at the end, measuring his pace so that the tom could match him.

His sharp eyes spotted the cat before Southpaw scented it. "Splendid!" he said. "One of your chaps, what? Let's get you two introduced, what say . . . oh. Blast. It's him. Oh well, too late to change course, must make the best of it."

Before Southpaw could make further inquiries, the smoky-grey cat had strolled over in their direction.

"Evening, Tommy," said the grey, eyeing Southpaw with some distaste.

"Top of the evening to you, Dippy," said the peacock curtly.

The grey cat's whiskers stiffened, but he ignored the peacock, turning to Southpaw. "I'm His Excellency Billi Bunter Singhji, Esq, KCB, MBE, OBE, KCS, of the Diplomatic Cat Corps, resident of Golf Links (with lifetime access to the Golf Course). My friends call me Bunter; you may call me Mr. Diplocat. Your credentials?"

"Me?" said Southpaw, puzzled. "What's credentials?"

Thomas nudged him with his beak. "Feller wants your name and designation, what?" he explained.

"Ah!" said Southpaw. He leaned forward to touch whiskers, but the Diplocat's ears quivered and he stepped back ever so slightly. The tom made the best of it. "I'm Southpaw, of the, ah, roofs of Nizamuddin, second drainpipe to the left on the Sender's stairs, currently, um . . . lost."

"Thomas," said the Diplocat, "he's a Common Cat?"

Thomas's feathers rustled slightly in the breeze, and the peacock raised his beak. "A very uncommon one, as you'll discover if you ask him about his travels, Dippy," he said. He looked as if he would have said more, but his attention was caught by a commotion towards the left, where a pride of

THE HUNDRED NAMES OF DARKNESS

peacocks had emerged from over the treeline.

"Sorry, old chaps, seems I'll have to say cheerio and pip-pip, what? Looks like Any and Much need me." He cocked his head to one side, listening on the bird network, "Oh dear, oh dear, oh dear, Birdbrain's got stuck in a bunker again. That's Bulbul, sweet feller but not the brightest beak in the nest, know what I mean? Southpaw, we shall meet at Philippi. Third hole to you. Dippy, introduce him to the others, there's a good chap."

"But he's just a commoner, Thomas!" hissed the Diplocat.

The peacock's feathers shot into a menacing fan, and the Diplocat took a hasty step backwards. "So sorry about that," said Thomas, "glitch in the system, got to get it fixed. So you'll take care of this little feller, what say?"

He looked at Southpaw with a kinder light in his eye. "You'll be all right, old chap. Dippy here'll show you around, get you some rations, won't you, Dippy? Take care of yourself, Southpaw." And he ran off, his claws racing lightly along the ground.

Southpaw's whiskers tingled as he received a crackle of irritation from the Diplocat, but when he sneaked a sideways glance, the grey fur was impassive.

"Step this way, please," said the Diplocat, setting off at such a pace that the kitten had to break into a gallop every so often just to keep up. They moved across broad swathes of green, through a deserted monument, and over tempting expanses of sand that the kitten would have loved to have explored, except that the Diplocat refused to slow down.

By the time they reached their destination, which appeared to be a grand old banyan tree whose roots spanned the top of a hillock, Southpaw's legs were trembling from the exertion, and the tomcat's hunger pangs were acute. The Diplocat said, "Stay here," tersely, and stepped stiff-legged to the back of the knoll, clearly in search of something. The cat flopped down between two large tree roots, his tongue hanging out as he panted. When he began to clean his fur, he realized he was still trembling, and he wondered whether the Diplocat would bring him something to eat. He didn't think so; the grey cat didn't seem very friendly.

Squirrels flashed up the trunk of the tree, darting blurs of grey and silver, chittering as they eyed Southpaw and made their way to higher branches for safety's sake. The tom's tiredness lifted a little in the cool shade of the banyan, and his whiskers started to whisper to him of the whereabouts of prey.

The Golf Course was rich in small animals, and Southpaw's mouth watered as a field mouse darted out, its black nose whiffling when it scented cat. He took a peek around, but the Diplocat was nowhere to be seen.

Cat etiquette required that he ask the Diplocat's permission before hunting on his turf, and Southpaw refrained from climbing up into the tree to see if he might find bird's eggs in a nest. It took some effort to rein in his instincts when two field mice darted across the roots, one chasing the other, but the cat held back. There were woodlice marching up a dry branch, and guiltily, he ate them, reasoning that it wasn't hunting really, just snacking.

The woodlice made his belly rumble, and instead of taking the edge off his appetite, they made him realize how hungry he was. He hadn't eaten since long before the visit to the vet's office, and his mouth watered at the signs and scents of so many mice and shrews. The tom shifted his position, pressing his belly down on the tree root in an attempt to stifle the rumbles.

The Diplocat stalked back across the tree roots, making no attempt to hide his annoyance. "Can't find the other cats," he said briefly. "The chaps are usually here, can't think what's happened to them."

Southpaw raised his whiskers. "Dipp—Mr. Diplocat? Might I have permission to hunt?"

The grey cat took a step back. "Permission to *hunt*?"

The tom wondered whether the cat rules were different here on the Golf Course and if he'd said something wrong. "I'm sorry," he said meekly. "It's just that I've been sick and haven't eaten much over the last few days, and there seemed to be a lot of mice here—but I wouldn't dream of trespassing on your territory, or poaching on your preserves."

The grey cat's tail was waving wildly from side to side. "Hunt! He thinks . . . You think I would eat a common or garden mouse? How dare you! I've never eaten anything in my entire life that hasn't come out of a tin or a packet! Norwegian sardines! Danish ham! English pilchards! And you insinuate that I would lower myself and eat this . . . this . . . common food, hunting for myself like any cat from the gutter? I don't know what Thomas was thinking, bringing you to me. Oh go on, eat as many mice as you like. Kill as much vermin as you please. Just leave me out of it. Hunt! He thought I would actually hunt the damn things! My paws and whiskers!"

Southpaw felt sorry that he'd hurt the Diplocat's feelings, but just as he was about to offer an apology, the dry leaves rustled, and a fat, young, juicy rat ran out from behind a branch.

The tom's instincts kicked in, and in a flash, he was on the rat, slamming it out of the air with a wickedly fast paw. In two blows, it was dead, and the tom tore into his kill with a ferocity born of his extreme hunger.

It was the best meal he had ever tasted. Fresh, juicy, singing with the flavours of grass and rare herbs, tender enough to satisfy the most demanding of cats. Southpaw had finished well over half of the kill before he recalled his manners.

"The prey in your part of the world tastes of sunlight," he said, using the formal speech Miao had whacked into his head when she taught him the etiquette of hunting. "Shall I save a haunch for you? I know you would rather have cat food, but the lore says I should . . ."

His whiskers stung as the Diplocat crackled with indignation. The grey cat's back was arched and his tail rigid.

"I think," he said, "that I might be sick. That is the most disgusting proposition anyone has put to me, much less a common cat from the gutter. Tell Thomas I did what I could for you, but this is too much. Good day to you. Pray continue with your meal. Ugh."

And the Diplocat stalked off, his tail held high, his whiskers radiating disapproval.

IT WAS SOME TIME later, with his stomach pleasantly full, that Southpaw began to consider what he should do next. He washed his paws, and his whiskers, and his tail, and watched the butterflies darting from one blade of grass to another while he turned the matter over.

The Bigfeet's cars had scrambled his sense of direction; his whiskers felt as though they had been whirled around and returned crinkled at the ends after one of his trips to the vet. It was the way they rushed around the place, going so fast that his whiskers couldn't keep up with the scent trails. Overpasses were the worst; going over them made his head throb and his stomach ache. He had been too sick on his first few visits to the vet to notice or care, but when he was back to his normal self, he wondered how the Sender could stand it. He had asked Mara, imagining that it would be much worse for her, with those long Sender's whiskers. She was guarding him, watching the Bigfeet bandage his paw. When they'd finished and left the room, she licked the fur around the edge of the bandages so that it lay flat and didn't tickle him too much.

"It's horrible, isn't it?" she said sympathetically. "I used to get the worst hairballs because the speed turned my stomach, but then I discovered that if I sang very loudly and yowled at the top of my lungs, my whiskers didn't vibrate so much. That helps."

The tom's paws kneaded the grass as he thought of the Sender, and of Nizamuddin. He unfurled his whiskers, but it was as he had feared—the distance was too great to allow him to link. But he kept his whiskers unfurled, letting their tips question the winds, and slowly, his ears flicked towards the east, and his nostrils flared, as though he might be able to pick up the scents of the dargah, the canal, the colony. He was too far off for that, but he felt the silent pull in the whiskers over his eyes, the light but insistent tug that told him home was towards the east—a long distance away, but at least he had an idea of the direction. Perhaps he could ask Thomas, the tom thought. But he would have to find the peacock, and as he let his whiskers explore the territory, he began to understand how vast the Golf Course was.

The Bigfeet appeared to have left as the light faded; he could hear their voices in the distance, but this side of the Golf Course had emptied out. Southpaw assimilated his surroundings. There was an abundance of prey, acres of space, and provided one kept out of range of the Bigfeet and other predators, he thought he'd be safe enough.

A butterfly hovered in the air by his nose and Southpaw swatted it away. Two more fluttered by, tempting in their rainbow coats. The cat gave into temptation, chasing the Angled Castors as they bobbed above the daisies and the wild weeds. He made small darting pounces at the butterflies, glad of the chance to stretch his paws after the meal. He had once caught a Yellow Orange Tip, and had no wish to repeat the experience—its wings had fluttered in his mouth, leaving a thoroughly unpleasant powdery taste. But chasing and pouncing and catching were three completely different things, and Southpaw enjoyed the exercise, until the sun slipped below the horizon, and the sound of a hundred and more birds calling from the trees announced the end of the day.

He stopped in a sand bunker to do his business, reflecting that it was very kind of the Bigfeet to provide so many places for the Golf Course cats to use as litter trays. As he hopped out of the bunker, he noticed a Bigfoot in the distance. It was running towards him, uttering one of the strange incantations Thomas had mentioned. The tom wondered if he should stay to chat, but on reflection—the Bigfoot was gesticulating with some urgency—he decided to take cover behind the wide roots of a banyan tree.

THE SCRATCHING WOKE HIM out of what had been a remarkably peaceful nap. The squirrels and snakes had left him alone; they were either wary of the stranger, or more polite than Ao and Jao back in Nizamuddin, who could seldom resist tickling the ears of the sleeping cats with plumes. The space between the thick, gnarled roots was so comfortable, the earth under him cool and soft, like the best of beds.

Southpaw stretched to his full length, feeling the strength come back into his injured paw. To his surprise, the brisk walk with Thomas Mor had done it some good; he could feel the muscles respond. The moon peered down at him through the tops of the chamror tree, as white as the flowers that bloomed among its dark, glossy leaves.

His eyes liked the dark better than the sunlight, perhaps because he had learned how to hunt at night. Without the distractions of glare, the white light of day, the Bigfeet's constant noise, even if they weren't physically present, Southpaw could turn all of his mind to the intricacies of stalking and hunting. Even the tips of his whiskers felt sharper, more alive, after sundown.

The scratching came from all around him, as though the roots of the banyan and the chamror had entwined to form an island in the middle of the activity. Southpaw stared into the darkness, and his fur stood up, slowly, as if it had been touched by the last of the icy winter winds. He felt his tail fluff, his heart-beat speed up as it did when he and Hulo sometimes stumbled on a larger predator than they had expected on a hunt night.

At first, he could see only the eyes, glowing like fireflies in the dark, not far off the ground—perhaps no more than the height of the thickest of the banyan roots. Moonbeams reflected back from the eyes, the way they would in the black waters of a lake, so that he was surrounded by points of light. The smell was as thickly layered as paint; rich, oily, unpleasantly musky, like freshly turned earth where something rotten had been found underneath the clods. There were many of the oily trails, and slowly, Southpaw realized that the snuffling sound he had heard in his sleep came from the creatures. He raised his whiskers, letting them uncurl and curve into the night air: bandicoots, but more of the great grey rodents than he was used to facing in Nizamuddin.

He slid his claws out, preparing for battle if need be. The snuffles shifted an octave, intensifying and then slowing. The creatures seemed hushed, waiting for something.

In the long grass beyond the banyan tree, at the start of the smooth expanse of turf that marked what Thomas had called a "golfing hole," one of the creatures grunted. It was a question, and it was answered by another set of grunts, closer to the roots; these were rough, menacing in a way Southpaw couldn't understand.

He backed until he was almost pressed up to the massive trunk of the banyan, glad for the cover it gave him on one side; he still had three flanks open, but if it got to paw versus claw, he might have a chance.

"It's a new boy," said a rusty, hoarse voice.

"It doesn't know the rules," said another voice, grunting.

Southpaw's fur crawled, and he saw that the creatures were shuffling in his direction.

"Not so fast!" he called, trying to keep his mew firm. "I do not wish to attack you since this is your territory; but come too close, and I'll defend myself."

The scuttling stopped, and he sensed that the bandicoots were assessing him, their tiny whiskers probing him for weaknesses.

"It doesn't belong here, the new boy doesn't," said a third voice. This one was unpleasantly unctuous. "It hasn't been introduced, has it? It isn't with the other cats, is it?"

"It isn't," said the hoarse voice, consideringly. "It's all on its own."

"It hasn't paid the price," said the second voice. "You can smell it on its whiskers—it's eaten, in our territory, and it hasn't paid the price. Cheater!"

"If it's alone," said the unctuous voice, caressingly, "then it's ours, it is."

The bandicoots chittered, and Southpaw's hackles rose. He let his fur inflate, and growled in low warning.

"I don't know what price you mean," he said. "I didn't know this was your territory; Thomas said he'd introduce me to the cats, but he was busy. But what is this talk of prices? You're just long-nosed rats, you lot."

He didn't care how many of them there were in the dark, though it seemed like several large runs of bandicoots to him, judging by the volume of the grunts and snuffles. No bandicoot, thought Southpaw, fury rippling through his fear, was going to talk to a tom—a hunting tom, a blooded tom—in this manner.

"Rats, it called us!" said the first voice, its grunt angry.

"The new boy doesn't know who runs the Golf Course," said the second voice.

"We should show it, then," said the unctuous voice.

Southpaw heard the scrape on the earth as the bandicoots shuffled forward. He saw the glowing eyes start to come towards him, and felt his flanks tremble: there were far too many of them! He brushed the fear from his whiskers and hissed at them.

The bandicoots swarmed over the tree roots, and now he could see their black beady eyes up close. They were small, and would have reached only halfway up one of his paws, but he remembered his hunts with Miao and Hulo. "They're terrible warriors on their own," Hulo had said once as he'd cleaned out a bad flesh wound, scouring it with his tongue to make sure it would not rot, "but they're such cowards, bandicoots, they like sneaking up on you in gangs. Nasty little creatures, attacking in packs, howling for help if they get into a brawl on their own. Ugh, and their fur's so oily. They leave a bad taste in your mouth!"

And then they were rushing at the tom. Southpaw unleashed his battle cry—he had borrowed it from Hulo, but he was quite proud of the imitation—and prepared to swat his opponents. He smacked the first wave of bandicoots off the ground, sending them flying back into the grass. He swatted the second wave, and the third; but the bandicoots kept on coming at him, and the feel of their tiny pink paws on his fur began to disgust him. The moon illuminated the brown hordes, some swarming up the roots nearby and trying to get behind the cat so that they could rush him from the rear. Their grunts and snuffles took on a dangerous edge; the stink of their fur was sour in his nostrils. Southpaw backed, and found that he was pressed up against the tree trunk. A prickle of unease ran through his fur, and he felt himself tremble: surely this was not the way he was going to lose in battle, nibbled and pulled at by these cowardly creatures?

"You wouldn't dare fight me if there weren't so many of you!" he snarled, shaking off a few who had climbed onto his back, using his fur to haul themselves up. More than the scratches they had started to inflict on his skin—which hurt no more than going through a prickly pear hedge—it was their touch that made his fur crawl, and he felt a sudden sick sense of helplessness, at not being able to avoid their naked clutching paws.

"They wouldn't, indeed," said a polite voice behind him. "Off with you lot, or I'll wake the owls. Where's Chhota Poonch?"

The bandicoots snuffled frightfully, grumbling and complaining, but they began, reluctantly, to move back. A few jabbed at Southpaw's fur and paws vengefully as they left.

"Come on, step up," said the handsome Bengal cat who emerged from behind the banyan tree. He was a stately, plump cat, with an air of authority, black rosettes gracing his beautiful golden fur. "I know you're there, Poonch, I can smell your black tracks ruining the jasmine-scented air, my friend."

There was a sullen grunt, and one of the bandicoots reluctantly turned around.

"There you are, leading valiantly from the rear as usual," said the Bengal cat pleasantly. "What's the meaning of this ruckus, Poonch? I thought we had an agreement, my long-snouted friend. What was it again—yes, say it out loud, I want all of your lot of ragamuffins to hear it, since they've obviously forgotten all about it."

"The agreement doesn't hold, Mulligan," said the bandicoot with the unctuous voice, rubbing his paws together. "We would never attack a Golf Course cat, oh my whiskers, no, no, no. But a stranger, who hunts on our territory, without a permit from Chhota Poonch, you must see that . . ."

The tip of Mulligan's tail twitched very slightly, but it was a sharp twitch, and the second bandicoot stopped snuffling immediately.

"*Our* territory?" he said, his purr so soft that Southpaw knew someone was in trouble. "Poonch? Do I hear Chamcha right? Since when has the Golf Course become your territory?"

The third bandicoot cut in, his voice smooth. "Small misunderstanding, everything can be explained, no need to bring your claws out, it is all Chamcha's fault," he said.

"You interest me greatly, Moonch," said Mulligan, his mew bored but his eyes gleaming in the dark.

"Of course this is your territory, we have always said, this is the kingdom of cats, yes? And ourselves only humble squatters," said Moonch, slinking forwards, his nose twitching eagerly at Mulligan. "We live at the pleasure of the Golf Course cats, we die at the command of the Golf Course cats, that is the way it has been for my father, and my father's father, and his father, and all of us who have lived on the Course for so long, so very long . . ."

"Moonch," said Mulligan, his whiskers administering a light smack. Southpaw could feel the tingle of annoyance in the air.

"So there is no question that this is your territory, yours and the other esteemed cats, and of course the peacocks, the Mor family whose claws and feathers we worship," said Moonch, oiliness seeping into his whiskers.

"No question," said Chhota Poonch, gesturing with a sweep of his tail to the bandicoots to return to their runs.

"But as you see," continued Moonch, his tail lowered obsequiously, "we are in great need of space. Our cousins have come visiting, and sometimes uncles and auntyjis also, and you know how it is, you cannot say, now you must go, it would be the height of rudeness."

"Moonch," said Mulligan, his tail waving dangerously, "I am not interested in the intricacies of the bandicoot joint family system."

"Yes, yes, of course, saheb, why would you—scion of such a proud species, even if though, these days, there are not so many of you or the illustrious peacocks, so sad—be interested in our overcrowding problems?" said Moonch, his belly brushing the ground in a way that made Southpaw cringe for the bandicoot. "But you can see for yourself what the outcome of such inflow has been. When Chamcha said 'our' territory, he meant only that there are so many of us here that we are feeling an obligation to look after the place, keep an eye on things, make sure that in your absence all is well, yes? No one is sneaking in from frontside or backside? Because, saheb, after all, you are busy cats, you cannot be everywhere on the Golf Course, and this is our duty, to serve you in whichever way we can, to travel to this place and that place and make sure that at least one of our clans—mostly us bandicoots—is always there."

There was something about Moonch's oleaginous voice that made Southpaw feel very sleepy, and he found his whiskers nodding in agreement at the bandicoot's persuasive arguments. It seemed reasonable enough, the oily voice made good points—but what was that the bandicoots had said? Something about a price. He hadn't paid the price, in their territory; there had been something about running the Golf Course.

But Moonch continued, rubbing his paws together, his scent heavier than the other bandicoots, filling the heavy spring air and adding to Southpaw's odd tiredness, and whatever the bandicoots had said to him faded out of his memory. It was such an odd voice. Flat, he would have said, dull; just as Moonch's heavy aroma was not offensive, merely pervasive, driving out all other scents from the place. Southpaw blinked, and some instinct made him stretch and move quietly to the far side of the banyan tree trunk. He could see and hear the bandicoots as clearly as before, but he was a little out of the way of Moonch's voice and scent. A light breeze, one of the last of the delicate night breezes that would freshen the nights and touch them all with delicious coolness before the heat of summer brought its burning force to bear on the earth, played around the trunk of the banyan. It brought the aroma of magnolia and jasmine along with it, and cleared the tom's aching head.

"Very persuasive, Moonch," said Mulligan, his striking tail switching back and forth, "and let us suppose that for a moment, I ignore the scent of trepidation emanating from the burrows over there, while Poonch and Chamcha wonder whether I'm going to actually let my whiskers believe your pleasing fara-diddle. None of this twaddle explains why a Golf Course cat was attacked by a complete thuggery of bandicoots."

The ivory moonlight shone strong on the Bengal cat, and Southpaw saw the grimness in Mulligan's hazel eyes.

"But a thousand apologies," Moonch said, turning to Southpaw. "We thought we were merely defending the sacred land of the Golf Course cats against an intruder."

"No," said Southpaw slowly, his fur prickling in remembrance, and the whiskers over his eyes waking from their somnolence, "you said—or at least Poonch said—that I didn't know who ran the Golf Course, and you would show me."

Mulligan spat, and arched his back, the gleam in his eyes positively dangerous.

"I've warned you, Poonch! Remember how your tail was shortened in the first place!"

Southpaw's whiskers bristled, sensing a shift in the wind. He peered into the darkness and his eyes widened: it couldn't be his imagination, could it? Were the bandicoots waiting and listening at the very mouths of their burrows? Even his eyesight wasn't good enough to penetrate that far into the dark earth and the long, shivering grasses, but he caught the thick black scent trails, like brushstrokes around the rim of the burrows, and he was sure. They were waiting, their eyes like small coals in the dark, for some sort of signal. The scents were shifting, becoming muddier, thicker, exuding a sourness like the ooze at the bottom of an old puddle: the bandicoots were sullen, not liking what Mulligan had said one bit.

Furtively, he slid his claws out, taking care not to let them click on the tree roots. If it came to a fight, he and Mulligan were probably as outnumbered as he had been on his own, but the tom didn't mean to let the Bengal cat handle the—what had he called them—thuggery of bandicoots on his own. Two sets of teeth were better than one, eight sets of claws could rip and shred more flesh than four.

But Moonch had oiled his way in between them and Poonch. Southpaw had the strange sense that an urgent message passed between this bandicoot and his fellows. He thought he heard Moonch say, "Not yet!" in an urgent snuffle, but he might have been wrong.

"Oho, but I am now fully seized of the matter! What a mix-up, what a blunder, what a misapprehension you were under," said Moonch, his whiskers sending small ingratiating twitches Southpaw's way. "How were you to know who ran the Golf Course, no, no, no, you are fully blameless. The name of Mulligan may be famous, every blade of grass knows his esteemed clan, but you as an outsider—oho, of course not, you would not know who runs the Golf Course. We know. Poonch knows. Chamcha knows. And we were going to take you to the esteemed clan, but how were you to know, small wonder you attacked us, but of course, no blame attaches. We will accept apology, any time, no problem, any friend of the Golf Course cats is a friend of ours, what are a few scratches here and there?"

Mulligan's tail twitched uncertainly, as he stared first at Southpaw, then at Moonch.

"I didn't attack you!" Southpaw said, his mew so indignant it came out as a hiss. "Your friends attacked first, I only defended myself."

Moonch looked down and dug at the ground with his long snout, not meeting Southpaw's eyes.

"Whatever you say," he said soothingly, "it shall all be as you say. I can see your whiskers are still mostly black, only one or two white, young toms have such hot blood, yes? But of course, no need for apologies among friends, and any friend of Mr. Mulligan's is a friend of ours, all you have to do is to twitch your whiskers and we are at your service." Behind him, Poonch grunted. It was a contented sound, as though the bandicoot had been given something that he had wanted all along.

"It would take all night to uncomb the tangles in this matter," said Mulligan, his whiskers truculent, "and I don't have all night. Thomas Mor told me Southpaw would be somewhere in these parts, and just so that we understand each other—any cat found on the course, whether of the clan or not, is to be considered a Golf Course cat until we mark him as an intruder. Is that clear?"

"Yes, yes," said Moonch smoothly, "we shall treat all cats we meet exactly as they deserve." Southpaw's whiskers went up. Moonch's voice had been as smooth as ever, but there had been the tiniest of shifts in his scent; a sudden flash of dark anger, or had he imagined that, too?

Mulligan lowered his head, the ears held upright so that he could listen at the widest range possible.

"Moonch," he said, "how many bandicoots are there in your clan? Have the burrows expanded? I haven't been this side for such a long time, and it seems . . ."

"Not at all!" said Moonch hurriedly. "You're smelling the old runs. A rat snake lived on that side of the tall grasses, and he must have left behind many small corpses of prey. None of us go there, of course. If you're smelling the skein of scents from the bushes near the water hazard, that is where the rats used to live, until they . . . they shifted. After the rat snake . . . he left too. Some time ago. These snakes, so restless."

"I thought there were a lot of you," said Southpaw, his nose picking up on Moonch's unease. And there it was again, a sharp, hastily concealed but unmistakeable flash of anger, leaving a stain of black scent in the air. Then the breeze started up again, and jasmine's dazzling white perfume filled his nostrils.

"So did I," said Mulligan, and there was a distinct menace in his purr. "Poonch? The cousins who came visiting you last year, before the monsoons? Did they leave, or are they still here?"

Moonch snuffled before Poonch could answer. "Mulligan saheb!" he said. "You do us too much honour! I am so delighted, so touched—no cat, not even your honourable father and mother, no, no, no, none of you have ever asked after our families. Would you care to visit my humble abode one of these days, perhaps share an earthworm or two with us?"

Mulligan was silent for such a long time that Southpaw felt the unease spread in the air. His fur felt cold, touched by a hundred tiny beady eyes, and he felt that there were watchers whom they could not see, listeners taking care not to snuffle or grunt.

Then the Bengal cat spoke, and his mew was friendly enough. "It is kind of you to invite me, Moonch," he said. "I may take you up on your invitation one of these days, before summer falls upon us. It seems to me that my clan has neglected this part of the Golf Course, for far too long."

They heard Poonch's nervous grunt, and then Moonch answered, his whiskers taut, his snuffle more sure this time.

"But of course, Mulligan saheb, at your pleasure," he said. "We have not felt the neglect in this tiny corner of our ... your ... territory, but you and your clan will always be received in the appropriate manner. You must come. All of you must come. There are so few of you left, are there not? I remember tales of the days when every hole on the course had a clan of cats guarding the tee, but then times change, life moves on."

"Some things don't change that much," said Mulligan, stretching and stropping his claws on the roots of the banyan tree. "The Golf Course will always be home to the peacocks and us cats, and the snakes will always patrol its borders, near and far. Along with the bandicoot clans, Moonch. It has been many generations since all of our tribes and clans have shared these wide greens, these vast acres between us—peaceably, I might add."

"Of course, of course," said Moonch, and Chamcha snuffled his assent, too. "You are in charge here. We are but your humble servants." He rubbed his paws together again and turned, lowering his belly and tail to the ground. "All of us," he added, "every last bandicoot here is most conscious of who is in charge." Southpaw started; his whiskers had received the smallest of stings, and he thought he had heard Moonch add as he scuttled away, "For now." But Mulligan didn't seem to have heard; the Bengal cat lay stretched out over the roots, his eyes fastened on the burrows in the distance.

The bandicoots snuffled and grunted as they left. The scurrying of their paws faded, but the thick scent trails lingered in the air.

Southpaw stood up, meaning to thank the Bengal cat.

"Sorry," said Mulligan, stretching and sitting up. "Terrible way to meet us, you know, being at the mercy of those thugs. Yes, I heard what Moonch said, but your whiskers are very, shall we say, expressive, and indignation quivered at the tips of them. Oh well, the fur hasn't flown, and it's only this part of the course that's infested with the beasts. You have these outbreaks every so often—one year it was the peachicks, running around and leaving claw-marks all over the tees, one year the club cats had six or seven kittens per litter, and this year seems to be blessed with a barrage of bandicoots. Up to each clan to curb its numbers, spread out so that they don't inconvenience the rest. But look at me, rattling on and on. You must be hungry, Southpaw. Shall we head off and join the others? Mashie and Niblick had just begun hunting when I came here to find you—Thomas got the news across to us via Major Mynah a little late, he's been busy these days. You'll like Mashie, and you'll find Niblick's part of the course rather smashing. He has most of the sand traps, lucky fellow, and access to the clubhouse too. Would you prefer rats, mice or bird's eggs for your *chhota hazri*—your morning repast?"

Before Southpaw could say a word, his stomach sent out a hopeful rumble; it had been a while since the rat he'd offered to share with Dippy.

"That's a yes, then!" said Mulligan, his mew rather pleased. "Follow me!"

The two cats set off, heading towards the far end of the course, where a cluster of Bigfeet monuments beckoned to Southpaw enticingly, their vast empty stone interiors promising good hunting. The tom turned once, pausing when Mulligan stopped to comb some burrs out of his tail, to look back at the banyan tree, but the grounds were tranquil and hushed. A keel-back snake slithered past, its vivid green scales matching the colour of the grass in the rough. If the bandicoots stirred, they did so underground, hidden from view. As the toms walked towards Mulligan's friends, Southpaw took the memories of their glowing eyes, their grasping paws, that insidious, menacing smell, and set them to rest.

CHAPTER FOURTEEN

The Bonds of the Earth

The Bigfeet were fast asleep when Mara slipped away, in the early hours of the morning. They were used to her sojourns by now, and let her go in and out of the house without fuss. But they smelled of relief when she came back home, and she tried to thank them by spending some of the night on their bed, curling up on the pillow until they had gone to sleep. It was one of the many curious aspects of the lives of Bigfeet that they chose to waste the time between moonrise and moonset, sleeping the night away instead of resting during the day, as more sensible creatures did.

In her kittenhood, Mara had patiently attempted to train the Bigfeet into playing with her during the choice, sweet hours just before dawn, but they had not seemed to appreciate the gifts she had bestowed on them, the songs she had sung as enticement. The Chief Bigfoot was as challenged on this front as the lesser Bigfeet, and often came into the house just when

Mara was settling into a much-needed mid-morning nap. As the seasons passed, the Sender gave up on trying to change the Bigfeet. Instead, she sacrificed the early hours of the night, napping with the Bigfeet until the moon was at its zenith, or until the peaceful hours before dawn; and she slept in the afternoon instead of the morning, so that she could accompany the Chief Bigfoot and help her with household inspections.

Before she left the house, Mara performed a small sending, one that had become a ritual over the last few moons. The Sender ignored the acrid stench from the Bigfeet's bonfires, the sawdust and the dried, dead sap on the branches joining the ever-present smells of tar, cement and turned earth.

She raised her whiskers, sweeping them back and forth slowly and deliberately. She stood at the open window, and she closed her eyes, giving her sense of smell and touch full play. In the Sender's mind, the roads that led from Nizamuddin to the home of the vet took slow shape, until she had the layout firmly fixed between her ears. Then she opened her eyes and deepened the scan, her whiskers reaching out and probing for any signs of her quarry. She had done this every morning, and every night since the Bigfeet had come back with the scent of tears on their skin, and an empty cage. It might take her all of summer to find him, but until she had located Southpaw on the grid, the Sender would raise her whiskers and search every last inch of Delhi, if that was what was required. She moved lightly among the pigeons and crows, the mice and the sleeping cats of Khan Market and Lodhi Gardens, sending so discreetly that none but the most alert sensed her presence. The bats in the Lodhi tombs stirred uneasily, their radar picking up the light probing of the

Sender's whiskers, but when nothing appeared in the doorways of the ancient tombs, they relaxed their leathery wings and went back to their slumbers.

It was some time later, as the morning heat warmed the window sill where Mara sat, that she gave up on her search for Southpaw. There was no despair in her whiskers; only patience as she straightened them and padded down the stairs to meet Beraal.

FOR A MOMENT, WHEN she saw the black-and-white queen, Mara almost snarled. The slender warrior cat sprang so lithely from parapet to parapet, intent on her hunting, that the Sender recognized her only when she drew close enough to catch Beraal's scent.

Beraal moved so fast that she seemed like a ghost shadow, her fur melting into the dim light of dawn. The shrew she was stalking fled, dodging to left and right, trying to use the gaps in the bricks as cover, but Mara saw a paw shoot out, stabbing once, twice. Then Beraal dropped down, growling an instinctive warning as she held her kill in her mouth. The shrew's head lolled to one side; only the fur on its neck had been touched.

"That was a fine, clean kill!" said Mara, with some respect in her mew. Though Beraal had taught her the basics of hunting, from opening gambits and endgames to the five classic paw-and-claw strikes, the Sender's knowledge of the Double Slash or the art of YowlClaw was mostly theoretical.

Beraal stopped snarling, and she dropped the shrew on the ground, patting it once to make sure it wasn't playing dead.

"Enough for both of us," she said, and her purr was satisfied. "I picked up a fine, fat rat right near the taxi stand, and carried it back for Hulo and those two before coming out to hunt."

Mara thanked Beraal, but refused to do more than nibble daintily at the shrew. Her Bigfeet had fed her well, and she would not have taken the warrior's kill in any case; she remembered her night of hunger, out in the park, and she knew how little the other cats had to eat. Her whiskers touched Beraal's lightly, in thanks, and she settled back on her haunches, happy to know that her mentor would have a full belly. "My Bigfeet would feed you all," she had said wistfully to Beraal, on one of her first night patrols. But Beraal had said:

"If it reaches the point where our ribs and our backbones stick together, we will come. Katar said your Bigfeet fed him well; but we are not house cats, and our paws stop at the threshold of the Bigfeet's houses, no matter how kind they are to us."

Watching Beraal eat, Mara thought she understood. The relish with which the warrior queen supped was not just because of the tenderness and sweetness of the shrew's flesh. The meat tasted sweeter for the pleasure of tracking and then besting your prey. Mara's whiskers quivered in memory of her own kills, though these had been humble—a few moths, the odd cricket, and winged beetles that she had learned not to eat since they gave her hairballs.

"Is it hard to find enough prey for you and the kittens?" Mara asked.

"Harder now," said Beraal, her tail swishing sadly as the two queens padded down the silent back alleys, past the iron grills and the small patches of green that linked the Bigfeet's homes. "But when I was in my first few years as a young warrior, learning the hunt from Miao, that life was as rare and rich as any of us could want."

"If it weren't for the Bigfeet, even now, we would have happy hunting," said Beraal. "But the crows have become aggressive, and driven off many of the pigeons; we kill the latter for meat, not so often the former. The rats and mice have fattened on the Bigfeet's garbage heaps, but we must hunt with the Bigfeet's eyes on us, with the Bigfeet taking over our old hunting grounds— and so the rats thrive, and we grow lean. But making one, two, three kills a night was common enough in the old days, and besides, how else would we know our terrain unless we hunted and quested through it?"

Beraal's nostrils and whiskers were vibrant as she shared her memories. "Your whiskers are never so much alive as when you hunt," said the warrior, her emerald eyes gleaming. "Nor is your nose as keen at any other time; nor do you see so much so clearly."

It was true. Mara could feel her own nose twitching, and as they took the bends and curves of the alleys, pausing only to avoid a few early-rising Bigfeet, she felt her whiskers take in the neighbourhood that had sheltered her clan for so long.

They were moving out towards the back of Nizamuddin, where the Bigfeet's homes ran alongside the canal. Gradually, Mara felt her fur begin to rise, tugging sharply at her skin. She had not been this side before in her careful, brief patrols with Doginder, but there was something about the air, fetid as it was, that felt familiar.

She heard water lapping along the banks, and her whiskers pulled taut as they neared the bridge. Far away, on the other side of the dargah, the dogs barked, and Mara shivered.

Beraal pressed her nose against the Sender's flank. "Is it too open for you, Mara?" she asked. "You're used to the comfort of being inside four walls; shall we go back?"

But Mara's hackles were rising, and the Sender seemed unaware of Beraal as she walked, stiff-legged, up to the bridge. Beneath its flat grey concrete expanse, the black waters swirled.

"It's not that it's too open," she said. "But this is where . . ." She remembered dogs barking, and once again, she remembered her mother's mews, frantic, the scrabbles as the older cat fought for her kitten's life.

The fine hairs inside Beraal's ears rose, in surprise. "This is where the Bigfeet found you?"

Mara was crouched on the stone parapet, shivering despite the warmth of the summer morning. The Sender's whiskers pointed downwards, at the opening to a pipe embedded in the embankment. The pipe was made of stippled cement, and though the mouth gaped open, it was jammed with flotsam from the canal—bright pink plastic bags, smudged newspapers, faded biscuit packets, brown glass medicine bottles, discarded banana leaves and desiccated marigold garlands from the temple.

A cheel swooped overhead, his wings skimming the high poles of the bridge; he somersaulted and looped upward, towards the rising sun. Far beneath Mara, the waters foamed and hissed, spewing grey foam up the banks.

Beraal watched as Mara's white whiskers curled outwards, searching for something that was long since lost. All that was left of the Sender's kittenhood under the bridge was memories, and detritus. Beraal did not attempt to comfort the Sender. She washed her tail, grooming the long black fur, savouring the unexpected pleasure of hunting after so long, and kept an eye on the sky and the road in case any predators, Bigfeet or bird, threatened the Sender's reverie.

When Mara came back up the bank, picking her path carefully up the rough concrete and the dry mud, Beraal was pacing, her whiskers extended in the direction of the Bigfeet homes on the other side of the road.

"If the Bigfeet had not found me that day," said Mara, and her mew was low and thoughtful, "perhaps I would have been part of the clan; perhaps my scent would not have been strange to any of you."

Beraal rubbed heads with the Sender, and turned so that their whiskers entwined. Her deep emerald eyes met and held Mara's gaze. "Without your mother, as tiny as you were when we first heard you cry across the airwaves of Nizamuddin from the Bigfeet's house, you would have perished in a day, Mara," she said gently. "Between the dogs and the cheels, the crows and the Bigfeet, between hunger and the hazards of living in the open, between predators and sickness, very few kittens survive the first few moons of their lives all alone. Never let sorrow settle on your whiskers for what never was."

A car rumbled by, and a line of dogs gambolled down the road, barking as they jostled one another. Beraal dropped to her belly, and Mara, following her cue, took cover behind a large dustbin. The dogs passed; a cow meandered by, and two Bigfeet pushed their brightly coloured ice-cream carts down the road, as the koels and bulbuls murmured overhead in the branches. Nizamuddin was almost awake.

"This road will soon be so crowded that you'll wonder how we ever crossed," Beraal said to Mara as they trotted over to the row of Bigfeet houses that faced the canal. These houses carried an old-fashioned air about them; many were only one or two storeys high, unlike the more recently built homes, and despite the faded, peeling paint, there was something welcoming about their small courtyards and the wide balconies.

They stopped in front of a cheerful, tiny plot, the brick walls scrubbed white and clean, the steps covered in chalk designs. The door was open, though there were no Bigfeet in evidence. An old dog, venerable and so advanced in years that she did no more than open her eyes once and blink in acknowledgement at Beraal, lay snoozing on the upstairs balcony. Downstairs, a pair of parakeets chattered in a cage; potted plants made up a small but pretty garden; and a wide earthenware birdbath with birdseed scattered on the earth outside its rim testified to the fact that the Bigfeet who lived there liked animals.

"I wanted you to see this, Mara," said Beraal. "Do you like the house?"

She watched the young Sender curiously.

Mara's nose was twitching, and her eyes were wide as she took in everything. "It is very different from my Bigfeet's home," she said, "but it has a warm, welcoming feeling to it, as though many creatures have walked into it over the years."

Beraal settled down on the pavement, considerately moving some distance from the birdbath so as not to frighten the bulbuls and sparrows away. Mara found a spot near the wall, and they watched the world go by, the Bigfeet clattering over the canal bridge, the pigs grunting to one another as they woke up and began rooting through the garbage piles for breakfast.

"I brought you here because this was where Tigris lived," she said.

Mara's whiskers rose, and she peered with even more interest into the house.

"The last Sender before me," she said, her mew quiet. "The one who never went out."

Beraal turned so that her paws covered Mara's smaller ones, and she began washing the little cat thoroughly.

Mara let herself be washed; Beraal had often washed her when she'd been a tiny kitten, and she remembered the feel of her teacher's rough tongue on her fur far more clearly than she remembered being groomed by her own mother.

"We all thought that Tigris stopped going out," said Beraal, in between washings. "Miao, who had grown up knowing her before she became Nizamuddin's Sender, was terribly worried at the time. She said that sendings had become more real to Tigris than the world itself, and that for a few Senders, this could happen. Their whiskers could lead them into places so beguiling that the world around them seemed flat and dull in comparison. Or for some, though I didn't entirely understand what Miao meant, sendings became safer than their ordinary lives."

Mara blinked. "Yes," she said, "you can't be hurt when you're sending, it's just your whiskers taking you for a walk.

But when you're here, out in the world, you're like every other cat. The dogs bark at us, the Bigfeet rush around, and crows and cheels can drop down any time from the skies. It isn't easy."

Beraal was listening intently. "I see," she said. "Now I understand—perhaps that is how it was for Tigris. She lived here, among Bigfeet who were kind to her, and she could visit the clan through her sendings, and over the years, she stopped visiting us in any other way. But it was not good for her."

"Miao said that as well," said Mara, and her fur prickled with unease at the thought of how she had spent most of her first year indoors, content to watch the world from the safety and comfort of her home. In the cage in the courtyard, the parrot chattered, its intelligent eyes watching them as it attempted to imitate Beraal's deep mews.

"If I haven't hunted for a while," Beraal said, "my paws begin to itch and my flanks grow soft instead of taut. Once, I had to stop hunting to heal a battle wound, a bad one. I'd dealt with an insolent tom who strolled into our midst from Lodhi Gardens, acting as though he owned the place. Of course I sent him yelping back with very little fur on his tail, but he landed a few telling bites when we brawled. For many moons, I could not hunt, could barely even patrol Nizamuddin, and my whiskers began to get tangled. I started at small, insignificant noises; my teeth chattered at every least little thump and bump; and worst of all, I began to fear the dark, when I had once owned the night. Perhaps that was how it went with Tigris, for her whiskers twisted, and sometimes her sendings were so strange, so odd that it was as though she could no longer tell her dreams—or her nightmares—apart from her sendings."

"Poor Tigris!" said Mara. A shiver ran through her orange fur, despite the warmth of the day. She remembered the incidents when Begum had said she'd been sending in her sleep, and for the first time, she wondered how far her whiskers would have knotted if she hadn't eventually stepped out. "Everyone says she was such a great Sender, but to stay trapped inside your house forever, never being able to go out . . ." Mara pinned her ears back, not liking the thought.

"But Tigris did go out," said Beraal, grooming her long fur and claws carefully. "You know the bats whom you met in my house? Pola, Drac and the rest? Their clan goes back almost as many generations as ours does, and they told me that they often heard her. She did not send to the clan in her later years; her sendings became more infrequent, perhaps because she knew that they thought her behaviour was odd. But she stayed in touch with her friends the sparrows, and with some of the mynahs, and indeed, with a few of the bats."

Mara looked from the house to the banks of the canal. It was not such a great distance.

"She came out in the evenings, often, if she could be sure that none of us were around," said Beraal. "The bats say that Tigris was always kind. However much of a tangle her whiskers had got into, however hard the burden of sending had become for her, she would greet the sparrows every day, and even chat with the carriage horses when they went by. And they say that she met a handsome tom one day—a stranger who was passing through or some such—and that he enjoyed her stories greatly. Tigris was a marvellous storyteller, Mara."

The Sender's green eyes were intent, and her orange tail flicked lightly from side to side. The cats moved closer to the wall when a laughing crocodile of schoolboys wound its way down the road, but the young Bigfeet did not notice them, and they let themselves relax again.

"The bats say that some moons after the handsome tom had left, Tigris left the house, too, and made her home elsewhere."

Mara raised her ears. "Under the canal," she said.

Beraal brushed her whiskers with her own. "Under the canal," she said. "Where she had her only litter of kittens, of whom only one survived. And that one became Nizamuddin's Sender."

The sparrows kicked up the dust near the birdbath, letting it sift through their feathers. They ducked their beaks into the water from time to time, enjoying the dust bath, hopping and chattering.

Mara had raised her whiskers involuntarily, but there was nothing—no scent from the canal, after so many seasons, to remind her of Tigris or her kittenhood. The Sender huddled, thinking back. "You're a Sender," her mother had said. Mara remembered the low murmur, the gentle, loving touch of her mother's whiskers, as clearly as the sound of the traffic that had rumbled and thundered over their small, snug home under the bridge. She pressed close to Beraal's flank, and her fur warmed, just as it had when her mother had washed her all those moons ago. And Tigris' deep, steady voice came back to her: "It's not an easy life," she had said. "It's an interesting life."

Then there had been the dogs, and the Bigfeet, and Mara had forgotten those days under the canal. It came back to her; Tigris's blue eyes had been far away, and her whiskers had stilled as she spoke. Her mew had trembled slightly: "It's not an easy life." She had not been speaking mother to daughter, Mara thought. She had been speaking Sender to Sender. She had nuzzled Mara, and washed her to sleep, easing all the day's small aches and worries, and Tigris had promised that she would teach Mara all that she knew.

Mara had been staring out towards the canal. She shivered, and turned to Beraal: "Why did Tigris feel she had to leave her house to have her litter? Wouldn't she have been more comfortable there? Her Bigfeet wouldn't have minded, would they?"

Beraal ducked as a cheel flew a little too close overhead. "Her Bigfeet would not have minded, and the bats couldn't say why—Tigris never told them. But you know what my whiskers tell me? They say that Tigris left because she wanted her kittens to be born outside, just as she was. Perhaps she knew that if she'd had her kittens inside the Bigfeet's house, she would never have stepped out, and she would never have let her kittens step out, either."

"But she must have been scared of the outside by then, if she'd spent so long living inside, away from the clan," said Mara.

"Yes," said Beraal, "I can almost feel what that fear would be like, on my fur and on my whiskers. And though we'll never know, perhaps Tigris wanted more than a comfortable home for her kittens. Perhaps she wanted you to live a different life, one where you could shake the fear of the outside from your paws and whiskers."

"Really?" asked Mara, and her whiskers rose a little.

"Yes," said Beraal. She hadn't known Tigris very well, but from what the bats had said to her, she had begun to understand the courage it would have taken for the other cat to leave the safety of her Bigfeet's home.

"She never told me she was a Sender," said Mara. "But she said she would teach me what it meant to be a Sender. Before the dogs came for us."

Beraal stretched, and as gently as she could, she rubbed her nose and whiskers along the length of Mara's flank. "That was brave of her," she said. "To teach you what it meant to be the clan's Sender, Tigris would have had to return to sending herself. She would have had to raise her own whiskers, in order to show you how to control yours."

The Bigfeet inside the house were stirring, and Beraal's ears flickered. Mara and she rose and stretched; it was time to return to the kittens. They padded in companionable silence down the road, but Beraal had made Mara feel much better. They left the house that Tigris had lived in for so many years behind them, and as they passed the canal bridge, Beraal paused, raising her whiskers at Mara questioningly.

"We don't have to rush," she said. "Hulo's with Ruff and Tumble, and though they bully him dreadfully he's really quite good at looking after them. Do you want to go back to see your home again, before we go?"

The pigs grunted and shifted down below, and the stink rose thick from the canal.

"I don't need to," said Mara, and to her surprise, she found that she meant it. "Everything that was special about my mo—

about Tigris—is here, in my fur, on my whiskers, in my memories. I remember the way she brought back fresh kill, and how happiness sang in her fur when she and I lay curled up together. She told me that my whiskers would take me everywhere, and they have. She came outside for me, and perhaps we would have both been Senders together."

Beraal felt a sharp pang run through her fur; how much easier this winter would have been for the clan, if there had been Tigris as well as Mara to guide them! But the sense of loss was as brief and as fleeting as a stray scent caught and tossed aside by the winds.

"You may never have been taught by Tigris," she said in a soft mew as they moved on. "But you have her blood, and her skills, and just as Tumble has my colouring, perhaps Tigris gave you her whiskers. It is something, to be a Sender; and something more, to be the daughter of one of Delhi's greatest Senders."

Mara felt her tail go up and her ears rise in happiness. She had been imagining Tigris's life indoors, and thinking of her only memories of her mother. "If I am the daughter of a Sender," she said, her whiskers glad, "perhaps I am not so strange after all."

They left the canal, and Mara felt a lightness in her paws and fur. She let the last of the canal's sounds and smells touch her flanks, and then she said a silent goodbye to her old home.

Ahead, the warrior queen slowed abruptly, hunching up her shoulders, her vibrissae rising in alarm. She signalled to Mara to get down, and the Sender obediently dropped behind one of the abandoned termite heaps that dotted the verge. The two raised their heads, and Mara took in a deep breath, puzzled. It was a bird, but she could not tell whether it was predator or prey. It waddled along the ground, its talons digging into the dirt, and from time to time, it flapped its brown and gold wings.

"What is it doing?" she asked, confused. The bird seemed to be a young cheel, but Mara had never seen one of the great sailors of the sky on the ground before, so she wasn't sure. As she raised her whiskers inquiringly at Beraal, the bird bobbed up and down, pumping its wings more strongly, letting its gold-flecked wingtips graze the dusty ground. Mara squinted at it, narrowing her green eyes. The cheel had begun raising itself up and down, as though it were doing push-ups with its talons.

Beraal gave a soft, amused mew. "That's Hatch," she said. "Tooth's son."

Mara watched Hatch pirouette on his talons while he pumped his wings even faster.

"Is he wounded, or is that some kind of mating dance?" she asked, fascinated.

"Neither," said Beraal, though her own whiskers were twitching in laughter. "He's challenged in the flying department. Hatch?"

The cheel stopped dead in his tracks, and then he turned warily in their direction. He pushed his wings up awkwardly, peering at Beraal.

"We were just passing when we saw you," said Beraal, "so I thought we'd stop and say hello. How's Tooth?"

Hatch stared at her, his beak agape.

"I'm Beraal," she said patiently, "and this is Mara. We're friends of your father's, after a fashion."

Hatch closed his beak and mumbled something that might have been a hello.

Mara thought he might be annoyed that they had interrupted. "Don't let us stop you if you're practising your flying," she said, extending her whiskers kindly in his direction. "We can wait here while you take off. We don't want to stray across your flight path by accident. Besides, I've never seen a cheel actually take off from the ground, your dad and the squadron seem to live in the sky."

Hatch said, "Whatever," miserably, but he didn't move.

Mara stared at the fledgling, wondering what she had said to make the young cheel's feathers droop. He smelled tired to her, and truculent, and beneath that, he just smelled sad.

Beraal flicked her ears lightly and said, raising her whiskers only a little so that Hatch wouldn't be able to hear her, "Hatch has had some trouble—as I was saying earlier—in the flying department."

But Hatch had sharp ears. The fledgling drew his wings even closer around him and mumbled, "Can't. Don't wanna." Then he turned his back on them, ruffling his feathers with some meaning.

Beraal stretched her spine, savouring the feel of the sunlight on her back, and turned to go. "We won't bother you any more, young Hatch," she said, and began to stroll away.

Mara studied the cheel's rigid back, noting the sweep and strength of the wing feathers, the fully fledged tail feathers, the powerful muscles in his talons.

"A moment, Beraal," she said. The young queen stepped

around the termite mound, circling until she and Hatch faced each other. The fledgling clacked his beak, irritably.

"You can't, or you don't want to?" she asked.

Beraal fluffed her fur in warning. Hatch was Tooth's son, and far from being part of their clan, they weren't even the same species. His problems were none of their business. She had her whiskers up, and was about to let Mara know that they should leave him alone, when the fledgling spoke.

"Whatever," he said, but his golden eyes scanned Mara. "Who cares?"

Mara sat down, settling herself on her haunches and looking up inquiringly into Hatch's eyes. Beraal felt a sudden prickle of fear; the Sender had left her throat bare and vulnerable, and Hatch was a cheel, a predator with a sharp, lethal beak, almost fully fledged.

"You haven't answered my question," said Mara calmly. She began grooming her whiskers and cleaning her ears. "Can't? Tried and failed? Never tried? Don't mean to try?"

Hatch spread his wings out and then let them drop. Mara continued to wash herself, and after some time, she said, "I might care."

Hatch said, "Whatever?" cautiously.

Mara flicked the tip of her tail casually and stretched until all her muscles had been fully wrung out. "I was answering your question," she said. "I might care, because I'm curious. You look like a fine, fit, well-muscled young cheel to me, and it makes me wonder: don't you want to join the others in the sky?"

"Can't," mumbled Hatch.

"Oh no, Mara, don't do that!" Beraal's mew was anxious, her whiskers suddenly stiff with fear.

Mara ignored her. The Sender let her long white whiskers unfurl, slowly, until they brushed the very edge of Hatch's feathers, ruffling the pinions. The cheel clacked his beak furiously and raised his wings to their full span—but Mara continued with the lightest of strokes, and to her amazement, Beraal saw Hatch drop his wings. Instead of attacking the Sender, he shuffled from one talon to another, and combed his feathers out.

The cat and the cheel watched each other for a while, his golden eyes holding her green ones steady, and it was Mara who turned away, blinking.

"Your wings are fully formed," she said, "well-fledged and ready to lift you up into the sky, where you belong."

Hatch said hoarsely, "So what?" He made a half-turn, but he did not turn completely away from Mara. The mynahs chattered and squabbled on the low-running parapet of the canal, and the pigs grunted lower down as they jostled each other on the banks.

"See my whiskers?" Mara said, spreading her long white whiskers out, leaning forwards a little so that he could see the delicate, curved whiskers that graced her forehead as well. "They are as long and as white as your wings are strong and well-muscled."

Beraal, who was keeping a wary eye on Hatch just in case he should lose his temper—raptors were notoriously short on patience, and he was, after all, the son of Tooth and Claw—spoke. "Mara is the Sender of Nizamuddin," she said.

THE HUNDRED NAMES OF DARKNESS

"Her whiskers go further than ours can reach, and she walks further than any of us can with our paws."

Hatch blinked and preened his tail feathers, trying not to look impressed. "Yeah," he said, inspecting a talon. "Whatever."

Mara flicked her ears, listening as the first few cars and bicycles began to pass them, and as the Bigfeet inside their homes began to stir. She looked over at Beraal, and knew that her mentor was just as alert; they would soon have to leave, or risk tangling with the Bigfeet on their way back to their homes.

"We don't know each other, Hatch," she said, "but when I saw you, the first thing I noticed was not your wings; it was the way you looked at the sky."

The pupils of Hatch's eyes went so dark that they almost crowded out the gold, and the feathers on his pileum fluffed slightly.

"Don't look up much," he mumbled.

Mara let her gaze travel upwards, watching as the cheels performed a complicated set of arabesques, Claw leading one half of the squadron high above the canal, Tooth teaching the newest flyboys how to do double and triple rolls over the roof-tops of Jangpura.

"You try to keep your eyes on the ground," she said, "but every few moments, you can't help yourself—you take a quick look at the skies, at Mach and the rest exercising their wings. I know what that feels like. I used to play with my toys, curl up with my Bigfeet, but then I would stray back to the windows and doors, or let my whiskers stretch into the air so I could watch the cats of Nizamuddin. My whiskers took me anywhere

I asked them to, but my paws, like your wings, would not carry me out with the rest of my clan."

Hatch peeked at her, ruffling his wings slightly.

"You're out here now," he observed.

"The Sender didn't go out for all of her first year," Beraal said quietly, inspecting the termite mound. "She used her whiskers to connect with us and travel elsewhere, but she did not step out of her home until very recently."

Hatch took a few steps forward, bobbing up and down on his talons.

"Scared?" he offered.

Mara raised her whiskers again, and let them brush Hatch's feathers. This time, he did not flinch or call out in warning.

"I smell fear on your feathers, and it smells the same as the fear that I carried on my fur for so long, the fear that held my paws still instead of letting me join Beraal on her hunts, Katar on his long patrols, Hulo on his explorations through the dargah," she said. "But do you see the mynah, over there?"

He was marching up and down the length of the parapet, his yellow-stockinged legs flashing jauntily in the morning sun. His brown jacket bobbed up and down on the parapet, and the yellow legs gave him a dashing air, compensating for his garrulous chatter.

"See him," confirmed Hatch. "Hear him, too. Yammers a lot."

Mara rose and uncurled herself, shaking out her paws.

"He's not at all like you, is he?" she said.

"No!" said Hatch, horrified at the thought. He bobbed uneasily on his talons, rather faster than before.

"Then why, young Hatch, are you waddling around like a mynah, or a sparrow, or a Babbler?"

Hatch's eyes gleamed, the gold burnished by anger. When he called out, it was the keek of an adult cheel, not of a fledgling.

"I'm a cheel!" he said, and they saw the ripple of the muscles behind his feathers as he erected his wings.

"Then why aren't you up in the sky where you belong with the other cheels?" Mara said, her mew so quiet that Hatch had to lean forward to hear the young queen.

"Sky's so big," he muttered. "Might fall out. Besides, other birds don't like me. Tooth says I'm a freak. Not like Mach." He peered at Mara. "My sister," he elaborated. "Squadron Leader already. Started as Flight Lieutenant. Got promoted fast. I'm a cadet. Never flown. Don't like flying."

"From the time I was a kitten," Mara said, "I thought it was the fear that kept me inside. I had better whiskers than most, just like you have a broader wingspan than most of the cheels up there, and there was nothing wrong with my claws or my teeth, but the world seemed too large, too frightening, and I didn't want to meet the clan because they thought I was really strange."

"Yeah," Hatch said gloomily. He understood.

"But it wasn't the fear of the outside that kept me trapped at home, alone except for my Bigfeet and the few cats who visited me," said Mara.

Hatch leaned forward, rocking on his talons. His black and gold eyes were puzzled.

"You're looking at it the wrong way," she said. "You don't have a flying problem, and you're not really afraid of the sky, Hatch.

You might think you are. I thought I was afraid of the outside, but that wasn't what was wrong. You and I, Hatch, we didn't have a problem with fear, or being outside, or being in the sky."

"We . . . didn't? Uh. You said 'we,' like, us two," said Hatch, bobbing up and down.

The Sender stood up and stretched to her fullest extent, letting her own powerful forelimb muscles show.

"We have a memory problem," she said. "Until someone reminded me, I'd forgotten what I was. And you've forgotten what you are. You're not a sparrow, cleaning its feathers in the dust. And you're not a mynah meant to spend your life marching up and down on the ground, yammering at the other birds. You're a cheel. You belong in the sky. And most of all, you're a predator, Hatch. Remember that."

As Beraal and she left, they heard Hatch, talking to himself.

"Predator," said Hatch thoughtfully, testing his wings and flexing his talons, though he stayed on the ground. "Predator, huh?"

He sounded happy.

CHAPTER FIFTEEN

A Thuggery of Bandicoots

The course sprawled across more open land than Southpaw had ever seen, and he understood that it might take him many moons to discover the secrets of all its acres. In the daytime, he gave the Bigfeet a wide berth. He watched their antics, fascinated by the peculiar calls and the thwack of the club upon the ball; but he kept to the safety of the rough, and did not attempt to go too close to them. Early on, he had tried to make friends with one of them, retrieving a ball that the Bigfoot had smacked into the rough scrub; but the Bigfoot began yelling and thumping, and didn't seem pleased at all. Since then, Southpaw had left them alone. He slept in the old monuments that dotted the greens, ignoring the susurration of the wings of the bats, who stirred in their sleep when he came by for his afternoon naps. Hunting was rich and easy, and though Southpaw kept a wary eye out for the large rat snakes and cheels, he found few predators. His whiskers sang to him every morning of the hidden delights of the day ahead, and he often woke up at night with the fur on his paws prickling in anticipation of whatever he might find, meet or hunt under the benign gaze of the moon.

Far away from the place where he had met the bandicoots, a grove of fig trees overlooking the fifth hole became his base. The branches of the intertwined ficus trees offered shelter to owls, squirrels, bee-eaters, parrots, coucals, treepies and dozens of different insects. He often slept in its shade, and at night, when he was tired of roaming the course, he explored the tree itself. He was soon on good terms with a family of scops owls who uttered soft, pleased whuks when they saw him.

The Horned owls, Hobson and Jobson, were less friendly, but they did not attack the tom. He felt their yellow eyes on him sometimes at night, and he often watched them, too, learning from the swift, deadly skill with which they hunted rats, moles and shrews. It was a good life, a comfortable life, but often, he raised his nose and sniffed at the air, as though the scent trails of the clan and the warm smell of Mara's fur would be conjured up by the intensity of his longing.

"HOW LONG WILL IT take me to get home?" he asked Thomas Mor when he met him next, pointing with his whiskers in the direction that whispered to him most of Nizamuddin.

"Where's the rush, young whippersnapper?" said Thomas, striding ahead, his plumes bobbing behind him. "If it's the wall you mean, it's no more than a few days' journey—half a moon, I'd say, because you'll have to stop and rest that paw of yours, young fellow. Yes, yes, you never complain, that would be bad form, but it slows you down, doesn't it? Fine over short distances, but you couldn't cross more than one hole a day on the course without needing to rest. I twisted a claw once, when I was a young nitwit of a bird—tried to steal a golf ball off the greens, it was so white and so tempting, what—and it was dashed agony, having to hop around like a hoopoe."

Southpaw stopped when the peacock stopped, both of them watching the Bigfeet practise their shots. The safest place, he'd begun to realize, was behind the Bigfeet—except for the novices, who were easy to spot because they smelled nervous and made the most racket of them all. There was no safe zone around the beginners, who were capable of landing golf balls anywhere at all. One stepped up to the tee, and flailing his hands in a way that reminded Southpaw of a beetle knocked over on his shell, struggling to get back up, hit the ball with immense force and no judgement at all.

Southpaw and Thomas, settled comfortably in the shade of a ruined tomb that stood near the tee, watched the ball rise almost vertically into the air.

"What goes up must come—oh well, apparently not," said Thomas philosophically, as the white golf ball disappeared into a koel's nest.

There was a mellifluous cry of surprise from the nest, and a brown-and-white dappled head rose, daintily. "Which admirer has left such rare gifts for me?" said the koel, trilling.

Thomas hunched slightly, trying to avoid being seen by the koel. "Kooky's very sweet," he muttered to Southpaw, "but she's not quite—you'll see what I mean. She's a sub-tenant of the bulbuls, in a sense—steals their nest whenever they're away."

"Was it you, darling Thomas? My absurd little bird, too shy to speak your heart!" the koel trilled.

"Worms and grubs and centipedes!" Thomas said under his breath, but he raised his superb head, bowing so that his emerald crest bobbed in Kooky's direction.

"I cannot claim credit," he said. "It was the Bigfoot over there. He's having trouble with his tee shots."

"Of course he is!" said the koel, her sweet voice trilling gladly. "Of coooourrrse he is! Love will do that to a bird, or a Bigfoot, and it is the season of sighs and songs. O Bigfoot! Thank you for your fine gift—see how love overtakes him? See him run, for fear that he will look up and swoon at the very sight of his beloved? Such a dear little Bigfoot! Such a shy little Bigfoot! Had a bird ever had such a lover?"

Thomas let out a stifled cry of annoyance. "He's off to the second hole, Kooky, he's taken a mulligan because he can't find his ball. Er. He can't find his ball because you're sitting on it."

"The lover leaves for fear that he will betray himself," said Kooky simply. "As for the gift—I would be a cruel harpy indeed if I spurned the gift of an egg! Shall Kooky break her lover's heart, even if he be Bigfoot and perhaps too large to share her love nest with any degree of ease? No! I shall love the egg he has left behind; if I cannot have him, no matter. I shall have his fledgling when it hatches."

Thomas raised his tail, and the dazzling colours flashed out for a moment. The peacock almost danced in exasperation.

"Kooky!" he said. "We've been through this last year, haven't we? That's not an egg, it's a golf ball! It isn't going to hatch!"

The koel uttered a reproach, her song liquid, beautiful and running to several verses.

"It did not hatch last year because he was not the right one!" she said, her feathers smoothing protectively over the golf ball. "He was not worthy to give me an egg. But this Bigfoot—how long has he come to this very hole, day after day, hoping for no more than the right to hear a few nazms, a few couplets, from my beak? I will sing to his egg. I will sing to the egg that he has left me, as a token of his undying love, and you'll feel so silly, won't you, when it hatches."

"I'll feel extremely surprised if it hatches, Kooky my sweet," said Thomas drily. "But I wish you joy of your nesting. We'll be off, then."

"It must be so," said Kooky, a trifle dramatically, flinging her tail feathers up and spreading her wings over the nest. "My lovers all leave me, because they cannot bear to see me return the favours of another. Go, Thomas, we shall meet again, you know you always come back, like a moth to a flame."

"I always come back, Kooky," said Thomas, his voice rising to a screech, "because this is the first hole! All of us who patrol the course start from here!"

Kooky laughed, a tinkling, musical sound, her beak clacking in perfect rhythm.

"They all say that," she said fondly to the golf ball, tucking it in under her feathery backside, in between the bulbul's eggs.

Thomas said nothing until they were safely out of earshot, and then the peacock stopped in the green hedges between the third and the fourth hole, letting out an anguished shriek.

"That's better!" he said. "The peahens refuse to come to the first hole any more because she drives them bonkers. But there's no harm in our Kooky, it's only that she flutters so. We're right at the edge of Mashie's territory—you've met him, of course?"

"Not often," said Southpaw, his whiskers dropping, his mew tinged ever so slightly with regret.

Southpaw had met Mashie and Niblick. Like Mulligan, they were friendly enough, bright-eyed, purposeful cats who patrolled their territories with much care, and extended their hospitality freely to strangers. But the Golf Course cats lived an entirely different life from the Nizamuddin clan. The land teemed with everything a cat might need—prey, shelter and water, and there were few natural predators, barring the Bigfeet. There were few cats, too, and each kept to his or her own territory, meeting infrequently if at all. They rarely linked, using their whiskers only in times of emergency. The clubhouse cats, led by Colonel Bogey, were kind enough, but their lives revolved around the Bigfeet who worked in the kitchens, and Southpaw shuddered as he saw how easily they let themselves be petted. They were sleek, feeding on the rich scraps from the Bigfeet's plates, but the brown tom could not understand why they would choose to sequester themselves in the confines of the clubhouse when there was so much else to explore.

"What was your life in Nizamuddin like, young chap? Living among all those Bigfeet, no greens, no open spaces—can't have been easy, what?" Thomas had trouble trying to imagine a life away from the calm spaciousness of the Golf Course.

Southpaw sat down, and washed his fur as he tried to help Thomas understand, the bird grubbing up worms from the ground for a light snack as he listened.

"The Bigfeet aren't easy to live with, true," he said, his whiskers waving outwards as he remembered. "We often hid from them on the rooftops, and we feared their loud voices, the harm they could do with their feet, their blows. None of you know what it is like to go hungry here, or to search for clean water."

As he talked in low, soft, reflective mews that were almost chirrups, the sounds and smells of home, the constant thud and grumble of traffic, the Bigfeet's unpredictable ways, the difficulty of hunting for prey when the prey itself was starving or too thin to be worth the trouble—all this and more came back to him. And in a great rush of longing, everything he missed came back to him, too: the skein of caring that connected the cats, an invisible but unbreakable thread. He could almost feel the shadows cooling his fur as the cheels of Nizamuddin sailed overhead, hear the slow sensual melodies and the quicktempo, warbled ragas of Qawwali and Dastan clearing their throats as they taunted the dogs in the dargah. And he could feel Mara's whiskers brushing his own; he remembered how good it had felt to be able to come to the Sender after a long night's hunting or patrolling, to nestle into her soft orange fur and be washed until he fell asleep.

"We were all so close," he said, and absently, his paws kneaded the ground as he shared his memories. "I miss them so very much, especially Mara. I wish I could tell them where I am."

Thomas spread his tail out, the high plumes allowing him to hear everything Southpaw said, and much that the tom hadn't put into mews, but that drifted out into the summer air on the tops of his whiskers all the same.

"If you never went back to your clan, could you be happy here, Southpaw?" he asked.

The brown tom felt the cool grass under his paws; even in the worst of the summer, the Golf Course held secret patches of coolness and comfort, and he knew without having to ask that there would be ample shelter for all who lived here through the monsoons, ample protection from the biting cold of winter.

"What creature could not be happy here?" he said, but the scent of sadness rose briefly from his fur. "There is good hunting, and peace; the Bigfeet do not crowd us or bother us. The trees and the shrubs would make a thousand cats happy; the air is filled with calm, and birdsong, and at night, the bats tell tales that make my whiskers rise in laughter. At home, we had to fight for every scrap that we could call our own, and often the moon would sink in the morning, and the sun would come up, and my belly would hang to the earth, still empty for all the night's hunting. I have had a full belly since I came here, but . . ."

He stopped, and washed his tail furiously.

"A full belly, but an aching heart," Thomas finished for him. The peacock shuffled his claws uneasily, raising and lowering his magnificent plumes. He turned his sinuous head and answered the distant call of one of the Mors, asking them to wait for a few moments.

"Your whiskers do you proud, my striped friend," said the peacock. "They hold the scent of the clan, despite the comforts of the course. Oh well, I had hoped you'd be our guest at least till the monsoons—what beauty, Southpaw, as the rains roll across the courses, and we have most of the greenery to ourselves, since the Bigfeet stay away in the heavy downpours. But if your heart draws you home, I have nothing but respect for that, old son. I'll get the Mors to show you the softest path to the wall, and from there you'll have to make the crossing back home yourself. Whiskers up, we'll soon have you home, though why you would prefer the Bigfeet with their giant termite heaps when you could have this, I don't know. Don't suppose we can persuade you to stay—no? Very well, then."

They were approaching the sixth hole, taking a thickly overgrown path that wound past one of the abandoned pepperpot tombs. It was late afternoon, and the worst of the heat had left them. Here in the shade, the grasses whispered to Southpaw to stay; he saw a rat snake wriggle off in the distance, startled by their march through the long shrubbery, and knew he would miss this earth, the many riches of the course, the abundance it so freely offered the creatures who lived here in the wild places strewn among the Bigfeet's manicured greens.

Thomas's plumes started to rise off the ground at the exact moment that Southpaw felt his whiskers stand up in warning, and his fur trembled all the way down to the skin. The yowl that rent the air was long, anguished and familiar.

Thomas wasted no time with screeches; he skittered along the ground, his plumes streaming in the evening breeze, and

Southpaw followed him, careful not to press down too much on his injured paw.

The ixora bushes shook, their dark, silky green leaves parting sharply. Mulligan shot out from between the branches, snarling, his eyes wide as he howled. Shock radiated from his whiskers, so strong that Southpaw flinched, as though his own head had been soundly smacked.

"My home!" the Bengal cat howled, spitting and spinning through the grasses. "They have my home!" His rosettes rippled as the evening sun fell on the three, illuminating all of them, setting Thomas's plumes on fire until the grasses seemed to flash blue and green.

Southpaw's fur shivered, and then he smelled it—some distance away, towards the water hazards where he and Mulligan had first met. Rising up like a black, oily fog, overpowering the light lure of the golden magnolia flowers and the sweet smell of the grasses, stronger than the markings of the bats who had made the pepperpot ruin their summer home, there was the unmistakeable stench of bandicoots.

"A Mor! A Mor!" cried Thomas, beginning to dance. His high shrieks silenced Mulligan, the Bengal cat trembling as the peacocks picked up the call along the length and breadth of the course.

"They will not challenge you," said Mulligan, coming back to himself now that he was in safer territory. "They won't come into your territory, or stray across Henry's boundaries. I should have trusted my nose, I should have listened to my whiskers. They told me that there were too many of them; the stink from the burrows, when I finally got there! But this place is so large, I've been over in the south corner all spring. So many of them, so many new families added over the winter, over the spring, so many runs and burrows across the place that you can't make a dash for it without twisting your paws! And the pythons have gone! Gone, killed, I don't know which; there were only the broken shells of their eggs, and a few scraps of snake-skin, as dried up as the eggshells were old and covered with dust. They won't risk a war with your kind, Thomas, they're cowards, after all. But they have my home; they've moved in, lock, stock and snout. It belongs to them, my part of the course, and given the numbers of them coming in every day—the tunnels, the new roads they've built—they might threaten Mashie or Niblick. Curses on them all!"

His fur was trembling, but the Bengal cat had recovered some of his poise. When he washed his paws, he took care to go over the claws, and to make sure that every knot of fur on his rosettes was licked back into place.

Thomas stopped dancing, but he kept up the warning shrieks for a while, and by the sound and the distance of the responses, Southpaw understood that the peacocks were drawing a boundary, re-establishing the lines of their terrain for the benefit of the intruders.

The evening breeze changed direction, and the filthy, oily stink came back so swiftly that it almost gagged Southpaw. His tail swished back and forth, and then he met Mulligan's gaze, and the brown tom understood.

"It's the bandicoots," he said. "The bandicoots have attacked."

Mulligan turned, his proud form silhouetted in the evening light, his long tail swinging from side to side.

"They won't stop there," he said. "Moonch and Poonch want all of the course—every bit that doesn't belong to the Bigfeet—and there aren't enough of us cats to drive him and his kind out. Soon, this will belong to the bandicoots, too. They've been coming in for many moons, from all over the city."

He and Southpaw spread their whiskers out, and the evening breeze confirmed what they smelled: not a dozen runs, not a few large burrows. There were more than a hundred bandicoot runs already on Mulligan's old territory, and they smelled the fresh-turned scent of newly dug-up earth. The bandicoots were taking over.

CHAPTER SIXTEEN

The Sender of Paolim

T he night was muggy, the heat of summer making the air oppressive, and Mara's dreams were uneasy, flitting from one blurred image to another.

The bats chittered past, brushing her fur the wrong way with the edge of their wings. "Everything must go," said Theda, her snout sniffing at the hot winds of summer, her pearly fangs bared in a snarl. "I smell heat and dust and blood and sadness. Leave, Mara, leave."

Southpaw scrabbled under a pile of dried leaves and earth, emerging from a deep burrow marked by the telltale tracks of bandicoots. "Couldn't you find me? I've been here all the time, such a long time." He reached towards her to caress her neck, mewing, but the leaves made a dry sound, like twigs or bones scraping together, and the pile flew up to cover him. She heard his paws scrabble desperately, under the leaves, but no matter how much he flailed, his paws and then his beseeching brown eyes slowly disappeared as he sank back into the tunnel, and all she could hear was the sound of his claws, scratching under the uncaring earth.

Kirri's giant shadow loomed over her, the mongoose's obsidian eyes flaring as she displayed her long, sharp claws. "When the trees bleed, it's time for you to go," said the mongoose. "Hurry, but remember the hunt price."

"The blood price?" said Mara. In her dream, Kirri was three times her size, so that the cat could see each silver bristle, the scimitar curve of her claws. Kirri slashed, and Mara felt blood well up on her flank. There were three gashes, deep and painful.

"We all bleed, Sender. Blood is easy to spill," said Kirri, "The hunt price will be higher." Her voice was fading, her fur rippled into the dust.

Perhaps it was the intensity of the dreams, or perhaps it was just the heat. But when Mara woke up, the Sender's whiskers had taken her elsewhere.

Her whiskers caught the scent of clouds pregnant with rain, the musk rising from damp earth, the subtle silver-and-blood fragrance of fish and frogs. Mara blinked, but the world she had woken into refused to shift back into the solid outlines of her room, the Bigfeet's house, Nizamuddin. Light and water, the water iridescent with the last of the twilight glow from the sky; clouds rolling across the horizon, backlit by crimson and gold rays as the sun sank down over emerald fields, and beyond it, the sweetly black, fragrant river. Her paws were damp; she lay on rough, unpainted boards, and overhead, a pair of kingfishers flashed by, stabs of blue and gold in the monsoon downpour.

There was the lightest of touches on her whiskers and the Sender flinched, her own claws extending in instinctive response.

"Something told me I hadn't seen the last of your fur," said a familiar purr. Magnificat stretched, shifting so that she moved back under the shelter of a wooden ledge—just as battered as the boards, its cheery blue paint cracked and peeling—closer to Mara. The two Senders, one's fur still bleary from sleep, the other's vivid green eyes flashing as they caught the reflection from the lightning, were far back enough to stay dry as the early monsoon clouds rolled across Paolim. The rain drummed on the waters of the Chorize, and the narrow fishing boats moored to the buoys in mid-river bucked and spun, like flying fish.

Mara used her paw to smoothen her fur, realizing that she hadn't groomed since that morning. "My whiskers seem to like your village, Sender," she said. The smell of the fatigue she'd felt earlier clung to her fur, but she could feel some of her alertness returning. On the other side of the river bank, Mara saw the undergrowth darken and become an even more vivid green as the rains sluiced down. She straightened her whiskers, enjoying the fresh, clean bite to the breeze, so different from the Delhi air, and scrabbled as she turned towards Magnificat, meaning to apologize.

"No need," said the Sender of Paolim, her fat, fluffy tail flicking away a few stray raindrops, "you were sleeping when you landed—smacked down from the sky in a perfect landing, I noticed. Quite impressive, but it doesn't explain why you keep coming back. It's like having a kitten following me around in a year when I didn't plan on having a litter, except that no normal kitten would insert itself into my best fighting and fishing moments."

Mara jerked as the thundering roar of the ferry's engines started up, cutting in over the drumming and hammering of the rains, but she recovered herself quickly, curling her tail around so that she could groom the mud out of it.

"Magnificat," she said, letting her mew stay as meek as possible, "my sendings are not in my control, my whiskers often lead me into trouble. I don't know why they keep bringing me here, but we are both Senders; perhaps they want me to learn something from you."

Magnificat's green eyes gleamed. "I teach no one," she said, and her purr had menace in it. "None of my kittens have been Senders, Mara, and I had to learn how to handle my whiskers on my own."

Mara asked, "Didn't your mother teach you?"

Magnificat watched the ferry push away from the far bank, turning in an ungainly arc, the rain spattering its cheerful blue decks.

"I was born near the sea as the gales raged and the ships sent their anchors down fathoms deep, as the waves lashed the shore, or so I was told," she said. "My mother was too frail for childbirth, perhaps she had caught some illness; she did not survive, and my whiskers recall not even the faintest trace of her scent. A fisherman found me, and took me back to his boat. He had a cat, an old sea salt who loved riding out with him when he took his nets out, and she was kind enough to me. It is from her that I know the story. He was caring, as Bigfeet went, but careless, absent-minded. When I was not yet old enough to say more than a few meeps, he took me to the fish market as a treat, and haggling over a fine kingfish, he forgot he had brought me there."

The ferry bucked as it cut through the waves; the rain had swelled the river's waters, and the tide came almost to the jetty, where the two cats sat, the white fur and the orange fur close together.

Mara listened, her eyes intent. "Come," said Magnificat, strolling closer to the edge of the jetty. "We'll cross, I have business on the other bank."

They stepped on to the ferry, walking past the pilot, who gave Magnificat a friendly if respectful pat. "Here," said the Sender of Paolim, settling herself comfortably on a fat coil of rope, "this is my place." Mara's paws were curling, despite herself; the orange cat had never had to walk on a surface that rocked gently (and sometimes not-so-gently) underneath, and she felt most unsettled. But she found a comfortable spot, in the centre of a discarded lifebelt. The Senders watched as a few Bigfeet trickled on to the ferry, the rain streaming off their umbrellas.

"They'll take some time," said Magnificat. "The Bigfeet never seem to listen to the tides; they have to see and hear the ferry before they come out, and I often wonder why they don't listen to the water instead of waiting for the boat."

"My friend Southpaw says it's because they don't have whiskers," said Mara.

"That would explain a lot," said Magnificat, cleaning her own, fine set with some pride. "Poor creatures; they have no fur, either, and that can't be comfortable in any season, going around like cats who have the mange. So now you know my story."

"But you hadn't finished!" said Mara, her green eyes hoping for more. "When did you know you were a Sender? How did you learn to manage your whiskers?"

Magnificat stopped washing her whiskers and started on her paws. "I had no idea that I was a Sender!" she said. "The fish market was welcoming, to kittens as well as to cats, and you could grow fat on the scraps from just the morning's work—sup lightly on scales, snack on bones, feast on discarded fish heads. The Bigfeet threw away the best bits, but then they're like that, there's no telling which way they'll jump next. I often woke up and found that I'd sent myself from one fishmonger's stall to another and had to twitch my whiskers to come back. As I grew older, my sendings grew more ambitious, and sometimes I'd wake up on a fishing boat, sometimes I'd wake to find that I was hovering above the fishing nets. But I had no mother, no siblings; I thought this happened to every kitten."

"Me too," said Mara quietly, but the ferry engine sputtered into life just then, and her mew was lost. The river stretched out on either side, its shining, rain-fattened waters slapping against the stern of the boat, like a marine lullaby.

"As my whiskers grew, so did my journeys, and some of them were rich and strange indeed," said Magnificat. She had gone back into the past, and her whiskers raised, she shared her stories with Mara. There was the time when she'd interrupted the quiet evensong of a cluster of dignified Portuguese church cats with her loud wails, and the time she had inadvertently tumbled into the middle of a merry party of market cats. On one memorable occasion, she had been chasing a mouse, and found herself sending in mid-pounce, arriving in the middle of

Carnival to hover over a giant papier-mâché lobster. Often, she had discovered herself sailing with the fishing fleet, her whiskers yearning for the sea as much as her paws yearned for the river. But she had little control over her whiskers; they were as wayward as the wind.

"It used to be that they led, and my paws followed, even if I didn't mean to go on a sending," said Mara, and Magnificat, startled, brought herself back into the present. The fine vibrissae over her eyes stood up as she surveyed Mara. The ferryboat's pilot went down into the engine room, starting up the ferry.

"A Sender who drops in without willing it, her whiskers longer than most," said Magnificat, "needs something, even if she doesn't know what it is. Your fur smelled of understanding, also recognition, when I was telling my tale. Who trained you, Mara, or were you untrained as well?"

"I never knew my mother, though she was the Sender of Nizamuddin before me. Tigris and I parted ways when the dogs attacked her under the canal," said Mara. Her scent changed as she thought of the past, of that terrifying time before the Bigfeet gave her a home. "Beraal taught me what she knew of sending and helped me with whisker control; but she is not a Sender, though she and the old Siamese warrior, Miao, understood what it meant to be one."

"Solantulem told me what it meant to be a Sender," Magnificat said, her purr tender as she talked of the friendly tomcat who had strolled out from a smart cafe in Susegad one day and shown her the sights. For Magnificat, accustomed to a life split between hunting on the red roofs of Paolim and fishing off the banks of the Chorize, or sailing further down where the fishermen put their boats out to sea, the lives of the cafe and restaurant cats were a revelation. Most of them struck deals with the cafe owners, bartering their services as rat catchers for scraps and leftovers; they lived well and partied hard, their voices often raised in raucous song along the balcaos and rooftops of Susegad. "Solly," she said, as they stepped off the ferry, "had been something of a jazz aficionado himself, scatting with the best of the Bigfeet. He'd known Saudade, the legendary Sender of Goa, and Solly put it so well, one night when we were hanging out with the boys on the roof of the local bar. He said, "What do you think, Green Eyes, your whiskers send you places just because it's fun? You're a Sender; when your whiskers send you somewhere, it's for a reason, or because the clan needs you to roam further than the cats can on their own four paws."

BACK ON SHORE, THEY strolled back, chatting amicably.

"When did you know what it meant to be a Sender?" asked Magnificat, bounding up the stairs that wound up the low hill towards a church. She stopped when she reached the red stone porch, settling in under the eaves as though she belonged there. Mara checked when some Bigfeet tramped up the stairs, wondering whether they should leave, but Magnificat offered her head to be scratched, and kneaded her paws in pleasure when the Bigfeet obliged. "Most of the ones here are friendly," she told Mara, who was watching in astonishment. "You need to watch out for a few, but many of them like our kind."

Mara let the calm of the place seep into her fur; the cool evening breeze, fragrant from the rain, the emerald fields that stretched out as far as the eye could see, buffalos moving placidly across the muddy earth, the ferry's low reassuring honk in the distance, the egrets circling like friendly winged spirits overhead.

"Begum explained what it meant to be a Sender," she said, combing her whiskers out, "but it was only after I stepped out into Nizamuddin, and felt what they felt, hid with them from the Bigfeet—ours are not as gentle as yours—and learned what it was to hunt for prey that I became their Sender. But a Sender is supposed to help the clan, and I cannot help them out of the trouble they face this summer."

Magnificat, who was licking her white fur and repairing some of the damage done by the rain, looked out across Paolim.

"A Sender cannot prevent trouble, especially the kind that drags along, bumping in the dust behind the Bigfeet," she said, her whiskers gleaming as they caught a few raindrops. "I learned early on that I could not stop kittens from falling into the river, or from being hunted by little banded goshawks. I could not stop toms from brawling too freely in Panjim and having the Bigfeet chase them out with brooms or worse; there is nothing Senders can do to help cats who squander their lives by stepping onto the highway without looking left and right, or those who fall from the palm trees, who slip on the tiles of the roofs."

Mara felt her whiskers fall, her tail droop. From the time she had first seen Magnificat, whirling as she fought a cobra on the roof of a Paolim house, there had been something about the Sender's fierce spirit that had drawn her strongly. Magnificat swaggered through her territory, as though the roofs, the ferry, the fields, the walls and even the Bigfeet belonged to her. Until she felt the disappointment in her whiskers, Mara had not realized how worried she was about the Nizamuddin clan. What had drawn her back to Magnificat again and again was the feeling, deep down inside, that Goa's fierce Sender, this fearless white cat, would know what to do.

"But if you are any kind of Sender, then you will also learn that there is more you can do for the clan than you suspect. Not long after my whiskers had turned white, there was the incident of the fishing cats further off, by the sea. The Bigfeet had stopped going out with their boats, and the cats were growing thin, their ribs beginning to show, for lack of their usual fare. They asked me to wave my whiskers at the Bigfeet, and make everything go back to the old ways."

Mara widened her green eyes, staring at Magnificat's impressive whiskers. "But even I can't make my whiskers get through to the Bigfeet!" she said. There was awe in her mew.

"Neither can I," said Magnificat. "But there was little point telling the fishing cats this—since I was friends with the fishermen, purring at the Bigfeet when they talked to me in their loud booming voices, the clan would not have believed me. Instead, I sat out on the seashore with my whiskers stretched wide for an entire night, and in the morning, I said to them that the sea had whispered its secrets to me. The sea had said that it was tired of the fishermen's boats, and it was sending them back to shore; the Bigfeet would go back, since the waves had rejected them, and the seafaring cats must keep the Bigfeet company in their hour of need."

The rain had slowed to a drizzle, and the faint trembling of her fur told Mara that her sending would end soon. The Senders watched a group of children run laughing up the road, splashing through the mud and spinning round and round in the last of the showers.

"They believed you?" said Mara.

"They did indeed," said Magnificat, yawning and stretching her forepaws, "and it worked out very well for them. As the Bigfeet shifted inland, the cats became foragers and hunters in their villages, chasing palm rats and shrews over the thatched houses, settling into the lanes near the marketplace. The ones who had fishing in their blood, and whose fur could not settle without the sound of the sea, they stayed with the fishermen, or became ship's cats, but the rest settled without fuss elsewhere. They did not need my whiskers, or any sendings; all they needed was for the Sender to tell them what they already knew, deep in their hearts and their tails, had to be done."

"My clan has to leave Nizamuddin," said Mara, and a sudden shiver ran the length of her fur; this was the first time, in any of her mews or purrs, that she had claimed the Nizamuddin clan as her own. "The Bigfeet have built their houses over the old hunting grounds, and there is neither food nor water, nor room for the next generation of kittens. They cannot roam the roofs the way they used to, nor can they live on the ground in peace. They have to go, and they look to my whiskers to tell them when and where. But though I walk through the streets and neighbourhoods of Delhi every day, in my sendings, how shall I know which is the right place for the clan? And how shall I take them there? What clan moves out of its territory?"

Magnificat's eyes took on a ferocious gleam as she eyed the sudden emergence of clouds of insects, dancing over the puddles that the rain had left behind. "The prey will be fat and juicy after these rains," she said. "I wish you could come hunting with me, but even the most real of sendings has its limits. Mara, I have never wished to be any Sender's teacher or mentor, and you cannot follow where my paws have taken me as a Sender anyway. But I smell your caring for the clan on your fur as you tell your tale, and that is all that matters."

Mara stretched her own paws, and stood up, preparing to end the sending. She felt a little disappointed, but also soothed, as though Magnificat had washed her fur and untangled the knots that had been bothering her.

"I cannot give you advice," said Magnificat, her tail swishing from side to side, "but if your whiskers have brought you this far, then they will know where your clan should go next. Trust them; let them lead you, and when you reach the right place, your blood will sing yes, your fur will settle itself, your paws will relax and let you rest. As for the clan, perhaps your Delhi cats are not used to moving, but in Goa, our clans let the winds take them where they will. Some cats have lived in one village all their lives, and we say that they cannot bear to lap the water from other wells, but many shift like the sand on the beach, becoming a shack cat in one season, a ferryboat cat in another. The clan will move, never fear; they have paws, all they need is for your whiskers to show them the way."

The palm rat stood up on its hind legs, sniffing worriedly at the wind. Magnificat's eyes glittered.

"Caught my scent," she said, cheerfully, "now to give it a sporting chance. Rat! How fast can you run? If you reach the foot of the stone cross before I do, I promise I won't eat your tail, otherwise beware the bite marks."

And she was off, her long tail swinging jauntily in the monsoon winds, like the whitest of white banners.

"Goodbye, Magnificat!" called Mara as she shimmered out of view. "And thank you!"

Mara's fur felt warmed, her whiskers settled as she ended the sending. She heard the splash of the river, and then she was back in her house.

THE SENDING HAD BEEN exhausting—she had gone too long a distance, stayed too long. Mara swayed, aware that she was falling asleep on her paws, and then the floor came up obligingly to meet her. The Bigfeet were there; she heard the click of their shoes as they came to her side. Their concerned voices reached Mara from an immense distance away, and she dimly felt them touching her nose, to see if she was unwell. "There's nothing wrong with my nose," she wanted to tell them, "it's only the tiredness of sending and summoning, that's all." But though she opened her mouth, she fell asleep before she could mew. The Bigfeet cradled the Sender and carried her back to her basket.

When she heard the sounds, Mara struggled to open her eyes, though it felt as if a thick blanket lay across her eyelids. Her whiskers strained to rise, and gave up. She turned, wrapping her paws around her head so that they covered her ears, and she fell down the black well of sleep. The Chief Bigfoot came in to check on Mara, worried that the sounds from the house—made by packers, who had cardboard cartons out in the bedroom and the kitchen, and had already emptied the living room—would have upset the cat. But the Sender slept heavily, her ears closed, her ribs moving in slow, deep breaths.

She woke once, rising unsteadily to her paws, the fatigue wrapped so tight around her that she didn't attempt to smooth her sleep-ruffled fur. Her whiskers would not rise; her bones ached, and Mara shuffled over to her litter box and then her water bowl with legs as stiff as if she'd been a venerable old cat with white covering her muzzle.

The sound penetrated slowly through her tiredness. The babblers, led by Sa, were singing their hearts out in the park. Mara listened, her ears twitching, but it took a while for the meaning of their song to sink in.

"So long, farewell, please let us take our leave

We have overstayed our welcome in Nizamuddin, we believe

The Bigfeet have chopped our old homes down and built over everything

Eviction notice has been served, so now we must take wing

But thank you for the grubs, thank you for the trees

Thank you for the shrubs, and for our days of ease," trilled Sa, Re, Ga and Ma.

"No need for sadness, no need for doom and gloom

We're shifting nearby only, backside of Humayun's Tomb

Any time our old friends feel like a change or rest

Please feel free to invite your good self to be our honoured guest

One small advance tweet, to check our nests are not indeed full?

And to welcome all of you, we shall gladly do the needful," finished Pa, Dha and Ni.

The babblers hopped onto the top of a bus, settling themselves with much fluttering of wings and gentle squabbling over seats on the luggage that was lashed to the racks. Mara saw two grey, striped shapes join the babblers; Ao and Jao snuggled up together on a lumpy sack that contained cabbages. The bus rumbled by the park every day, swinging across the road towards Humayun's Tomb. The cats hated cars and buses, and preferred the long walk to the tomb, but the birds often took the bus to visit the endless stream of cousins and second cousins once removed from a different nest or branch of the family who lived in the peaceful, verdant gardens that surrounded the old monument. The Sender watched numbly as the squirrels and the babblers left, unable to do more than send a tiny twitch of farewell in their direction.

She knew she would feel bad about the babblers and the squirrels leaving Nizamuddin later, but at this point, her whiskers were leaden, unable to sense or feel very much. The Sender stumbled sleepily into the drawing room, looking for her Bigfeet.

Mara stopped at the edge of the carpet, her tail waving uncertainly back and forth. The furniture that she used as scratching posts, appreciative of the effort the Bigfeet made to provide her with the best, had been wrapped in thick layers of cardboard. The bookshelves stood empty; large cardboard cartons were stacked one upon another. It was a disturbance, a rearrangement of the order she was used to, and even through the fog that had enfolded the Sender, she wondered uneasily what it meant.

And then she forgot about the crates, as the smell reached her nostrils, making them flare, washing every last speck of fatigue away. Mara was wide awake, her blood racing, her tail up and lashing from side to side. The air of Nizamuddin was thick with smoke, and when Mara twitched her whiskers, she smelled green sap and sawdust, the acrid odour of smouldering wood and bark.

CHAPTER SEVENTEEN

Ashes and Departures

K atar used the roughest part of his tongue, rasping at his fur savagely, pulling at the knots and smoothening them out, but it was of no use. Woodsmoke infiltrated his fur; the ashes had mingled with the grey, and no matter what he did, the smoke clung to his skin and to his whiskers. It would not leave him, any more than it would leave Nizamuddin.

His attention was caught by the harsh keek of an adult cheel, calling out its protest against the smoke curling upwards into the air. The cheel was a handsome bird, his gold-and-brown feathers dappling the blue sky, and he flashed past the roof-tops, using the merest flick of his wingtips to skim around the columns of smoke. Something about the way he flew seemed familiar, but Katar couldn't place the bird. He assumed the cheel was one of Tooth's new flying officers.

A prickle touched his whiskers, reminding him that he was late. The tom gave his fur a last, hopeless tug, combing the ashes out as best as he could with his paws. Checking once for Bigfeet, he let his whiskers unfurl, wearily getting onto the Nizamuddin link.

"How bad is it?" he asked without preamble. "Beraal, Hulo, Qawwali?"

There was a crackle on the line as Beraal joined in. Tiredness poured from her whiskers, too, and Katar could feel it even if he couldn't see the black-and-white hunter. "The kittens are all right," she said. "There was no risk of fire—the Bigfeet were only burning branches and twigs—but the smoke got into Ruff's eyes and Tumble's nostrils, so they both needed attention. We're staying out near the canal, though the pigs have left. They've gone upstream."

The canal's waters upstream were a thick industrial sludge, so tarry that Katar had once, at the height of summer, seen a family of pigs cross through the waters as though they were wading through mud. It stank of the harsh aroma of petrol.

"It's bad in the parks," said Hulo, his mew rough with exhaustion. "The whine of the saws hasn't stopped since morning. The trees have lost their limbs, the sap pours down their bodies, and the small fry have either left or sought cover. Not that there's much cover left if you ask me. The babblers have already gone along with Ao and Jao to Humayun's Tomb. Ao tried to fight the Bigfeet, if you please, as if they would pay much attention to something his size, but they cut down his tree anyway."

Katar felt a weight descend on him, as though something heavy had pressed down on his fur, and it was some moments before any of them spoke. Ao and Jao were the oldest of the

THE HUNDRED NAMES OF DARKNESS

squirrels of Nizamuddin, residents since Miao's time, and were among the very few of their kind who had outlived predators for almost eight years. Katar's whiskers trembled as he imagined the squirrels chittering, forlorn, in the bare fork of their tree, deprived of the shelter of the branches, the comfort of the places where they stored their stocks of food for winter, the company of their friends, the mynahs, the baya weaverbirds, the bulbuls.

"The nests?" he asked, dreading the answer.

"All gone," said Hulo, and the link crackled with the tom's sadness. Hulo was a great stealer of birds' eggs, and considered unprotected nestlings fair game, but he and the mynahs also exchanged gossip, and he loved their concerts. He would sit on the roofs, adding his own loud voice to the mellifluous musical soirees of the bulbul family.

The birds would leave, too, Katar thought.

Qawwali took over, his mew slow and heavy. "It has not been so bad for us at the dargah," he said, "there were few enough trees here, so the Bigfeet had less to chop down. But, Katar, the young toms of our clan have been leaving all through winter, and while it is traditional for them to go off on long hunts to prove their worthiness, many have not come back. They have chosen to stay in Khusro Park and turn pigeon-fanciers; to settle down in the shade of the bungalows where the Bigfeet live beyond the overpass; to move further and further away from the place where we thought they would raise their litters. The smoke has driven deep into the dargah, and while the old alleys can support the few of us who are left, it is only us who still stay—the ancient families, Katar. There is my family; Dastan and his boys have a corner of the Ghalib Academy to themselves; even Abol and Tabol talk of moving."

He coughed, and Katar could sense how badly the smoke had affected the old warrior; the grey tom's whiskers rose in sympathy, as they heard the harsh rasp of Qawwali's chest.

"I worry about the rats," said Qawwali, his whiskers quavering. "Time was when I could despatch them with one swift blow, and when they would scurry away at the merest whiff of our scent. But now they are growing bold, Katar, there are no young warriors and queens left in the dargah. If it was not for Tooth and his companions, they would strut around the streets as though the fragrance shops sold perfume only for their wretched tails! But such is life. One mustn't complain too much. If you'll excuse me, Katar, I will take my leave. Must do something about this cough, it makes me sound like a wild dog, not a respectable old cat, yes?"

After he left, Katar had to will himself to continue.

"What shelter and food do we have left for the summer?" he said. "In the parks near the dargah, there is little enough left. The trees have been stripped by the Bigfeet, or torn down to make more of their houses."

"The rats and the garbage dumps," said Beraal, "that's all we have left."

"It's bad this side," said Hulo. "Beraal's litter is the only one that survived this year, but when Tabol talked to me of leaving, she said many of the young queens felt that there was nothing left for them in Nizamuddin. Especially the ones who had seen their litters waste away from hunger, or had their kittens killed by the Bigfeet's cars. What can we do, Katar?"

Katar's whiskers sagged, but he made himself come back onto the link.

"You know what we have to do, Hulo," he said.

"Leave Nizamuddin," said the black tom, almost growling. "But where shall we go? Qawwali would share his food with us gladly, but there isn't enough. There won't be enough when next season's kittens come along."

The air seemed to shimmer with heat, and they felt a ripple of electricity go along the link, as though a strange cat had leaned in and touched her whiskers directly, tip to end, to their own.

"Nizamuddin cannot hold the clan any more," said the Sender, joining the link. "If you stay here over summer, the older cats will die, and few of your kittens will survive the time from the monsoons into the winter. The trees have been whittled to matchsticks, and if there is no room for the birds, there will soon be no room for us."

"Us?" said Katar. "You live with the Bigfeet, Mara."

"Indeed, I do," said the Sender. "But I have walked through Nizamuddin often, sometimes with Doginder, sometimes with Beraal. My nose is almost dead from the stink of the smoke the Bigfeet have spread today, but if you will let me, Katar, I would like the pleasure of greeting you formally. May we touch noses and tails?"

On the roof, Katar's ears prickled as he heard the approach of another cat. He turned, rising as he swivelled. An orange cat with bright green eyes watched him with interest, her long whiskers signalling friendly greeting.

"Hello, Katar," she said. "I thought it was time we met, since I've already met Hulo and Beraal. I wasn't alone, Hulo, Doginder saw me to the stairs. He's gone off for a long run—he wanted to get the stench of the burning wood out of his head, but he'll be back soon."

Beraal felt her whiskers swell with pride. How far her pupil had come, she thought, from the days when a tiny orange kitten struggled to control her wayward sendings, and feared setting a paw outside the safe boundaries of her home.

Katar lowered his head, and let the Sender brush his fur. She did so very carefully, touching his whiskers only lightly with her own, but he felt an electric crackle—the Sender's power—course through his fur all the same.

"It is good to see you out, Sender," he said.

"I should have come out sooner," she replied, her mew grave and sad.

"You are here now, little one," said Hulo over the link. "But what can the clan do? We are not birds that we can take to the air and fly wherever we please."

The Sender stretched her whiskers out, so that they could all sense her over the link, the three clan elders, the dargah cats listening with some curiosity, the little queens, the toms.

"We have paws," she said, "and whiskers. They can take us further than you might think. In my sendings, I have seen much of Delhi. The Bigfeet may have shredded the shape of your old lives in Nizamuddin to pieces, but there are other places."

A young queen, one of the skinny market cats who was often seen tagging along with Tabol's family, broke in on the link.

"We can't lope all over the city looking for places that suit us better," she said. "Who will find these places for us?"

Katar took over the link, his whiskers suddenly calm and strong, despite the acrid air, the heat, the emptiness of his own belly.

"You forget," he said, "as we all had forgotten in the years of plenty. When Tigris grew silent and retreated to her Bigfeet's house, none of the clan suffered. The prey waxed fat in those days, and the Bigfeet in the market fed us instead of showering us and the strays with kicks and curses. We have forgotten what it means to have a Sender of Nizamuddin. Your whiskers are longer than ours, Mara."

The rumble was so loud that every cat in Nizamuddin heard it: the sound of heavy machinery, digging up the stumps of the trees; then the whine of the saws started up, the noise making their whiskers ache.

"For all of our sakes," said Beraal, before the link shut down and the cats went back to their business, "I hope your whiskers will tell us what to do before the worst of the heat hits, Sender."

KATAR SAT SLUMPED, HIS fur dull from the ashes. He watched the Sender spread out her whiskers. "For Southpaw?" he asked. Beraal had told him that the Sender scanned the skies every day. "Yes," she said. "It is hard to find one cat in a city this large—hard enough to hear only our kind, when you have the chatter of the monkeys, the stray dogs, the slow speeches of the cows, the clamour of the birds, not to mention the Bigfeet. But there are so many clans of cats in the city; so many of us slipping silently through the lives of the Bigfeet. Southpaw might have made his home with any one of them."

Katar blinked, and combed his whiskers, trying to imagine the city that lay outside the boundaries of the canal and the tomb, beyond the lines of scent that had marked the borders of his life and the lives of the clan for as long as he could remember. He knew about the other clans near Nizamuddin, but had met only those who had passed through on their journeys elsewhere.

"Have you visited the clans around Nizamuddin recently?" he asked.

"All of them," said Mara, thinking of her last stroll, when her whiskers had taken her to the back of Khan Market, where the restaurant cats took long naps in the shade and occasionally taunted the busy, bustling, anxious government colony cats. "The Race Course cats near Safdarjung's Tomb are very dashing, but the stable cats have had many litters this year, and our clan is too large to be welcomed. There is the clan who lives near Isa Khan's Tomb, but they are very solemn, and seldom mew loudly, and the kittens would disturb them greatly. The clan who lives near Ashram is very friendly, but they throw midnight parties—you've heard their late-night caterwauling—and enjoy their brawls very much. They would feed us, but they would fight us just for the fun of it. The Supreme Court cats, Affit and Davit, have extended their deepest regrets over the situation in Nizamuddin—that's Affit, he always talks like that—and suggested that we join them in their chambers whenever we like. But unfortunately, their Bigfeet have shifted from paper files to computers, he says, and there has been a running shortage of rats for some moons; we would not want to add to their troubles."

Katar listened, his ears flicking in interest. "Why would the rats be affected?" he asked, diverted despite himself.

"Davit says that the rats like nibbling on fresh matters. The computers give them nothing to eat—the wires aren't tasty—and the old cases are too dry."

As Mara continued, a map of the world outside the one he had already known began to take shape for Katar. He felt his fur settle, and he curled up, allowing himself to rest. For the first time since winter's sharp teeth had settled into their flanks, he began to believe that the clan would find a way through this tangle.

The grey tom looked out over Nizamuddin. The Bigfeet's homes on this side, near the cool, vast lawns that surrounded Humayun's Tomb, were calm and relatively untouched. But Katar had spent some of his youth here, and remembered a time when he and the other hunters would have been able to cross the roofs without effort. Now the buildings went up so high that only the monkeys could even begin to find a way through the jungle of cement and brick. All over Nizamuddin, the greenery he had remembered, had disappeared over time, leaving behind this bare landscape.

The heavy, humid wind assaulted their nostrils yet again with the stink of bonfires, and Katar tried, unsuccessfully again, to scrub the smell out of his fur with his tongue. His whiskers tingled; he could not imagine staying on in Nizamuddin any longer, even though he could not see where the clan might go.

HULO HEARD DOGINDER'S EAGER bark before he saw him. "Hang on a tick, Hulo," Doginder called. "I'll come around the back—oh wait, shortcut."

The tomcat, pausing on the stairs that led to the Sender's house, closed his eyes and flinched as Doginder charged the bougainvillea hedge. "That's too high, Doginder," he said.

"Not at all!" said Doginder, panting as he made his run-up, his tongue flopping out in between barks. "Now that I've switched from being a Rescue Dog to being a Guard Dog, I've been practising leaps and bounds, this is going to be— ouch, all right, maybe not." Stuck in the middle of the hedge, Doginder wriggled with all his might, trying to get his belly out of the branches. He made it, finally, and bounded up to Hulo, knocking over a small cactus in its flower pot with his tail. "Just as well Ao and Jao aren't here, they'd have been calling me all sorts of names by now. I miss them, though they seem to have settled in at Humayun's Tomb quite happily—one of the mynahs brought a message. Has the Sender shared her plans?"

"Not yet," said Hulo. "She's busy with her Bigfeet; says that she thinks they're moving house."

He hunched his fur around him, feeling miserable, though he didn't want to share his sadness with Doginder. There were too many creatures leaving Nizamuddin, he thought. The babblers, the squirrels he had known for most of his life, and now the Sender.

Doginder's tail stopped its joyous waving. "Mara's going?" he said in dismay. "I wanted to tell the Sender that I'd been offered a position at the dhaba. Guard Dog, you see, they need someone to deal with the rats, and they picked me! No leashes, no chains, all I can eat, though I have to say there's a limit to how much leftover butter chicken you can take, and so long as I chase the rats off, I'm free to do what I want. Must say it's a relief, I'd been on short rations for a while. That's changed, see?"

He turned to his side, so that Hulo could see how rapidly his jutting ribs had been replaced by the beginnings of a promising paunch.

"Impressive," said Hulo. "So your lot have also had trouble finding prey?"

Doginder sat down and scratched behind his ear. "Ever since winter!" he said. "The prey's thinned out, not that we could survive by hunting alone—I've often wondered how all of you manage. The garbage dumps used to be reliable joints, if you don't mind fast food, but there's been too much competition this year, what with the rats lining up at one end and the monkeys swinging by whenever they get chased out of their neighbourhoods, the crows, the mice. There isn't enough for anyone but the Bigfeet in Nizamuddin any more. I'd have had to leave if the job hadn't come through."

He scratched with considerable thoroughness, and added, with great pleasure, "Good job, that, and I've made friends with a young chap. Fine pup, wants to grow up to be a Ferocious Attack Dog, since I've resigned from that post. I have a new designation now. Which do you think sounds better? Guard Dog, Dhaba? Official Guard Dog? Guard (Official) Dog? Yes, that sounds about right. G(O)D, Dhaba, Nizamuddin."

"Excellent," said Hulo. "I'd better be off, Doginder. Glad you've found a nice billet."

"Me too!" said Doginder. "I would hate to leave Nizamuddin, no matter how much it changes. I was born here, just like you."

Hulo's whiskers went up. "You feel that way, too?" said the tom, his battered ears swivelling towards Doginder. "My whiskers drop when we talk about leaving. I was born in the alleys of the dargah, and the smells of meat and perfume, the bustle of Bigfeet, the clamour of the call to worship and their raucous chatter every morning as they set up their shops, the cheels overhead, even the stinky canal—it's hard to make my paws believe that we'll have to leave."

Doginder trotted alongside Hulo.

"It's easier for some of the dogs," he said. "They don't mind. They said that if we'd been pups at a breeder's place, we'd have had to go to different houses anyway. And the pedigrees say that the Bigfeet separate them from their mothers; they leave home almost as soon as their eyes open. They're right, but I like it here, even if the Bigfeet do make a ruckus. I like breathing the air of home."

They parted, but Doginder's bark echoed in Hulo's ears for a long while. "The air of home," he thought, his whiskers cast down, "the air of home." He felt the thinness of his own ribs as he walked, the slack folds of his stomach hanging down. The previous night, he had gone over to Beraal's, and watched Ruff and Tumble assuage their hunger pangs by licking at a plastic bag, which had a ghost tang of milk. The food he brought back was no longer enough, and though Beraal was back to hunting, she, like the toms, had nothing to hunt.

Custom held them in its claws; he had met cats outside of Nizamuddin who thought little of hunting songbirds or mice they had grown up with, but the clan followed the old traditions. They slaughtered pigeons mercilessly, considering them vermin, like the rats. But they would not kill the bulbuls or the mynahs, nor would they do more than occasionally tease the babblers or the squirrels; the songbirds were not fair game, and even in a summer of starvation, none of the cats had considered changing their hunting habits. This was a question of habit more than kindness. Growing up in a time of plenty, he, Katar and Beraal had been taught to stalk only birds who flew in from elsewhere, visiting strangers. As the old trees went down, one by one, the flame trees and the fig trees, the neem and the laburnum and the silk cotton trees, there were fewer birds in Nizamuddin, especially those that could be considered prey. The flocks of plump pigeons who had once been so plentiful that they fluttered like grey, noisome clouds around every rooftop, dwindled, and then disappeared.

There was no help for it; the clan would have to leave, and now that the Sender had become so much closer to the clan, perhaps her whiskers would tell them where they would find home next. Hulo could feel in the depths of his fur that this would be a killing summer, a deadly monsoon, and his blood whispered to him that he could not stay; and yet his whiskers rippled insistently into the past, bringing back memories that told him he could not go. The hunger that gnawed at him every night was one matter; the sight of Beraal's kittens, with their slack bellies, Tumble's lethargy and dull eyes, was another. He padded off towards the market, walking more slowly than he usually did, mapping the neighbourhood—the park, now dusty and dry in the absence of grass and trees, where the Bigfeet played games of cricket, the empty place where the Cobra's Tree used to stand, replaced by a three-storey building. He marked each curve of the road, each bend in the canal, breathed in the tang of mutton curry and garbage, jasmine blossoms and tar, not realizing he was mapping the scents of Nizamuddin, storing them up against the day when they would be forced to leave.

MARA POPPED HER HEAD out of a cardboard box and growled at the Bigfeet. "I am going to live here forever," she told them crossly. "Don't imagine you can win me over with your fancy scratching posts and those intriguing toys you're dangling over my head! I don't want to leave my house!"

The Bigfeet cooed at her sympathetically, and one of them squatted near the box, dangling an enticing toy inside it. Mara turned her back on them, digging up the cardboard floor mutinously.

"How could you do that without asking me?" she said, ignoring the way in which the toy—a green felt mouse attached to a red plastic wand—smacked her hopefully between the ears from time to time. "All I had to do was nap for a little while, and you pack up everything? You haven't even asked if I'll miss the park. All right, it was a crowded park and I had to dodge the Bigfeet, but it was mine, wasn't it? Go away. Quit swatting me with that admittedly fine, irresistible toy—hey, wait, don't take it away! Come back! That's my green mouse, you hear? Give it to me!"

Soon, she was batting the mouse around the carton, delighted with the thwacks it made. Her Bigfoot jerked the mouse up and

Mara pounced at it, happy to see that the strength had flooded back into her paws and limbs. The mouse skittered off the sides of the carton and bounced in the air. Mara wriggled her backside and chased the toy, flying around the new sofas that didn't smell at all of either the Bigfeet or her own fur. She made a note to herself to fix the scent problem, and then the green mouse popped up from behind the sofa. "Game on!" she said, mewing ferociously.

The mouse squeaked and scurried across the ground, the Bigfeet careful not to step in between Mara and her green felt prey. For a moment, the Sender thought she should lower her whiskers and stalk off, just to show them how upset she was at the idea of leaving Nizamuddin and the clan, but then the red wand rose enticingly and the green felt mouse whirled across the doorsill. Mara laid her ears back and shot across the sill. Before the Bigfeet could draw it back, she had it, and was lying on her back, batting it between her paws. She wrapped her whiskers around it, and smelled the catnip inside the mouse. "That's a dirty trick," she said to the Bigfeet, who had followed her out onto the balcony. "You know I love catnip! I know you're trying to bribe me, and—this is delicious."

The game allowed her to relax, but later, Mara stared unblinkingly out over the park, thinking of Beraal. She had dodged the traffic and braved the dogs to go and see her mentor, not wanting to leave with the Bigfeet without making her farewells. Beraal had raised her head wearily; her black-and-white fur was matted from the humidity, and she had not bothered to untangle or comb herself. "They're underfed, Mara," said Beraal, "and my milk is almost at an end. If we don't find hunting grounds soon . . ." Mara had understood that the Clan would face some hardship, but Beraal's next words had helped her see how grave their situation was.

"We must leave Nizamuddin now," Beraal had said. "It will be hard, our claws will dig into the soil and try to hold on as we walk away, but I have nursing kittens. And if they are to survive, then my whiskers say we must leave, or else Ruff and Tumble will die before the monsoons. I cannot hunt for them as well as myself; there is not enough food for all. With the Bigfeet's racket and their incessant construction, we've lost almost all of our old shelters. At the height of summer, when the heat is at its most fierce, Hulo, Katar and I will have to choose. Do we hunt for the clan, or do we hunt for our own survival? If we come across prey, or stray scraps from the Bigfeet, will we link and let all of the other cats know? Without us, the clan will not survive; but even with us, the clan will have to fend for itself through the worst months. The old and the ill will die. Those who are injured in the next few months will die. And most litters will not survive."

Mara's fur had gone cold, despite the heat of the evening. She had known this, but the despair in Beraal's mew made it seem inevitable. The wind blew hard, a dry, desiccating wind that rasped like a fevered tongue across all of them.

"The right place is close by, Beraal," she said. "I can feel it in my whiskers."

"Take us there soon, Sender," said Beraal, curving her belly protectively around her kittens. "Another few days of starvation, and these little ones won't be able to stand up, leave alone walk."

Mara had left with Beraal's mews ringing in her ears. She ate well, and when her Bigfeet cuddled her, she butted her head lovingly against their legs, forgiving them for deciding to move out of Nizamuddin without consulting her. They switched on the air conditioner. She sat in front of the vents, letting the cold air ease the terrible heat of the day, and she purred at her Bigfeet. But the Sender's thoughts returned time and again to Ruff and Tumble, and how they had lain there so still and listless while she and Beraal mewed and murmured.

The next day, when the packers began loading her Bigfeet's furniture into the truck, Mara shivered, but she did not protest. And when she was placed gently into her cage, she did not yowl, or send the few remaining squirrels dropping from the branches of the trees with the force of her sendings, as she would have in the past. Instead, she raised her whiskers, and linked once.

Katar was out on the walls of a Bigfeet's house, hoping to steal some small scraps of meat from the wedding feast that was being prepared. Hulo, sitting with Qawwali in a quiet courtyard in the bustling dargah, paused in mid-conversation. Beraal looked up, pausing in the middle of washing Tumble. The Sender's mew was calm and her whiskers steady, as she bid them farewell. "This is your Sender speaking," she said, and all around Nizamuddin, the cats listened to the young queen who had finally claimed them as her clan.

"I don't know where my Bigfeet are taking me, or where you will make your next home, but I'll send to Katar and all of you when I do know. This has been a long, hot summer for you, a season of desperation and ashes. But even the longest summer ends; the rains will soon be here, and I promise that you will welcome the monsoons from your new home. Hunt as best as you can, eat as much as you can. Keep your strength up, and make sure that your paw pads are well-cleaned and toughened. You'll need them for the journey ahead."

Doginder left his post at the dhaba to race behind the Bigfeet's car, offering his friend a 21-bark salute. Behind him, a tiny stray with long ears and solemn brown eyes pelted grimly in Doginder's wake, taking his duties as a Ferocious Attack Pup very seriously. Then the car turned the last corner, and the truck rattled off behind it, and Nizamuddin's Sender was gone.

WHEN MARA WOKE UP, she was in her old basket; the stuffed monkey that had been her only friend before Southpaw had marched in to her room so long ago stared up at her, its glass eye winking; but the house smelled different.

The Bigfeet laughed and scratched between her ears, and scratched under her chin, and Mara wriggled on the cool marble floor, as happy as a kitten. She stretched, letting her tail extend to its maximum length, and looked back at the living room. If you put a few scratches into the covers on those new sofas, and knocked a heap of books over so that the friendly chaos of the old house was retained, Mara thought, it might feel like home. It was bigger than the old place, and there was more room for her to scoot around on her belly. Her worst fears had been assuaged that morning when the doorbell rang, and the Chief Bigfoot came in. Mara was very impressed with the powers of the Chief Bigfoot: she hadn't been in the car, or in the trucks that had brought the Bigfeet's furniture, so she must have navigated between Nizamuddin and whatever this new place was on her own.

The Bigfeet were leaving the room, without her permission, yet again. One of their worst flaws was their inability to recognize that they were supposed to ask her before they ended a play session, but Mara made allowances for them. The house was new, and they, too, might take some time to settle in. And the balcony, much wider and larger than the small terraces in her previous home, beckoned. The Sender settled herself into the cool earthen embrace of a flowerpot, tucking her tail and paws in neatly.

A jarul tree formed a hospitable roof, spreading its wide branches over the balcony. Some of its lush mauve blossoms had fallen on the floor, and Mara found that they made respectable scratching pads. Java plum trees, white fig trees and white frangipanis bent their heads together in the large park that faced the house. She heard a few Bigfeet, and saw their cars drive by, but this place seemed much quieter than Nizamuddin's bustling, noisy streets had been. The jarul branches caressed the balcony, forming a natural ladder on one side, while a goolar tree with its scaly bark and red figs offered a staircase on the other side.

She wondered whether to spread her whiskers out, to let them scan the area for her, but she was still cramped from the cage and the car journey. The goolar staircase was tempting, and Mara padded down its twisting length, deciding to go for a short stroll wherever her whiskers wanted to take her. Perhaps she could even tell how far she was from Nizamuddin. Downstairs, she yawned, stretching until she had stretched the sleep out of her fur. She cleaned her paws thoroughly, then raised a hind leg above her ears, to make sure that she did each side with care and attention. She watched the road until she was sure that she understood the Bigfeet's rushing, intermittent traffic patterns. Then she crossed, and when she found a break in the long high wall that ran the length of the road, Mara went through.

The place felt strangely familiar, in a way that told her she had travelled these routes before through her sendings. She spread her white whiskers wide, her green eyes abstracted as she took in the scents of the air; this place was home to dogs as well as Bigfeet, but the only clan of cats she could find seemed to be much further away. She wrinkled her whiskers at their scent trails. Instead of criss-crossing each other, with the rich overlay of smells and scents forming a tapestry, the cats who lived on the other side of the road appeared to roam vast swathes of territory on their own. Their brisk, no-nonsense scent trails met only at the borders and boundaries of their terrain. There were other networks of scents hovering in the background—the intricate lacework left behind by clusters and clans of bats, a heavy, oozing set of trails, thick as ropes, strung out across the terrain, that indicated small predators— but so many, Mara wondered? The links between birds of different feathers opened up, shining like skeins of spider silk, as delicate and as intricately woven. This would bear exploring, the Sender thought. She let her whiskers lead her through the greens and the roughs, but she didn't attempt to steer her whiskers in any particular direction.

The dargah tugged at Mara's vibrissae so suddenly that the Sender was taken off balance—so she wasn't that far away!

337

A few of the Bigfeet's roads stood in between her and Nizamuddin, but her old home was perhaps a day, perhaps two days' journey away, as the cheel flew. Beraal's quiet purr came back to her, one of the pieces of wisdom the warrior queen had passed on during their training lessons: "Never measure distance by the way a crow flies." Mara, curious, had asked: "But why not? Don't crows make long journeys?" "They do," said Beraal, "but as for whether they'll take the straight route or some road that twists like an earthworm in the rain, depends on the crow. Watch the cheels instead; they fly straight and true."

The Sender's whiskers twitched uncertainly, making a hesitant foray into the long line of trees and bushes that lay behind a monument. And then the tips of the whiskers began to vibrate as if they were reaching for something. The high red walls of the monument beckoned to Mara; acacia bushes rustled, their dry branches telling her to hurry up.

The Sender's paws brushed against the thick, tough scrub, and led her into a world of green and grass and trees. In the branches of a white fig tree overhead, a sleeping peacock screeched once, and went back to its dreams. The Sender let her whiskers sweep past the greens, their soft velvet grass ringed by shrubbery and high trees. The moon shone down on the Golf Course, and illuminated the monuments where the bats made their homes. Something pulled her on, though she dearly wanted to explore. There were tangles of scents; owls, watchful and wary, the sinuous paths of rat snakes and keelbacks, and then black ropelike tracks she had picked up before. The Sender had a sudden flash of understanding. Bandicoot runs criss-crossed parts of the course, winding through it the way the yellow ropes of ambar bel, the strangling creeper, would sometimes cover and then choke a tree.

But her whiskers wouldn't let her stop. They drew her on, deeper and deeper into the course, and the moon shone even more brightly, and the Sender felt something in her fur rise and prickle with sudden happiness. "Over here," her whiskers whispered to her; and as she hovered over the roots of an ancient banyan tree, she knew why she had come so swiftly across the way. The tips of her whiskers tingled, as though they had been caressed by the brush of a head she knew so well, and had missed so much.

"I couldn't believe my whiskers when they caught your scent. But it is you, Mara, isn't it?" said the dear, familiar voice. She saw his shape, and Mara felt her tail rise in the air, her whiskers spread out in gladness. The brown tom, sleek, alert, a full-grown warrior, turned, and the moonlight caught his striped flanks and the scars that covered his ears and sloped down across his nose. The Sender's cry of greeting rang out over the Golf Course, waking the baya birds and startling the owls. She had finally found Southpaw.

CHAPTER EIGHTEEN

Twists in the Tunnel

The white ball soared high, clearing the water hazard effortlessly, skimming the glossy canopies of the khirni trees.

"Shot!" called Thomas, the peacock's plumes raised in approval, the eyes on each feather nodding in applause. Southpaw stared at the ball, following its descent automatically, calculating that it would reach the greens and roll within a foot of the fluttering flag where the rest of the Bigfeet stood.

Mara's head appeared from behind Thomas's tail. "Why are the Bigfeet hitting balls with sticks?" she asked. "The Bigfeet in Nizamuddin use their hands and feet."

Thomas shuddered, his plumage rustling green-and-gold. "Your Bigfeet back there were probably playing something else. Volleyball, or football, or one of those games," he said, making them sound like diseases. "This is golf. And that was a great tee shot." The peacock craned his sinuous neck, trying to see where the ball would land.

"I see," said Mara, her green eyes following the ball with interest. "Did the Bigfoot mean to send it into the middle of that burrow? Only it looks like he'll have to use the other end of the stick to dig it out. It's gone in deep."

It had, and they watched in surprise as the soil crumbled even further. A whiskery brown snout popped up. At the edge of the green, the Bigfeet yelled, shaking their clubs at the bandicoot. But before any of them could reach the burrow, the bandicoot had fled underground, absconding with the golf ball.

Thomas' screech must have carried from the second hole all the way down to the seventh, at the other end of the course. "That ball was in play!" he called to the bandicoot, his claws kicking up the dust as he danced in anger. "It mustn't be moved, shifted from the lie or otherwise tampered with, you mange-ridden, rat-faced, short-whiskered thug, that's against the rules! Don't you know anything about golf?"

A brown tail made an insolent gesture in the peacock's direction, before disappearing from view.

"That is the best shot I've seen all morning," said Thomas, his temper showing as he opened and closed his plumes, snapping his tail around like a fan. "And that dashed beast had the infernal nerve to disrupt a possible birdie! No, an eagle! I've a good mind to report him to the Committee!"

Mara had been tracking the subtle bulges of the earth as the bandicoot made his escape.

"You'd never find him," she said, her nose following the

scent of the fresh-turned burrows. "That run goes deep and long, under this green and all the way beneath that hill over to the next one. They're all over the course, aren't they? Why haven't you killed them yet?"

Thomas Mor's eyes flashed as he stared at the Sender. Mara made him uneasy. First, she'd popped up over Southpaw's ears, and settled above the branches of a tree. He found that disconcerting; he liked his cats to stay on the ground, instead of behaving like blasted bats or birds, popping out from mid-air. Then she'd physically strolled in to meet Southpaw, instead of doing that dashed sending number that made the feathers around his eyes and his crest itch madly, which was an improvement. But she had taken him and the other peacocks aback, by extending her long, fine whiskers and picking up on the lay of the land as though she'd been living here as long as the clubhouse cats.

"Your greens—where the Bigfeet play their games—are surrounded by scrub and thick forests, aren't they?" she had asked at once. "Do the Bigfeet use all of the land, or only the parts that they've groomed so neatly?" And of course she was right; the Bigfeet seldom ventured into the tangled bushes that grew near the boundary walls, and they left the beautiful old ruins alone, for the most part. "Only some parts," he had said, puzzled. "So who runs the course?" she had asked. "The peacocks, of course, but who else? The owls? The birds of prey?" Thomas had bobbed his tail indignantly. "Your kind does," he said. "It's the cats and us." The Sender had been polite about it, but he'd caught the twitch of dissent on her whiskers, he wasn't some young peachick with unfledged quills!

"Indeed," she said. "Then how is it that the thickest and most extensive scent trails belong to the bandicoots? The Mor clan's trails are clustered in parts of the course; the scent trails of the cat clan barely show up, they're as faint as the trails of the koels, and they run in single lines—one cat to every two of your golf holes, by the smell of it."

He had not liked that—bad form, swaggering into someone's territory and telling them who was the boss of what, especially when she'd got it all wrong. There had always been cats on the Golf Course; it belonged to them (and the Mors) as much as it did to the Bigfeet. Perhaps there'd been this little business of the bandicoots; his brother Henry Mor seemed to have got his feathers into a flap, squawking about how they'd overrun the place, but Henry had hated all rodents ever since he'd eaten a dodgy rat and spent three days repenting at leisure. Thomas knew his duties, though, and he'd brought it up with Colonel Bogey, back at the clubhouse.

The majestic black cat had yawned and said, his purr soothing, "Kind of you to mention it, Thomas, but really, aren't we making a fuss about nothing? You don't see any bandicoots showing their whiskers over here in the clubhouse, do you? They aren't ordering the Bigfeet around, are they? Not eating up the T-shirts and the tees and the golf balls in the Pro Shop, mmmm? If you ask me, they'll hang around for a bit and get bored. Bandicoots, they're the sort you find infesting racecourses, stables, public parks. Golf courses? They wouldn't know their irons from their woods, my dear chap. Yes, yes, I know all about Mulligan's unfortunate incident. But—just between my whiskers and your feathers—he's not one of us, is he? Those Bengal cats, so excitable. The pythons—really. Whoever heard of a bunch of rodents knocking off some of the toughest snakes in the world? Did you know their ancestors came from Burma? Must have gone off for a spot of vacation, mmmm, but the idea that bandicoots got the pythons is, frankly, ridiculous. Nothing against Mulligan, such an imaginative fellow, what? Not really the clubhouse type at all, though of course he'd be welcome to drop in for a plate of fish fingers, do let him know I said so."

That chat had made him uneasy—the Colonel was such a snob—and Mara's query only increased his discomfort. Thomas took a half-turn around the edge of the scrub. From the tilt of Southpaw's whiskers, he could tell that the brown tom was turning Mara's question over too: why hadn't the bandicoots been killed?

"We cleared a few runs out of the area that we patrol," Thomas said. "Henry and the rest of the gang spent a day or so, but it wasn't that hard. Odd thing, but they abandoned their runs fast enough, almost as soon as we killed the first few. I suppose they don't like the smell of their own blood being shed."

Mara settled herself on the dry grass, watching the Bigfeet as they milled around.

"Where did they go?" the Sender asked.

"Go?" said Thomas, startled. "I have no idea, Mara, I didn't ask them to leave me a blasted forwarding address. We told them to clear out, and they did."

Southpaw fluffed out his whiskers, addressing the peacock. "I know where they went," he said. "They moved into the old rat burrows near Mashie's territory, and they built new ones."

He turned his head, displaying the scars that criss-crossed his fur. "I had to fight a bunch of them the other day. Mashie thought he'd cleared them out, but they're cunning creatures. They waited until he'd moved on—there's only so much territory he can patrol on his own—and they shifted back into the runs. They were startled when they caught my scent, but they grew belligerent when they realized it was only me. I rousted them out of their burrows, but I haven't been there for the last few days. Something tells me they're probably back in residence."

The Sender raised her whiskers, and Thomas watched her uneasily, as the vibrissae trembled delicately. The heat touched Mara's fur, and for a moment, her intent orange head seemed incandescent, as though flames rippled over it.

"They are," she said. "But, you'd better see this for yourselves. Thomas, will you walk with me?"

The peacock swung his tail back and forth, but the Sender had already started off, skirting the fairway of the third hole. They were, he realized, moving crossways, towards the fifth hole. A well-dressed mynah peered at the party, startled, and continued on its afternoon saunter across the scrub.

"I haven't been here for almost a full moon," said Thomas, looking around with interest. The first, sixth and seventh holes were his territory, while Henry and the cousins hung out on the tenth, eleventh and twelfth holes. The clubhouse lay behind them, as they made their way up to the massive trees that lined the fairways; he heard the reassuring chatter of wagtails, and saw a few stray hoopoes.

The Sender stopped at the edge of the scrub, her whiskers indicating that he and Southpaw should look out at the course.

"Everything seems in order, Mara," Thomas said, puzzled. The greens were undisturbed, if a little rough. The bunkers were smooth and all seven of them seemed well-raked. He wondered what the Sender wanted them to see, and then his plumes went up. Seven bunkers? Seven of them? He couldn't remember offhand how many there had been the last time he'd come this side, but surely there couldn't have been more than three, or four at the most?

"So this is where they've set up their home base," said Southpaw. The tom scratched at the grass, staring at the expanse of sand ahead of them. He stropped his claws with the eagerness and frustration of a born warrior who knew that this wasn't the right time to go into battle, but who had the enemy well in his sights.

Thomas turned away, and then back, but the vision that met him stayed the same. The three extra "bunkers" weren't sand traps at all, and hadn't been built by the Bigfeet. The white sands that heaved before their eyes had been part of the green before it was stripped of its grass, and the creatures that made the sands undulate were bandicoots. A black sea of them, their runs spreading like a blank, white gash across the greens.

The peacock called out, a despairing screech that made the few Bigfeet on the green raise their heads and listen.

"They can't just scurry in here as if they own the place! If they're here, and if they're infesting the Barakhamba, the other tomb buildings, and half the courses, they'll be at the first hole and the clubhouse soon enough!" he said. But even as he screeched, he was making calculations.

"Too many burrows," he said, lowering his tail so that it was held parallel to the ground. "Even if Henry, me and all of the peacocks across the Golf Course tried to dig them out, we wouldn't be able to tackle all of them. And we'd draw the Bigfeet's attention, if we waged our battles during the day. And you don't have enough cats to take this lot on—begging your pardon, Southpaw—but there's not much you, Mulligan, Mashie and Niblick can do against this sort of invasion. Perhaps if the clubhouse cats joined in—but no, even assuming the Colonel decided to join us, there still wouldn't be enough in the way of troops."

He lapsed into silence, pecking absently at the ground, so preoccupied that he didn't even bother to chase a grass snake that had strayed into the area. The snake checked when its tongue scented the peacock, and it fled, making wide, wriggling loops across the fairway.

"What we need to tackle this lot," he said, "is either two extra prides of peacocks—hard to get, mind, though I suppose we could ask over at Tughlaqabad whether some of the distant cousins would care to fly down—but it's a long way off to the forts, and I don't know how many of the pride remains in those old ruins. Pity we don't have a proper clan of cats, what the course used to have, way back then. Those were the days, Southpaw; you had one family to every hole, sometimes large ones, and it did my tail feathers good to see the kittens tumbling around the place. Kept the rats on their toes, they did.

But there's no point expecting Mashie and Niblick to produce a clan out of thin air, what?"

Southpaw's brown eyes met Mara's green ones, and they held each other's gaze, a question passing between the two cats, asked and answered.

"We have a clan," said Mara quietly. "They are about to lose their old homes, Thomas. They could help, but only if they would be welcome here."

Behind them, a cat mewed in disbelief.

"You must be a Sender," said Mulligan, stepping into their little circle. The Bengal cat was in woeful condition. He had a thin, haunted look to him; and even his proud rosettes seemed dull, his beautiful golden fur matted. "Only Senders talk like that, or have such long whiskers."

Mara hesitated, but Southpaw came forward, offering Mulligan a friendly head-butt. "She is," he said. "She's the Sender of Nizamuddin, and she's my friend. But why do you doubt her?"

Mulligan stared at the bandicoots, at the upturned earth, the ruinous mounds that made even the hoopoes and the wagtails step lightly, treating the ground with caution for fear that they would tumble into a fresh hole or an old run.

"I have heard Senders can do many things," he said, his mew a hoarse rasp, "but long as your whiskers might be, they cannot conjure up an entire clan of cats in an instant. You might know of a clan in need of a home, we might welcome them—there is space enough, food enough, if we could wrest our homes back from these encroaching thugs—but which Sender has ever had whiskers powerful enough to drag an entire clan across the city?"

Thomas Mor nodded his head, setting his feathers to

dancing again. "Very true," he said. "Excellent idea, but the point is—your clan is over there, somewhere, and you're over here, whiskers and all. You have as much chance of bringing the two together as we do of diverting the Yamuna and flooding these dirty rats out of here."

Southpaw stretched, and gave Mara a light, affectionate head rub, ruffling her whiskers gently.

"Sender," he said, "they're right. How do you plan to bring the Nizamuddin cats here?"

Mara yawned and arched the kinks out of her back.

"I have to go now," she said, "my Bigfeet will worry if I'm not home for dinner. Rest well tonight, and don't get your whiskers, or feathers, into a tangle. The Golf Course will have its clan before the full moon wanes, one way or another. Southpaw, would you like to come back with me? Just to see the new house?"

The two cats slipped easily away, moving with such lightness over the grass that the hoopoes didn't see them or sound an alarm until Mara and Southpaw had passed by. Mulligan felt his whiskers tingle with hope, but then he happened to look at the bandicoots again.

Their runs were massive, spreading like stains across the course. Thomas Mor gave voice to the thoughts in Mulligan's mind: "If there are so many of them here, how many runs might there be elsewhere? How long have they been planning to take over the course?"

The peacock and the Bengal cat left in silence. Much as they hoped they could believe the Sender, neither thought it was likely that a clan of cats would fall from the skies, like monsoon rain.

MOONCH SURVEYED HIS KINGDOM, satisfaction oiling out of every pore and whisker.

"Who would have thought, Chamcha?" he said, snuffling in the direction of the new runs, where they hoped to connect the fifth hole with the part of the Golf Course commonly known as the peacock hole. "All of this for me."

Chamcha made a somewhat pointed snuffling noise, and Moonch corrected himself. "Us," he said, "of course, of course, what I meant was we have availed of all this for the sake of family only. From now on, no more hiding in drains, or living a dozen to one tiny little rat hole, no? Is the digging done?"

Poonch raised his snout and said, a little meekly, "Moonch, maybe we are going too far? Today the Bigfeet were yelling, shouting, all because their feet keep going into our burrows. And then the repair work; some of our teams are working night and day just to patch up the holes left by the Bigfeet. Shouldn't we be more careful? Build only in the parts of the course where there are forests and fewer Bigfeet?"

Moonch squeaked in indignation, and Chamcha squeaked hastily.

"No wonder they call him Chhota Poonch, the Short-Tailed One," he said to Chamcha. "He lost his brains when they bit off his tail. Poonch, what do you think the point of taking over the Golf Course was in the first place?"

Poonch blinked, his beady black eyes confused, his ears curving into two pink, defensive shells.

"But we only wanted more space for our families," he said, "not the whole Golf Course, surely? I thought we just wanted to spread out a bit so that we weren't so cramped, but then these other clans started coming in from all around Delhi. It worries me. In fact, Moonch, I was thinking . . ."

Moonch bit him, hard, on his stump of a tail, making Poonch squeak in terror.

"Who asked you to think? Did I ask you to think?"

"Did *I* ask you to think?" said Chamcha, emboldened.

"Shut up, Chamcha," said Moonch, kicking at the ceiling of the burrow so that sand and dust dislodged itself from the roots of a tree and landed on the bandicoot. "Point is, Poonch, you can't see the big picture. You are only seeing as far as the gutter; I am seeing much further. You're worried about the Bigfeet? But what can they do against us?"

"They might . . ." began Poonch.

"Might what?" said Moonch. His snout jabbed aggressively at Poonch, making the other bandicoot step back. "Might threaten us, like those foolish cats? Very silly they looked, didn't they, Mr. High-and-Mighty Mulligan, Mr. Since-When-Has-The-Golf-Course-Become-Your-Territory Mulligan, where is he now? Cowering for shelter with the peacocks! Stealing birds' eggs because he and his fine furry friends are too scared to fight us. Your Bigfeet, I'll tell you what will happen with your Bigfeet. We'll dig up their precious course, and they'll stop playing, that's all that will happen. All the more room for us. Chamcha, remember after we're done here, we'll start digging up the clubhouse. Tell everyone to make that top priority."

He stood in the centre of the bandicoot run, liking the way it had disrupted the peace and serenity of the greens. The chambers extended far beneath the ground; aunts, uncles and cousins chattered noisily at one another in the galleries.

THE HUNDRED NAMES OF DARKNESS

Poonch said, "Moonch, but even if the Bigfeet aren't as numerous as our clans, what if they bring more of their kind in? And what about the peacocks? Won't they attack us? The cats—there aren't so many of them, but I fear that brown tom. He slaughtered half a burrow of relatives, even if they were only distant cousins thrice removed. If the Bigfeet and the cats and the peacocks get together . . ."

Moonch snuffled along the burrows, searching for something. "Stand back," he said to Chamcha and Poonch. "Don't get too close, but see this and marvel at my brains." He took them through a winding set of tunnels, going deeper and deeper into the earth. They stopped outside a wide chamber, buttressed by roots on three sides, the roof partly open. Sentries guarded the entrance and the roof, their whiskers on high alert. "See?" said Moonch. "I've made all the necessary arrangements. Good, no?"

Poonch grunted, his eyes dismayed. "But why would we need such elaborate hiding places and burrows? Our lives were going well, Moonch. All we needed was a little more space, maybe some more hunting grounds, but this is going too far. You're preparing for war."

Moonch turned away, his squeak dismissive. "You were always the timid one," he said. "I was the one who had to plot and plan and think for us all. If we'd stayed with you, we would have remained in the gutter only. There are sentries posted all around this set of burrows, and it's off limits to everyone but me. If the Bigfeet threaten us, then we'll rest here until they go away again."

Poonch quivered, but he stood his ground. "And the rest of the families? Those clans who came here because you invited them? This is very clever, this hiding place just for us, out here where only the oldest families of rats have their homes. But what about the rest? You brought them here; it's because you asked them to come in that all of the digging and disruption started. If the Bigfeet attack, or the cats hunt us, it will be because of *your* marvellous plans, Moonch!"

Moonch flew at him, and Poonch squeaked in pain as the other bandicoot bit savagely at his tail and his back.

"So much jibber-jabber, chitter-chatter," said Moonch, spitting out some of Poonch's fur. "Now you listen, okay? Maybe you're satisfied with crawling to the peacocks and the cats all the time—'Yes, saheb! No, saheb! A few scraps from your beak will suffice, saheb!'—but you tell me, why shouldn't the Golf Course belong to us?"

Poonch was backing away, his beady eyes on his escape route, but he paused. "Because it doesn't belong to any of us, Moonch, it belongs to all the clans, and it always has—even you must see that! The peacocks and the snakes, the koels and the cats, us and the field mice—we have all been here for generations. More space for us, that I understand. But why can't we share? The peacocks and the cats have been here as long as we have."

"The cats!" said Moonch. He grunted, an unpleasant sound, and raised the short, bristly hackles on his back. "I would like to see those two toms suffer," he said. "They carry their whiskers as though they belong here by right! Their fur oozes their dislike of us, their contempt for our kind; they detest the way our burrows take over everything, instead of seeing how beautiful it is, how right, how proper, that the bandicoots should inherit the earth. Grass! Flowers! What nonsense. All that space going to waste, instead of being packed shoulder to shoulder with bandicoots. Some day soon, Mr. Mulligan and Mr. Southpaw will scrabble in front of me. Just you wait."

The three bandicoots left, Moonch signalling to the young bandicoot sentries that they could go off duty.

Deep in the bowels of the earth, there was a soft, scurrying sound, and the pitter-patter of feet even smaller than the bandicoot's own delicate pink paws. If Moonch had gone further down the twisting passages and stepped into the chamber, he might have caught a familiar smell: the scent trails, ancient and robust, from the warrens of the rats who had lived underneath the Golf Course for many years, unseen, disturbing no one, their lives uninterrupted until now. The rats had shuffled closer as Moonch spoke, and though they were silent for a long while, once they were sure the bandicoots had gone, the passage filled with shuffles and low squeaks.

CHAPTER NINETEEN

Full Moon Rising

Tooth circled the canal, sailing down one bank and up the other. He saw a flash of movement and dived, his eyes never leaving his target. "Kill probability, 70 percent . . . 80 percent . . . 90 percent . . . mission accomplished!" The cheel swooped upwards, the limp body of a rat between his talons.

It would probably be the last kill of the night; though the full moon shone brightly enough, there had been little enough prey all day, and his senses told him there would be little more. His feathers did not ruffle with satisfaction: killing rats was too easy. Nor would the meat stretch far. It was not enough for him, or for Claw, or for Mach and Hatch, even if Mach and Claw did their own hunting. There had been no birds' eggs this summer, no sizable prey, and Tooth refused to scavenge at the dumps that had kept so many in his squadron going. "That's for the vultures," he had said, his keeks angry and sharp.

He saw Katar, picking out the tomcat from between the canopied trees. Once, the trees were so thick around the area that all they could see from the skies was a tightly woven mat of green, hiding Nizamuddin's rooftops from view; now all they could see were the bare discoloured scabs of the Bigfeet dwellings, the sullen black snakes that meant roads and traffic.

Katar looked up, and Tooth saw the tomcat pause, waiting for him. The cheel ate his snack on the wing, and swooped down, glad for the excuse to get away from his own dark thoughts.

The tomcat had an air of excitement about him, and his whiskers prickled with news. "Southpaw's been found!" he said. "The Sender got through to us over the link. Her Bigfeet have moved to the Golf Course, and she says the Golf Course cats need us—something about an infestation of bandicoots. The clan's leaving tonight. I'd hoped you and I would meet before we left, Tooth."

The cheel flapped his wings, turning on the concrete pipe he was using as a perch. "That is good news for your clan," he said, his keen eyes taking in the change in Katar. It seemed that the grey tom, and the other cats, had become that much thinner every time he touched his talons to the ground, as though Nizamuddin had become a home for shadows. But he felt something shift in his feathers and in his breast. He had made friends with the cats late in his career—as a young Group Captain, he would not have dreamed of stopping for a chat with a common mouser. He'd met Miao when he had already spent some seasons as Wing Commander, and now, he could not imagine the days going by without a word with someone or the other in the clan. Tooth had friends in the skies, but he would be lonely when he touched down once the clan left.

He groomed his feathers, pushing those thoughts out of his head. "The course is some distance, though," he said. "How will you know the way?"

Katar raised his ears and leaned forwards, his tail up like a flag. "I was hoping you'd ask," he said. "The Sender's already arranged it, but perhaps you'd like to meet one of our helpers. He's the chief helper in a way, and he's doing quite a special job."

Tooth raised his tail feathers inquiringly, wondering whether Katar wanted to introduce him to a new cat. The cheel would have made his excuses, not wanting to get his talons tangled in the cat clan's business, but he hesitated. He would like to say his farewells, he thought.

Katar padded through the alleys that led to the dargah, but then he turned down a separate route, taking a twisting path that led to an abandoned baoli to the side of the dargah. "We'll leave from here," he said. "The Sender has made her own arrangements for when we get closer to the Golf Course, but we worked out what to do for the first leg. We won't have to wait long—most of the clan is here, and our guide should arrive any moment."

Some of the dargah cats were preparing to leave along with the Nizamuddin clan, the cheel realized; he could see Dastan with his family, Shayar and Jigar, among them.

Katar turned his whiskers upwards, towards the night sky. Tooth, perched in one of the niches, caught the beat of wings, and peered at the moon, wondering if the owls were out on one of their sorties.

A handsome young raptor streaked out from behind the moon's bright, shining face. He closed the gap so rapidly that Tooth felt his wingtips quiver in grudging respect—even more so when the kite soared upwards and did a double roll, skimming through the electric lines dexterously, avoiding the hazards of the satellite dishes on the Bigfeet rooftops, hovering with absolute precision over Katar's head. The stranger had a dashing tilt to his head, his plumes a trifle long at the back, but fashionably so, his talons burnished and his wings neatly groomed, despite all his fancy flying.

Tooth wondered why Katar and the clan had called in a stranger, presumably some flyboy from Defence Colony, and he felt irritation ruffle his feathers. He folded his wings grimly and waited for the stranger to present his respects.

The young raptor hovered above Katar's ears, about to land. Then, as though he had heard the older cheel's annoyed thoughts, the flyboy raised his wings, saluting Tooth. He threw his head back and let out a wild, triumphant keek, and he shot upwards again, taking off and spinning as soon as he'd gained some height. He looped one loop, a second—double roll—and went for the triple, swinging dangerously and dexterously between the electric wires.

Tooth felt the feathers in his chest suddenly tighten. He stared at the raptor, at the familiar clutch of the boy's talons, the messy plumes at the back of his neck, and he shot into the air, calling out in terror. "Hatch!" he cried. "What in the name of thunder and lightning do you think you're doing? Come down this moment!"

The raptor shrugged his wings, in a defiant gesture, ignored his father and took the triple. He slid between the cables with a feather's length to spare, and together, the two cheels soared higher, until they were black shapes against the moon.

In the air, Tooth could speak freely, and he did, when he could get over his shock. "You could have died! You could have hurt yourself, sliced a wing!"

"Chill, Dad," said Hatch, feathering the leaves on the branches of a tree with the skill of a much older pilot. "I thought you and Claw wanted me to get off the ground, so quit yelling at me."

"I did! I'm so proud of you! How long has this been going on? Why didn't I know? The cats chose you to be their wingman—do you know how that makes my heart and feathers swell with pride, my son? Why didn't Mach tell me?"

"Whatever!" said Hatch, diving towards the ground. He gave Tooth a look that said with some clarity, *parents*!

"Wait!" called Tooth, diving behind him. "All right, son, I'm sorry. I was taken by surprise—your mother will be so proud—all right, all right, I'll stop. But there's just one thing: you have to tell me who taught you to fly like this!"

Hatch hovered, his wings spread out so that his father could catch up. The two cheels flew wingtip to wingtip, in absolute precision. "I learned from the best," said Hatch. "There were lessons every single day, and I watched that cheel fly for hours until I was sure I knew his best moves. Then I met someone who told me I'd better get my wings in the air and off the ground, and so I did. Why do you want to know, anyway?"

"Because," said Tooth grimly, "whoever that son of a twig is, and whatever else he may have taught you—superb hovering, great sense of space, beautiful take-off, by the way—I'm going to tear his head off with my claws for being irresponsible enough to teach you that triple roll. You could . . . you have no idea how dangerous it is, Hatch, Stoop died that way!"

"Yeah, Slash told *you* that the time you did the triple roll," said Hatch, rolling his wing over as he prepared for landing. "I was watching, that time and all the rest of the times. You're awesome in the air, Dad. Everything I know, I learned from you."

And Hatch was on the ground, his talons wide, grabbing the soil in a perfect landing.

The clan had waited patiently for the two cheels to finish their conversation. Katar raised his head questioningly when Hatch landed.

"We should probably go, Katar," said Hatch. "Nice of your Sender to ask me along for the ride. She's the reason I took to the skies—I'll tell you the full story some day. Dad?"

Tooth had his golden eyes fixed on his son, the cheel's wings spread out, ready to lead a clan of cats on what promised to be an interesting journey.

"Yes, son?" he said, his voice wobbling slightly.

"Maybe you and Claw should come too," he said. "I did a survey of the Golf Course yesterday. Plenty of room for all of us. The squadron's doing fine under Slash, and Mach's great as his second-in-command. She has her place with the squadron in Nizamuddin. But those dudes over there, they could use a few predators. Got a bandicoot problem, the Sender says."

Tooth preened his wings, thinking. "We'll come and visit soon," he said. "Son, I'm sorry I pushed you so hard to fly when you didn't want to. Seems like you're doing fine on your own."

"I'm sorry I took so long, Dad," said Hatch. "First, it was scary having you and Claw for parents—living up to the best pilots in Nizamuddin, like, no pressure, right? Then there was my name."

Tooth's eyes glowed golden. "Your name?" he said.

"Yeah, it's like, 'Hatch,' like I just came out of the egg or something," said Hatch, inspecting his talons.

"Ah," said Tooth.

"Then I figured, like the Sender said, what keeps us stuck isn't the fear of the sky or being cross because your parents gave you a lame name—Mach got the cool one, but whatever. It's like she said—she's a pretty cool cat, that Mara—we're predators and we've got to be okay with that in our heads. So it didn't matter what I was called. Even if it's really lame."

Tooth stepped forward and lightly touched his son's shoulder with his wing.

"Off you go," he said. "Lead them well, remember that their paws will go more slowly than your wings."

"Yeah," said Hatch. "Well, whatever, then."

Tooth waited till the cats were ready to leave, and till his son was almost ready to rise into the skies.

"Hatch?" he said.

"Yeah, Dad?"

"It's Hatch, short for Hatchet," he said. "Machete, and Hatchet. That's what we named you, because you two were the sharpest beaks in the nest."

"Whatever!" said Hatch as he flapped his wings, but all of them, the cats and the cheel, heard his unmistakeable delight as he sounded a loud keek across the velvet sky.

THE MOON HAD TRAVELLED across half the sky, and the Bigfeet had long since gone to sleep when Mara broke off their absorbing game of Hunt-the-Lizard. The house lizards didn't mind being stalked by the cats at all, once they had all agreed on the rules: neither Southpaw nor Mara could climb higher than the pelmets, or place a paw above curtain height. This allowed all of the concerned parties hours of fun; the lizards enjoyed the thrill of darting all the way down the wall, just to tease the pair, and it was good exercise for Mara and Southpaw. The Bigfeet had welcomed the brown cat fondly when Mara brought him back from the Golf Course, but though he enjoyed the titbits they offered him, he preferred romping around without them or the Chief Bigfoot watching their expeditions.

"We have to go," said Mara, thanking the lizards politely.

"No, we don't!" said Southpaw. "Your Bigfeet won't be up for hours. I'd just figured out how to use the lampshade as a perch, Mara, can't we keep playing?"

"The time for games is over," said the Sender, and her whiskers were so solemn, her green eyes so serious, that Southpaw let his tail drop, meekly following her onto the balcony.

The moon hung in the night sky, large, friendly and so bright that Southpaw wondered if the Bigfeet had found a way to polish it, just as they did their silver. (He and Mara had recently spent an afternoon watching with fascination as the Chief Bigfoot tackled this task.)

"That will help with the war," said Mara. "We don't have much time to lose. You should eat; there's leftovers in my bowl, and you shouldn't go into battle on an empty stomach."

"War?" said Southpaw. "Battle? What are you talking about, Mara?"

"Eat," said the Sender, and she would say no more until he had scoured the bowl clean.

When Southpaw had finished, she leaned over and washed his face, cleaning his whiskers instead of letting him do his own grooming.

"It will be a hard night for all of you on the Golf Course," said Mara, "and you must be ready. Southpaw, when you go back, first you must wake up the peacocks, and then . . ."

When she had finished, Southpaw was looking at her in such a way that the Sender felt her fur ruffling.

"Is something wrong?" she said. "Your fur crackles with anxiety, and with something else. Is it the battle plans?"

"The battle plans are fine," said Southpaw. "I won't have much trouble carrying them out." He rubbed his head against hers, but she could feel the stiffness in his whiskers. When he spoke, his mew was quiet and meditative.

"You've been my friend for so long," he said, "that I forget you are the Sender, too. It worries me."

Mara wrapped her tail around his, comfortingly.

"Don't worry about the battle," she said. "You're all warriors, and if the plans go off correctly, your reinforcements will come in at just the right time."

Southpaw's tail flicked once, hard, from side to side.

"It's not the battle that scares me," he said. "It's not what might or might not happen on the Golf Course. It's what you're planning to do, Mara, that makes my whiskers tremble in concern."

The orange queen stood at the balcony railings, and her gaze travelled out and upwards.

"There is no need for concern," she said. "I'm a Sender, and this is what Senders do. You handle the battle, and I'll take care of my whiskers. I've done this before."

Southpaw had stood up, stretching, ready to leave, but at this, he turned around. His mew was almost angry.

"Yes," he said. "I remember the first time you came to the aid of the Nizamuddin cats as their Sender, and how you summoned Ozzy into battle."

"Well, then?" said Mara, washing her paws, and letting the claws slide out as she prepared herself for what would come next.

"I also remember how you slept afterwards, and how long it was before your whiskers came back to normal," Southpaw said grimly.

But the Sender didn't seem to be listening. Her ears flickered once, idly, in his direction.

"Let me do my work, and you do yours," she said. "I don't tell you how you should slash at your enemies, or when you should feint, or bare your teeth. Go, Southpaw, or you won't be able to rouse the peacocks in time."

"But . . ." he began, his tail still switching from side to side.

"Go!" said the Sender, and she snarled at him, her hackles rising.

Southpaw's back stiffened. He padded over to the goolar fig tree and left without so much as a head-rub, though if Mara had looked in his direction, she would have seen how often the brown tom turned back to look at her, how his whiskers quivered sadly.

The Sender did not look towards the goolar fig tree even once. Instead, she closed her green eyes and raised her whiskers, sending them out towards Old Delhi. The moonlight fell on her, catching the tips of her long white whiskers, turning them a shimmering, iridescent silver.

KATAR KEPT THE CHEEL in his line of sight as they wound through the sleeping lanes of the dargah. They had agreed to move in groups of four or five, so that they could break up and scatter more easily if there were Bigfeet or traffic along the way. Beraal was in the forefront, and she sent him a quick flicker of reassurance through her whiskers.

The tom fell back, wondering how they would manage the rest of the journey. The Sender had told them not to worry. "It's all arranged," she had said. But he, Hulo and Beraal would have to handle the situation on the ground, and he wondered whether they could keep so many cats under control. The clan hunted in separate groups, and only came together or linked in times of great trouble. They had never undertaken a journey in a group this large, and Katar found his whiskers trembling at the thought of the many things that might go wrong. Even the Sender did not know the exact route; the Golf Course was a large place, she had explained. Though her whiskers had explored it, she did not know it well enough to stroll back and forth between the course, Nizamuddin and her own Bigfeet's house the way she had been able to travel between Nizamuddin and the zoo.

He fell back, realizing that they had reached the last of the alleys that led out of the dargah. His paws slowed of their own accord, and his paw pads caressed the rough gravel and the stones lovingly. He paused, letting the clan overtake him, looking around, wanting to take in all of Nizamuddin on his whiskers. Here he had come as a tiny kitten, following Miao around and demanding to be taught the basics of climbing and hunting before his paws could do more than wobble. This was where he, Beraal, Hulo and Miao had spent many moons and seasons meeting their Bigfoot friend, before the Bigfeet had shut down the tiny shrine and sent the fakir away from the neighbourhood. He turned, his whiskers running over the beloved roofs of Nizamuddin, committing the last of the trees to memory.

Katar's whiskers tingled, telling him they were reaching the edge of their territory. He started walking again, moving towards the front. The clan would need encouragement. Their paws and whiskers would tell them not to cross, and it would take them an effort of will to move past the bounds of Nizamuddin, to leave the old scent markings behind.

Behind him, Hulo said, "A moment, my friend."

He turned, and when he saw the great black tom, his shaggy head bowed, sitting in the lane with Qawwali, he stopped.

"My paws will not go any further, Katar," Hulo said. "My ribs and my skin might stick together, but I was born here, and my whiskers will sigh forever for Nizamuddin, no matter how fat the feeding elsewhere. Don't tell the others until they've reached the Golf Course, or more will waver. But Qawwali here needs me, Katar, between him and me, we'll find enough food—we'll live like princes once you greedy lot with your fat bellies have cleared out, yes? No, Katar, no sad farewells. No whisker rubs. You know I won't stand for any of that nonsense. I'll come and visit all of you once you settle down. Go, my friend. Lead them to safety."

If he raised his whiskers to say goodbye, Katar thought his heart would break, and so he didn't. He walked on without turning, and as his paws clicked across the cobbles on the sleeping streets of Nizamuddin, he thought of how he and Hulo had fought back to back in the war against the ferals, of the way they had brought up Southpaw, of the times they had brawled, or lined up hoping for the favours of the same comely queen.

Katar's ears flicked and he let his tail lash several times; then he turned again and raced back as though his paws had wings. Before Hulo could let out a warning mew or the least of growls, Katar had touched his nose lightly to Hulo's whiskers. He rubbed his old friend's neck, and felt Hulo return the head rub, once.

"Look after Beraal's kittens for me," said Hulo. "Tumble needs more care than Ruff. Make sure she gets it."

Hulo had kept the kittens alive through the past few hard months. Now it was Katar's turn to help Beraal bring up the pair.

"I will," said Katar. "When you get tired of the air of Nizamuddin, when your whiskers long for a change, come and visit."

Hulo raised his own whiskers in farewell, and in good humour. "Who could tire of the air of Nizamuddin, Katar?" he said. "The rich stink of Bigfeet! Their incomparable perfume, going back centuries! Where else would you find such a fine aroma?"

And then Hulo and Qawwali strolled back down the alley. Katar looked up; Hatch was waiting, hovering at the edge of the rooftops.

The tomcat went ahead, walking out of the ancient alleyways, even though he could feel his whiskers pleading with him not to go beyond the boundaries, not to leave the familiar, beloved scents of home behind. The grey cat padded past the sleeping Bigfeet who had found shelter on the pavements, as homeless, helpless and as scrawny as any of the strays, and stood at the edge of the road. Behind him, Nizamuddin called; ahead, the road sloped upwards, towards an overpass that smelled of cars and gravel and other grim Bigfeet artefacts. His whiskers caught the scent of trees and open spaces quite some distance away, but these were masked by the harsher smells of petrol, Bigfeet clustered together, and the bitumen road.

Hatch flew down, and perched on a signboard. "Katar," he said, "I know the cheel's route to the Golf Course, but you cannot take that road—you would fall off the overpass and have to leap a few buildings. It doesn't seem practical for cats. Did your Sender tell you what route to take?"

"There must be a Bigfeet route of some kind, aside from the sky roads you cheels follow," said Beraal. Her whiskers, like Katar's, twitched nervously; the urge to let their paws take them back home was strong, and it was hard to override the silent, insistent call of instinct.

Katar could smell her anxiety, and his own paws were stiff with worry. He spread his whiskers out, but they were no use to him; he did not know the terrain of the Golf Course, and he wondered which route the Sender wanted him to take. "If you flew very slowly, circling back from time to time," he said to Hatch, "perhaps we could use our noses to read any scent trails the Bigfeet or other animals might have left. Wouldn't we be able to reach the Golf Course that way, even if we had to go in fits and starts?"

Hatch ruffled his wings, trying not to let his own concerns show. This was his first mission, but how was he going to get a bunch of cats who couldn't follow his flight paths across to the course? "We could," he said cautiously, "but I've done a few surveys, and the question is, what part of the course do you need to go to? There are five possible entries, and if we go to the wrong one, your clan might need to walk an extra day before you meet Southpaw and the others."

"I don't know," said Katar. Hatch hunched over, pulling his feathers up over his head for a second, and then his golden eyes blinked, accepting what the grey cat had said. He flapped his wings and rose up into the sky.

Katar raised his whiskers, and Beraal said quietly, behind him, "Mara travels so easily using her whiskers that she may not have realized it would be harder for us to stay in touch with a cheel. But if the Sender thought Hatch would be able to guide us, then perhaps we should try, and soon, otherwise the clan will grow restless, or lose heart."

The heavy breeze changed direction and Katar's nostrils filled with the scents of an unfamiliar world. The grey tom turned his head, but instead of looking back at his home, he faced his clan. The toms were terrifyingly lean; the queens had thin bellies; the kittens were listless, underweight. And yet, they looked back at him with trust, and some let their pink nostrils quiver as they, too, inhaled the aromas of an unknown future.

"Hatch?" he called.

The cheel, who had been idly practising flying in concentric circles, came back, hovering close by the cats.

"Beraal's right," Katar said to the cheel. "If the Sender thinks you can lead us to the course, we should try, at least. Perhaps you could fly in short hops?"

"Whatever," said Hatch, agreeably. "But we should leave now, if we want to reach before the Bigfeet stir."

Katar hesitated, and then he put his tail up, pretending a confidence he did not feel.

"Beraal, take the rear, so that any stragglers can be returned to the group," he said. "Kittens to the front, nursing queens right behind, and I'll expect all of you toms and queens who are healthy to take the flanks and sides, just in case we need to fight anything on the way. No need to look behind you, Abol, from now on we must keep our eyes and whiskers forward. All right, clan, let's go."

The grey tom walked out of Nizamuddin, and he felt his whiskers flare with sadness, as home stretched its beseeching fingers out to him. He refused to let himself slow down, though, and set a brisk pace that forced the other toms and queens to move just as fast. Before they could mew their farewells, they had crossed the vast, empty road, and they were on the concrete pavement, gingerly skirting around the Bigfeet who slept in their rags under the shelter of the overpass. Katar could feel his pawpads curl as they padded across the rough, unfamiliar gravel of these roads, the pitted concrete slabs of the pavements.

They crossed another strip of road, Beraal reminding Katar to check for Bigfeet and their cars, the night lamps casting glowing pools of light like oases in the darkness. Before them, the road bifurcated into two dull grey ribbons, and Katar hesitated, his paws unsure of which path to take.

"Hatch!" he called, but the cheel was a distant speck, far away in the sky. It was hard to tell which road he was flying over—hard enough to see him against the night sky, in the first place. The tom felt his fur stand up in dismay; they would have to wait until the cheel discovered that they weren't following him. He felt his paws curl at the thought that the clan was very conspicuous—passing Bigfeet might not have spotted one or even two cats, but no predators, and certainly no Bigfeet, could miss seeing an entire clan of cats.

"If there's any trouble at all," he mewed softly, indicating that the toms and queens should pass the message on to each other, "hide in the ditches until Beraal or I mew an all clear." They should have practised splitting up into groups, Katar thought, his whiskers rippling with discomfort, or finding hiding places. It had seemed so simple at the time; they would cross to the Golf Course and settle into their new home. He and Beraal had talked to the clan about the need to wait until the cats of the Golf Course offered them territory, to ask permission before they hunted anything at all; but they had never moved a clan of cats from one place to another before, and neither of them had thought to practise other manouevres.

High up in the sky, Hatch seemed to pause and veer sharply away. Katar watched him, puzzled by his erratic flight path. Then the grey tom's tail switched back and forth, and he growled softly, unable to believe his eyes.

As clear as the stars, as sharply etched as the moon, the forms of five cats began to materialize in the night sky, far above their heads. Katar heard the mews and growls of others in the clan; they could not smell these strangers, who dotted the sky like a line of the Bigfeet's colourful paper kites, but they could see them—a calico, a half-Siamese, a plump tabby, among others.

Katar slashed at the air, his teeth bared in a fighter's challenge, but even as his claws sliced at the horizon, he knew it was no use. The sky-cats were too far away.

The calico was moving closer, looming out of the sky, and Katar felt a sudden tug on his whiskers. He backed, snarling, until he was up against the metal posts of one of the Bigfeet's signboard. The calico hovered over the clan, and it seemed to him that her image flickered in and out, her fur oddly blurred, especially around the ears and tail.

"Well done!" she mewed, her ears up at a jaunty angle. "You must be Katar; the Sender of Nizamuddin said I'd find you and Hatch here. Mara's planned this Sending so that none of us get our whiskers too tired, though I hope her own can keep us going until you get to the Golf Course. Is that the cheel listening? Hatch, we're taking the route over the overpass—this way, around the roundabout, up past Khusro Park, got that? Umrrow Jaan will take over the next leg of your journey, then Jalebi will step in until we get closer to the Golf Course, and Mara can take you through that last stage. Quite astonishing, your little Sender,

I don't think we've had a group sending or summoning in Delhi for centuries. Katar, we Senders will stay low enough in the sky so that you can tell us to slow down or hurry up, depending on how fast the clan's paws can carry them, and we'll tell Hatch to fly fast or slow as you need. Well, what are we waiting for? Let's get on with this before dawn breaks and the Bigfeet find you out and about."

"To the Golf Course!" mewed Katar, feeling his fears ebb from his whiskers. His tail was up, and though they had already walked some distance, he felt that he could lead the clan all night, if necessary. The grey tom's paws clicked on the pavements, tapping out a happy tattoo as he followed the cheel and the brisk, shimmering figure of Begum, the Sender of Purani Dilli. And the cats of Nizamuddin followed him and Begum, their paws taking them further and further away from home.

CHAPTER TWENTY

The Belly of the Beast

Moonch inspected the sand trap, his snout quivering as he traced patterns across the smooth rake marks, blurring them. "Chamcha!" he called. "This could be a possible place for my burrow. Make a note of it, will you?"

Chamcha grunted, cautiously. "Of course, Moonch," he said, his tail curling in an obsequious way. "You wish to move your quarters again? The birdsong disturbed you? Or was it that the sun slants in the wrong way?"

The bandicoot twitched his snout; he rolled a small ball of sand between his pink palms.

"You have any objection, Chamcha?" he said. He snuffled twice, sharply. "Because you should think very hard before you voice an objection, no? What is the point of having a hundred bandicoot families at your beck and call if you can't beck them and call them, yes?"

"But I am nobody to object," said Chamcha hurriedly. His tail showed signs of bite marks, and he twitched the tip nervously, as though he was scared of acquiring a few more. "I am only your humble, obedient servant, Moonch, whatever you say is fine by me. If you tell me to move your burrow to the top of the koel's tree, we will oblige. If you tell me to move your burrow to the clubhouse, it shall be done forthwith! It shall all be as you say, Moonch, please forgive your humble servant if he has given offence."

"Slinky, bite him," said Moonch lazily. A bandicoot with a sly, conniving air about his eyes sidled up to Chamcha and took his tail up. Delicately, Slinky sank his teeth in to the tip, his black eyes feeding on Chamcha's squeaks of pain.

"I am nobody to object, too," said Poonch, his grunt calm, even belligerent. "And yet, one of us must, Moonch. The Bigfeet have noticed how deep our burrows go—some of them were walking around the other day, taking note of how many runs we had in each hole. They won't run away as easily as the cats. If we cut back on our burrows, if we moved off the fairways and the greens, they'd probably leave us alone. But there are too many of us—and who are these new families anyway? Chamcha and I haven't invited them, so you must have. It seems like every bandicoot in Delhi is showing up on the Golf Course."

"How dare you!" squeaked Moonch. "This is my burrow! This is my Golf Course! I'll invite whoever I please!"

"You're inviting trouble," said Poonch. His grunt had deepened; he rubbed his pink paws together in some nervousness.

"You don't want to hear this, Moonch, but it's all going out of control. If we don't get the newcomers out of here, and if we don't stop building, the Bigfeet or some sort of predators will attack. We could live here peacefully for years if we'd just show some sense."

"You were always a coward," said Moonch, contemptuously. "Haven't I planned ahead? If the Bigfeet try anything, I have my retreat in order. You're forgetting what I am, Poonch, I think ahead."

Poonch straightened up, and he held his tail in both paws as he stared at Moonch. "I know what you are," he said. "But can't you stop, Moonch? All we wanted was a small part of the course where we could breed in peace."

"That's what you wanted, fools like you and Chamcha," said Moonch. He seemed to have lost interest in his former friends; his pink ears were cupped as he listened for something. "I always wanted the full course, all of it. A place for the bandicoots and the rats, only for us."

"Why couldn't we have shared?" said Poonch. "The rest of them do—the cats, the owls, the peacocks. Everyone shares their territory."

Moonch grunted, a noise of satisfaction. "That's because they are fools," he said. "So smart of you to mention the owls and the peacocks." There was a sudden screech from above ground, and then more. "We made a decision some days ago— Slinky and me." The owls began hooting, and Poonch heard Hobson's angry screeches. "We thought: these birds have too much territory. They strut around, fluffing up their feathers, and do they show us respect? No. I am a humble creature. I eat only a few beetles every day, only a handful of woodlice, some grubs, whatever birds' eggs might be going around—simple, honest food. All I ask for is respect, yes?"

The screeches intensified, becoming more frantic, as the peacocks called to one another.

"And if it is not forthcoming, then we must take steps, yes?" said Moonch. His black beady eyes exuded a calm certainty. "It occurred to me that there was no need to build tunnels around the place, joining them up. If we took over the peacock's territory, then we could tunnel through. Much simpler. I am a simple creature, after all, a bandicoot of humble, simple tastes."

Abruptly, the screeches stopped. Poonch had no love for peacocks, but he felt a shiver run through his fur. The new settlers, those who had streamed in over the last few days, were far too eager to brawl and fight and spill blood as long as it was not their own.

Moonch drummed his tail on the floor and looked up at the sandy roof. "What's taking them so long?" he said to Slinky. "They were supposed to report back immediately to tell me that they've taken over. I plan to have all the fairways under my control by morning, and then the clubhouse—those cats . . ."

He stopped in mid-squeak. The roof shook, and dust began falling into the centre of the burrow.

"Careful, you fools!" he grunted. "Step lightly, step lightly, no need to thump across the bunker!"

The sand began to stream steadily down, and Slinky ducked. Cracks started to ricochet across the ceiling. Poonch stared up—and then he had to fling himself onto the floor, to avoid the claw that ripped through the roof. For a moment, the claw hung there, as curved as a scimitar, as sharp as a rat's tooth, and then it disappeared upwards, taking part of the roof with it.

"That was no bandicoot!" said Poonch.

"That was no peacock!" said Chamcha.

In the distance, they heard the sound of paws scurrying—away from the burrows, not towards them.

"Wait!" grunted Moonch. "I haven't given you permission to go! Guards! Get them."

A peacock screeched triumphantly. "A Mor! A Mor!" called Thomas, his cry carrying across the Golf Course.

Moonch whirled around, rubbing his paws together. "Slinky, get all of the families up and out! All of them! At once!"

An answering call came rippling back, and then another, and then a third, until the air resonated with the sound of peacock screeches. And then the yowls started. Huddled in the burrow, the bandicoots who had rushed out from their galleries and chambers shivered, as a cat hurled a challenge into the night.

"Cowards!" snapped Moonch, his tail quivering. "It's only one cat, we can take it down like that."

The caterwauling intensified, and from the north, another cat joined in. The bandicoots muttered and jostled one another.

"Two!" said Moonch contemptuously. "And there are so many of us. Remember how those two ran for their lives? Remember the fear in their whiskers?"

Another cat started up, and slowly, the sounds grew, until they formed an image in the minds of the bandicoots. Outside the burrow, a circle of cats stalked round and round, closing in on them.

"Moonch," said Slinky, "I'll just go and check on the other burrows, shall I?"

"You yellow-bellied, weak-furred, cowardly excuse for a . . ." Moonch began, but then the roof shook again and the sand poured down, in such strong drifts that the bandicoots started to cough and sneeze. They swarmed for the exits, frantic to get out of the tunnels.

Moonch stayed where he was, his black eyes glinting. He waited until the burrows had emptied, and he urged the few bandicoots who were hanging back to go. "Never mind me," he said, his squeak suddenly acquiring a noble tinge to it. "Yes, yes, there's a risk that the roof will fall in, but you must get out safely. Go, my friends, go. I'll follow later."

He waited, listening. The tunnels held the lingering, oily residue of bandicoot fur, and he heard the squeaks of relief as they tumbled out. Then the squeaks changed to cries of fear and despair. He listened, his pink ear quivering, as the peacocks cried "A Mor! A Mor!" and the bandicoots scurried here and there, as the cats caterwauled and yowled in triumph. And when Moonch saw blood darken the sand of the walls of the tunnels, he combed his whiskers, pleased that he had managed to escape.

He heard Southpaw's growl close by, and peered out, careful not to risk his whiskers by getting too close. A black flood of bandicoots streamed out of the burrows, some hysterical with terror at the scent of so many cats, making for the walls. They would slip over, or tunnel under, and find a place for themselves in the sewer systems nearby, or on the canal banks.

Southpaw held two bandicoots in his jaws. He stood near a grey tom whose claws were out. Spinning through the fairways, a black-and-white cat whirled, spreading destruction in her wake. She moved so fast that Moonch felt his own stomach clench; the warrior queen and the other cats were everything that he had been brought up to fear.

Beraal yowled, hurling a string of war cries into the air, and her paws wreaked havoc wherever she went. "This feels like the old days, Southpaw!" she called. "I've missed being a warrior so much! Oh look, Katar's got them on the run on the other side of the greens!" There, too, a river of bandicoots pushed and jostled one another as they fled the cats on one side, the peacocks on the other.

The cats stalked along one side of the field, and Moonch blinked, kicking back the sand with his hind legs so that he could burrow down and stay hidden. To the other side, the peacocks ran, making for the burrows on other fairways. A high screech alerted him to the danger in the skies; Hatch soared above the Golf Course, scouting for bandicoot runs.

The bandicoot climbed deep into the burrows, kicking sand over the bodies of those who had died in this one-sided war and fallen back in through the crumbling roof. Moonch pushed back a hanging taproot, and squeezed through the gap in the earthen wall. It didn't look as though it was large enough to lead anywhere, but he emerged on the other side into a wide gallery. From the gallery, a long, narrow corridor bearing the signs of fresh scrape marks, but only a few paw prints, as if to indicate that it had been used by only one or two bandicoots, led deeper still.

Moonch descended through the earth, letting the musty scent comfort him. He scurried through the scraped-out corridors with their low ceilings, using the ends of the roots that poked out through the walls to help him pass through, but he didn't rush. The bandicoot stepped into a wide gallery that had been built with some care. It was large enough to hold four or five bandicoots in comfort, well stocked with a selection of fine foods—hand-picked fungus, dried wild mushrooms, plant tubers and some grubs, squirming in a deep-dug pit. The walls were lined with bits of wool from the Bigfeet's clothes, leaves, grass and other detritus patted together to make a snug nest. There was ample ventilation despite the depth of the burrow; it had been built to take advantage of two enormous tap roots, and chimneys of a sort had been constructed by removing some of the sand around each root.

Moonch surveyed his lair with satisfaction, and then, rubbing his palms together, he stepped into the next chamber. His whiskers twitched with pleasure when he thought of how clever he had been. It was a pity about the bandicoots who had died, but there were always more. His burrow was well-stocked; he would wait until the peacocks and the cats—officious beasts—had left. If there were bandicoots left above, they might die, too, but there was no shortage of bandicoots in Delhi; more would join him at need, in the seasons to come. And they had dug plenty of burrows all around the course. Moonch felt he might take an evening walk along the burrows every so often, once the fuss had died down.

He heard a scuffling sound, like paws running over a wall, and the patter of feet, but those sounds grew more distant.

Moonch rested in the comfort of the scrape he had made in the burrow's loose earth. He thought there might be a few of his kind left, after the carnage, and in the fullness of time, he, Moonch, who had imagined a better life for his clan and his kind than any of the other long-snouted ones, would bring the bandicoots back again. Different ones, perhaps, but there was little difference between a Slinky and a Chamcha.

There was a scraping noise from the tunnel that led back into his wide, comfortable gallery, and behind the other wall, the one that led to an old set of abandoned rat runs he hadn't bothered to examine, a quick, rushing patter. "Who's there?" called Moonch.

"Nothing to worry about," said Poonch. "I'll be with you in a minute." The scraping sound continued; then there was a series of rapid, muffled thuds.

"What are you doing?" asked Moonch.

"Only a few security measures," said Poonch, grunting with the exertion. Moonch heard him work his way out of wherever he was; and then he smelled Poonch's fur above, and looked up.

Poonch peered down at him, through one of the gaps in the roof, where a large root dangled down into the chamber. His snout was scratched and bloodied.

"You're all right, Moonch?" he said, chuffing from exertion. "Came out of the battle unscathed, I see."

Moonch twitched his whiskers, trying to read Poonch's scent. His hind legs, he found, were alert and ready for battle, though he wasn't sure why.

"I got lucky," he said, his grunt wary.

Poonch's black eyes blinked. "Yes," he said. "Bandicoots like you often get lucky, Moonch, very lucky. They get lucky when they haul themselves out of the sewers and the gutters and start to boss their friends around. They get lucky in wars where they send other bandicoots out to do the mucky work of fighting, and bleeding, and dying. They get lucky when they discover a place better than the stinking, cramped quarters they came from. Some of them stop right there, you know? Some stop when they have a fine, clean burrow of their own."

"What are you talking about, Poonch?" said Moonch. "Babbling like a babbler, on and on and on."

Poonch went on as though Moonch hadn't let out a squeak.

"Some never do stop, Moonch," he said, his shoestring tail poised over his head. "Some get greedy after they get lucky. They want more, and more, and still more, and they forget that luck runs out. They put everything that really matters into danger because they can't stop wanting more, their bellies never full no matter how much they might stuff their snouts. They put everyone into danger, except for their own precious selves, and they dream dangerous dreams."

He moved away, his snout disappearing into the darkness. Moonch heard another sound, one that made his own ears stand up in alarm. Poonch was digging with his hind legs, and Moonch remembered how large those legs were, how well-muscled, how much sand and earth they could bring down with them.

"Chhota Poonch," he called, "stop that at once! You're bringing the roof down on this place."

"If I do it right," Poonch called back, "you will be buried forever, locked up into the earth so that you can never harm anyone else again. The fairways run with the blood of bandi-coots who followed you, Moonch, the Bigfeet's greens are black with the blood and guts of bandicoots whose only fault was to accept an invitation you sent them. You've been lucky, Moonch. Very lucky."

Moonch grunted, a hard, angry noise.

"Nonsense," he said. "You won't bury me, Poonch. I built this place, and I know where all the doors are. You won't sleep much, because you'll know that my whiskers and my teeth are after you, and one day, when you do sleep, I'll catch up, and that will be the end of your treacherous, betraying ways."

He climbed up to the tunnel that led to his chamber and crawled in. Poonch waited, pausing in his labours, allowing his hind legs a rest.

Moonch squeaked in fury, "The exit's blocked! Poonch, that was your doing."

"You ordered this place to be built," said Poonch. "I was the one who built it. Don't bother trying the other exits, they're firmly sealed. Except for the ones in the far wall, the ones that lead to the ancient rat runs. You never bothered to talk to the rats, did you? I did, half a moon ago. They didn't seem to like your plans, Moonch. They didn't seem to think it was a good idea to draw the Bigfeet's attention to their quiet, ancient runs, places that had been left undisturbed—until you got here. In fact, they didn't seem to like the idea of you taking over their most ancient chamber at all. But I'll let them explain the matter to you."

Moonch scrabbled to go up the walls, but they had been well made. It would take a lot of digging before he could bring them down. He scraped with his hind legs, frantically.

Poonch started up again, aiming his hind legs with some care at a single spot on the roof. Clods of earth started to rain down, and then larger and larger pieces.

Moonch grunted, and Poonch heard the sound of claws scraping against stone.

Inside the chamber, the earth crumbled slowly, leaving bald patches in the far wall. Moonch scurried back as the wall began to collapse. He saw one small black nose, sniffing and questing, then another, then a third; and then there were too many to count. What was left of the wall heaved as though it was alive, and then the brown, wriggling mass of rats turned their whiskers in his direction. Their eyes were beady, and questioning, and not at all friendly.

"Poonch!" cried Moonch. "The rats! The rats! Get me out of here."

"But you were the one who didn't want to leave the Golf Course, Moonch," said Poonch. The loosened earth poured into the centre of the chamber, burying Moonch in a mound of dirt as the brown circle of rats shuffled closer and closer still. Then Moonch disappeared from his view, covered by the earth, and by the busy rats.

There was a frantic scrabbling. It was quite some time before the scrabbling stopped.

The rats squeaked, and Poonch heard a final, feeble scrape of claws. Then there was silence, and only the taproots stirred, like slender fingers reaching out of the earth.

Epilogue

"What a summoning!" said Umrrow Jaan. "This Sender of Nizamuddin—I suppose she's the Sender of the Golf Course now—bless her whiskers, I haven't been picked up and whirled around in the air like that since the time I went to sleep in my Bigfeet's holdall and found myself being dumped on the upper berth of the Rajdhani Express! It's so impressive, Begum, it took all five of us to summon *her*, and she lifted her whiskers like she'd been doing this all of her life—and boom! You, me, Jalebi, Spook, Baoli—right here! I swear, if she'd noticed them she'd even have picked up the Viceroys."

The Viceroys were a tribe of goats who lived in Mehrauli, and exhibited signs of deep derangement. Curzon was given to bouts of trouser-eating; Wavell made up for his tendency to butt heads with everybody by having an exceptionally soft nose; Canning had hard little horns and ate rusty nails for breakfast, and Mountbatten had something of a roving eye, not to mention an omnivorous appetite.

Begum flickered in and out, looking around at the Circle of Senders. "Just as well the Viceroys weren't here," she said. "They'd have driven us mad, and been of no help at all; the bandicoots weren't going to be chased away by a handful of bleating old goats. We're done here, aren't we? We should probably go back to our own homes; I hope the Sender isn't too exhausted."

Begum's whiskers crackled with concern. She couldn't imagine the kind of power it would take for one Sender to summon five more. Of course, it had made it much easier for the five of them to guide Hatch, going between him and Mara, than if Mara had tried to send to him on her own from the Golf Course. And except for Umrrow's belief that what the cheel needed as he flew to the Golf Course was a consolidated dose of Sender gossip, it had worked perfectly. With Mara raising her whiskers from her home near the Golf Course, the Senders had set up a chain of links between the young Sender and Hatch. But it had never been attempted before. It was probably justified, the Sender of Purani Dilli thought, thinking of the vast bands of bandicoots they had seen as they'd left the battlefield.

The fairways were strewn with the corpses of the bandicoots, but the greens were finally peaceful. The Bigfeet would be puzzled, though they would probably leave the cats and the rest of the Golf Course's inhabitants alone, Southpaw thought, as he took stock of their troops. He had found that the Bigfeet rarely cared if rats, mice or bandicoot were slaughtered, though they would make a fuss over an injured pet or a missing cow.

The peacocks and the cats had sustained injuries, but suffered no losses. Hobson, the more fierce of the owls, had come out to help the cheels, but disoriented by the daylight, had attacked the stump of a tree with immense savagery. Before Southpaw could explain that he'd made a mistake, Hobson had declared himself the winner, and popped back into his hole, hooting in triumph.

"Famous victory, what?" said Thomas Mor, strutting around the course. "Did you see Henry and me peck the blighters to bits? That should be a warning to anyone who breaches the Rules of Golf. And these dashed blighters did! Rule 1-2: Must not exert influence on movement of balls or alter physical conditions. That includes tunnelling under the greens, blast it!"

IT WAS COLD, AND voices whispered in the dark. Kirri loomed over her. The mongoose's claws made shadows on the wall; her silver throat was streaked and clotted with blood. The creature who lived on the black mountain panted, and his hot breath scorched her fur. A cobra rose up, and Magnificat screamed, flying through the air to attack the snake as its fangs struck at the Sender of Paolim. Bandicoots scurried around in Mara's basket, climbing up her fur, swinging from her whiskers, pushing their pink snouts against her paw pads.

The Sender opened her eyes with some effort, and all the creatures of the night disappeared.

She was lying on the stone floor of the balcony. A sleepy koel called once, twice, from the branches of the tree. She had come home from the Golf Course, stumbling as she climbed the goolar fig tree, to find that her Bigfeet had gone out, perhaps for the evening. The Chief Bigfoot would come in the next day to feed her and play with her.

All of this went through Mara's mind as she tried to raise her whiskers. She couldn't. When the summoning ended, she had felt the blood start to drain from her paws. Calling one cat down to help would not have tested the Sender's powers; calling and holding five Senders for so long had drained her. Her whiskers trembled incessantly, and she could do nothing to make them hold still again. A coldness settled into her fur, despite the heavy heat of the summer night, and she curled her paws around her belly.

She wanted to call out to Southpaw. Somewhere in the dark, on the other side of the road, she could sense that her friend searched for her, his whiskers slightly bloodied, a little bent, fresh scars on his fur. She had seen that much, and then the sky had spun around, the stars had wheeled and rearranged themselves.

Mara felt her tongue begin to dry out. She wanted water. Her bowl was over to the side of the balcony, a blue plastic bowl with a wide rim. It was a few feet away. It was too far away. She raised her head, and tried to mew, but no sound came out.

Then she felt the steady rasp of a tongue over her head, like the comforting touch of the towels the Bigfeet sometimes used to bathe her. She hadn't heard Southpaw come up, but he must have followed very soon after her. She felt his whiskers touch her own, and she felt her whiskers rise again as the pain ebbed from their tips and from the tender fur on her face. "You have to come back, Mara," Southpaw said. "Come home now, Sender."

She felt his paws on her fur, and then he bent his head and washed her nose, her head, her eyes and whiskers. The tom worked steadily, calmly, breathing life back into her nose, her mouth. "Come home to me, Mara," said Southpaw.

When she woke, briefly, out of that deep sleep, his reassuring mew was the first thing she heard. The summer night was cooler than she had expected, and crickets chirped in the distance. But Southpaw had curled himself around her body, cradling her protectively. His brown eyes measured the darkness as though he would hunt each one of the Sender's nightmares down if they showed themselves; but the night showed him nothing but the ghosts of bandicoots.

The Sender rested, letting Southpaw wash her, letting his touch and the firm rasp of his tongue bring her strength. Once, she opened her green eyes and brushed his scarred, furry, beloved face with her own whiskers. They rested that way all through the night, the Sender and her warrior tom.

When she woke that morning, she purred at Southpaw, and he purred back. "Sender," he said, "you may walk outside as much as you please, and fight as many bandicoots as you please, and hunt as often as you please. But if you ever go to those borderlands at the edge of summoning again, I will clip your whiskers myself."

Mara blinked her green eyes at Southpaw. "No one tells a Sender what to do, Southpaw," she said gravely. Then she washed the scar that ran from his pointed ears to his whiskers with care and love. "Except, once in a while, her tom."

When she stretched and rose to see if there was anything left in her food bowl, Southpaw's brown eyes narrowed, and his whiskers flickered. Mara said nothing, and he didn't raise his voice in a mew or a snarl, but both of them saw the same thing.

Her fur was smooth and clean, the orange glowing in the morning sunlight. Her rounded belly was untouched, and her paws were pink and healthy. The Sender had seen the war of the bandicoots from a distance, intent on holding the link between Hatch and the Circle of Senders. But the strain of the summoning had left its mark. Mara's long white whiskers unfurled, vibrating, unharmed, except for the tips, which had turned the colour of smouldering ashes.

SOUTHPAW STROLLED ACROSS THE greens, waiting politely for the Bigfoot to take his tee shot. "Splendid!" he said. "Remarkable how he always manages to hit the pine tree, just so, every time. Perfect aim for a Bigfoot."

Thomas Mor bobbed up and down in frustration. "He wasn't aiming at the pine tree, old chap," he said. "It's a tee shot, you see? He was trying to get it over to that side, where the green is. That's the point of the game."

Southpaw's whiskers twitched in disagreement. "Don't think so," he said. "I think he's got a bit of a soft spot for Kooky, frankly. He keeps sending her golf balls, and one of these days, she might even hatch one."

Thomas spread his tail out and clicked it shut, like a fan. The Nizamuddin clan had fitted so easily into the life of the Golf Course that it was hard to imagine a time when Beraal wasn't prowling the perimeters or when Katar wasn't trying to knock some sense into Ruff and Tumble's whiskery heads. Tooth, Claw and Hatchet had settled in on the roof of the Barakhamba Tomb, clearing the course in short order of the last of the rat and bandicoot infestation, and keeping the population of pigeons and shrews down to an acceptable number. They went back often to Nizamuddin, to catch up with Mach and her squadron of cheels.

All was well in Thomas's world, except for one minor issue, the acacia thorn in the turf grass: the cats had absolutely no understanding of the Rules of Golf. They were civilized about it, staying off the greens and the fairways, though every so often one or the other of them succumbed to the temptation to use the sand bunker for a certain purpose. But they had no sense of the importance of tee shots, or the lie of the land, or when to take a drop shot. The peacock's gorgeous plumes rose as he surveyed the blue skies, watching the clouds roll in, wishing the only member of the clan with a feel for golf were there.

Hatchet flew down to Thomas, his beak almost clattering with excitement. "You missed something, Thomas!" he called. "What a rousing game—that Bigfoot cleared the water with his tee shot, and then he made it out of the bunker and straight onto the green!"

"I wish I'd seen that," said Thomas wistfully. "Did he sink his putt?"

There was a brief pause, and Hatchet said, "Didn't quite catch that part of the game." The cheel shifted nervously, his feathers flapping awkwardly. "Right then, got to go, Thomas, see you around."

"Not so fast, young fellow, not so fast," said Thomas, edging around the cheel.

"Why are you sneaking up on me from behind?" said Hatchet crossly. "No, wait, don't look there. I'm not sitting on anything, really I'm not. Oh well, yes, I am."

He hopped away, and a white golf ball rolled across the greens.

"Hatchet," said Thomas sternly, "this has to stop, what? Conduct unbecoming of a raptor, hey? You can't go off stealing golf balls! Ruins the game!"

"They're so tempting," said Hatchet plaintively, preparing to fly off again. "Sorry, Thomas. It's out of love of the game, you know that."

"Once and for all, Hatchet, they aren't eggs!" screeched Thomas, as Hatch soared into the blue skies.

The thunder rumbled, and Southpaw sniffed at the air. He would just about have time to make it back to the Sender's house before the rains came down. The brown tom hurried off, pausing to say hello to Katar and the kittens.

Katar sauntered across the rough, followed by Ruff, Tumble, and a pair of mynahs.

"They're new," said Southpaw, while the mynahs bobbed politely in his direction.

"Yes, well," said Katar, his whiskers held at a defensive angle, "they've been listening during Ruff and Tumble's training sessions, and it seems that they're enthusiasts when it comes to hunting."

Southpaw stared at the clan's leader. "Katar," he said, "you're teaching mynahs how to hunt birds?"

"Lower your whiskers, lower your whiskers," hissed Katar,

"of course not. We're learning how to hunt beetles, and worms. We'll get to—what you mentioned—much later. When the mynahs aren't listening."

Tumble shot off to chase a butterfly. The listless kitten Southpaw remembered from Nizamuddin had undergone a complete transformation. It took the collective energies of Beraal, Katar and Southpaw, with some help from the owls, Hobson and Jobson, to keep track of her movements. And Ruff had filled out—he could almost keep up with his mother during their war games these days.

Southpaw would have stayed, and perhaps even joined in, but there was a tiny ripple in the breeze.

His whiskers tingled, and so did Katar's and Ruff's and Tumble's.

"THAT WAS LOTS OF FUN!" a ringing, sleepy mew said, right in their ears. "I'M SORRY YOU COULDN'T FIND ME, MAMA, I'D GONE TO SLEEP AT THE BOTTOM OF A CARDBOARD BOX. AND I MET A BEETLE! WE'RE BEST FRIENDS NOW, DO YOU WANT TO MEET HIM?"

Southpaw let out a happy whiffle, letting his whiskers rise. "She's up," he said to Katar, unnecessarily.

"So we heard," said the tom. "So did every bird and mouse in the neighbourhood, Southpaw, she's even louder than her mother! You'd better be off, or she'll start demanding to know where you are, and you know how loud she can get when she's crying."

"I do," said Southpaw, with some feeling. At three weeks, young Monsoon, who had arrived with the rains, making as much racket as the thunder, had a way of making her presence felt.

On the balcony, Mara stopped Monsoon's chatter by the simple expedient of holding the kitten down with a paw and washing her tiny nose and whiskers. Monsoon stopped sending, but she continued to squirm until she had broken free of her mother's grip. "Mama, will you tell me that story again? The one about how you and I and Tigris all have long whiskers because we're special?"

"At bedtime," said Mara, rolling Monsoon over with a paw so that she could have her belly washed. "You've already heard it thrice today." The kitten squeaked, but subsided, liking the rough rasp of her mother's tongue across her wriggling tummy.

The Sender paused when she saw the familiar shape cross the road. Her green eyes were tender as she watched Southpaw cross the park and climb up the goolar tree to join his daughter.

AUTHOR'S NOTE

Though all the characters in *The Wildings* and *The Hundred Names of Darkness* are fictional, they are based on strays I've met and grown to love over the years. The stray animals in India's cities live, very much like homeless humans, in the margins, unnoticed, sometimes unloved, often in need of vaccinations, food, care and affection.

If you'd like to help, here are a few organizations that accept donations of money and of time:

RED PAWS RESCUE, DELHI: *www.redpawsrescue.com*

BLUE CROSS, PUNE: *bluecrosspune.blogspot.com*

PAWS INDIA: *www.pawsindia.org*

ACKNOWLEDGEMENTS

That unholy trinity: Meenakshi Ganguly, Kamini Karlekar, Peter Griffin.

The parents, Tarun and Sunanda Roy, Tara, JT, Rudra, Antara, Neel and Mia, for the encouragement, and for being kind enough not to hint that I should grow up and get a real job.

Margaret Mascarenhas, for sharing the Calvim house, her poetry, her Goa and Max with me. And for introducing me to Delilah, queen of the rooftops, pillow-stealer, incomparable warrior who met the greatest hunter of them all much too soon.

Ina Puri, for asking what Mara intended to do about the bandicoots.

Tripti Lahiri, for conjuring up Chancha and Meenchi.

David John Godwin, keeper of the flame in a swiftly tilting industry; Anna Watkins, Heather Godwin, Caitlin Ingham, Philippa Sitters, for all the many kindnesses.

David Davidar, Rachna Singh, KD Singh, Ninni Singh, for loving books as much as you do.

THE HUNDRED NAMES OF DARKNESS

Pujitha, Bena Sareen, Aienla, Simar, Hohoi, Hina, Ravi, and all the other Alephbets.

The incomparable Prabha Mallya, for the illustrations and for walking through the hundred names of darkness with me one Delhi summer's day.

Amanda Betts, my editor at Random House Canada, for the constant encouragement and thoughtfulness, and for laughing in all the right places. Kelly Hill, for reimagining the wild-ings in her stunning cover designs; many thanks to Louise Dennys and Anne Collins for championing both books, and to all of the Penguin Random House Canada team.

The Akshara Theatre, Anasuya Vaidya and all the perform-ers of *The Wildings*, for giving the cats all nine of their lives.

The home team: Anita Roy, Arjun Nath, Doc, Keshav Palita, Kriti Monga, Mitali Saran, Ruchir Joshi, Salil Tripathi, Samit Basu, Shovon Chowdhury, Prem Panicker.

William Dalrymple, for letting me borrow a few Mehrauli goats.

Salman Rushdie, whose books lit up my imagination, and whose courage continues to be an inspiration. Thanks for your generosity and the kindness you've shown these wildings. The real Ferocious Attack dogs: Doginder, Alpha, Laddoo, gentlest and warmest of souls. And Oliver, who lives on in my memories.

And always, every time: Devangshu, without whom I would never find the words.

Nilanjana Roy is the author of *The Wildings*, winner of the Shakti Bhatt First Book Award, and a collection of essays called *The Girl Who Ate Books*. She is the editor of *A Matter of Taste: The Penguin Book of Indian Writing On Food*. Nilanjana lives in Delhi with three independent cats and her partner.